SOME WOMEN'S HEARTS.

BED-TIME STORIES.

BY

LOUISE CHANDLER MOULTON.

WITH ILLUSTRATIONS BY ADDIE LEDYARD.

Square 16mo. Price $1.50.

"Mrs. Moulton's 'Bed-time Stories' are tender and loving, as the last thoughts of the day should be. They are told simply and sweetly. All of them teach unselfishness, faithfulness, and courage. 'What Jess Cotrell did,' and 'Paying off Jane,' are perhaps the best; although 'Mr. Turk, and what became of him,' is such a sympathetic revelation of a bit of child life, that we are half inclined to give it the first place. The stories are not for very young children, but for those old enough to think for themselves; and the influence they exert will be pure, gentle, and decidedly religious. The dedication is very graceful." — *Boston Daily Advertiser.*

"It is long years since we were a lad; but, as we have read these tales, we have dreamed ourself a boy again, have exulted with some of the young heroes and heroines of Mrs. Moulton's coinage, and have wept sweet tears with others, just as, we have no doubt, many a boy and girl will do who takes our advice and secures this delightful budget of stories out of their first savings. Parents, who appreciate the difficulty of providing suitable reading for young people when they are at the doubtful age which Burns describes as being ''twixt a man and a boy,' will find Mrs. Moulton one of the most graceful and thoughtful purveyors of an elevated literature, especially adapted to the wants and tastes of their bright-eyed and quick-witted sons and daughters." — *Christian Intelligencer.*

"Very delicately and prettily are these stories for children told. . . . Children, the kindest and sharpest of critics, will willingly read them too. And not on the other side of the Atlantic only, but on this, and in every land where the English language is spoken. Real stories these for real children, not namby-pamby, teachy-teachy little tales, but regular stories, full of life, told in the good old-fashioned, diffuse, delightful manner." — *The London Bookseller.*

In Preparation.

MORE BED-TIME STORIES.

Sold by all Booksellers. Mailed, postpaid, by the Publishers,

ROBERTS BROTHERS, Boston.

SOME WOMEN'S HEARTS.

BY

LOUISE CHANDLER MOULTON,

AUTHOR OF "BED-TIME STORIES."

The sense of the world is short, —
Long and various the report, —
To love and be beloved;
Men and gods have not outlearned it;
And, how oft soe'er they've turned it,
'Twill not be improved.
R. W. EMERSON.

BOSTON:
ROBERTS BROTHERS.
1874.

CAMBRIDGE:
PRESS OF JOHN WILSON AND SON.

TO

A FEW BELOVED WOMEN,

IN WHOSE FAITHFUL HEARTS I HAVE FOUND THE TRUTH AND LOYALTY THAT ARE FRIENDSHIP AND THE UNSELFISHNESS THAT IS LOVE,

I OFFER THESE PAGES, IN WHICH SOME OF THEM, PERHAPS, MAY SEE THEMSELVES AS I HAVE SEEN THEM.

L. C. M.

MAY, 1874.

CONTENTS.

	PAGE
Fleeing from Fate	1
Brains	131
Twelve Years of My Life	157
Little Gibraltar	208
Household Gods	225
The Judge's Wife	258
A Letter, and what came of it	289
Out of Nazareth	321

SOME WOMEN'S HEARTS.

FLEEING FROM FATE.

CHAPTER I.

ELIZABETH.

DUSK was settling down upon the great, roomy house in which the Fordyces lived. It was a May evening, but chill, with some lingering breath of the vanished winter, and a bright fire was kindled in the great open stove. A servant brought in lights, and placed one on the centre-table, and another on the mantel. They revealed the group in the room quite clearly. A set of merry young people were these Fordyces, — pure blondes, all of them, except one who stood at the window, and who was not a daughter of the house, though her name was also Fordyce.

Kate Fordyce was the eldest of the party, and besides her there were two other sisters, and two brothers, — all Saxon, and rosy, and merry. They were teasing each other good-naturedly, laughing a great deal, and saying a good many things which passed with them for wit, because it takes so little in this respect to satisfy those who are ready and waiting to be amused.

The girl at the window paid no heed to them. She

was looking intently out towards the lovely, lonely hills, where the rosy glow of the sunset still lingered. A little at one side, as the window framed the landscape, was her uncle's iron manufactory, from which a red light streamed high, and sparkling cinders rayed off and glittered through the dusk. She always liked to look out of this window at this hour. The manufactory, prosaic as it might be by daylight, gave to the evening landscape a weird picturesqueness. Its mystery allured, as well as its brightness. Then there were the hills, — not the one on which the village of Lenox stood, — but the distant, solitary ones, where free winds blew, which wild birds haunted. Their aspect made her sad, oftentimes; touched her to pain; and yet she used to say that if her ghost could come back she knew it would walk among those hills. To-night, however, and a great many other times when she looked at them, they seemed to her like prison-walls, shutting her in from the world, — the world which must be somewhere, and mean something besides woods, and slopes, and waters, — the world which held excitements the thought of which thrilled her pulses, triumphs which fired her fancy, delights which haunted her dreams. Would she ever, ever know any thing about it; or was Lenox to be all her world?

She was not unhappy. Her feeling was not positive enough for that. She was only beset by the longing to eat of the tree of knowledge of good and evil, — the longing which is always the inheritance of an imaginative youth.

No one in the Fordyce household was at all unkind to Elizabeth. In a certain fashion they all loved her. If there were an imperceptible dividing line between them and her, it was she, not they, who drew it. For they were not of her kind. Their father and hers had been brothers, and certain family traits were reproduced in them all. But this girl had taken something from her mother which did not run in the Fordyce blood,—a fine and keen imagination, a capacity to enjoy and to suffer, of which they knew nothing. She was not heeding now their merry nightfall talk. Her thoughts were far away, tilting in some great tournament of life, living in some other world of poetry, and passion, and love, and woe.

She dared sometimes even to utter longing prayers that a door might be opened into this world of her dreams. It was almost the only prayer she ever said, except the Lord's prayer, which she still repeated every night as simply as a child. Of deep spiritual experiences, of mental conflicts, she knew nothing as yet. She guessed vaguely at her own capacity for emotion. I am glad that I can show her to you once, while still all her sorrows lay before her.

"What does Queen Bess say?" her Cousin Kate asked at last, going up to her and breaking in upon her revery.

"What about? I have not heard a word you have been saying."

She turned as she spoke, and her face fulfilled the promise of her voice. To do that was something, for the voice was no common one. It was not sweet, simply, but low, and clear, and tender. You felt that it indicated a deep and thoughtful nature.

She was a tall, slight girl, this Elizabeth Fordyce, whom her cousin called Queen Bess. She had dark gray eyes, which sometimes seemed hazel, and sometimes black. They were shaded by lashes so long that they cast a shadow. Her complexion was clear, but not fair. She had no color in her cheeks, except when some strong emotion stirred her, and then a glow, deep and warm as the heart of a summer rose, would suffuse them. Her lips alone were bright always. Her head was proudly set on her slender throat. Her hair was soft, and dark, and abundant. Her features were not faultless, but one who cared for her would never remember to find fault with them. She had a low, womanly brow; too broad, perhaps, for some tastes. Her mouth was not small, but the bright, mobile lips expressed every passing shade of feeling.

I have told you all this, and yet I am conscious that I have given you no true conception of Elizabeth. I can only trust to your learning to know her as my story goes on. In those early days, when, as I said, all her troubles lay before her, she neither understood herself, nor was understood by any one else. Perhaps no one loved her quite well enough to take the trouble of studying her. Her individuality was too decided for her to be generally popular. Nor had it even been the fashion in Lenox to call her pretty. Her cousins — with their full contours, their pink cheeks, and yellow hair — were spoken of as "the handsome Fordyces;" but no one meant to include Elizabeth when this phrase was used. And yet she had a charm of her own for those who had ears to hear and eyes to see. As she turned to ask what her cousins had been talking about, her eyes and cheeks brightened, and the Fordyce blondes paled beside her.

Kate answered her, speaking in a pretty, eager way, which seemed like a reminiscence of the time when she was fifteen; but then she had been kept young by over-much petting, though she was twenty-four now, and the eldest of the Fordyce sisters.

"We are talking about our May picnic. We must have it on Thursday, or we can't, by any stretch of imagination, call it May-day, for the month goes out on that day. We were discussing the propriety of asking Elliott Le Roy. He is boarding at the Gilmans, you know."

"But we have always said we never would ask any of the summer boarders, — birds of passage, here to-day, there to-morrow, and caring nothing for any of us. For my part, I think the one charm of the May picnic has always been that we had only Lenox people, who had known about one another all their lives. I don't like strangers."

"You think you don't, I know; but there isn't one of us who longs to see the world as you do. After all, Mr. Le Roy isn't exactly a stranger. He belongs to us and to Lenox in a certain way. He is a cousin of Uncle Henry's new wife. It's very different, don't you see, from some one of whom we know nothing? I suppose Aunt Julia's having settled here was what attracted him to the place. He keeps house in New York, she says, — has an elegant establishment, though he is a bachelor. But he is an author, and he has so many associations and engagements in the city that he couldn't get on with his work there, and, as it was something he was in a hurry to finish, he came here for the quiet."

"An author!"

Elizabeth grew excited, though neither her face nor her manner gave evidence of it. She was only eighteen then, and full of enthusiasm; very young, too, of her age, because she had lived so much in a world of fancy and imagination, and known so little of the coarser realities of actual life. To her dreaming soul an author meant something a little less than divine, — a sort of demi-god, to whom she could have offered incense like a pagan.

"What does he write?" she asked, with suppressed eagerness.

"Oh, political things, I believe, and essays on history. I heard Aunt Julia say that he was a philosophical historian, or a historical philosopher, I forget which. But there's no doubt about his cleverness, any more than about his money. She says he is a real man of the world, too, — very fascinating to women, as it is, and he might be very dangerous if he were not so cold. He has never loved any one, and does not care to marry. He is a good comrade, she says, and generous in a certain way; but that comes of his brain, — his heart was forgotten and left out when he was made."

Long afterward Elizabeth remembered those words.

"I don't see why there should have been any question about asking him," she said, quietly. "Very likely he will think the whole thing a bore; but his belonging to Aunt Julia gives him a claim to the courtesy of an invitation. For my part, I hope he'll come. I confess I should like to see a real, live book-maker."

Bell Fordyce, the second daughter, laughed merrily.

"There," she cried, "you see Queen Bess is as very a woman for curiosity as the rest of us. We will have the picnic on Thursday, and we will ask the book-maker. Dick, you must see about it to-morrow; and you and Rob must give all the rest of the invitations. We girls shall have enough to do in making our part of the good things; for I don't suppose even authors are above eating at a picnic."

"Why haven't we seen this Mr. Le Roy before, since he is a family connection?" Elizabeth interpolated, pursuing, as her habit was, the subject which interested her.

"Oh, he only came on Saturday. I suppose Aunt Julia would soon have brought him round, or we should have met him there, for I guess he goes to her house every day; but now she will be as busy about the picnic as we shall, and I suppose we shall see him first on the shore of the Mountain Mirror."

Then began a discussion about cakes and salads and receipts; and Elizabeth turned back again to her window, for in this direction no one expected any thing of her. So she withdrew into herself, and began to fancy what this man of the world, this scholar, this author, would be like. How could people tell that he had no heart? How unfair to pronounce such judgment when they really knew nothing about it. Just because he had never loved any one yet,—as if every line were long enough to fathom a deep nature.

She was quite prepared to make a hero of him, and hitherto she had known only book heroes. It was more than twenty years ago,—I am writing in the year of our Lord 1873,—and even then Lenox had begun to be a tolerably well-known summer resort. But of the people who came and went, the Fordyces, living at some distance from the village, and taking no boarders, saw very little. There were, among the stalwart Berkshiremen, not a few in whom the elements of the heroic were not wanting,—men of brains, and soul, and culture,—but Elizabeth had seen them so often that she had grown used to them, and so never paused to speculate upon their possibilities. This new-comer represented to her the unknown, which to a fine and fresh imagination is always the admirable.

CHAPTER II.

AT THE MOUNTAIN MIRROR.

THURSDAY dawned clear and bright,—warmer than any day of the month had been before,—a perfect time. Elizabeth looked out of her window in a trance of delight and expectation. The lonely, lovely hills had never seemed so fair, so full of promise. The sky was a deep, lustrous azure, over which now and then some bit of white, fleecy cloud drifted. Elizabeth repeated snatches of verse to herself as she dressed. She could not sing, but she recited in a chanting tone, which was in itself full of musical suggestion.

She put on a pure white dress. Somehow she felt as pure and fresh herself as the new day out of doors, — the new day, washed with God's dews, and freshened by His winds. She was as simply glad and expectant as a child; so she suited her attire to her mood. She brushed her soft hair away from her forehead, and coiled it into a net, through whose slender meshes all its beauty was visible. A branch of coral fastened the lace around her throat, and was her only ornament. She might have sat for a picture of Undine, but for the soul, already awakened, which looked out of her luminous eyes.

She went downstairs, and found the rest all ready for it was nearly nine o'clock, — Rob and Dick Fordyce in their cool, gray suits; Kate in violet, Bell in pink, and Emmie, the youngest one, in sea-green; for the three graces were prejudiced against dressing alike, and they had been bright enough to discover that azure is not of necessity the one idea of blondes.

They ate their late breakfast in a desultory way; one and another jumping up at intervals, to put some forgotten or neglected thing into the lunch-baskets.

About half-past nine they finally got themselves off

in a large, comfortable wagon drawn by two horses, the three seats of which held them all without inconvenience. As the residences of the various guests were scattered in different directions, no rendezvous was attempted until they should reach the picnic ground. I will not bore you with any attempt to make you see the Mountain Mirror with my eyes. You may be fortunate enough to go some day to a picnic in Lenox, and behold with your own this deep, still tarn, which reflects for ever the lofty peak that rises directly from its western shore, the lesser hills at the east, and the solemn, watching, cloud-swept sky high over all.

The Fordyce May picnic was held, year after year, on this enchanted spot; and to climb the Peak, and look from its summit over the wide-spread landscape, was the fatigue which always earned them the right to their repast. So they arranged at once, upon arriving, baskets and hampers in a cool, shady place, and then made ready for their mountain scramble. Presently the rest of the company began to appear. Elizabeth looked eagerly at the Gilman carriage, but found it quite empty of interest for her, containing only Hannah and Selina Gilman and their sandy-haired brother. Half a dozen other well-laden wagons followed; and, last of all, a light buggy, with a vicious-looking black horse, driven by the only stranger of the party.

Elizabeth Fordyce sat very still in her place under the trees, while her cousins went forward to welcome Mr. Le Roy. She saw a tall, elegant-looking man, dressed in speckless white linen, — a man with the unmistakable grand air she had associated with him in her fancy. This hero, whose very name, before English spelling corrupted it, was *Le Roi*, the king.

"A Saul, than his brethren higher and fairer," she said softly to herself; and just then her cousin Kate brought him up to her.

"Another Miss Fordyce," Kate said gayly; "my Cousin Elizabeth."

Elizabeth looked up, and met the gaze of a pair of cool, speculative, yet reticent blue eyes, which told no secrets and held no smile, though the lips below were parted and revealed glittering rows of teeth. He was very handsome,—that was her first thought; very satirical also, was her second. He would be intolerant of sentimentality or weakness, some instinct told her. Well, she had one gift, that of being able to keep silence; and she need not expose any vulnerable points to his shafts. She rose with an air as lofty as his own, and gave him her hand. That momentary contact sent a curious thrill through her nerves, — not repulsion, but as certainly not attraction, — prophecy, perhaps. She did not try to analyze it as she sat down again, and he passed on with his merry guide, to be made acquainted with the rest of the party.

"See how he will let Kate bore him," thought Elizabeth to herself, "just because she is handsome. Good and sweet as she is, she could have no comprehension of such a man or such a career. How is it that, even with the best men, beauty answers for every thing?"

She forgot that her own face had not seemed unlovely when she looked at it in the glass that morning. She came nearer to envying her cousin's yellow locks, and pink and white prettiness, and eyes of china blue, than she had ever come before to a feeling so mean. She really wanted this Elliott Le Roy to be interested in her. Not that she was thinking of him as possible lover or husband, — Elizabeth was too proud to have such thoughts a spontaneous growth in her mind, — but she wanted to attract him enough to make him talk with her, and give her a taste of that wine of life which he had quaffed so long that surely its tang must linger upon his lips. If her eyes were not blue, or her hair yellow, she had at least the ability to appreciate him; but probably he would not care to find that out. Just as she was becoming disgusted with herself for this phase of envious feeling, he came back to her, quite alone this time.

"They are getting ready to climb the Peak," he said, carelessly. "Do you go, — or shall we stay behind in the shade, and let the rest look at the view for us?"

That "we" stirred Elizabeth's pulses a little. He had elected himself her cavalier, after all. But her calm, pale face betrayed no eagerness or excitement.

"*I* must go," she said, rising. "They would not give me my dinner, else."

"And you expect to be hungry by and by?"

He eyed her critically as he spoke, beginning to admire her composure and self-possession, — qualities which he had expected to put to flight at once in any country girl whom he might honor with his attention.

"Most unromantically hungry," she answered, smiling, "I always am on May-day."

Le Roy lifted his brows.

"So this is May-day? I really thought that had been a month ago, when I saw the streets full of young Hibernians, with paper wreaths on their bare heads."

"Oh, yes," she replied quietly. "That was May-day in New York. It takes most fashions a month to travel to Lenox. It is too cold here for flowers to bloom on the first of May, and we never call it May-day until there are blossoms enough to crown our queen. We always make a wreath of violets for Kate, and they are less blue than her eyes."

"Queen Katherine and Queen Bess, — I find myself among the royal family."

She did not answer. She fancied that she detected a shade of satire in his tone, and it stung her sensitive pride. By this time the rest of the party had all started. The three graces had given up Mr. Le Roy to Queen Bess very willingly. They were a little afraid of him, and found themselves more at ease with their village cavaliers. He had cut an alpenstock, as he called it, for Elizabeth, and another for himself, while they had been talking; and now they started for the climb, just enough behind the others to be out of ear-shot.

For a while they were both silent. Elizabeth carried little of the small coin of society, and she was resolutely on guard. Mr. Le Roy was thinking about her; just, perhaps, on account of her silence. She interested him because she was so unlike the women to whom he was accustomed; so doubly unlike any one whom he could have expected to meet in Lenox. He was used to have women strive to please him, offer perpetual incense at his shrine, — but this girl was evidently indifferent with an indifference which he could not believe to be assumed. She was gathering flowers and leaves as she went on, — a spray of dog-rose, a clump of violets, a stalk or two of wild lilies of the valley, anemones, a columbine, — he noticed the artistic grace with which she grouped them. She walked with a free, grand tread. Her voice was cool and clear, her accent perfect. How had it all come? His wonder culminated in a question.

"Were you born in Lenox, Miss Fordyce?"

"Born and bred," — she answered, lightly, — "as native a product of the soil as these violets. Indeed, I have never been out of Berkshire county in my life."

"And, I presume, do not care to go out of it, since it has suited you so well?"

His eyes expressed the admiration which something in her quiet self-respect forbade him to put into plainer language. She smiled.

"There, at last, your penetration is at fault. I do want very much to go away from Lenox. I should want, when I am old, or tired of the world, to come back here again, and die under these skies. I think I could not rest quietly in my grave, unless I were buried in the shadow of these Berkshire hills. But in the mean time I do long to see something of life. I was interested to meet you to-day, because you came from the great world outside, and I fancied there would be something of its atmosphere about you, making you different from the men to whom I am accustomed."

"And you are disappointed?" he asked; and then waited for her slow-coming answer with an interest for which he mentally scoffed at himself.

She looked at him thoughtfully and deliberately, before she spoke.

"No, I do not think that I am. You are not just what I fancied, but there is something about you which is not of Lenox."

He wondered in what respects he had failed to realize her conception of him, — whether he were less than she had thought, or more, — but he saw no encouragement to ask the question in her quiet eyes; if indeed his own pride had not stood as much in the way as her reserve. Just then he registered a vow, mentally, that before the summer was over he would know just what she thought about him, just how much power he could gain over her. The affair began, even in this early stage, to interest him keenly.

Do not commit the error of fancying that his heart was touched. His cousin had said, you know, that a heart had been left out when he was made. However that may have been, he certainly had not as yet developed any sentiment for Elizabeth Fordyce; but his curiosity was thoroughly aroused about her, and his masculine vanity, of which he had no small share, was up in arms. Before the summer was over, not only would he know her thoughts concerning him, but they should be what he pleased to make them.

The encounter gave new zest to the prospect of his summer campaign. He had planned to go to Newport later in the season, after his literary work should be accomplished; but there would be time enough for this little innocent game of hearts before August.

Not a single throb of pity moved him, as he watched this young, imaginative, fresh-hearted girl standing at length on the summit of the Peak, and looking off over the landscape, her dark eyes shining, and the swift color of excitement staining her cheeks. He began to think her really handsome, as he saw her now, in contrast with her three cousins, whose beauty had been so much more striking at first sight. *They* were "well-blown," as he phrased it to himself. The sun had treated them as he usually does light-complexioned, thin-skinned women. Their delicate little faces were flushed and scorched, till they looked like full-blown peonies; and there was an unpicturesque disarray about their general get-up which certainly put them at a sad disadvantage.

Queen Bess looked as cool as when she started. Her white robes were unstained. The flowers in her hands, even, were not withered. She stood there, looking off towards the world she longed to try, with her wide eyes and her glowing cheeks, — an incarnation, surely, of pure-hearted, high-souled, graceful womanhood. And

Elliott Le Roy speculated about the phases of feeling through which she should pass before he had done with her, as coolly, and analytically, and selfishly, as if that fine, strong nature of hers had not held capacities for joy and sorrow which he could no more comprehend or measure than one could fathom the ocean with a lady's ribbon.

The whole party went down the Peak in company, after half an hour's restful enjoyment of the view. Mr. Le Roy was thrown with Kate and Bell Fordyce; or perhaps he let himself drift into their neighborhood just to see if it would pique Elizabeth. It vexed him a little to perceive that it did not. She was just as calm and bright as when she had climbed up the height at his side, — silent for the most part, as she had been then, but with a face full of enjoyment, eager eyes which swept the landscape, and yet with gentle words and attentive air for every one who particularly addressed her. "Wild thing, shy thing," he called her to himself, remembering a line of an old song. Would any one ever tame her? Would she ever come and go at any man's hest, — lay her heart in any man's hand? If so, and he were not that man, it would be easy to hate him.

At the foot of the Peak she sat down again, and began to make the violet-wreath for which they had all been gathering blossoms, but for whose twining no fingers were so deft as her own. Preparations for dinner were going on. A fire was kindled amid difficulties and laughter. A kettle was hung on some crossed twigs, and girlish heads bent over baskets and hampers. Mr. Le Roy looked on for a few moments without offering his assistance, and then lazily sauntered over to Elizabeth.

"So you don't help to get dinner?" he asked her.

"No, my part is to make the wreath, and arrange the flowers for the vases. I always put out fires when I try to kindle them; and I think I can't be one of the wicked, for whatever I do does not prosper, in a domestic line, at least."

"I think you could kindle some fires that many waters could not quench, neither could the floods drown," Le Roy said, slowly, watching her cheeks for a blush which did not come.

"Could you get me some water from the spring for these vases?" she asked, trying her flowers into one of them, so coolly that he could not tell whether she had comprehended him.

"Don't send me away for cold water," he said, pathetically. "I get enough of that here."

Elizabeth laughed.

"Oh, you must do something as well as the rest, if you want your dinner. Kate is Queen bee, and she won't allow any drones in the hive."

"Cruelty, thy name is Miss Fordyce!" he sighed, with a dramatic air; but he took a pitcher and brought her the water, notwithstanding. When he came back she made a diversion by filling her vases and putting them on the table; and then the crown must be adjusted to Kate's golden head; and by that time dinner was ready.

For the hour or two after the feast fate was unkind to Mr. Le Roy. He had no opportunity to get Queen Bess to himself; and he was one of those men for whom nothing is so stupid as a general conversation. He revenged himself on fate by doing his utmost to disturb the peace of mind of Miss Emmie, the youngest Fordyce, by pouring into her ear the most absurd and unmitigated flatteries, which she swallowed just as children a little younger do candy, regardless of whence it comes, but with eager and unsophisticated delight in its sweetness. He soon tired of this too easy game, and managing to get the ear of his cousin, Mrs. Henry Fordyce, the most carelessly good-natured of matrons, he asked in an undertone, — "Jule, would it be any harm for me to invite one of those Fordyces to drive home with me?"

Mrs. Henry considered a moment. "I don't believe it would," she said at length. "To be sure you never saw them till to-day; but they are my nieces, and you are my cousin. No, I don't see any harm."

Of course Elizabeth was the "one of the Fordyces" whom Mr. Le Roy had in his mind, and wanted to have in his wagon. He went up to her, armed with her aunt's approval.

"I wonder if you would have confidence enough in my skill as a whip to trust me to drive you home?" he asked, adroitly, as if he were suggesting the only possible objection to his arrangement. "I spoke to Julia about it, and she thought you would be safe enough. She has sat behind my horse two or three times; but there are not many things of which she is afraid."

Miss Fordyce considered a moment. It was not quite the thing, even in primitive Lenox, to drive with a gentleman so nearly a stranger; but then he was her aunt's cousin, and he was an historical philosopher, or a philosophical historian, she had not found out which yet, but she wanted to find out. Yes, she would go.

They started a little earlier than the rest, for they found they were agreed in disliking to take other people's dust; and it would be equally objectionable to lead the cavalcade, and inflict on simple-hearted followers the annoyance they shirked for themselves. So they solved the problem by starting half an hour in advance of the time appointed; and though they took the longest way home, and made a considerable detour even from that, they were standing at the Fordyce gate, and quite ready to welcome the three Graces on their arrival.

Soon after they set out, Elizabeth plucked up courage and asked Mr. Le Roy about his books. He saw the eager light in her eyes, and smiled secretly. So it was as an author that she was interested in him. That might answer for the world, but he chose to make his first impression upon her in his private capacity as a man.

He answered carelessly, — "My books are not books at all. The papers I am writing now may possibly be put into book form some time; but the Bostonians are to have the benefit of them first in the shape of lectures before their Lowell Institute, — dull old lectures about the history of a certain epoch. For the rest, I've only written articles for the monthlies and quarterlies, and a lecture now and then. Did Cousin Julia delude you into thinking me an author, and so make all Lenox ready to be shy of me in advance?"

"I don't know about the delusion. She certainly said you were an author, — at least Kate told me so, — and I cannot see any thing incorrect in the statement, according to your own showing. I suppose Addison was none the less an author because his best energies were given to a daily paper."

"Oh, if you are going back into the classics, I cry quarter. I foresee I shall find you too clever for me."

A smile flickered round his lips as he spoke, which vexed Elizabeth and made her silent. She was willing enough to be laughed with, but it would not be easy to win her forgiveness for man or woman who should laugh at her.

They bowled along for a little while under green trees over the still country road. Le Roy had understood her silence, and was thinking how to redeem himself. Presently he said, with a complete assumption of frankness, — "I vexed you just now, but you vexed me first. My ideal is so high that I feel myself a tyro, and it sounds like satire when any one talks to me of authorship. Let us cry quits and begin again. I *have* seen some really great men. When I was in England I heard Robert Browning talk, and Tennyson. Which do you like best?"

"I don't know. I think I should say Browning; and yet Tennyson has written two verses which move me more than almost any others in the language."

"What are they?"

He asked the question in a quiet, matter-of-fact way, and she answered it as simply as if she had not been a young girl, talking to a man whose fascinations had already proved too much for many a woman's peace:—

"Oh, let the solid ground
   Not fail beneath my feet,
Before my life has found
   What some have found so sweet;
Then let come what come may,
What matter if I go mad,
I shall have had my day.

"Let the sweet heavens endure,
   Not close and darken above me,
Before I am quite, quite sure
   That there is one to love me;
Then let come what come may,
To a life that has been so sad,
I shall have had my day."

"Jove, how that girl could love!" Le Roy said to himself, listening to the quivering voice, watching the changeful color. "I should like to see how she would look when once her whole nature was waked up."

When her voice died on the air, which seemed to hold the echo of its melody a moment after the last word was spoken, he looked at her steadily, till the clear eyes drooped.

"You are tempting fate with that prayer, Miss Fordyce. You stand in the east of your life, and already I see the rose of dawning. But you are cool of head, if warm of heart, and I think you will not go mad."

She did not answer. His longing to tame this "wild thing, shy thing," was growing on him. I wish Elizabeth had had a mother just then to say a prayer for her happiness; for Elliott Le Roy was a man pitiless as death, and what he longed for he generally attained.

CHAPTER III.

A COSTLY EXPERIMENT.

Mrs. Henry Fordyce looked out of her window the forenoon after the picnic, and saw her handsome elegant cousin sauntering in at her gate. She was weak enough to feel a little pride in her relationship with him, — in his talents, his breeding, his good looks, his grand air, his magnificence, generally speaking. She knew that half Lenox was envying her her kinship with him; and few things are more delightful to a naturally constituted woman than those which tempt her erring sisters to break the tenth commandment. She received her visitor with impressment.

"I looked for you, Elliott. I thought you were sure to come and tell me how you liked Lenox."

"What I thought of your husband's nieces, you mean," he corrected her, with a smile which held a little covert satire.

"Well! if you choose to put it in that way. I saw that you drove Elizabeth home. Don't you think the others handsomer?"

"Yes, I suppose so, if they weren't such duplicates of each other. I like individuality."

"They are a good deal alike. People call them 'the three Graces,' you know, — or 'the handsome Fordyces.' When they say those things, of course they don't include Elizabeth."

"Does that hurt her feelings?"

"How absurd. Would she say so if it did? But really I doubt if she cares, she is so full of her day-dreams."

"And the others are not dreamers, — real blue and gold, flesh and blood. Jule, it is warm, and I am lazy, — just in the humor for gossip; which, after all, men like quite as well as women, if only the subject is interesting. So let me lie back here in this great easy-chair, and you tell me about Elizabeth Fordyce. She has excited my curiosity, just because she is so unlike the rest of them. How is it that she hasn't the family beauty?"

"Why, you see her mother was a Nugent, and that's where the dark eyes and hair, and the reserved, dreaming temperament come from. She's very like a picture I've seen of her mother. There's but little Fordyce about her, poor thing."

"It *is* unlucky, if her face is her fortune; but perhaps she has money?"

"Not a dime of her own. I've heard rumors since I

came here that she wasn't fairly dealt with in that matter; but Henry wont talk about it. You see her father and the uncle she lives with were in business together, and just after her father's death there was some embarrassment about money matters, and the firm came near being insolvent. So it was made out, somehow, that no money was to come to her; but then her uncle took her home, and has done by her just the same as by his own children; so, after all, there is no fault to be found. They've all been good to her, only I don't think they understand her very well. They say she's queer."

"I suppose she likes her life?" he asked, with secret curiosity.

"I don't quite know. She was eighteen last spring, and Kate told me that she had been restless ever since to get away and do something for herself. She would have gone before now, only that her uncle was so opposed. But she has been studying with all her might to fit herself to go as a governess at the first good opening."

Elliott Le Roy smiled at the thought of some of Elizabeth's cool, little ways, and crisp, curt speeches. The governess element did not appear to him to be very strongly developed in her character. Having found out all he wanted to know, he got up lazily.

"What, you are not going?"

"Yes, I'm afraid I must. It's a bore, rushing round in the sun, and you know, Jule, how I like to sit in your cool, quiet parlor; but I must not quite forget all social laws even in this Berkshire Arcadia. It becomes me to inquire about the health of the Fordyces after their picnic."

As he walked along, however, it was only one of the Fordyces of whom he thought, and that one, Elizabeth. He had said to himself, yesterday, "How that girl could love!" and he was curiously tempted to try the experiment of making her in love with himself. He fancied her petulant little ways; her pretty insubordinations; the shy sweetness of her rare and hard-won tenderness; and then the triumph of her full and free surrender. Once it came across his mind that it wouldn't be so very bad a thing to marry her. If he married at all, it *must* be a woman who would not fetter him, — who would demand little, and take what he gave, thankfully. He had bachelor ways, single-man tastes, which he would not be willing to sacrifice to any one. A girl in his own set, well posted as to her dues, would not be satisfied with any such half conquest. But this "wild thing, shy thing," would she not be easy to content, once that a man had tamed her? If some one were to save her from her governessing career, and surround her with elegance and luxury, how gratitude would deepen and sweeten her love.

That reflection, by the way, showed how little he really knew of women. Gratitude and love run in parallels. There may be room for both in the same heart, but they never touch, nor do I see how one can deepen the other.

Mr. Le Roy laughed, a cynical little laugh, all to

himself, as he came to the Fordyce gate and the end of his revery at the same time. After all, what did he want of a girl with whom he certainly was not in love,—who, at best, would be more or less of an incumbrance? Still, it was only Miss Elizabeth Fordyce for whom he asked at the door; though the rest might be supposed to hold equal claims upon his courtesy.

He was shown into a little room which, by tacit consent, had been abandoned to Elizabeth. It was furnished with quaint, old-fashioned furniture, which had been her mother's. A bookcase, well filled, was one of its adornments. Ivy-vines had been trained over the windows, into leafy cornices for the soft, white muslin curtains. The few chairs were all easy-chairs. The windows were open, but Elizabeth had a Southern temperament, and liked warmth, so there was a little grate with a tiny soft-coal fire, clear and bright; and, near the fire, her delicate cheeks flushed by its glow, sat Elizabeth. She had no means to make expensive toilets, but she had the tact to make effective ones. Her dress was white, with violet ribbons; and a violet odor floated out from her filmy handkerchief. Her eyes kindled when she met Mr. Le Roy, and then drooped again; and her visitor took in the whole picture,—room and furnishings, and graceful woman,—and scoffed at Lenox for not having found out, before this, *who* was the handsome Fordyce.

The shy eagerness of her welcome charmed him. He sat down beside her, and began to talk to her about some of the books lying on her table. He found that she had both read and thought, though her high estimate of his ability made her diffident of expressing her own ideas. Once or twice, however, she flashed into passionate earnestness. Once was when he took up a volume of Goethe.

"So you like the grand old German?" he said.

"Like him!" The dark, gray eyes flashed, the cheeks flamed. "Mr. Le Roy, I hate him!"

"I presume you do not question his genius?"

"The more genius, the more shame!" she cried, hotly. "A man that could coolly go to work to win one woman's heart after another, just to see how love would affect each different type, and then throw them away like squeezed oranges. I try to think good will always triumph over evil, in the end; but I have often wondered whether there were soul enough in that man to be worth saving. Mind he had plenty of; but it is not mind to which the saving promise of immortality is given."

"So you think trifling with a woman's heart is the unpardonable sin?"

"I don't know," she said, slowly. "God forbid that I should pronounce any soul's sentence. Still, I know but one worse crime in a man than winning a woman's heart for pastime."

"What is that? Your code of morals interests me."

"To marry a wife without loving her," she answered, in a still, controlled voice, but with cheeks and eyes aflame. "When a woman found herself trifled with and deserted, pride might come to her rescue, and her day and chance for happiness might not be quite over, — for, romance about it how we may, women, and men too, do sometimes love more than once. But, deceived into a loveless marriage, what is there for the wife to do but to die? I think I could never forgive that wrong on earth or in Heaven."

"How if a woman marries a man without loving him?"

"She wrongs him, surely; and her own soul yet more. But the cases are not parallel. Love is not so vital to a man; and, besides, I firmly believe that any husband who has married a wife with a free heart can win her love if he tries."

"Your experience must have been very limited; how have you formed your theories of life?" he asked her, wonderingly.

"They are only theories, as you say. I cannot tell how they would stand contact with actual life. But they were strong enough to make me hate Goethe."

She rounded her sentence with a smile, and then took up some delicate sewing, and began stitching on it, as if she considered the discussion finished.

Mr. Le Roy drew "Men and Women" from his pocket, and opened it first to "Evelyn Hope;" that hopefullest poem of love and woe which poet ever penned. Afterwards he turned a few pages to the "Toccata of Galluppi's," and read it through. Two lines stayed with Elizabeth, and kept her company long after he had bidden her good-morning, and gone away, —

"Some with lives that come to nothing, some with deeds as well undone,
Death came tacitly, and took them where they never see the sun."

Would her life come to nothing? Was she one of the "butterflies" to "dread extinction"? Her existence, just then, seemed laid upon her as a burden, not given her as a blessing.

Elliott Le Roy went out again into the June sunlight. He was becoming singularly interested in Elizabeth; but it was precisely in the Goethe fashion of wishing to try experiments with her.

"It would almost pay to marry her," he said to himself, with his cool little laugh, "just to see what kind of wife she would make. She talked desperately and defiantly enough, but she would be very submissive, I think, when she couldn't help herself. It's the way with these high-mettled, true-blooded creatures, whether horses or women. Once well-broken to harness, and there's no end to their faithfulness and submission. I'd trust her. But she wouldn't give away that heart of hers in a day."

He walked on, switching off dandelion-heads with his light walking-stick. Lenox was more exciting than he had expected. Perhaps he could not make Elizabeth care for him, even if he tried; but at that thought he smiled a little scornfully to himself. He had found women so far very easy to win, though he had won them not to wear, hitherto. So far in life he had loved and ridden away; but curiously enough he did not for a moment contemplate pursuing this course with Elizabeth. If he won her heart he quite understood that he must pay the legitimate price for his triumph. Nor did this prospect very much trouble him. Partly because — come how those things may — she was so essentially thorough-bred that he could trust her to be equal to any position in which he might place her; and partly — though this was unacknowledged to himself — because even his Mephistophelian nature was not wholly free from the human longing to be loved, to have one human creature to say a prayer for him if he were in peril, or drop a tear for him if he were dead. I think, too, that even this man of the world would not have been quite bold enough deliberately to resolve on trifling with such a "being of spirit, and fire, and dew," as Elizabeth.

Still, whether in the character of trifler or man in earnest, he went day after day to the Fordyce dwelling. He read to Elizabeth, and talked to her. The country ways learned to know his horse's footsteps, and the people, for a radius of ten miles round the village, grew familiar with the handsome, haughty face of the horse's master, and the slight, dark-haired girl beside him.

Elizabeth's soul was in a strange tumult. All of life had become savorless to her except the hours when he was beside her; and yet with him she was never quite happy or at ease. She wished in one breath that she had never seen him; while in the next she shivered at the thought of what Lenox would be when summer and he had taken flight together.

"Do you love me, Elizabeth?"

He asked her this one day, in a half-reckless mood; piqued to do it, perhaps, by her inscrutable self-possession. It was six weeks after the picnic, — six weeks during which there had not been a single day when they had not met. In August he was to go to Newport; and now it was the middle of July. They had been talking of this, and it had seemed to her as if something tight round her heart were strangling it. She sat silent, because she had not self-control enough to speak calmly; and into this silence his question fell, — "Do you love me, Elizabeth?"

She grew very pale, and her voice shook as she answered, — "God help me, I do not know. I never cared for any one else, and I don't want to part with you; but I had thought love was something more, or different. Can't you help me to understand myself, Mr. Le Roy?"

The soft pleading in her eyes moved him. Her helplessness was so appealing, her voice so faltering, her face so pale and sweet, that Elliott Le Roy came nearer to loving her in that moment than ever he had before. He took her close into his arms, and kissed her, — a long, silent kiss, — his first. He felt something, but I think he feigned more; for his was a nature to which shams fitted themselves as a garment.

"I think you do love me, Elizabeth. Is it not so?"

With his eyes and lips on hers, the whole magnetism of his nature swaying her towards him, she answered under her breath, — "If you care for my love, Mr. Le Roy, I think you can keep it."

And in saying this she told him neither more nor less

than the truth. If he had honestly loved her, honestly cared for her love, it would never have failed him. She did not yet know herself; but he had all things in his favor. He satisfied her pride, — he fulfilled the demands of her taste, — her heart might easily be his by right of discovery, if he chose to enter in and take possession.

Would he choose?

For a moment a vague longing for the possible sweetness there might be in a true love, a true home, came over him, and his manner was very tender.

"Shall I be a grand dame enough for your sphere in life?" Elizabeth asked humbly.

"If I had not thought my rose perfect, should I have tried to gather it?" he said in answer. "There are other flowers in other gardens, — I have chosen here."

He had not said one word about his love for her, but Elizabeth had not noticed the omission. Nor had he left such words unsaid from any conscientious scruples, any doubts of himself, but simply because they did not come naturally to him. He was not an affectionate man; and just here was the reef on which, had all her skies been fair, all her winds favoring, Elizabeth was sure, soon or late, to come to woe.

Underneath all her delicate shyness, her nature was tenderly affectionate, and, where she deeply loved, very demonstrative as well. She would never have wearied of the manifestations of affection; while to be fond and caressing, or even to endure such things patiently for any length of time, was not in Le Roy's mental constitution. Elizabeth's instinctive and refined womanliness was sure to keep her from wearying any man with unsought caresses; but it offered her no security against that hunger of the heart of which one dies at last, just as surely as of bodily famine.

The time for discovering this lack had not yet come, and she fancied herself very happy as she sat at Le Roy's side, and heard him tell how she had interested him from the first. Nor was he insincere in this talk. If I have given you the impression that he was a man with *no* good qualities, *no* tender human feeling, *no* respect for moral obligations, I have failed to render him to you fairly. The trouble about correctly understanding people is that there are no pure temperaments; no one is altogether bad or altogether good. The bad preponderates fearfully in some natures; but no man is left to live on earth when he is quite a devil, or fails of translation when he is all a saint.

Sitting beside Elizabeth, in those first hours after he had won her, Le Roy certainly felt a tenderness for her, a real interest in her, which he had never experienced for a woman before. It was far enough from the grand, self-sacrificing devotion of a nobler man; but it was the best he had to give, — let us do him justice.

As for Elizabeth, thinking of her in those hours, one wishes over again that she could only have had a pure, wise, good mother. Poor child! She was not in one sense ignorant. She had read and thought in her way, and framed her fine-spun theories; but she knew so sadly little of her own heart.

And this engagement was but the type of half those formed by young girls of eighteen the country over. They do not guess what true love is or should be, — they mistake for it their first heart-flutter, — they do not comprehend their own natures, or divine what they will need when they come to the full stature of their womanhood; and yet they are very honest, and mean all they say when they utter, in their ignorance, that solemn vow which neither Heaven nor man could help them to keep, until Heaven or man should be able to make the sun move back on his course, or the streams flow upwards towards the mountain tops.

CHAPTER IV.

HER MANACLE.

The next day, after the understanding arrived at in the last chapter, was Thursday; and Mr. Le Roy started for New York in the morning. Friday afternoon, the last train brought him back again, and he went over in the gloaming to see Elizabeth. She trembled a little when he came to her side. It gave her a curious feeling to meet again, after his brief absence, this man, in whose hands her future lay. The agitation of her manner made him think of the fluttering of some newly caught woodland bird. He called her again, in his thought, his "wild thing, shy thing," and experienced some of the pleasant excitement he had expected to feel in her capture.

"Did you know you were to wear my fetter?" he asked after a while. "I went to New York partly for the purpose of providing myself with a manacle for your securer binding."

"I think I shall not want to run away if you are good to me," she said, in a low, shy tone.

"And I, you see, do not mean you shall run away, whether or no. I shall hold on to you like Fate."

He laughed as he spoke; but he and she, in those two sentences, had unconsciously struck the key-note of their two lives.

The ring he put upon her finger was the conventional diamond solitaire, but unusually large and brilliant, for Le Roy was rich, and not niggardly. Elizabeth had the intense love for beautiful things, which inheres in such temperaments as hers; but the ring, handsome as it was, gave her a singular feeling of discomfort. It seemed to watch her, like a great, fiery eye. She felt as if, in some subtle, inexplicable way, that eye were her keeper. She was never quite the same self-willed, independent girl after she wore it. It was as though, like a conquered fort, she had given up her defences, and hung out now the colors of the enemy. Not that she allowed these thoughts any room in her consciousness. She imagined herself very happy indeed, only some occult influence had changed her from her old self.

Perhaps, as the days went on, Le Roy may have felt this subtle change. At any rate, the two weeks which followed his betrothal were duller than he had expected. Some sauce piquante was wanting. He was precisely one of those men, to whom the chief charm of any object consists in the winning of it, — once his, it was apt to pall upon his fancy. For six weeks past there had been a certain kind of excitement about long morning sessions in Elizabeth's little parlor, listening to and drawing out her quaint fancies and crude theories, afternoon rides behind his high-stepping horse, and evening lingerings under moon and stars, amid falling dew, and air heavy with summer odors. But now, that all these things were orthodox, and he knew that it was expected of him to pass a good share of his days at Elizabeth's side, he began to grow tired of it all. He thought of the little girl in Sydney Dobell's song, who asked, —

> "Is she changed, do you think, papa?
> Or did I dream she was brighter before?"

and would have liked to pat the aforesaid little girl on the head for expressing his idea so well. Still, he contrived to satisfy all Elizabeth's demands, — partly, perhaps, because she knew so little of the ordinary ways of love and lovers. Then, too, her nature was generous, and not exacting. Moreover, she had logical foundation for an entire faith in him. She had neither fortune nor social influence, nor did she think herself in the least handsome. She thought, therefore, that the love which had sought her out, in spite of all these disadvantages, must be deep, if silent. So she went on, fancying herself altogether happy; but something had changed about her, she knew not what. She was quiet and submissive to an authority, recognized, if new; and, after all, the tamer had nothing to tame. It was a household bird, which came and went at his call, and wore his manacle willingly, but he could not fancy her his "wild thing, shy thing," any more.

One day, in the first week of August, he stopped at his Cousin Julia's on his way to Elizabeth.

"I am off for Newport to-morrow, Jule," he said, when she came into the room, "and I thought I'd look in on you a few moments before I went away."

"Are you off with Elizabeth?"

"No; without her."

"You know what I mean, — is it all over between you?"

Le Roy laughed. "Oh, no; it is all impending. I want to be married the last of October. I hate bridal tours, and all similar exhibitions of one's self to the million; so I want the wedding just when it will be pleasant to go back to town. Elizabeth will have enough to do in the mean time, and there is no reason why I shouldn't have my usual five or six weeks at Newport."

Mrs. Henry Fordyce looked at him for a silent moment; then she said, with an expressive lift of her eyebrows, — "Upon my word, you are a cool lover. But Queen Bess can't blame me, whatever comes. I told the Fordyces, before they ever saw you, that your heart was left out."

"If that be true of me, you will at least acknowledge

that I did well to select a wife who will not demand that I should dance perpetual attendance upon her. Elizabeth knows little of the ways of the world; and, thank God, she is neither exacting nor demonstrative."

"Neither exacting nor demonstrative, is she? Elliott, I quite understand the estimate you put upon my penetration; but, trust me, if *that* is your opinion, *I* know Elizabeth Fordyce better than you do."

A sarcastic smile crossed Le Roy's lips, but he suppressed it before it had time to rouse his cousin's ire, and said, with the air of one willing to listen to reason, — "You may be more than half right; but at any rate, the thing is done, and I came this morning to ask your aid towards its being well done. If I have sometimes questioned your penetration, you know I have never questioned your taste. The future Mrs. Le Roy will not be a woman of fashion; but some society she must see, and I am unwilling to be mortified by her toilets. You have lived in New York so long that you will understand just what she ought to have. I want you to help her with her preparations. Suppose you go down with her next week, and arrange about dressmakers, and the like. I will give you some blank checks, and you must see that she has every thing which she needs."

"But how will Elizabeth like this supervision?"

"I will make that all right with her. Of course I don't mean that her taste is to be set aside in the matter; only you must tell her what and how much she requires, and make sure that she has it."

Elizabeth swallowed a little pang at the announcement of her lover's approaching departure. She did not speak just at first, but he saw a quiver of pain flutter round her sensitive mouth, and I think he was human enough not to be sorry that she would regret him.

"I thought you understood all that, dear," he said, kindly. "My plans have been made for this sojourn at Newport from the first. I am to meet a party of friends there. It was an arrangement before I left New York. It will give you all the more time for your preparations. The last of October I want to take you home."

"My preparations will not be much," she said, a red spot burning on either cheek.

"But I want them to be a good deal. Mrs. Le Roy will not be shut up in a convent, and I want her properly made ready for presentation to her husband's friends. I have been talking to Julia about it this morning. She will go to New York with you, and help you shop. To save you trouble, I have left the sinews of war in her hands, and she will see to all the bills."

"But, Elliott," — she called his name very timidly, for she had not spoken it often, — "I don't like you to do this. I should feel so much happier if you would just let me have what my uncle chooses to give me, until — afterwards."

He silenced the pleading lips with a kiss.

"I want you to be prepared for afterwards," he said, resolutely, though not unkindly. "If you are ready to give yourself to me, and let me take care of you for life, surely you need not oppose my pleasure in this trifle."

She looked at the great diamond eye glittering on her finger, — her manacle. The color came and went in her cheeks. She shut her lips firmly to keep them from betraying her by their quivering. Her eyes grew moist. A tenderer, more generous man would have understood her well enough to spare her this humiliation; but Elliott Le Roy was not tender, or in any large sense generous, and he silently waited for her acquiescence. She did not venture to blame him, even in her heart. He did not know how she felt, and of course it was not to be expected that he would. And perhaps, after all, he *had* a certain right to make sure that she would not mortify him. So she said at last, very quietly, — "I will give up my own will in the matter to yours, and do as you and Aunt Julia tell me; but I *wish* you had not desired this thing."

He ignored the last part of her sentence altogether, and only thanked her for being such a good, sensible little girl, just as he had felt sure she would be, when she came to consider.

After all, the weeks of his absence passed quickly. It was not in the heart of woman, least of all such a beauty-loving woman as Elizabeth, not to be interested in all the elegant things which were purchased so lavishly for the future Mrs. Le Roy. Nor, indeed, was she quite enough in love to have her lover's absence take away all the brightness from her life. She understood herself so little that she was not conscious of any lack in her experiences; but there were depths in her nature which Elliott Le Roy, let him love her never so well, could not have sounded. And yet, if he *had* loved her generously and fondly, she would have gone through life beside him, and he would never have lacked any thing in her eyes. It is almost always easy for even a man, who is not the right man, to hold a woman's heart, if he will but love her enough.

Twice a week Le Roy wrote to her, and she was very proud of his letters. They were not love-letters, though he always addressed her as the one to whom his future belonged; but they were very brilliant letters, full of wit, and observation, and satire. She was proud that he should thus give her of his best; and her answers, though she was not vain enough to perceive it, paid him back his own coin with usury. Elizabeth, in her modesty, had never understood her own capacities; but Le Roy began to discover, during this correspondence, that it would be in her power to dispute the bays with him on his own ground, if she chose.

Early in September he came to see her for a day, and admired the progress of her trousseau, delighting Mrs. Henry Fordyce with his unqualified approval. He gave her at this time a second commission, — bridesmaid dresses of the loveliest blue silk for the "three Graces."

"Not white?" she asked; for colored dresses were less in vogue for bridesmaids then than they are now.

"Decidedly not white," he answered. "White is

for Elizabeth, alone. They will be grouped around her, and it is my fancy to have my pearl set in turquoise."

Elizabeth opened her gray eyes a little wider when he told her that his absence was to be still farther prolonged. He was going to the White Mountains with the same friends whom he had joined at Newport. She did not utter a word in opposition; but he answered the unspoken protest in her eyes.

"You are busy, my Queen, and I should only be in your way. Besides, you know these are my last months for enjoying myself *en garçon*."

She looked at him gravely. "Am I to be a burden to you, Mr. Le Roy, — to stand in the way of your enjoyment?"

"Not at all, foolish girl; only to change its nature a little, perhaps;" but he thought to himself as he spoke, that even this last was extremely unlikely to happen.

So he went away again, and the preparations went on.

He extended his trip into Canada, and was gone a week or two longer than he expected. Then there were arrangements to be made in New York for the reception of the bride in her new home; so that somehow October was over before a positive time could be fixed for the wedding; and it came off at last, on a November morning, gloomy and despondent, which of itself seemed to Elizabeth's imagination to presage ill.

The "three Graces," having made their own toilets at an earlier hour, assisted at the bride's, by their presence and comments; but a quiet little dressmaker, who had set most of the stitches in the white robes, put them on. Elizabeth stood up at last, fair and pale as a snow image, with a wonderful radiance of shimmering silk and falling lace about her. Mr. Le Roy came to look at her before her uncle took her to church; his most gallant, debonair self, on this occasion, quite ready to pay her compliments.

"Am I all right?" she asked him, a little anxiously.

"If the other Queen Bess had been a tithe as fair she would never have died unwedded. But you look like a wraith, — unreal, illusive. Will you 'slip like a shadow, a dream, from my hands'?"

"Not now," she answered. "If you should tire of me, by and by, who knows what I would do?"

"Well, at least you shall wait for that," and then he took her in his arms, and kissed her for the last time as Elizabeth Fordyce. Did his kiss lack any thing, or did some secret whisper of destiny make itself heard just then in her soul? She clung to him an instant, in a strange passion of emotion; was it regret for the well-known past, or dread of the untried future, — who knows? She only said, — "I shall have no one in the whole world an hour hence but you. God help us if we are making a mistake!"

Elizabeth Le Roy came out of the church, where she had stood, a pale pearl, among her cousins, brave in blue and gold and in their young, strong, healthy beauty, whose brilliance no sentimental sorrows would ever dim, — among them, but not of them, as she had been for so many years. She came out, leaning on her husband's arm, and the keen, penetrating November air seemed to strike to her heart with a sudden chill.

She had speculated sometimes, as what girl does not, in her dreaming girlhood, about her wedding morning; but somehow her fancies had never been any thing like this reality. Still she tried to believe that she was not only very prosperous, but very happy.

Mr. Le Roy, wealthy, elegant, critical, had chosen her, — her, out of the world full of women he knew. He was going to take her from the stillness and inaction of which in those long, dreamy years her very soul had grown tired, and carry her into the thick of life, — such a life of stir, and tumult, and endeavor as she had longed to try. What did it mean, that fate should so have filled her cup to the brim? Why, to her of all others, had this brilliant destiny opened? And what ailed her, that she was not fuller of self-gratulation, that she could take it so quietly?

They went home, and ate bride-cake, and drank champagne; and then Elizabeth went away to take off her misty robes. One last look her husband had of her in those garments, as she turned at the foot of the stairs to speak to him, her drapery, white and fleecy as a cloud, falling about her, — a tall, slim shape, with gleaming eyes, and hair of silken dusk, and face of lilies not roses, save where the lips had budded red. She looked too much like a spirit. Le Roy was glad when she came back again in her travelling dress, and they went away.

He had been quite ready to fulfil his engagement with Elizabeth, rash and ill-considered as in his secret soul he had already begun to think it; but the whole matter of the wedding had bored him, and he was glad to be done with it. He had not enough of faith or spiritual insight to have the words of the marriage service impress him with their solemnity, or even touch him by their beauty. It was simply a necessary evil, with which he was thankful to be done. He was rejoiced that Elizabeth did not cry. It was like her good sense, he thought. But, indeed, she had not loved any of the Fordyces enough to melt into tears over them. The hills, as lonely as herself, were the friends to whom her heart was knit the most closely: and as she stood at the old window for a few silent moments, looking out towards them, over her eyes there "began to move something which felt like tears." But she turned away resolutely. She was bidding them and her past good-by. Who knew what heights of joy, what depths of woe, her soul would touch before she should see those hills again?

Their long car ride was a strange bridal journey. During those monotonous hours, Elizabeth had plenty of leisure to think of what she had done. Now and then she stole a look at her companion's handsome, inscrutable face, as he bent over the newspapers with which he had provided himself at the second station. It did not cross her mind that he was an uncommonly inattentive bridegroom. She knew very little of the world's usages. She had never been accustomed to be watched and tended, and she did not expect very much in that way even from him; but she would have liked him to talk to her a little, to satisfy her doubts of herself, if such satisfaction were possible. She was suffering, as she rode along, from a singular oppression, — a dread, lest she should not be elegant enough to please him, — should shame him by her ignorance of the ways of that world in which he moved.

She struggled with these doubts and fears in silence, for it was not her nature to make much ado about her feelings. She had always borne whatever she had to bear without words. A woman more exacting, more accustomed to be an object of interest, would have demanded Le Roy's attention, told him her thoughts, constrained him to soothe or reassure her. It is possible that this course would have suited him better, though he did not understand himself well enough to think so. At least, it would have given him an interest of some kind in the affair, and an occupation. As it was, he began to feel himself ennuied. He would have liked to think it a respectable proceeding to take himself off to the smoking-car, and enjoy a cigar or two in peace. Since this would not quite do, he began to watch Elizabeth covertly over the edge of his paper.

She was always handsomest when she talked. Now her face was colorless and motionless, and it lacked that perfect classical regularity which makes repose statuesque. The excitement of capture was all over. His "wild thing, shy thing," had been curiously tame and submissive ever since she had worn his ring on her finger. He felt in his heart that he might be tempted by too much submission to become a tyrant, and he wondered if the instinct of serfdom belonged to Elizabeth. He was destined to find out some day.

He asked himself, in a vague discontent, to what end he had hastened their marriage. Why could they not have remained engaged for a few years? Then he remembered that he had felt impelled to hurry matters because Elizabeth had had it in her mind to go out governessing, and plumed himself anew on the right he had earned to her gratitude, by having saved her from this career. At length, out of very shame, he roused himself from this train of thought, and pointed out to his wife some familiar object. They were nearing New York.

Elizabeth had understood from Mrs. Henry Fordyce, that Mr. Le Roy had a handsome establishment, but she was hardly prepared for the quiet elegance of the house on Madison Square to which he took her. A housekeeper, stately in black silk, received them; and Le Roy, bidding his wife welcome home, with more of tenderness than he had shown her at any time during the journey, told her that Mrs. Murray had managed his household for years in a way that could hardly be improved; therefore, there would be nothing for the new queen to busy herself about but her own pleasure, — the prime minister behind the throne would take all trouble off her hands.

Whether or not she liked this arrangement, Elizabeth submitted to it silently. Mrs. Murray led her upstairs to her own room, — a spacious chamber, — from which opened on one side an elegant sitting-room, on the other, Mr. Le Roy's dressing-room. Strangely enough, a passage from the Bible came into her mind at that moment, — "All these things will I give thee if thou wilt fall down and worship me."

Just then, in a rush of enthusiastic emotion, she thought it would be only too easy for her to worship her elegant, handsome husband, from whom all her good gifts came. She felt a new thrill of tender thankfulness for the love which had elected her to share the half of this man's kingdom, which brought to her eyes some silent tears. If she had married him with any thing short of the entire consecration of her whole being, she had erred from pure ignorance of her own nature. But if either this man or this woman had loved with that unqualified surrender of self, which is so entire and so holy, that it is little less than religion, and which is so mighty that, felt on one side only, it has before now made of marriage a saving ordinance, I should not have had my story to tell.

CHAPTER V.

AFTER FIVE YEARS.

FIVE years had gone by, — years which the locusts had eaten, as they say in Provence, — aimless, profitless years, which yet had brought Elizabeth from eighteen to twenty-three, and wrought, I was about to say, some subtile changes in her character. But I correct myself. I think all our possibilities are latent in us from our birth. Most of us are many-sided, and circumstance, like the turn of a wheel, brings uppermost now one side of us, now another. Elizabeth Le Roy fancied that she was not what Elizabeth Fordyce had been, but then Elizabeth Fordyce had not known herself.

Of these five years she had kept no record. Elizabeth was not the kind of woman who keeps a diary. She could not ease her pain by spreading it over reams of paper; or by self-pity solace herself into a sort of luxury of woe, practically almost as desirable as happiness. The long, slow years had eaten into her life, but she had made no sign. Some scenes were seared upon her soul, — some words burned into her heart so deeply that she thought not even the river of Death could wash them away; but neither the world nor even her own household knew her as any thing but a prosperous, elegant, haughty, silent woman. Only Elliott Le Roy knew that the Queen Bess he found in Lenox had been neither haughty nor silent. Did he ever think with a pang of regret of the vanished girlish sweetness?

She came downstairs, on the fifth anniversary of her marriage, with her toilette carefully made, as usual. Her soft, heavy black silk trailed after her soundlessly as she walked. Dainty laces made a white mist at throat and wrists; her jewels were pearls, quaintly set. She had a singular charm for the eye, though she was not, never had been, a beauty, as her husband had once told her. It was the only outbreak of coarse sincerity in which he had ever indulged, — the only time vulgar truth had come, strong and passionate, to his elegant lips. They had been married scarcely two years then; and Elizabeth had not yet lost her faith in his love. From the first he had left her a great deal to herself, and she had almost always borne his absence patiently; but this one time it entered her mind to remonstrate. He was going away on a pleasure trip, and she begged him either to stay at home, or to take her with him, with an exacting earnestness to which she had never accustomed him, and which some brutal instinct, rising to the surface and overpowering his suave polish of manner, impelled him to put down at once.

"It is certainly not my fault, Mrs. Le Roy, if you are poorly entertained," he said, coolly. "You have at your disposal your time and my money. As my wife, society is open to you."

"But I am not your wife for the sake of society," she had persisted. "For what did you marry me, if you did not care to have me with you, — if our lives were to be apart?"

All that was demonic in Le Roy's nature, and that was no little, looked for a moment out of his eyes in contemptuous silence, then burst from his lips. "By Heaven, what *did* I? What summer day's madness was it which made me fetter myself to a woman not rich, or distinguished, or even handsome?"

She thought, for an instant, that she should fall helpless at his feet; then pride brought the color back to cheek and lips.

"So you did not love me?" she asked, slowly.

"Did I? — I have forgotten."

The words stung her with their contempt, till cheeks and lips grew white again; not with faintness this time, but with a white heat of passion.

"I told you once," she said, speaking each word with slow distinctness, "that for a man to marry a woman without loving her, was a crime which I, for one, would never forgive, on earth or in Heaven."

Le Roy looked at her, and feared the spirit he had roused. He would have given a good deal to unsay his own words. As it was, he could only eat them. He spoke more hurriedly than was his wont.

"Elizabeth, we are behaving like two children. If I had not loved you, why on earth should I have chosen you? If I loved you once, is it likely to be entirely over in two years? Don't exasperate me into saying things which will cause ill-blood between us. You take the surest way to wear my love out when you are exacting, and make me feel my chains. Remember how free a life I had led before I knew you."

And she, proud woman that she was, feeling herself altogether his, too reserved and too self-respecting to turn anywhere else for comfort, altogether helpless in her dependence upon him, suffered him to seal a hollow truce upon her lips; but after that day she never again urged him to stay at home.

Since then she had been three years his wife, —just as entirely his, subject to his pleasure, bound to hold up his honor, as if they had loved each other with that love which makes marriage a sacrament. She almost hated herself when she thought of it. And now it was the fifth anniversary of those mistaken nuptials.

The last three years had gone by her like a long and evil dream. That one outbreak on her husband's part had never been followed by any other. He had treated her with all outward courtesy; but he was like the French chevalier who killed more men in duels than any other *beau sabreur* of his time, and who always smiled as he slew. No chronicle, had she kept never so many, could have recorded the times when she felt the merciless pressure of the iron hand under the velvet glove, — when his keen scorn struck home to her heart; his merciless politeness froze her; his forgetfulness, which seemed born of contempt, goaded her to madness.

Sometimes she had prayed to die, with a passion which it seemed should have opened Heaven; but not even Death wanted her.

After a long time, suffering seemed to have deadened her nature. Le Roy came and went, and she scarcely knew it. Sometimes he talked to her, but his words were vague to her as dreams, — polite, inquiring, sneering, it mattered not, — they made no impression. She ceased to shrink, even on the rare occasions when his lips touched her mouth, or he took her, his property, into his arms with some sudden sense of that loveliness of hers, which the slow years had brought to something paler, purer, and more striking than of old. Nothing made any difference to her, — nothing seemed worth while.

She woke up this afternoon, — because it was her wedding-day, perhaps, — and wondered what this long and entire absence of emotion had meant. Was she dying, or slowly going mad. Better death itself than this hopeless apathy.

She went back upstairs, and opened a wardrobe in an unused chamber. Her wedding-dress hung there. She looked at the shimmering white robes and frosty frills of lace, until they carried her back to her old self, and the feelings and emotions of the old time. Something in her nature seemed to break up, as the streams do when the winter frosts are over. She felt tears gathering in her eyes, those eyes which had been dry so long, and she wiped them away with a thrill of thanksgiving. Then she shut the door, and turned its key on the ghostly, gleaming bridal fineries, and went downstairs again, and sat in the lonely grandeur of her drawing-room, at a window opening upon the street.

How many weary hours she had sat there during

these slow-paced years which had gone by her. She had watched funerals there, and weddings; beggars and republican princes. That window had shown her strange sights. Startling contrasts were to be seen from it, even now; but she did not stop to marvel at them. It seemed natural that there should be changes in the world, — only for her there was no change, and that was stranger than all.

She began to ask herself what it meant. For what reason was she here, always here, — here where she did not want to be, and where no one wanted her, — far away from all the landmarks Fate would have seemed in early days to have set for her, and yet held here by the iron clutch of Fate itself? All sorts of chances and changes happened in the world, — deaths and births, fortunes made and lost, unexpected discoveries, hidden things brought to light, — but for her nothing save the same dead level, the life she hated, with not even a breath of wind across the desert sands.

Then suddenly as if another than herself had asked it, the question came to her, — why did she stay here? Why not go on to the next oasis? Somewhere over a cool fountain the palm-trees rustled, the water of life waited for her lips. Was she imbecile? Had she no courage? Why had she sat still so long, and let the years go by her, never once trying to take destiny into her own hands, — growing old, and hopeless, and despairing, but never struggling to help herself? Did God make her a coward, or only a woman, — or were the words synonymes? Did she not deserve all she suffered? Why had she married Elliott Le Roy in the first place? But, looking back, she saw that she could not justly blame herself for that. Her eyes had not been opened to what love might be by any feeling deeper than she experienced for him. She remembered what a knight, without fear and without reproach, he had seemed to her when she first met him, — a Saul among his fellows. She had neither understood her own heart then, nor had any standard by which to measure him.

Is it not true that women are marrying as unwisely every day? Some find out their mistake, and are still indifferent; because to them life is in the abundance of the things a man possesses. Will such women's heaven, I wonder, ever be more than meat, and drink, and raiment?

Others, in these mismated ranks, never understand themselves. They find life a tread-mill round; but they do not guess that it holds any deeper joy or subtler woe than themselves have tasted.

But she did know, — this poor Elizabeth. She had found out. She understood herself but dimly, even yet; still she knew that there was something in her crying out for ever with a cry that would not be silenced, — an inner self, dying slowly, for want of room to breathe. She wondered again why she had stayed so long.

She had no child to look at her with its father's pitiless blue eyes, whose possible meanings she knew so well, now. If she had had one, she could have borne on for that, and drawn strength from the thought that she was suffering for another's sake, not her own. But now she suffered for no other. Le Roy did not want her; or, if he did, wanted her only because of his own pride; and surely he, who had been in all things so utterly self-seeking, deserved nothing at her hands. Her own self-respect she would preserve. Her own honor should be unstained; but she was not held in the old grooves by any fiction of honor or duty toward him. He had put those to flight long ago. Why, then, did she sit on there idle, with the great gay world of chances and changes outside, and grow old and hopeless, losing all the years that should be young and glad, doomed to a thirst which no fountain was given her to quench?

She might have asked herself as well, if she had been wiser, what she could possibly gain by going away? To go away from her keeper would not free her from her bondage. She could only drag her chain with her. Morally and legally, the fetter would be upon her still; and would the simple gain of not seeing one man's face compensate her for all she must give up, — her position of worldly ease and high repute, — the luxuries of which long use had made necessities, — all the good things of this world which belonged to her as Mrs. Le Roy? But she was inconsequent by nature, as women almost always are. Roused at last from the torpor which had so long held her motionless and silent as death, with no throb of feeling beyond a vague, sad wonder at herself, she now began to long passionately to get away. But where should she find any door of escape? Did God, who sent an angel to open Peter's prison-house, keep in His Heaven any messenger of deliverance for her?

She heard the street-door open to the master of the house, and she sat still and waited for him. The emotions of the afternoon had left their impress on her face. Perhaps she had never in her life been so handsome. Her eyes sparkled feverishly. Her cheeks glowed. Her lips were vivid crimson. Her husband came in, and his observant look rested upon her. He bowed to her with an air of gallantry which seemed to her so hollow, that her very soul rose in rebellion against it. He said, as he bent before her, — "I congratulate myself, Mrs. Le Roy, on having your face in my drawing-room. It has blossomed anew to-day."

"Do you know what day it is?" she asked, coldly.

"Let me see, — fifth, sixth, seventh of November, is it not?"

"It is the fifth anniversary of our marriage."

"And in honor of that your roses have bloomed? I congratulate myself that you have retained through five years of matrimony so much sentiment for me."

"Sentiment for you!"

She got up and stood before him, a slight shape, with her soft lengths of black silk falling around her; her gleaming eyes, her cheeks, where burned the roses he had praised. Her voice was low, but awfully distinct. Her words dropped into the silence like stones into a well.

"I will tell you just how much sentiment I have for you, Elliott Le Roy. I hate you. You took me, a warm-hearted, honest girl, ready to love you. But you did not want my love. You have chilled me, till now *my* heart is ice, too. I only want one thing in this world, and that is to get away from you."

"Take care, Elizabeth."

She looked straight into his eyes, and saw a red gleam kindle them. His face was livid. His lips were set. But she only laughed a bitter laugh.

"No, I will not take care. I have taken care long enough; and lived in mortal fear of your cold, sneering words, and your pitiless eyes. I don't want to stay with you. Why *should* I stay?"

Le Roy smiled, — a smile which was not good to see.

"I will tell you why, but take a seat first, if you please. We are not upon the stage, and we can talk more at our ease in a less dramatic position."

She obeyed the inclination of his hand, and sat down. He went on, quietly, — "I will tell you why you should stay; because it is my pleasure. I do not choose to have my domestic matters in the mouth of every man about town. It is my will that you remain here, and I think you will not be mad enough to go away. If you left me without other justification than you could bring, do you think there is any capacity in which scrupulous people would receive you into their houses? There would be no one thing which you could do to support yourself. You could take your choice between starving and going back to Lenox. Perhaps your uncle would welcome you cheerfully, if he found you had forsaken your own home. Of that you can judge; you know him, probably, better than I do. I should scarcely fancy, however, that to go back among your old friends, under such altered circumstances, would quite suit you. About that you can consider, however. In the mean time, if you please, we will go to dinner. It has been waiting ten minutes already, and you had best understand fully that our affairs *shall not* be talked about in our kitchen."

He offered her his arm, and she took it, girding fiercely at herself. Why had she not courage to refuse to keep up this sham? Why was she still meekly obeying the man she hated?

Le Roy talked in his lightest and most sparkling vein while dinner was served. Jones — oh, the sagacity of our domestic critics — remarked downstairs, between the courses, that he guessed something had gone wrong with the master to-day, he was so extra smiling and smooth.

Elizabeth constrained herself to make answers when they were necessary; but she went on, meanwhile, with her own thoughts. Clearly, her husband would never help her to break from her bonds, and what could she do of herself? She had said once, that when she was old or tired of life she should want to go to Lenox and die there. But she was not ready to go there now, and face those familiar eyes. She felt herself strong and full of life, in spite of her despair; and she thought death might be too long in coming.

After all, was she not utterly helpless? She would have shown herself wiser to have gone on in silence, in the old, passive way. Now, of course, Le Roy would never forget or forgive what she had told him. Still, what matter? What could he do to make her life any more hopeless or barren than it had been so long? That night, when she had said her prayers, — the old, simple, familiar prayers of her childhood, — she added to them another, — "O God, thou who didst send the angel to Peter, open for me a door, — I pray thee, for thy mercy's sake, open for me also a door!"

She forgot, entirely, to say, "Thy will, not mine, be done." She was like some passionate child crying for the moon. If the moon should fall at his entreaty, the child's destruction would be sure and swift; but still the Father holds the heavens in their places, and rules the lives of men.

CHAPTER VI.

AN OPENING DOOR.

Three weeks went by without a single allusion having been made to the passionate words Elizabeth had spoken. Whether her husband believed them, understood them in their full significance, or regarded them as a momentary outbreak, born of "just the least little touch of spleen," she could not guess. He had ever since treated her with his customary smooth politeness. It had been seldom always that he gave her any thing positive to complain of, but she had thought sometimes that Torquemada himself never invented tortures keener or subtler than hers.

Le Roy had once questioned within himself whether the instinct of serfdom belonged to Elizabeth. If this instinct provides that the serf shall love his chains, assuredly she had none of it; for though she wore hers in silence, every day they galled her more and more, and her spirit grew more and more bitter and impatient.

"Was there really a God in Heaven?" she asked herself sometimes, "who *cared* for His creatures? Had He not rather framed some pitiless laws under which He had set His universe in motion, and then, sitting serene and far-off in His Heaven, undisturbed by any groans or sighs, left them to crush every offender against them to powder?" If she had only had a little faith; but for her, in those days, neither the sun shone by day, or the stars by night. Her heavens were as dark as her earth.

One forenoon Le Roy came in, and found her sitting idle and listless, as usual.

"I am off to-day," he said, "with a party of gentlemen for Havana."

"And I?" she asked, lifting her eyes to his face.

"You will of course remain in your own house. You

will find that every necessary arrangement has been made for your comfort. You need not be troubled with any cares concerning money. Mrs. Murray is competent for all indoor details. Jones will supply any outside wants. You will find your credit excellent at all the places where you are accustomed to trade; and you need have no anxiety about any thing."

Elizabeth understood him fully. She saw that she was not to be trusted with money, lest she might use it to baffle her keeper's will. She spoke the thought which came uppermost.

"You might as well send me to a private mad-house at once."

He smiled, his cool, cynical smile.

"Oh, no, I do not think that will be necessary. Such things have been done, when women have shown themselves incapable of understanding their own interests. In such a case a husband, of course, would not hesitate; but you, I think, will be wiser. You have speculated a good deal about social questions. You used, I remember, to have quite fine-spun theories of life."

Poor theories, she thought, — where had they brought her?

She sat silent, and watched her husband as he moved round the room, selecting a few things he wished to take, and restoring others to their places. She began to feel a sort of curiosity about their parting, thinking of herself in a vague, questioning way, as if she were a third person. Would that man kiss this waiting, watchful woman when he bade her good-by, she wondered. It was not that she wanted the kiss, or even shrank from it. She felt a wholly impersonal curiosity, such as I suppose every one of us may have felt about ourselves, in moments when emotion has grown torpid and observation is wide-awake. It was not his habit to make affectionate farewells; but then he had never gone on a sea voyage before; and she believed there was some tradition about connubial kisses before long partings. But, no; when he was quite ready he only said, with that irritating, condescending politeness, which always nearly maddened her, — "Good-by, Mrs. Le Roy. You must manage to amuse yourself. I hope you will not be dull during my absence."

And then he was gone.

Elizabeth sat still where he left her. Her face was like marble, but her soul was in arms. *He* could wander where he liked, — he need not even go through the idle ceremony of consulting her. His own pleasure was his only law. For her there was no freedom of choice, no change of place such as she would welcome, even though it were only change of pain. She, this rich man's wife, had not a paltry hundred dollars at her command. Here she was, shut in by these brick walls, held fast by Fate; and outside, still outside, was the world, as much beyond her reach, with its great and strange delights of chance and change, its bewildering excitements for heart and brain, as it had been when she lived among the lonely, lovely Lenox hills.

Just here I want to protest against being supposed to endorse the course of my poor Elizabeth. I tell you the story of a living, breathing, suffering woman; but because I show her to you as she was, you have no right to conclude that I show her to you as I think she ought to have been. Unquestionably she would have been nobler had she striven to conquer her fate, instead of sitting and longing vainly for means to flee from it. Many, many faults she had. She was rash, undisciplined, wanting in faith as in patience; and yet, just such as she was, I loved her very deeply, and would rather pity than blame.

For a week after her husband went away, she sat alone, and brooded in a kind of passionate despair over the circumstances which environed her, at feud alike with Fate and with Providence. Then there came to her a letter with the Lenox post-mark. This was a rare event, for during her married life she had seldom heard from Lenox. She had not cared so much for any of the Fordyces, that it had cost her any special pain to let them drift out of her life. If she had been very happy, she might possibly, after the manner of women, have liked to summon them as witnesses of her felicity. As it was, she had acquiesced willingly enough in her husband's opinion, that "it would just be a bore to have them there; country relations always wanted showing round, and it was the most tedious thing in life;" and therefore none of her cousins had ever visited her. She had always sent them gifts at Christmas time; and upon the announcement of Kate's marriage to a well-to-do young Berkshireman, a handsome silver set had gone to her, in the names of Mr. and Mrs. Le

Roy. But this letter from Lenox was not in the chirography of either of the "three Graces."

Elizabeth broke the seal, and first of all there fluttered into her lap a piece of newspaper. She took it up, and read the announcement of her uncle's death; and after it a long obituary, setting forth his excellencies as husband, father, man of business, member of society at large.

"Poor old uncle," Elizabeth said, with a sad smile, "he has departed this life with all the honors."

Then she took up her letter again. It was in two sheets. The first, which enclosed the other, was from a lawyer, whose name she recognized, but who was not her uncle's customary legal adviser. She remembered him as a man whose integrity stood in very high repute in Lenox.

His letter informed her that three weeks ago the late Mr. Fordyce had called upon him, and entrusted to his care eight thousand dollars, with the understanding that as soon as convenient, after his decease, it should be forwarded to herself in the form of a draft on some good New York bank. At that time Mr. Fordyce had shown no signs of illness, but, notwithstanding his apparently good health, had seemed to be impressed with a conviction that he had not long to live; and, for some domestic reasons, into the nature of which he did not enter, had wished to have this money conveyed to Mrs. Le Roy in such a manner that it need not come to the knowledge of even his own family. Doubtless the enclosed letter from her uncle, of the contents of which he himself was entirely ignorant, would make the whole matter clear to her. In a day or two after this interview, Mr. Fordyce had been seized with the sudden illness which terminated his life; and as soon as practicable afterwards, arrangements had been made for carrying out his instructions with regard to the money. Mrs. Le Roy would find the draft enclosed. The late Mr. Fordyce had provided for all the details; and Mr. Mills had only to request of Mrs. Le Roy an acknowledgment of the safe receipt of his letter and its enclosures.

With curious emotion Elizabeth took up the draft and looked at it, — a draft in due form for eight thousand dollars, payable to her order. Was there, after all, a God in Heaven, whose ears were not deaf to the cry of a weak woman's woe, — who heard prayers and answered them? Her uncle must have gone to Lawyer Mills about this matter just after those wild entreaties of hers, that the God of Peter would open to her also a door. And now her door was opening; for she never doubted for one single instant what use she should make of this money.

She broke open the dead man's letter next in order, and this was what it said: —

"My Niece Elizabeth, — I believe myself to be about to die. I cannot tell why this belief has taken hold of me, but I am sure that I am not long for this world. And, before I go out of it, I have an act of restitution to perform. When your father, my dead and gone brother James, died, if you had received your due, you would have had six thousand dollars. But the business was embarrassed at the time, and I thought that to put so much money out of my hands just then would ruin me. I took the responsibility, therefore, of deciding not to do it. I managed, by means that were not strictly legitimate, to keep the whole in my own possession. I did not mean ill by you, either. Your memory will bear me witness that I dealt by you in every way as by my own children; nor do I think the interest of your six thousand dollars, in whatever way invested, could possibly have taken care of you so well as I did. Still, to have it to use in my business at that critical time, was worth much more than the cost of your maintenance to me. So, as I look at matters, you owe me no thanks for your upbringing, and I owe you no farther compensation for the use of your money during those years which you passed in my house. For the five years since then, I owe you interest; and I have added to your six thousand dollars two thousand more, to reimburse you for your loss during that time.

"If my life should be prolonged for many weeks, I shall make arrangements for quietly putting you in possession of this sum; but I do not think it will be prolonged. I am acting upon a profound conviction that my days in this world are almost numbered. I had rather that this matter should not come to your knowledge till after I am gone. As I have not defrauded you of a single dollar, but on the other hand have, as I conscientiously believe, done more for you with your money than you could have obtained for it in any other way, I think I have a right to request you to keep the whole thing a secret. The most careful investigation of my affairs will not reveal the fact of any subtraction from my property. This fund is one which, ever since your marriage, I have been saving, gradually and secretly, for this very purpose. There is no need to toss my name to the geese of Berkshire; or even to make known to my wife and children that I had done something which, it may be, their notions of right would lead them to condemn. I acted according to my own lights; and I repeat, Elizabeth, I have not wronged you by so much as a dollar. If your husband must know this matter, at least let it go no farther. When you read these lines, I shall be standing, it may be, at your father's side; and for the reason that I was his brother, if for no other, I believe that you will deal gently with my memory. Your Uncle

"ISAAC."

Elizabeth's seldom falling tears wet the last words of this letter.

"Poor old Uncle Isaac," she said aloud; "you builded better than you knew. You have opened my door, and it is little to ask that not a soul on earth shall ever know your secret."

CHAPTER VII.

OUT OF THE CAGE.

Elizabeth had no conflict of ideas at this time. For her this eight thousand dollars had but one use, — flight from her fate; one meaning, — freedom. She felt as if Heaven itself had dropped this unexpected bounty into her lap. This was what she had been praying for. At last, in this great world of chances and changes, something had happened even to her. Now she could break her chains, elude her keeper.

The eleventh day of December, she stood on the deck of a steamer, outward bound for Havre. All her arrangements had been completed with a tact and secrecy and worldly wisdom which surprised herself. Not even Mrs. Murray's vigilance or Jones's curiosity had suspected her. Her outfit, the deep mourning of a widow, had been made at a University Place dress-maker's, whom she had never patronized before. She took off her diamond ring, and laid it in her jewel-casket. She locked drawers and wardrobes, and put the keys in an envelope, which she sealed and directed to her husband, leaving it in his desk. She left with it no word of farewell. She was utterly indifferent as to what he thought. She believed that he had no heart to be wounded. She credited him with no unselfish anxiety for her safety. As for his pride, he must nurse and solace that as he could. She felt free of him when once that great, glittering diamond eye was off her finger. She would take nothing of his, nothing except the plain gold wedding-ring, which was to corroborate her widow's weeds. Even the simple walking-dress which she wore to University Place, when she went to put on her mourning, was purchased with her own money. She left the house on foot, as if to take an ordinary walk; and that night dinner waited for her in vain at Madison Square, and she ate hers between blue water and blue sky.

Her name was registered in the list of passengers as Mrs. E. Nugent. As Nugent was both the name of her mother and her own middle name, she felt that she had a certain right to this designation, and was not exactly sailing under false colors.

The passage occupied thirteen days, and during that time she had ample leisure to arrange her plans for the future. The interest of her small fortune would be but a meagre support, she knew, even in Paris, where she had heard that the expenses of living were much less than in New York. Still, if a pittance, it was at least something fixed and certain, and she *could* live on it, if compelled by necessity. In the eager joy with which in those days she contemplated her freedom, she thought no life apart from her husband, whatever its privations, could be so comfortless or so barren that she would not infinitely prefer it to the fate she had left behind her. Still she believed herself to have resources. She had some knowledge of French,

— the imperfect knowledge a studious girl can acquire from such teachers as a country place affords. Her accent was bad, she knew; her grammar at fault; her ignorance conspicuous in every sentence she tried to frame. But these things would mend daily. Meantime, her French could not be much worse than the English of most of the language-masters whom she had been in the habit of seeing; and she thought her inaccuracies and inelegancies need not prevent her from seeking and probably finding employment as an English teacher in Paris. She had begun to acquire confidence in her own executive ability, which had stood her in such good stead in the last few days.

She withdrew herself during the voyage, almost entirely, from the rest of the passengers, as her deep mourning gave her an excellent excuse for doing; but more than one had noticed with an interest kinder than mere curiosity the young, delicate-looking woman, with her sad, sweet face, who knew no one, and whom no one knew.

"We shall see Havre to-morrow," the captain said, going up to her, as she sat on deck looking over the railing into the lapsing waters, alone as usual.

Captain Ellis was a man in his fifties, — such a man as the sea makes of material good in the first place, — cool-brained, quick-witted, clear-headed, large of heart, strong of muscle; above all, with no shams about him; entirely true, and entirely in earnest.

From the commencement of the voyage, Elizabeth's face had interested him, and her loneliness appealed to his sympathy. She might have been a daughter of his own, as far as years went; and this man, who was only the father of sons, felt for her a curious tenderness, though they had scarcely exchanged a dozen sentences. He could not bear to let her slip away from him like the waves in the wake of his vessel, and leave no mark. At least he must know whether she was going to a safe harbor.

I have spoken before of the singular charm of Elizabeth's voice. Captain Ellis felt it in the few words which answered him. Nothing in her manner, however, invited him to prolong the conversation; still, secure of his own good intentions, he determined to seem curious and officious in her eyes, rather than miss any possible chance of serving her. He stood beside her silently for a few moments, then he asked, apropos of nothing, as it appeared, — "Did you ever fancy that gray hairs might be an advantage, Mrs. Nugent?"

She gave, at the sound of the name by which she had been so seldom called, a slight start which did not escape his notice; but her voice was very quiet, as she said, — "I suppose every one longs for them, or for what they signify, who is tired of life. Any sign that one is nearing the end must be welcome."

"But I am not tired of life, Mrs. Nugent, or in any present hurry to get to any better place than Havre. I have found life a good thing. My days have been good days, and I am in no haste to end them. I like the salt, free wind, the wide sea, the watching sky;

and I will hold on to life while I may, always ready, please God, to die bravely when I must. Still I find an advantage in gray hairs, notwithstanding. But for them, and the fact that I am quite old enough to be your father, I should not venture to ask you, as I am going to, whether I can be of any assistance to you after you leave the ship. I suppose you will go on to Paris; and if you have no friends to meet you at Havre, perhaps there will be some way in which I can serve you."

Elizabeth looked up to him, a sudden rush of tears swimming in her dark eyes, her old, eager impulsiveness glowing on her changeful face.

"No one will meet me anywhere. I am all alone in the world, — running away from my destiny; but it seems to me God must have brought me so far, and perhaps He will help me on."

For a few moments Captain Ellis did not speak. Then he said very gravely and very tenderly, — "Tell me as much or as little as you like. But let me help you if I can. I have a wife at home, who is as good a woman as ever God made; and I had one daughter, who died before she had spoken a word except my name. If she had lived, she might have been about your age, now. I think I would not have let her take her life in her hand, as you have done; but I would have blessed any man who showed her kindness. For her sake, and her mother's sake, I would like to be kind to you."

"My father and my mother are in Heaven," Elizabeth

said, in a low voice, "and I had no one who cared for me very much. I cannot tell you my story; but I have done nothing which would have been unworthy of your daughter had she grown up to womanhood. If you will believe me, and help me, without knowing any more, I will indeed be thankful, for I am friendless. No soul in France has ever heard of me; but I think I shall do very well there, if I can manage the first steps. I have money enough to keep myself from absolute want, and my plan is to add to my income by teaching English."

Captain Ellis considered for a few moments before he said, — "I was trying to think whether I could get away from the ship for twenty-four hours, and I do not see how it can be done. But I will put you in the cars for Paris, and give you a letter to the American consul there. He happens to be an old friend of mine; but, even if he were not, you, as his countrywoman, would have a claim upon his care. I shall have to trust the business of getting you properly located to him."

Elizabeth had had the consulate in her mind before as the ark of refuge for an American citizen; but the captain's letter would make matters much easier for her, and she thanked him warmly. She had scarcely realized how lonely she was until she was taught it by the contrasting comfort she felt in the friendly interest of this stranger.

As she sat in the cars, in the early morning of the next day but one, whirling on toward Paris, she began, for the first time since she started on her long journey, to tremble in view of the untried life, the new, strange land. She had Captain Ellis's letter in her pocket, and he had given minute directions for her guidance; and yet it came over her, with a sense of awful desolation, that she was going into the midst of the world's Babel, the great, tumultuous city of which she had heard so much, all alone. In that seething, surging sea of human life, who was there to care if her little bark went down?

She pressed her face close against the car-window, and looked out over the strange, unknown land, up to the constant, always known sky, — God's Heaven, arching over all. She had cried out to Him before, in the bitterness of her despair, half doubtful whether He would hear or heed her; but she had never learned to draw nigh to Him as to a loving Father. It was strange that just at this hour, with the unaccustomed scenes of this new country before her, the murmurs of the almost unknown tongue buzzing in her ears, the faces whose aspect was so unfamiliar about her, she first began to have a near and sweet sense of the Friend who might be closer than all, — so that out of the very unrest of time and place, her soul drew nigh to the rest which is everlasting. It is not for any seer or psychologist of us all to explain the mental or spiritual experiences of another soul. Such analysis is beyond our weak vision; but the truth remains, by whatever means wrought, that for the first time in Elizabeth's life she felt herself ready to say, not as an idle form of words, but out of the depths of her heart, — "Thy will be done."

What that will was she did not know; or guess how widely she might have strayed from the path it had marked out for her. She was yet to learn her lesson of life through bitter sorrows; but she felt now that, however long or lonely the way she trod, she should never again experience the awful solitariness of a soul without God in the world.

She grew interested at last in the scenes through which she was passing, — the low, yet pleasant fields, where old women with blue umbrellas watched their cows, or shepherds with their dogs guarded the flocks; the odd little stone huts, scarcely six feet high, where the Norman peasants burrowed, with houses of substantial elegance interspersed now and then; forests, with their trees set out in rows; quaint costumes; picturesque churches; pretty railway stations, — every thing had for her the charm of novelty, the glamour which invests the unknown.

As she neared Paris, her heart began to beat suffocatingly; but she found the provident care of Captain Ellis had extended farther than she knew. A civil man, wearing the badge of a guard, came forward, and saved her all trouble with her luggage; and almost before she knew it she was in a *fiacre*, driving toward the consulate, in the Rue de la Chaussée d'Antin.

The consul received her with a courtesy, which became friendliness as soon as he had read Captain Ellis's letter.

"I think I know the very thing that will suit you," he said, "if it is not already taken up. A friend of mine, an American artist, left, three days ago, some quiet rooms, in a quiet old house on the Rue Jacob. He boarded with a French family, a man and his wife, who occupy the third floor, and who let him, at a very reasonable rate, a bedroom and a little sitting-room. If you could get it, it would be just the place to cast anchor in at first, — when you know Paris better, you can make a change if you choose?"

"I shall be thankful enough to cast anchor in any safe harbor, and stay there," Elizabeth said, gratefully.

"Then I will send a clerk with you at once. If unfortunately the rooms are engaged, and you will drive back here, we will see what else can be done. In addition to my interest in serving one of my countrywomen, any friend of Captain Ellis has a peculiar claim upon me."

Fortunately the rooms *au troisiéme* in the house in the Rue Jacob were not engaged, — most fortunately, Elizabeth said to herself, for she fell in love with the quaint old house at once; and her delight was intensified when she looked out of the windows of the little third-story back sitting-room, which was to be her own. In the rear of the house was a delicious old garden, shutting in a quarter of an acre of ground, in the very heart of the city. Over the high walls ivy ran luxuriantly, — a summer-house was in the centre, and flower-beds and shrubbery promised pleasantly for the spring.

She left the clerk, a voluble Frenchman, to make her bargain for her, and the matter was settled in five minutes. Her luggage was brought upstairs, and Madame

Nugent was at home in her two little rooms, with their brilliant cleanliness, their smoothly waxed floors, and inefficient little fires far within the deep jambs, sending frightened jets of flame up the chimneys. Her delight in it all was as fresh as a child's. She liked the odd furniture, — the bits of rug in front of bed, and easy-chair, and sofa, the inevitable clock and pair of candlesticks on the chimney-piece, the heavy chintz curtains about her little bed.

It was her first unalloyed taste of pleasant novelty, poor girl, and she had left no one whom she loved behind, — no one to mourn after, no one to be sorry for her. Her eyes grew bright as she looked around her, and a fresh glow came to her cheeks. At last she was out in the world for which she had longed. And she guessed so little what lay before her, — as little as we all divine of our to-morrows, God help us.

CHAPTER VIII.

THE DOCTOR DOWNSTAIRS.

"And madame has no friends in Paris?"

"Not one, good Madame Ponsard, unless you will let me call you by that name."

The flexible, tender, pathetic voice found its way to Madame Ponsard's heart, and a tear in her eye answered it before her words, — "I think madame may take that for granted."

"I think I may, for you have been very kind to me."

Elizabeth had just come home from giving an English lesson. She had five pupils already, though she had been in Paris scarcely a month. Madame Ponsard had procured them for her; and though they were *bourgeois*, they paid very well, and she considered herself in quite comfortable circumstances.

She felt a sense of freedom, of expansion, which exhilarated her like wine. She changed her habits with her mood. She was no longer studious. The books which had been at once the solace and the occupation of her past life, were left with that past behind her. She spent her leisure hours in wandering round the old Faubourg St. Germain, in the midst of which was the Rue Jacob; and taking in all the strange sights and sounds which everywhere met eye and ear.

Sometimes she went to Notre Dame, and idled an hour away pleasantly looking at the wonderful stone carvings on the exterior of the church, wondering whether the carver, fashioning here a saint, and hard by a devil leading some doomed band to endless woe, here a bird and there an evil beast, had builded with some pious purpose of making every thing that hath breath praise the Lord; or whether he had laughed a wicked laugh as he cut the incongruous shapes.

She developed, too, quite a love for harmless gossip. She liked to hear Madame Ponsard's voluble chatter about Monsieur Grey, the artist, who used to occupy her rooms; the charming widow on the first floor; the American doctor, whose apartment was just underneath them, and who used to come upstairs so often to see the artist, his compatriot, — such a clever man, madame said. Why, he had given her a *tisane* once for herself, and her throat had never been sore since.

It is possible that Elizabeth wanted to hear some of these often-told stories over again on this particular afternoon, late in January, when she took her work and went into madame's little sitting-room. But somehow the talk drifted first to her own affairs. There was a space of silence after Madame Ponsard had asked whether Elizabeth had any friends in Paris, — a space of silence which the French woman broke rather hesitatingly.

"And, — I beg pardon, but madame's face is so young, and her mourning so fresh, — I suppose Monsieur Nugent cannot have been long dead?"

"I lost my husband the week before I started for Paris," Elizabeth replied, in a tone which made her voluble companion feel that no more questions were to be asked. She bent over her sewing again, while Elizabeth looked idly down the street; for madame's sitting-room was on the front. At last she said, with a little color in her cheeks, — "I met a new face this afternoon as I came up the stairs."

"What sort of face?" madame inquired, with eager interest.

"A very good face, I should think. A man with kind-looking gray eyes, brown hair, and strong, resolute features, — not handsome, and not young."

Madame laughed, and patted softly together her pudgy little hands. "Good! good! That is the doctor downstairs. I know him from what you say. But he is not old, — not forty yet. Madame Nugent is so young, that what seems youth to me is like old age to her. Oh, but Dr. Erskine is not ill-looking, either."

"No," Elizabeth answered, musingly. "I said he was not handsome; but I think he is better than that. It is a face one can trust. How happens it I have never seen him before?"

"Some of the time he was away. For the rest, his hours for going out and coming in have been different from yours. But I am glad you like his looks. He is your countryman, and if you should be ill, that would be one grand comfort."

"For what is he here?"

"To study in the hospitals. Monsieur Grey said he was a great doctor in his own country; but he wanted to see some practice here; you know our surgeons are the most skilful in the world. It was last fall he came, and he said he might stay a year."

Elizabeth was ready to laugh at herself for the absurd interest and curiosity she experienced about this stranger, whom she had just met on the stairs; but then, in apology for her weakness, she thought how few human interests she had. And, after all, the face was that of a countryman. She began to think that there might be more in that tie than she had quite realized.

After this day she met Dr. Erskine frequently. Of course it is not to be supposed that he changed his hours of going and coming. A grave doctor of almost forty could not be suspected of watching from his window for the passing along the street of a slight, swift shape in black, and then of snatching hat and gloves, just for the sake of meeting on the stairs a white, young face, framed in by a widow's cap, and making to this, his neighbor, a silent bow. But somehow these interviews happened so often that this doctor, with whom she had never exchanged a word, but yet who was her countryman, grew to seem more closely her friend than any one else she had met in Paris. Some sure instinct told her that he was a man to be trusted all in all. How happy his wife must be, if he had one, — or his mother and sisters, — for she could not quite fancy him a man to have left a wife behind him.

Before February was over, an intuition told her that the American doctor, with his good, reliable face, might be destined to be more of a blessing to her than she had as yet fancied.

She had been married so long, with never a child to lay its bright head on her bosom, that she had ceased to think of this among the possibilities. And now, gradually, but surely, the knowledge came to her that before midsummer her baby, hers, would be numbered among the world's little children. At first she trembled with emotion, — half bliss, half a fear too exquisite for pain. Then another thought smote her like a blow. She had said in her passionate pride, that she would bring away nothing belonging to Elliott Le Roy. And now this child who was to come would be as much his as hers. Had she, then, sinned in coming away? Had she taken from him something which might have changed his life, wrought out his salvation, — something, at any rate, which it was his right to have? Must she go back? Was it her duty?

Then, with the ready sophistry which comes so easily to us all in the cause of our dearest wishes, she persuaded herself that he would have given the child no welcome, — that, if he knew all, he would very likely be thankful to her for taking it out of his way, — that, at any rate, it was hers, as it never could be his, and she was ready to pay the price for its possession. Now, indeed, she would have something to love, — something to be her very own, and fill heart and arms both full. Surely God knew just how much loneliness and solitude of soul she could bear, and had tempered His winds to her uses.

No more wanderings now round the old Faubourg, or in the galleries looking at carven stone or painted virgins. She had told her secret to Madame Ponsard; and the two women had bought, with real feminine delight, a store of lace and cambric and fine linen. Elizabeth kept on with her English lessons; for she was more ambitious than ever to make money, and add to her provision for the future. But all the time she was at home she was sewing away at the dainty little garments mothers have fashioned between tears and smiles since ever the world began.

She thought she was at last happy; but it would have seemed to a looker on the saddest thing in life to see her bending over her task in those deep mourning robes of hers; so young, so solitary, and yet so full of womanly hope and courage.

One April day, Madame Ponsard paid a secret visit to Dr. Erskine, and told him privately all which she herself knew of her boarder's history.

"Of course," she said, "you will be the one to attend her when her trial comes; and I thought it might be better if you should see her now and then beforehand, and get to seem not quite a stranger to her. *I* will open the way by being sick to-night or to-morrow, — and, indeed, I am troubled by a fearful indigestion."

Madame drew out a long sigh, and Dr. Erskine smiled as he looked at her black, bead-like eyes, and her fat, rosy, unromantically healthy face.

"I will come the moment you send for me," he said. "So, Madame Nugent started for Paris the week after she lost her husband?"

"Yes. She told me that much, one day. It was in answer to some question of mine; and there was something in her manner that made me think it would be just as well not to ask her any thing more, — though, indeed, as monsieur knows, I am the least curious of women."

Dr. Erskine looked smilingly after the good-natured little gossip as she trotted away. Then he turned back into his room and shut the door.

"At last!" he said to himself; and then he laughed, as a third person might, at grave, thirty-eight-years-old Dr. John Erskine being as eager as a boy about a new acquaintance.

"No wonder. The truth is, I have so few things here to think of," he said, apologizing to himself as Elizabeth had done before. Then he sat down at his window and looked out. It was about time for his neighbor to return from giving her English lessons.

That evening the *bonne* from the floor above knocked at his door. Madame Ponsard was very ill, — had sent for him, — would he come quickly?

He put a little case of bottles in his pocket, and, assuming an expression of grave interest, hurried upstairs. Madame Ponsard was lying on a horse-hair sofa, and Madame Nugent was bending over her anxiously, with fan and sal volatile. A humorous twinkle in Madame Ponsard's eye, as she began the woful tale of her sufferings, nearly upset Dr. Erskine's composure; but he maintained his gravity with a struggle, and at once mixed and administered a portion of medicine, — not very hard to take, as madame's satisfied expression sufficiently indicated, — and then sat down to await its effects.

They were almost immediate. In fifteen minutes madame sat up, declaring that she felt as well as ever, and that Dr. Erskine was a man the most remarkable she had ever seen. Then she introduced him in due form to Madame Nugent; and he lingered a half hour longer to express his delight at meeting a countrywoman, and to pave the way for future visits.

After that he spent an hour, as often as once a week, in Madame Ponsard's sitting-room, and Elizabeth was usually present. She tasted a pleasure in these interviews, which she did not attempt to analyze. For the first time in her life she was brought into close relations with a man whose intellect satisfied her, at the same time that she could entirely respect his moral qualities. He had two distinguishing traits, as was before very long made clear to her, — a will sovereign over himself as over others, and a tenderness which took into its shelter every living thing which was more helpless or more desolate than he, and which, she thought, must hold and cherish whatever was his very own with a devotion exceeding the love of woman.

Perhaps you are reading these lines without half comprehending how noble and how dangerous a man Dr. John Erskine was. Count over the men whom you know, and tell me how many you find who have inflexible wills, without being grasping, selfish, firm for themselves rather than for others, — or how many who are delicately sensitive and tender, and yet have strength to stand up grandly, and are not blown about by every wind. When you have counted this bead-roll of saints, you will know better whether I have given John Erskine rare praise when I have said that his will was as firm as his heart was tender. I called him not only noble, but dangerous; for he was such a man, it seems to me, as a woman like Elizabeth, who had been wounded so cruelly by the absence of the very qualities which he so largely possessed could hardly know intimately with safety to her own peace of mind. Just now, however, it appeared that she wore proof of mail, her whole heart was so full of yearning tenderness for the little being, her very own, whom the summer was to lay in her arms. It is possible that, after all, the chief danger may have been for Dr. Erskine.

CHAPTER IX.

WHILE THE MUSIC PLAYED.

It was the very last of June, when, for hours and days, death stood waiting in Elizabeth's little room; and Dr. Erskine fought with him, and at length won the victory. But for his wonderful skill, and still more wonderful care, as Elizabeth knew afterwards, neither she nor her child would ever have lived through those dark hours. For days both their lives seemed to hang on a very frail thread; but the poor young mother was delirious all the time, slipping from one wild dream into another; and when at length she woke to consciousness, the danger was past, and her week-old baby lay on the bed beside her.

She looked at the exquisite child as if that, too, were a dream. Then she put out her hand and touched the pink, soft flesh, and drew it back again, satisfied. The little morsel had rings of dusky, silken hair like her own, and faint, shadowy eyelashes resting on its cheeks. How eagerly she watched it, only mothers know. She and it were all alone. She scarcely dared to breathe, lest she should break the slumber which wrapped it like a spell. She lay there in a kind of ecstasy till it awoke, — not with a cry, but with a soft rustle, a stretching out of the little arms here and there, a low murmur, then wide opening eyes. Elizabeth looked into those eyes eagerly. They were the darkest of gray.

"Thank God," she said, under her breath. "The child is stamped mine, not his. It will not be like him in a single feature."

It uttered, just then, a little, twittering cry, in which she fancied she heard the music of the spheres. The faint sound brought in Madame Ponsard. Her eyes filled with tears when she saw Elizabeth's face of quiet content, and realized that the crisis was past, and the reign of hope had begun. But she only said with true French tact, going up to the bedside, — "So madame concluded to wake up and look at her little daughter? I hope madame is satisfied with the prettiest baby in Paris?"

"My little daughter, — my little daughter." Elizabeth said the words over to herself. A girl with her eyes, her nature. God save her from her fate! She would need to have a great many prayers said for her, this little one.

Two weeks more went by before Elizabeth could sit up, — and two weeks after that before she could go out into the beautiful summer, and gather the flowers of which the wide, rambling, old-fashioned garden, far down underneath her windows, was full. During all this time Dr. Erskine came daily, and brought in the sunshine with him, — sunshine blossoming in roses and jasmine, or globed in luscious fruits. And Elizabeth was happy, for the first time in her life, with an untold, indescribable happiness. She thought it was all because of the baby fingers with their waxen touches, the tender lips which drained her sorrow dry.

The baby, — whom she had named Marian Nugent, after her mother, but whom every one called "*mignonne*," or "*chérie*," or "little angel," — was indeed queen of the old house in the Rue Jacob. Madame Ponsard adored the little one. Childless through all her life herself, the instinct of motherhood, so powerful with women, came now to the surface, and overflowed in devotion to this child, born under her roof, and half her own, therefore, as she reasoned. Monsieur Ponsard drank less absinthe, and gave up a good many games of baccarat, to look wonderingly at this new importation from Heaven, this last and most touching of miracles. The gay widow on the first floor, even, came up to lay her offerings on the universal shrine. And as for the doctor, it became a customary thing not only for him to spend half his leisure time indoors, wherever the white-robed wonder might be found, but to take it down with him, and out into the garden, in his great, strong, tender arms.

Elizabeth's eyes and heart kindled over the new sight of a man so masterful and yet so gentle. When she got well enough, she used to follow down to the old garden, and sit there, and look after him and her baby, as they went to and fro among the flowers. Sometimes the little one would go to sleep, and then Dr. Erskine would bring her and lay her in her mother's arms, and stay and watch them both, and talk of "life, death, and the vast forever;" or Elizabeth would tell him stories of her old life in Lenox, — never, by any chance, of her sad married years, — making pictures for him of each old scene, till hills and trees and arching sky grew familiar to his thought as to her own. Then, when the afternoon began to grow chill, he would hurry them both in again, — these two, whom he liked still to call his patients.

So peacefully and blessedly August and September went by. Elizabeth never stopped to think what gave to this wine of life she was quaffing its so keen zest. Sometimes, when she loved her baby most, and was happiest in all its untold sweetness, an accusing prick of conscience would bring the child's father to her mind, — not as lover or husband of her own, not even as the cool, cynical Mephistopheles of her life, but purely in his aspect of the child's father, who had been defrauded by her act of all these delights which made her own heart so rich. But she tried to think that she had acted for the best, and that Heaven itself, in giving her the means of deliverance, had endorsed her course. Nor did these conscience pricks come often to sting their pain through her pleasure. For the most part she was entirely, overflowingly happy, as she had never been before, without thought or care for yesterday or to-morrow.

With October, the winds blowing down from the North Sea grew chiller; and it was only now and then that there was a day bright enough to take little Marian into the garden. But still Dr. Erskine continued his daily visits. Elizabeth declared that she was jealous, because the baby stretched out her hands to go to him, before she had ever accorded her a similar token of preference. It was a very good-natured jealousy which she felt, however; and somehow it gave a wonderful brightness to her face.

One day the doctor insisted that she should go with him for a ramble in the gardens of the Tuileries. Little Marian would do excellently with Madame Ponsard, he said; and Madame Nugent herself was certainly suffering for a breath of fresh air.

"He has a right to command you," Madame Ponsard remarked while the question was pending. "But for him neither you nor the child would be alive to-day."

So Elizabeth tied on her bonnet and went, — the first walk she had ever taken with Dr. Erskine.

They were very silent, as they wandered round the grand old gardens which Le Nôtre laid out in the seventeenth century, — Le Nôtre, whose dust long ago, let us hope, blossomed in roses. They went on till they came to Coustou's Venus, and sat down on the old stone bench near at hand, to look at that vision of sculptured grace. Then, at last, Dr. Erskine said, — "The time is nearly come at which I purposed to return to America."

Elizabeth felt a curious sensation of chill, though the October sun was shining. Just then the band began to play some slow, sad music. The time came afterwards when, standing face to face with death, as she thought, she seemed to see again those stately gardens, to look at Coustou's statue, and to hear the slow, sad music play, and Dr. Erskine's voice telling her it was almost time for them to part. It was the first time she had realized that he and she and Madame Ponsard, and the baby they all loved, were not to go on eternally, just as they had been going on for the swift, short two months which lay behind her. She drew a sharp breath, but she did not speak.

And the band played, and the October sun shone, and the prophetic wind blew from the north through all the trees, and after a while Dr. Erskine spoke again.

"I have no right, I know, to ask the question, but if you feel towards me enough like a friend to give me your confidence, will you tell me just this one thing, — was your marriage a happy one?"

"No."

She could not have spoken another word. She wondered how that one had got itself said through the chill that was stiffening her lips and turning her heart to stone.

After a little space, Dr. Erskine's voice came to her, low, clear, and yet, as it seemed, from far away, — "If you had said yes, I should not have told you what I am going to tell you now. I love you very dearly. I am thirty-eight years old, and I never loved a woman before. I should not have dared to say this to you if I had thought there was nothing but a grave between you and a man whom you had loved. But, if you have never been made happy, let me make you happy. I can. I will. Do you believe me?"

Did she believe him? Oh, God, did she *not* believe him? Had her punishment overtaken her?—for now she felt that in fleeing from Fate she had failed to evade Responsibility, or escape Retribution. She made a strong effort, and forced her lips to articulate the words which almost refused to come.

"I must not hear another word. I have no right."

"No right?"

"No, for my husband is not dead. I am still the wife of Marian's father."

She was frightened at the look his face took on,—such a look as she had never seen a man's face wear before. She made haste to tell him her story,—briefly as she could, but not sparing herself, or withholding any thing of the truth. And meantime the children wandered round with their *bonnes*, fashionable ladies passed with their cavaliers,—the autumn sun shone, the autumn wind blew, and the slow, sad music played.

When all was told, she looked timidly up into his face. Heavens! how sweet hers was! the dark eyes full of passionate appeal, the scarlet lips trembling. He was almost mad enough to kiss those lips then and there,—to tell her there was no law on earth so potent as that law of the soul which gave them to each other. Into the turbulence of his mood her low, pleading voice stole,—"Dr. Erskine, do you blame me so very much? I was young, and I thought I cared for him at first. Afterwards I know I ought to have been more patient; and I did very wrong to come away. But my punishment has overtaken me."

"Yours!" How his eyes kindled over her. "*Is* it a punishment to you? Do you care?"

"Do you think I could give you pain,—you who saved my life, and baby's,—and not care?"

"But for yourself, I mean. Elizabeth, have you any heart?"

The swift color flushing the poor, pale face answered him better than her low words,—"For myself I have no *right* to care. I deserve any suffering that may come; but you are blameless."

"Tell me one thing,—just one. If you were free, what then? Do you think I could have made you happy?"

"You are cruel. I will not think. God help me, I dare not."

The last words were so low, his strained ears could scarcely catch them. Just then Satan was tempting him sorely. He had not needed to be taken into any high mountain to see what for him would have outweighed all the kingdoms of this world, and the glory of them. He had never yet compromised with his conscience; but he was trying to do it now.

"Why should she not be held free, in this new world, from the old ties?" the Tempter was whispering. "You saved her life. Have you then no claim on it? Could you not make yourself a law to her soul? Does she not love you enough to obey you? You love her,—you would make her happy. That other man never loved her. God never joined those two together, — why should they not be put asunder? Are they not more utterly asunder already than even Death could ever make two who loved?"

He listened to these subtle whispers, coming gradually to believe in them, till the music ceased to play, its hour being over; till *bonnes* and children began to go away, and then he got up and gave Madame Nugent his arm.

As they walked, he said to her, — "Do you mean ever to go back to the old ties?"

"Never!" she answered, upon her first impulse.

"Then, — old things having passed away, — why should not all things become new? Elizabeth, you think I saved your life. Give it for ever into my keeping. You know how I will care for you and the child. I think I have a right to you. Oh, my darling, my darling, come and lay your destiny in my hands."

She turned on him eyes dark with unutterable woe. In her voice there was the faintest quiver of reproach.

"It is not your best self which is speaking, Dr. Erskine," she said, mournfully. "I think you care for me too much to tempt me, if you realized what you were saying. I will never do any thing to make myself unworthy to be Marian's mother; and, however we may reason about the matter, the simple truth remains. I am that man's wife, and no sophistry can make it right for me to hear words of love from any other."

She had uttered these sentences with an effort which

made her faint; but there was in them no faltering of purpose. After they were spoken, the two walked home in silence.

The next morning, a note was given to Elizabeth, which contained only these words: —

"You were right, and I was wrong. I would not tempt you to be other than you are, — the purest as the fairest woman, in my eyes, whom God ever made. I am running away, because I have not just now the strength to stay here. You will not see me again for two weeks. When I come back, I will be able to meet you as I ought, and to prove myself worthy to be your friend. JOHN ERSKINE."

Elizabeth was weak or womanly enough to press this note to her lips, in a sudden passion of love and pain. Then she caught up her baby, and kissed its soft, unconscious cheeks, talking her heart out to it, as mothers do, — as she could not have done to any one else on earth.

"Well, baby, dear, we must learn to do without him. He will go away across the great, wide sea; and we must be all the world to each other, you and I, — what an empty world, when he is gone out of it."

But either the sudden passion of her kisses frightened the child, or the sadness of her voice saddened it, — it burst into one of its infrequent fits of sobbing; and Elizabeth, taught unselfishness by motherhood, as women are, had to put aside her own pain, and comfort her little one.

CHAPTER X.

DUST AND ASHES.

Did the tender lips which Heaven had sent Elizabeth to "drain her sorrow dry," draw from her the passionate despair, the torturing unrest, of her mood at this time? I have sometimes thought so.

While she was happy, the little one had grown and flourished, — been a radiant incarnation of joy and delight. Now, in these days when it seemed to the mother as if all God's billows were passing over her, the child began to droop. She was never like herself again after Dr. Erskine went away. At first Madame Ponsard said, laughingly, that the little angel missed the doctor. But after a few days neither she nor any one else laughed when they spoke of the baby.

From morning till night Elizabeth held the little creature in her arms, watching the dark, questioning eyes, fondling the thin, transparent fingers, kissing the flushed yet wasting cheeks.

"Oh, if Dr. Erskine would but come back!" was all the time the burden of her longing. He had saved that little life once, — surely it must be, she thought, that he could save it again. For herself no matter. She knew now how easy it would have been to love him, — how dangerously near she had come to being willing to give up earth and Heaven for his sake, — and she thought that the blight which had fallen upon her child was the swift and sudden retribution for this sin of her soul. Oh, *must* this little innocent life pay the penalty for her? If only the child could be saved, she would go away with it somewhere, and never see Dr. Erskine again, — never even think of him, if she could help it.

Sometimes, in the midst of all this, her conscience asked her whether the sin for which she was suffering might not lie further back still. Had she not committed it when she fled away secretly from the home where God's Providence had set her feet, — the man to whom she had promised to cleave till death parted them? Well, she would do her best to atone now. If only her baby could be spared, she would go back and humble herself at her husband's feet. He should have his child, if he would, — he should pass sentence on her, and she would abide by it, — only let the baby live.

It was the old Romish notion of buying Heaven by sacrifice; and yet how naturally it comes to all of us in moments of anguish. Let but this cup pass from us, and we will drink any other, — only *let* it pass.

He was divine who, even in that first moment when agony beyond human conception forced from His lips this cry, added to it, — "Not my will, but thine be done." When this grace comes to mortals, it is the rainbow after the storm is spent.

Little Marian had been sick a week, when, one morning, Madame Ponsard looked at her more gravely than usual. "We must call a doctor," she said. "It will not do, to let this go on. Little *Chérie* is wasting away."

Elizabeth lifted her heavy, swollen eyes. "Is there no way to send for Dr. Erskine? I do not think any one else would help her."

Madame went down to the concierge herself, in her eagerness, and came back presently with slower steps.

"He left no word where he was going. He said he should be gone two weeks, and his letters must be kept for him. I think we ought not to wait."

"Send, then, for whomever you please. I believe that no one else will do her any good; still we can try. But you must make the strange doctor understand plainly, in the first place, that he must give up the case to Dr. Erskine, whenever he comes."

And then, as madame went out of the room, she burst into a low, heart-broken wail, — "He won't come, he won't come. God means my little one to die. And I have deserved it all."

Half an hour afterwards, a chatty French doctor sat watching Elizabeth's baby. He was heartily sorry for the poor young mother, and was kind to her, after his own lights. But he thought words would cheer her; whereas they went nigh to drive her mad. At last some cord snapped, and her weak nerves or her weak patience gave way.

"I cannot bear talking," she said, with a petulance which held in it something touching. "Please only tell me what you think of her, — whether she will live, — and leave us alone."

Good Dr. Bouffon was not disturbed. He hoped he could make allowance for ladies' nerves, he told Madame Ponsard afterwards. He answered Elizabeth with a calmness which she found intensely exasperating.

"It is impossible to say, dear madame, — quite impossible. She can never have been strong."

"Oh, she has been the healthiest little creature," Madame Ponsard interposed.

Dr. Bouffon bowed.

"Exactly, but health is not always strength. As I said, she could never have been strong. I have written the prescription which I think the case needs. For the result we must wait."

Then he bowed himself out. Madame Ponsard followed him, and Elizabeth sat holding her child alone.

Any other observer might not have considered its illness quite unaccountable. A first tooth was swelling its gums. A second summer had set in for a few days, burning October with the pitiless suns of July. There was a languor in the air which oppressed stronger constitutions. But Elizabeth associated the occult malady which was sapping the foundations of her darling's life with none of these things. To her it seemed a direct judgment from Heaven, — the execution of the sentence eternal justice had pronounced upon her. She lost sight of the beatific vision, which had once blessed her soul; of a Father, loving even while He chastened; and with something of a heathen's spirit, she set about offering her propitiatory sacrifice to offended Jove. She put out of her arms her baby, asleep now, and wrote to Elliott Le Roy these words: —

"Your child was born the 28th of June. I did not know of this which was to come when I left the shelter of your roof, or I should not have gone. The little one is very ill; and, feeling that she may not live, I think it right to give you the opportunity of seeing her, if you wish to, before she dies. Come, if you choose, to No. 50, Rue Jacob, and you will find her.

"ELIZABETH LE ROY."

Then, when Madame Ponsard came back, she told her story, and the contents of the letter which she wished posted. Madame was surprised and a little startled, but received the disclosure with the composure and tact of a French woman, and began calling her boarder Madame Le Roy as fluently as she had hitherto called her Madame Nugent.

Now, Elizabeth thought, she had given up her own will, — made the greatest sacrifice in her power. Now, perhaps, destiny would relent. But the days passed on, and brought with them no healing. The intense heat went by. It was clear, beautiful October weather, but still the child drooped, and daily the tiny hands grew more waxen, and the blue veins showed more clearly through the transparent temples.

On the afternoon of the fourteenth day, Dr. Erskine walked into the room where Elizabeth sat, as usual, holding her child. She lifted her languid eyes, but she did not speak. Not even a thrill of hope stirred her pulses. She felt in her soul that his coming was too late. He stood beside her, silent as herself, looking down at the child. Then he knelt, and counted its pulse-beats.

"Madame told me she was ill," he said, "but I did not expect to see her like this. I shall never forgive myself that I was not here to help you nurse her."

"It might have done no good," Elizabeth answered, so drearily that it went to his heart. "I think God meant her to die. It is my punishment. I have been altogether wrong. But now I have done my best to atone. A week ago I sent for *him*, — Marian's father. He will be here in less than three weeks if he cares to see her. Do you think we can keep her alive so long?"

She did not look at Dr. Erskine, or she would have seen a tense white line round his lips, which would have told her how he was suffering. He waited a moment till he could speak calmly. Then he answered her.

"We will try. I dare not promise you that she will get well. I think she is wasting away. She has your highly wrought temperament, and I could have told you that she never was strong."

"So Dr. Bouffon said, but I did not believe him. She has been so lovely."

"Yes, and it was partly her very frailness that made her so fair. But now you must give her up to me, and take some rest. Go down into the garden, and get the fresh air. Has there been no one to tell you how much her well-being depended upon your health?"

She gave the child to him obediently. For days Madame Ponsard had pleaded in vain to be allowed to hold her, and Elizabeth had clung to her obstinately; but it seemed another thing to trust her to Dr. Erskine.

Two weeks more went on, during which they watched together over that ebbing life. They seldom spoke to each other through this time; but now and then, out of the anguish of Elizabeth's tortured heart, would be wrung some cry which she would have suppressed before any witness but him.

"If she could but have lived," she would say sometimes, "to speak to me, to call me mother just once, I think I could bear it better."

Once, in the bitterness of her despair, she cried,—"Oh, if she were not quite so pure! If she had only lived to be soiled ever so little by human sin, I might hope to see her again,—but now she will go to the highest heaven, and I can never find her in all eternity."

To this Dr. Erskine made answer, or through him some holier voice spoke,—"I think the highest heaven is for those who have struggled and conquered, sinned and repented, rather than for those who have been spared alike all struggle and all pain. But I do not believe whole eternities can separate a mother from her child."

There came a morning at last when the baby's eyes did not open. Dr. Erskine felt the heart throb faintly under his fingers, but he knew it was beating its last.

He trembled for Elizabeth, and dared not tell her. She anticipated him.

"Doctor," she said, — and her voice was so passionless that it might almost have belonged to a disembodied spirit, — "I know that my darling is dying."

He bowed his head mutely. Her very calmness awed him.

"Is there any thing you can do to ease her?"

"Nothing. I do not think she suffers."

"Then will you please to go away? She is mine, — nobody's but mine, in her life and in her death, and I want her quite to myself at the last."

Sorrowfully enough he left her.

Elizabeth held her child closely, but gently. She thought in that hour that she had never loved any thing else, — never in this world should love any thing again. She wanted to cry, but her eyes were dry and burning, and not a tear fell on the little upturned face, changing so fast to marble. She bent over, and whispered something in the baby's ear, — a wild, passionate prayer that it would remember her, and know her again in the infinite spaces. A look seemed to answer her, — a radiant, loving look, which she thought must be born of the near heaven. She pressed her lips in a last despairing agony of love to the little face, from which already, as she kissed it, the soul had fled. Her white wonder had gone home. This which lay upon her hungry heart was stone.

An hour afterward Dr. Erskine went in, and saw the motionless mother holding to her breast the motionless child; and his first thought was that they had both died together.

But when he went up to take the child from her arms, Elizabeth clung to it with a passionate clasp. With infinite gentleness he entreated her to go out into the cool, reviving air, and leave for awhile her dead darling to the ministrations of Madame Ponsard. She obeyed him, in a patient, passive way, as if because to obey was less trouble than to resist; and he made her go down into the old summer-house. She sat there in utter silence, for an hour, conscious, as it seemed, of nothing which surrounded her, least of all of the tender pity in his watching face.

At last Madame Ponsard came down, and made a sign to him, and he got up and spoke to Elizabeth.

"Come, now," he said, "you may go back to the baby."

Her face lightened a little, and she got up and followed him.

The dead little queen of the Rue Jacob lay on her own tiny bed, made all fresh and sweet for her reception. She was robed in her richest garments, heavy with lace and embroidery, and in her hand was clasped a half-opened white rose-bud, as pure and pale as herself.

Elizabeth looked at her, and then turned to Madame Ponsard and Dr. Erskine, with such entreaty in her face, as brought the tears to both their eyes.

"Indeed," she said, "I am not ungrateful, but I shall have her such a little, little while. Mayn't I stay with her all alone?"

And so they both went out.

Once or twice, during the day, Madame Ponsard carried her something to eat or drink, and she took it with a sort of weary and patient submission, which was inexpressibly pitiful. Save for these brief interruptions, she sat all day quite alone with her dead.

At night Madame Ponsard went to her with a question. It was grievous to Madame's kind heart to see this silent anguish, which neither words or tears relieved, and which was so foreign to her own nature. She thought, if once the baby could be buried out of sight, Madame Le Roy would be able to cry, and by and by to grow cheerful once more. So she went to ask whether she should make arrangements for the funeral to-morrow or the day after.

The question roused Elizabeth.

"Not to-morrow," she answered, "and not the day after. I have sent for her father to see her. I will wait, and give him time. Let me keep her as long as I can. She was all I had."

So through the night, as through the day, she kept her solitary vigil.

The next morning Dr. Erskine came to her. There were the traces on his face of a conflict with himself, but his words to Elizabeth were few.

"I am going into Brittany for a few weeks. I think it is best."

"I think it is," she answered, drearily.

"Good-by, Elizabeth."

"Good-by."

The hand she laid for an instant in his was cold as death. No pulse quickened at his clasp, and she turned from him, as if even so few words had wearied her, to look again at the still face, the little dark-lashed eyes that would never open, the frozen lips that her kisses could never warm.

Dr. Erskine turned, and looked also, for a few silent moments, at the dead little queen he had loved so well, and served so faithfully. Then he stooped down, and pressed his lips to the tiny, stirless face, and was gone.

Elizabeth scarcely knew it when he went out of the room. For the time her passion of woe had absorbed every other emotion, save the one grim thought which would not be absorbed, — that Le Roy might be almost there, — that she was waiting for her Judge.

And so for two days more she sat there, — her arms empty, her heart faint with its hunger, her future so near that she seemed to feel an icy blast of its air.

CHAPTER XI.

A GATE OF FLAME AND A GATE OF FLOOD.

Toward noon of the third day after the baby died, Madame Ponsard came to Elizabeth, and asked her to go for a moment into her sitting-room. With a shiver running through every limb, Elizabeth got up and crossed the hall. She found herself face to face with Elliott Le Roy. She waited for him to speak.

The soulless gallantry which had stung her so often was gone in this crisis, from his manner; replaced, indeed, by a half-brutal hardness, which yet hurt her less than his mocking courtesy would have done.

"I came to see my child," he said.

It never entered Elizabeth's mind to spare him any shock, — she had always thought of him as without the capacity for feeling one. So she silently led the way to her own room, and pointed to the bed.

He looked for an instant at the little bit of pulseless marble lying there, with the white rose of peace in the sculptured fingers. Then she saw him grow white to the lips, and heard his cry, full of an awful passion of longing, —

"Dead! dead! Oh, God! my little child!"

She understood then, that even this heart of stone held the instinct of fatherhood. He could have loved his child.

She stole away noiselessly.

Whether he wept or cursed she never knew. When he came out, half an hour afterward, he was his hard, cold, mocking self again.

He asked a few questions regarding the time and manner of the baby's death; then went away to make the arrangements for its burial, which he communicated to Elizabeth in a brief note.

She did not see him again till he came next day to go with her to Pére la Chaise. They took the casket which held the little Marian with themselves, in the carriage which headed the short funeral cortége. They two, — alone at last with each other and the dead. But during all the drive neither of them spoke. Elizabeth was calm. It seemed to her that a mortal chill had hushed all the unrest and passion of her nature, — that she should never cry again, or smile, or care for any thing which went on around her.

But just at the last, when they were lowering her darling into the grave, when she heard the English minister say, solemnly, — "Earth to earth, dust to dust, ashes to ashes," she felt all this impassive coldness break up suddenly, and heedless of every thing but the little lump of clay, which she could never, never see again, she sank down beside the grave, and sobbed till she could sob no longer, and they lifted her up and put her into the second carriage of the small procession, where Madame Ponsard received her in her kind arms, and supported her all the way home, comforting and soothing her as only one kind woman can soothe and comfort another.

Le Roy went back in his own carriage, *vis-a-vis* with Monsieur Ponsard, who had left his wife to make room for Elizabeth, — went back, as he had come, in grim silence.

The next morning he came early to the old house in the Rue Jacob, and went into Elizabeth's sitting-room. He spoke to her with quiet decision.

"You will have to pack to-day; for we must leave at six this evening for Havre. A steamer sails to-morrow, and I have telegraphed to secure our places."

Elizabeth looked at him in blank wonder.

"Am I going back with you?" she asked.

"It appears to me to be the only thing for you to do, Mrs. Le Roy. Remember our marriage has not been dissolved. It binds us still, though its sole fruit is dust and ashes."

Elizabeth had made up her mind, beforehand, to submit herself to his judgment. She had found that for her freedom was not safety, even though she prayed every night not to be led into temptation. But now that the crisis had come, the struggle to submit was harder than she had expected. Every pulse was in mutiny. Still she offered no resistance; except that once she asked him if it would not embarrass him to take her back among his friends.

"Not in the least," he answered, coolly. "Not one of them suspects that your absence was without my knowledge and consent; or supposes me ignorant of any of your movements."

The man's cool mastery over circumstances astonished Elizabeth into another question.

"What did you tell them?"

"That an excellent opportunity presented itself during my absence for you to travel with some friends of your own, and as your health was not good, I had written to you to accept it."

"But the servants?"

"Thanks to your silence, they *knew* nothing, and I think they would scarcely have cared to retail their conjectures at the expense of my displeasure."

"But you did not know that you could ever find me," she said at last, amazed at his audacity.

Le Roy smiled the cold, glittering, cynical smile she remembered so well. An evil gleam of triumph shot from his pitiless eyes.

"I traced Madame Nugent without difficulty as soon as I returned from Cuba. I should have come for you, in any case, when I thought it time for you to return."

She had called this man the Mephistopheles of her life before; but never with such good reason as now, when he stood in front of her, smiling his mocking smile, exulting scornfully in his easy triumph. He had said once that he should hold on to her like fate, — and now she knew that she had never yet been entirely out of his power. Why should she engage in any vain struggle against his will?

From the very beginning of their homeward journey, destiny seemed to oppose itself to them, bringing to its aid all the perversity of inanimate things. A railroad accident, not serious, but most annoying, made their journey to Havre fifteen hours long, instead of six, so that when they reached their destination, towards noon on the fifteenth, the American steamer had been gone three hours.

Le Roy took Elizabeth to a hotel, where a fresh-colored maid, wearing a high Norman cap, brought her coffee, and went out himself to reconnoitre. He came in, half an hour afterwards, with his morning paper in his hand.

"There will be no other steamer from here till the first of next month," he said.

"Are we to wait here, or go back to Paris?" Elizabeth asked, feeling like a foot-ball which he and destiny were knocking back and forth between them, and waiting passively for the next push.

"Neither. My first thought was to go to Liverpool, and take the first Cunarder from there; but I see by a telegraphic despatch in the *Messenger*, that a steamer which left Hamburg last evening will stop at Southampton. We can sail for there to-night, after a day's rest here, and catch this German steamer for New York. Does this plan meet your approval, Mrs. Le Roy?"

"All plans are alike to me," Elizabeth answered, wearily. "If we are going to take the German steamer, may I telegraph to Madame Ponsard? She made me promise to send her word of my arrival here if I could. She thought we were going in the Fulton; and she will want to look out for news of us."

"Gratify your sentimental friend, by all means," Le Roy said, with a little sneer. "Write your dispatch, and I will see that it is sent."

Elizabeth wrote:—

"We were too late for the Fulton, and are going to Southampton to take the German steamer from Hamburg. Good-by."

She did not know why she said good-by over again by telegraph,—she certainly did not believe in presentiments, but some subtle foreboding of evil was assailing her, for which she did not try to account.

The next day, at Southampton, they went on board the German steamer, which set sail at quite a late hour in the afternoon. A heavy mist settled down with the twilight, and it was considered advisable to anchor the vessel between the Isle of Wight and the main-land. Early next morning they weighed anchor again, and in the process one of the crew lost his life. Owing to some mismanagement, the anchor ran out, whirling the capstan round with terrific force, and hurling the men in all directions. One was thrown overboard, and was supposed to have been instantly killed, as he never rose to the surface. This accident cast a gloom over the officers and crew, which any one familiar with the superstitions of the sea would readily understand.

"He's gone down below to tell 'em we're all comin'," one white-lipped sailor said to another; and the shadow fell upon them all. They were silent and depressed for days, though every thing seemed to promise a prosperous voyage.

Once at sea, and the confusion and excitement of embarkation over, Elizabeth settled into a strange, sad calm. Her presentiment of evil, though she had not forgotten it, ceased in any degree to absorb her thoughts. Every day, and all the day, she sat motionless and silent on the deck, looking into the troubled sea, or equally motionless and silent in her state-room. But everywhere she looked, into yeasty waves, or empty air, she saw one face only, — her child's. Madame

Ponsard, and the rest of them at the Rue Jacob; even Dr. Erskine himself came sometimes into the picture of which this face was the centre, but only as accessories to it. They seemed blank of human significance to her as the angles of a wall.

Of only one thing besides that face was she intensely conscious, and that was of Le Roy, — that he, her keeper, was breathing the same air with her, was carrying her home. How mad she had been ever to think that she could escape him. She wondered if through all eternity he would be beside her, and she should see for ever that face of pitiless power and mocking scorn. But it was very seldom that he came near her; and when they had been eight days at sea they had hardly spoken as many words to each other, beyond those demanded in the presence of others by the ordinary small courtesies of life.

On the afternoon of the ninth day, Elizabeth had come out of the state-room, and was standing quite by herself, looking into the surging autumn sea, but seeing only the one small face which for her filled sea and sky.

After a while she heard a wild and awful shriek, — the cry of fire, — horrible anywhere, but most unearthly and hideous in its horror far out at sea, when the flames are burning the one plank betwixt you and death.

By whom the cry was started, no one knew, but hundreds of voices took it up, and swelled it to a yell of madness and despair. A dense volume of smoke burst from the steerage, and then the flames broke through the lights, and leaped and crackled along the deck.

That first shriek had roused Elizabeth to something which was scarcely terror, — awful expectation, rather. Her foreboding was realized. Death was at last waiting for her. She had tasted the apple of life and found it bitter. What next?

She did not join in the wailing which went up to the unheeding sky. She no longer seemed to see the face of her little child. It had vanished like a vision. She looked down still into the sea, but she saw something else. Face to face with death, she seemed strangely enough to be living over again an hour of most intense and thrilling life. An October afternoon came back to her so vividly, that she seemed not to be standing on a burning ship, betwixt pitiless sky and pitiless sea; but sitting in a fair French garden, near Coustou's Venus, while the autumn sun shone, and the autumn wind blew, and the slow, sad music played, and through it all she heard Dr. Erskine's voice saying things which she had no right to hear. It was all so sweet, and sad, and wrong, — and now death was waiting for her.

How much had she sinned, she wondered. Was she past hoping for Heaven? God knew all, — temptation and sin and struggle, — God knew. Through all her turmoil and unrest, that thought filled her soul with a great calm. Simply as a child she said her prayer.

"Oh, God! oh, Father! suffer not my soul to perish! Take me home by flame or flood, as Thou wilt, but take me home!"

Meantime, a wild panic, of which she was altogether unconscious, had swept through the ship. From the very beginning of the voyage, when the sailor's life was lost at the weighing of the anchor, a secret terror had ruled the hearts of officers and crew. Now, with the first alarm, all presence of mind forsook them. The man at the wheel left his post, and the vessel being head to the wind, the flames swept back over her with awful rapidity. The captain was among the first to lose his self-command. Mad with panic terror, he attempted, forsaking all, to lower himself into a boat, and missing his foothold, was swept away. Then the wildest confusion began to reign. Boats were lowered, and some of them swamped in the very act of lowering. Those rushed into them who could, while others jumped into the sea, to escape the swift, hot pursuit of the flames.

At last Le Roy came to Elizabeth. He had been calm and clear-sighted through it all, waiting his opportunity. Now, as he thought, he saw it. A boat only partly filled, lay under the davits, on one side.

"Come," he said, pulling her along with him, swiftly.

He took a cloak from his own shoulders, and wrapped it round her, then lowered her from the vessel, and she was in the boat almost before she knew it. She looked back for him. He had stood aside for two more women. The officer in charge of the boat shouted,—"Keep off! We are full! another man would swamp us!" and at a sign from him, the men caught up their oars.

Just as, in defiance of the officer's warning shout, Le Roy was swinging himself down, the boat rocked away, and he touched the waves instead.

In an instant Elizabeth saw that white, satirical face, which seemed to mock even at death, looking up at her, with an awful light upon it, from the surging, fire-lit sea.

"Oh, save him! save him! for the love of God!" she cried, penetrated at last with the very passion and madness of terror, for that other life, not for her own. But no one noticed her cry. The rowers pulled away rapidly, and Elliott Le Roy went down, — as the captain had gone down before, — as hundreds of souls went down that awful day.

The engineers had been smothered at their posts among the first, so the steamer was going on all this time, at a rate of eight or ten knots an hour, as if she were trying to escape from the flames of her own burning.

She was an awful beacon, — a great, towering holocaust. The boat which held Elizabeth, pulled with all the might of its rowers in her wake. It was their best chance for a rescue; for she was a signal-fire of distress the like of which has seldom been kindled.

Still Elizabeth was calm and silent, but with all her faculties fully alive, — ready to live or die, as God willed, — anxious only, whether in life or death, to be in His keeping.

She should be glad, she felt, through all eternity, that Le Roy's last act toward her had been one of unselfish kindness. If she had any thing to forgive, she could forgive it all for the sake of that one moment. She had not loved him, nor he her; but, now that he was dead, she remembered how she had idealized him once, and began to look at him again in the old light, — to remember his power and exalt his strength, and see him master of circumstance, yielding only to destiny.

So the doomed steamer went on, grander spectacle in her death than she had ever been in her life; and the boat, with its dozen souls, pulled after her; till, just as night was settling down, the little company, faint with thirst and spent with rowing, saw a ship under full sail approaching the burning vessel, and rowed toward her with a strength renewed by hope. In an hour they got within hailing distance, and before the night had quite closed round them she had taken them on board.

The ship proved to be a French barque, taking a cargo from Newfoundland to the Isle of Bourbon. During the night sixty souls were received on board of her. Elizabeth looked anxiously at every one, to see if, by some Providence, the sea might not have given up its prey, but all were strangers. She thought then that she would have laid down her own sad life with unutterable content, but to see again in safety one face which had looked its last at her from the yeasty sea.

But Elliott Le Roy had gone down, with all the rest whom that day, by those gates of Flame and of Flood, Death led into the Land of the Hereafter.

CHAPTER XII.

FACE TO FACE.

No trace remained next morning of the fated steamer. The sky was as coolly blue as if no fierce flames had ever kindled a great funeral pyre below it. The sea was tranquil. The day was still. The officers of the French barque, seeing that they had done all they could, set sail for Fayal, intending to leave there the rescued passengers. But before that day was over they fell in with another barque, bound for Halifax, to which as many as could be accommodated were transferred, and among them Elizabeth.

So it came about that before Christmas her wanderings were over, and she went back again, a widow, indeed, and utterly free now, into that house from which she had fled to secure her freedom.

The excitement through which she had passed had roused her effectually from the apathy which had succeeded to the death of her little child, and which, otherwise, might not improbably have found its termination in insanity. She was in full possession of all her powers, — a sad woman, the colors of whose life had faded, but a woman who was mistress of herself.

She communicated to Mrs. Murray Le Roy's death, and the manner of it, leaving her to inform the rest of the household. Then she sent for her husband's man of business, desiring him to close up by spring, if he could, all the business details for which her presence would be desirable, as she wished to leave New York at the earliest possible moment.

The time had come to her now, she thought, when indeed she was done with life, and ready to go back to Lenox, and wait for death under those skies. She felt no desire to see any of the old faces; but her memories of the lonely, lovely hills appealed to her irresistibly. She thought she had tasted all the keen delights or sharp pangs which this life held for her; and now she longed only for rest. She wrote to Lawyer Mills, requesting him to secure for her a residence as near to her old home as possible; and learned, in reply, that the old home itself would be for sale in the spring. The youngest of the "three Graces," her cousin Emmie, would be married in February, and the widowed mother wished to give up housekeeping, and reside alternately with her daughters. So she began to look forward with homesick longing to the sheltered nook which the hills shut in, where she meant to pass the evening of her days, — this woman who fancied herself so old at twenty-five, that Hope and she had parted company for ever.

Sometimes, during those months, her thoughts went back to the old house in the Rue Jacob. Madame Ponsard would read of the destruction of the ill-fated steamer in which she had sailed, and believe her to be dead. That was best. She felt no inclination to write, and undeceive her. It was better to be dead to that old life, — dead as her youth was, and her heart within her.

6

Madame would be sorry, but she would grow gay again presently; though, to be sure, she would never forget her or the baby. Elizabeth knew if she should go back to Paris, after ten years had gone, she would find immortelles on little *Chérie's* grave, which madame would have hung there with pious care, — madame, who, childless herself, had loved that baby face so well. Still madame would be hearty, and healthy, and merry, and French.

And Dr. Erskine, — but she always stopped there, and told herself that she had no right to think of him at all. Of course, he would outgrow the old past, which had been only pain at its happiest, and love and woo some more fortunate woman; and that was best, too.

She was content; but, oh, the difference between that content which is born of resignation, and that other which is the paradise-flower of hope.

And so the winter wore away, and the spring, — and, at last feeling herself, with her share of her husband's fortune, quite too rich for her modest needs, Elizabeth went back to Lenox, and took possession of the old home, the purchase of which Lawyer Mills had in the mean time arranged for her.

She entered its doors, as it chanced, on the last day of May, the seventh anniversary of that day on which she had first met Elliott Le Roy. "Only seven years!" she said to herself, as this memory came back to her, — only seven years, and in them she had weighed the world, love, life, in her balances, and found them all wanting. She had come back at the nightfall, bringing no sheaves with her.

The summer came to her there, in the old home, — the brilliant New England summer, with its long, blue days, its flush of roses and flow of streams; the autumn, with its ripe fruits, and prophetic winds, and the haze upon all its hills; the long, white winter, keen and cold as death; and then the spring came again, and the summer.

This space had been for Elizabeth a time of healing. Its quiet had fallen upon her soul like a benediction. She had lived almost in solitude. The old friends who called on her could find no fault with the gentle courtesy with which she welcomed them; but she made her deep mourning an excuse for not returning their visits, and they did not feel free to repeat them. For the most part she was alone with Nature; and I think the dear old mother seldom fails to comfort the tired children who lean close upon her breast.

Insensibly, gradually, almost imperceptibly, Elizabeth grew towards peace; until, when the second summer came, she had begun to feel that her days were good days, — that there was a positive, pure joy in being alive, — alive where one could feel the sunshine, and hear the birds, and gather the roses. There were some keener delights in life, for which her hour was passed; but, just as they were, her days were not barren of enjoyment.

She thought a great deal about her little child; but now her thoughts of it were among her sweetest consolations. At one time she had longed to send over the sea for the little casket under the sods of Pére la Chaise, and bury it anew, where she could go often and stand above it in the long and pleasant grass. But as her health of mind and body began to be restored, she ceased to wish for this. She thought less of the bit of marble she had buried, with the white rose of peace frozen in its sculptured fingers, and more of the immortal little one, — alive, and free, and still her own, — still near her, perhaps; for she remembered and believed what Dr. Erskine had said, that whole eternities could not separate a mother from her child.

She thought, too, very often of Dr. Erskine, — for now she believed herself able to think of him unselfishly and abstractly. I told you, long ago, that this Elizabeth of mine did not understand herself; and all the experiences through which she had passed had still left her on the very threshold of self-knowledge. She thought, — because she never expected to see John Erskine again, or hear any words from his lips, and, so expecting, yet found that skies were blue, and bird-songs sweet, and summer days pleasant, and life had not lost all its savor, — that the old past in which she had felt so much for him was as dead as a dead day. She honestly believed herself capable of seeing him again without an extra heart-beat, — and I rather think she would have liked to try the experiment.

He, meantime, was daring to love her, because he believed that she was dead. He knew of the destruction of the ill-starred German steamer, and the loss of almost all her passengers. The short list of the saved had never met his eye; and he thought that Le Roy and Elizabeth had gone up together, through flame and flood, to stand at God's bar of judgment, for the final solving of the sad problem of their lives.

How far Elizabeth had been wrong, he did not know or question. He only knew that, whether her faults were great or small, she was for him the one woman in the wide universe of souls; and to that knowledge he trusted, as to a sure pledge, that he should find her again in some life, some world. So that all the living women on the earth, with all their smiles, their cheeks of tempting bloom, their lips ripe for kisses, were less to him than the memory of one sweet, sad face, with dark eyes which had never answered his pleading, and lips which he had never kissed.

He had staid in Paris for a year, after he returned from Brittany and found that Elizabeth had left with her husband, and the ship in which they sailed had gone down. He had not the courage, at first, to go back, and take up the burden of American work-a-day life; so he lingered on, in the French capital, until his mood changed, and he began to long for work as a means for his own healing. Then he went home; and through the winter and spring found himself full of business. A friend — the old Boston physician, with whom he had studied his profession — took advantage of his return to visit Europe himself, leaving his practice in Dr. Erskine's hands. So the Doctor was both busy and prosperous.

When the summer came, however, he was comparatively at leisure. Almost all of Dr. Gordon's patients went away to sea-side or mountains; and Dr. Erskine found himself able to take a few days of vacation for his own pleasure. He used them to make a pilgrimage.

Ever since his return, he had been longing to go to Lenox. His fancy was haunted by the pleasant pictures Elizabeth had made of it in the summer afternoons when she sat in the old garden of the Rue Jacob, her sleeping child upon her knees, while he watched and listened, — thinking then that she would be his, some day.

Now, it seemed to him that, if souls could come back to earth, hers would walk among those hills she had loved so well. He almost fancied he should see her, a radiant ghost, — a slight, swift shape, with pale, fair face, and luminous eyes, and hair of silken dusk, — the Elizabeth he had loved and lost. So he went to Lenox.

He left the cars at the railroad station in the village, and then walked across the fields by himself. He would not ask his way. He thought he could find the old Fordyce place, and know it from Elizabeth's descriptions. Presently the roomy old house rose before him, — the tall trees in front making a leafy darkness, the grassy pathway leading up from the gate to the front doorstone. He was sure that he had found the spot. Just so had Elizabeth described it. Just so, many a time, had it risen before his fancy, and he had pictured her, a gentle, serious child, going about under those trees; or, a thoughtful, pensive girl, sitting under them with her book.

The sun had just set. He turned to look at the clouds that kindled the west, and to wonder where, beyond them, she was, — his love.

Somehow the thought of her death had never much dwelt with him. He had never lingered morbidly over her possible sufferings. By flood or flame the agony had been short, doubtless; and he knew her well enough to believe the release had been welcome. He had loved, instead, to think of her as gone home, — translated into the sure refuge of God's peace, — her little one again in her arms, perhaps, as she sat among the heavenly gardens, where the very flowers of Eden made sweet the celestial air. Thinking of her thus to-night, as he had so often done before, the vision became very real to him, and he was scarcely surprised to see it taking form before him, as he turned back again to look at the old house.

Down towards the gate a shape was coming, like one he used to know, walking dreamily, and lifting its rapt face towards the sunset sky. He hardly dared to breathe as he drew near and watched this miracle of resurrection. Scarcely knowing what he did, he spoke at last one word, — "Elizabeth."

The uplifted eyes came back to earth. The dreamy footsteps paused. A heavenly smile curved the lips. A soft blush rose to the rounded cheeks. Do ghosts then blush and smile? He went forward, trembling with strange ecstasy, and they were face to face.

He touched the extended hand. The soft and slender fingers which trembled in his own were flesh and blood surely. The red lips, "dear and dewy," the eyes shy and sweet, — this was no ghost, no vision.

"I thought you were dead," he said.

"And I thought I should never see you again till we were both immortal," she answered.

Then there was a silence, which John Erskine broke at last; though his voice was hoarse with some secret struggle, as he asked, — "Were you both saved, — you and he?"

"He was taken and I was left," she said, slowly. "God knows why. My husband saved my life. He lowered me into the boat, and lost his own chance. We had both been wrong in our lives; but he was noble in his death."

"And you have been free all this time, — alive and free? Why did you never let me know? Did you never once think that your life belonged to me now?"

"I dared not think so. You know what I believed. I thought my darling was taken from my arms because I sinned, in those days, in caring for you too much; and it seemed to me God would be best pleased by my living out my life alone."

"And you meant to offer Him your own sad, solitary future, and mine, as a sacrifice of expiation? Oh, Elizabeth!"

"I meant only to offer Him mine. I thought you would be happy with some one else."

John Erskine's face kindled with a grand light.

"Child," he said, "I should have waited for you,—no matter through how many lives or worlds,—sure through them all that you would be mine at the last."

Then, for a moment more, he looked at her, in all her shadowy loveliness, and after that look some gust of emotion swayed him from his calm. His words were strong with a passion whose power startled her.

"Did you forget that our Father in Heaven pities us, as a Father pities his children? He *wants* to see us happy, believe it. You *are* mine,—my wife. Flame and flood spared you, because you were for me. Do you think I will give you up now?"

He took her into his arms, shy and startled, trembling like a girl of sixteen before her lover. Her very agitation calmed him, and he let her go before he had even kissed her lips.

"You shall come to me of your own free will, or not at all," he said, gently. "I called you mine,—*are* you mine, Elizabeth?"

Through the dusk which had gathered round them, she felt rather than saw his ardent, longing look. The moon, a pale crescent, was already high in the heavens, and one star glittered beside it. A late bird, going home, dropped a note full of hope and joy into the heart of the fragrant, dewy night. Half unconsciously she noted moon, and star, and bird-song, and the tender fragrance of the summer dusk. Had every thing believed and rejoiced in the Father's love except her heart,—and now had her hour come? Was her life at its flood-tide? She went through the shadows to Dr. Erskine, close into the arms that once more shut her in, — not passionately now, but gently, thankfully, with a clasp that claimed, and accepted, and would never again let her go.

BRAINS.

"YES'M!"

I turned with a start. I was quite alone, as I thought, and the fine treble of that odd little voice struck strangely upon my ear. I had been saying that I was tired of life, or some such repining speech, which I never allowed myself except in solitude, and this object at my knee answered me, "Yes'm!" I looked at her in amazement. She was a little morsel, scarcely so tall as a well-grown child of seven, but with a grave, mature, preternaturally wise face, which might have belonged to any age from fifteen to twenty-five. Was she goblin or mortal?

"Who are you?" I asked.

"My name is Susan Mory, ma'am, but they mostly call me 'Brains.' They say I've an old head to be on such young shoulders." And she laughed, a small, fine, queer laugh, as uncanny in sound as her voice. I was hardly yet convinced that she was human.

"How old are you?"

"Twelve, ma'am, last birthday."

"And what do you want, 'Brains'? How came you here?"

"I want to do your errands, ma'am. I heard you

needed some one; and your door wasn't quite shut, so I came in. Excuse the freedom." And here she bobbed me a droll little courtesy, quite in keeping with her voice, and her laugh, and the quaint correctness and propriety of her conversation. It was true I wanted an errand-girl; but what could this odd morsel of humanity do?

"What wages did you expect?" I asked, more from curiosity to see what estimate she put upon her services than with any serious intention of employing her.

"I heard you had been paying three dollars a week, and the girl boarded herself. I think I could earn as much."

"But she was a large girl," I said, in surprise. "She swept and dusted my room, carried home all my work, and shopped for linings and trimmings."

"Yes'm." She spoke with an acquiescent air, as if she thought the work I had mentioned was not at all too much for her. She seemed so ready and cheery that I couldn't bear to refuse her.

"Can you sweep?" I asked.

"If you'll try me, ma'am, I think my work will please you. If not, you know it's only to send me away again."

There was no room to dispute her assertion. I began to like the quaint, neat little creature, with her earnest, unchildlike face. I would question her a little more, I thought.

"Have you a home?" I asked. "Do you live with your parents?"

"With my mother. There are three of us, — mother, and I, and 'Body,' — I mean my sister Jane; she grew so fast, and was so careless and thoughtless, that father always used to call her 'Body,' and me 'Brains.' When the war broke out he went for a private soldier, but he was shot the second summer. We have eight dollars a month, you know, — mother's pension, — but that won't quite make us comfortable, and mother's delicate; and so I thought if I could do your errands, ma'am."

So she, too, had lost by the war, — she in one way and I in another. The thought made my heart warm to her yet more.

"You may come to-morrow morning," I said. "Come at half-past six, and ask the porter for the key of No. 10. You will find a broom in that closet behind the door, and you can get the room swept and dusted before the girls come to work."

"Yes'm."

Another droll little courtesy, and she was gone.

Then I went back to my thoughts again. They were a little less melancholy and self-compassionate, however, for the diversion. Yet I had lost so much. Before the war began my father had been one of the wealthy merchants of New York. He did a large wholesale business, mostly with the South, and when the crisis came it ruined him utterly. In the summer of 1861 we went to a little place in the country which belonged to my mother, and there he died. I think it was his trouble which brought on the long, slow fever from which he never rallied. Then, in that fall after his death, I had to decide upon my future. We had scarcely a hundred dollars in the world besides the little place which sheltered us, but which insured us only a roof over our heads. My mother was a delicate woman, accustomed ever since her marriage to be petted and waited on and tended. She was utterly broken down by her grief at the loss of my father. I must think for both and work for both.

I, too, had been accustomed to luxury, and never trained to any thing useful. I had received a fine-lady sort of education. I could play and sing, — with taste rather than with science. I danced well; I drew a little; I read French; I could manage Italian enough for a song; but what one thing did I know well enough to teach it? Not one. And even if I had, there were fifty applicants for every vacant situation in the department of instruction. Clearly I must do something besides teaching. I could not sew fast enough to earn much in that way. What was I good for? My self-esteem went rapidly down to zero, when suddenly a new idea took possession of me. I had one endowment which I might make available as capital, — taste in dress. I use the words in their highest sense. I not only knew what was pretty when I saw it, — I knew what would be pretty before I saw it. I had original ideas. In the days when I had been a leader of fashion in my own set, my dresses and my trimmings had never been servile imitations of French models. I had always invented something for myself, often for my friends. Schneider had said that my taste would be a fortune to any mantua-maker. It should be a fortune, then, to me.

I matured my plan and then communicated it to my mother. As I had foreseen, it vexed her sorely at first. But when I set matters before her in their true light, and she saw it afforded our only chance of comfort and independence, she began to look on the idea more favorably. She made only one stipulation, — that I should not attempt to carry out my undertaking in New York. To this I was quite ready to accede. The supercilious patronage of all my former friends would have been a burden quite too heavy to be borne. I should feel more comfortable, even if I made less money, to begin elsewhere. My scheme was quite an ambitious one. I ignored the proverbs about small beginnings, little acorns, and so on. I meant to storm success at the outset. I let the house which we were occupying for a year, and arranged to leave my mother with the new tenants until I was ready to come for her. Then I went to Boston.

I found vacant rooms in a building on Summer Street, in which nearly all the upstairs apartments were used by milliners and dress-makers. I had no references, but I engaged to pay my rent monthly in advance; and having paid the first month I arranged my rooms, and put my sign — "Miss Macgregor" — on my door, and downstairs at the lower entrance. I had hired a dress-maker to go on with me from New York, — one who had been in the habit of going out by the day, and had often sewed for me on common dresses. She could fit exceedingly well, but she would have been utterly wanting in the comprehensive ability necessary to carry on a business, and she made no pretensions to taste about trimming. She was quite satisfied to be hands, and let me be head, and would be contented with her weekly wages. In one of my rooms was a wardrobe bedstead which she and I were to occupy together till I could send for my mother. These arrangements made, I sent to the *Transcript* an advertisement setting forth the claims to patronage of Miss Macgregor from New York.

The evening the notice appeared I sat with it alone in my own room, — where, until it was time to retire, Miss Granger never intruded. The die was cast, and now I must go forward. For the first time a sort of passionate regret, a wild misgiving, took possession of me, and I cried bitterly. It seemed to me I had given up every thing I valued in life. If my social position, my New York acquaintances, had been all, I could have borne it without complaining; but I had resigned much more. Two years before I had experienced a new phase of emotion. Not to be romantic, or put too fine a point upon the matter, I had fallen heartily, and, I thought then, irrevocably, in love. I felt sure, too, that Horace Weir had loved me. There had been no engagement between us, but when he went away in the spring of 1860 to study for three years in the hospitals of Paris, — he was to be a physician, — I think we had both felt sure of each other's hearts, and looked forward to a future together almost as confidently as if we had been betrothed.

I felt that in giving up all my old associations and entering upon this new life I was giving him up also. If we had been engaged, I had faith enough in him to feel sure that he would have been changed by no change of fortune. But, as it was, I had not the shadow of a claim on him. We had never corresponded, and when he came back he would not know where to find me. I should drop out of his life. I will confess that I suffered keenly at this prospect. I would have clung to him if I could. For his sake I would have clung, if I could, to position and old associations. But the simple fact was that I could not. If I had been willing to starve genteelly myself, I was not willing that my mother should; and there was no resource but to go to work. Just then I took up a Bible lying near me, with some vague idea of finding in it comfort or direction, and, curiously enough, my eyes fell upon this passage: —

"And the Lord said unto Moses, Speak unto the children of Israel that they go forward."

I was just in the state of mind to receive these words as a special direction, — a sort of omen. I took them as meant for an indication that I had chosen the right path and must walk on in it. So I tried to be brave, — to cease to think of Horace Weir, — to suppress every repining thought, every longing for the old days of ease and luxury, and to content myself with the present. I trusted that I should succeed. I felt sure

I should, if I could but once make a beginning. I would let the old life go, and commence this new one bravely. I had used on my sign my middle name, Macgregor only. I trusted that if any old friends ever chanced to read my advertisement they would not associate Miss Macgregor, dress-maker, with Helen Macgregor Bryce, their friend of the old time. Perhaps this was a weakness; at any rate it harmed no one, and Macgregor was a more imposing name than Bryce would have been. To *be* imposing, to be elegant, to become the fashion, was my only hope. I had sold two diamond rings of considerable value for money enough to start me fairly; but if, in the two months to come, I could not secure a paying run of custom, I should have lost my last chance.

The very next morning a magnificent-looking dame walked into my room, stately after the manner of Boston, with a certain severe majesty appropriate to the hub of the universe. She was followed by two pretty young ladies. I had made a distinguished toilet that morning, and for stateliness it would go hard if I could not match her. She bowed loftily. I bowed loftily in response, and offered chairs.

"Miss Macgregor, I suppose."

Bow the second on my part.

"I saw your advertisement last evening, and came to talk with you about some dresses. Lubec has disappointed me so many times, that if I could find some one equally good who would be punctual, it would be a satisfaction to make a change."

Bow the third.

"Are you very busy, Miss Macgregor?"

"Not at all so. To-day is the first day I have been open, and you are my first caller."

Then followed a whispered consultation of the mamma with the tallest young lady. I knew they were debating whether it would be safe to trust a stranger whose work they had never seen, whose first patrons they were. I waited in apparent unconcern, watching the customers go in and out of the store opposite.

"You are sure," the lady began, again turning back to me, "that you would have no difficulty in fitting us for the first time?"

"I apprehend none, madam."

"And for trimmings, — what fashion-books do you use?"

"None. I have them all, but I invent my own styles for the most part."

Upon that the youngest daughter spoke in a pleasant, lady-like voice, —

"That will be nice, mamma. We shall not be copies of every one else."

"It would be better," the elder lady remarked, "if we could try some more common dresses first, but there seems to be no time. Could you get two light silks done for a wedding reception day after to-morrow?"

"Certainly, since, as I said, you have the fortune to come first."

"Then will you fit my daughters this morning?"

"At once."

I led the way into the other room, where Miss Granger sat waiting.

"White linen linings, Miss Granger," I said, with an air of command; "and please pin them on immediately."

Madam started at this with a gesture of alarm.

"Do you not fit them on yourself?" she asked. "Even Lubec always did that."

"By no means. There is no surer way to spoil one's power of adapting a dress to the figure. I stand at a little distance, and see that an artistic effect is preserved."

By this time Miss Granger was pinning on the lining over the slight girlish form of the elder daughter. She could fit well, and they must have perceived it. I gave a few hints and directions, and the work was accomplished.

"Will you leave the trimming entirely to me?" I asked, as the mamma shook the lustrous, pearl-colored silk out of its folds, "or have you a choice?"

"Leave it to her," I heard the younger daughter whisper, — "I know by her own looks she has good taste."

So it was settled that I should make the dresses as I chose. No sooner had they left than I began my task. I had only two seamstresses engaged besides Miss Granger; but we all worked. A few other customers came in, and I put them off until these two dresses should be finished. When done, they were to be sent to Mrs. John Sturgis, Beacon Street; and I felt that if they gave satisfaction I should have made as good a beginning as I desired. I trimmed them so differently that, though the silk was the same, the dresses were totally unlike, and yet equal in elegance. I sent them home the afternoon before the reception, and Miss Granger was kind enough to go with them and try them on, though that was not at all in her province. She came back and reported elegant fits and perfect satisfaction.

The next morning Mrs. Sturgis came for my bill. It was a matter on which I had bestowed some thought. I had questioned whether it would be the best policy to conciliate custom by the moderation of my charges, or to convey a sense of my own importance by their extravagance. One of my girls had formerly worked for Madame Lubec, who had stood at the head hitherto of Boston fashion. After a consultation with her, I had made out my bill, charging perhaps two or three dollars on a dress more than Lubec would have done.

Mrs. Sturgis ran over the items.

"You are a little higher in your rates than is customary here," she said; "but I suppose we must be willing to pay something for your taste. My daughters' dresses were the loveliest in the room. Can you make them some more next week? They want some walking-dresses, and I a dinner-dress."

"Not next week, I am sorry to say. I am more busy

than when you came first. I think I might promise for the week after next."

I had decidedly made a hit. After that customers came fast enough; and a good many of them spoke of the dresses Aggie Sturgis and her sister had worn at the wedding. I was able, in two months from that beginning, to bring on my mother, and to take for her a third room, — a small one which happened about that time to fall vacant, — so that she could be as retired as she wished. I completed this arrangement early in the winter of 1861, and for the two years between that time and the first appearance of little "Brains" in my establishment, I had been prospering beyond my hopes. But I was not happy. Success brought, indeed, a certain kind of satisfaction; but I missed sorely the carefree life of the old days, the liberty to follow my own tastes and ways, and I did miss Horace Weir. I had heard of him incidentally. He had come home from France, and was now practising his profession in New York. I would have given much to know whether he had thought of me, inquired after me, tried to trace me out. Vain enough it must have been if he had. I had given no clue to my present residence to a single old friend. Every one of them, to the best of my belief, had lost sight of me. I was wedded to a life very different from any of my early dreams. I had been successful, it is true, beyond my expectations. I was saving money. I could make my mother comfortable. I had little to do with the laborious details of my business. My task was to invent graceful fashions, —

to suit colors to fair faces,—to make charming toilets for girls living just such lives as I used to live once. God forgive me if sometimes I almost hated them,—if now and then a mad rebellious impulse seized me, and I cursed fate in my heart, forgetting that fate was but another name for Providence.

I had been in one of these murmuring moods when little Susan Mory interrupted my meditations with her fine, small voice. After she went away I relapsed into it only partially, and roused myself with determination at last, and went to my mother, to amuse her with an account of my droll little visitor. After all, mother had much more to bear than I. She had not even the diversion of business. She must sit through the long, slow days, remembering the past and all its good gifts and false promises,—stung by its contrast with the empty-handed present. How much more she had lost, too. What was the sentimental regret of a young girl over a love that had never even been declared, to a wife's sorrow and longing for the household tenderness which had been hers for a quarter of a century? As I opened her door I reproached myself for all my repinings.

I was glad to perceive that she was really interested about "Brains." She wanted to see her on the morrow, and began planning about garments we could give her to make over for herself and her sister.

The next morning, curious to see whether my small handmaiden had arrived, I put on my dressing-gown a little before seven, and looked into the work-room. I opened the door so quietly that she did not hear it.

She had swept the room carefully, and now she stood in a chair dusting the window frames. It was very amusing to see her grave, womanly patience and care, and her queer expedients to accomplish the tasks for which she was too absurdly short. As she turned round I said,—

"Good-morning, 'Brains.'"

She dropped instantly from her chair, and made me her droll little courtesy.

"Yes'm," she said, cheerfully, "I'm come. I've been trying to make it as clean here as usual." And she glanced at me interrogatively with her bright, thoughtful eyes, that looked so large and wistful in her queer, little, old-young face.

"Yes," I said, "you have made it very nice; I think you will please me."

When her morning work was done I took her in to see my mother, and her verdict was decidedly in the little one's favor. "She'll be the best errand-girl you ever had," she said to me after "Brains" had gone back to the work-room.

Time went on, and proved her right. Through all the winter she was the most faithful of little maidens. Never did pieces go astray, or bundles fail to reach their destinations; and she developed a remarkable capacity for matching dresses with buttons and braid, and similar trifles. I grew really attached to her, and would not have exchanged her for any other messenger of twice her years.

Early in March she took a severe cold, and began to

cough. I tried to make her stay at home until she was better, and let some one else take her place; but she insisted on coming. She knew just my ways, she said, and she was sure it didn't hurt her. She was going to get better of her cold as soon as there were some warm days. Still I was not just comfortable about her. I did not like the sound of that constant cough, — the color on her cheeks was too bright, — she was growing, too, into such a mere little shadow.

One morning when I entered the work-room I missed her. Some one else had been sweeping and putting away things, but it was not in the accustomed order.

"'Brains' didn't come. I'm afraid she's worse," Miss Granger said. They had all fallen into the habit of calling her "Brains," — the name seemed so appropriate, — there was so much thought, and care, and womanliness in such a little body.

Half an hour later there was a timid knock on the door, and in came a girl whom I had never seen before. I recognized her at once for the ten-years-old sister of my little errand-girl, — recognized her, as one often does, by some mysterious family likeness, which seemed to vanish when I looked at her more steadily. This one was a real, actual child, — large of her age, with full, rosy cheeks, and eyes round as beads. She came straight up to me, and delivered her message with the air of one who had been taught it carefully.

"Sister Susy is sick, and can't come. She is sorry, and hopes it won't put you to much inconvenience."

It was just like "Brains,"—the polite, careful message.

"And you are 'Body'?" I asked.

"Yes, ma'am,"—and she looked as if she longed to ask how I had learned her home name,—"Yes, ma'am; I am Jane, and they call me 'Body.'"

"Is Susy very sick?"

"Pretty bad, I guess, ma'am. She can't sit up, and she coughs most all the time, and mother sent me after a doctor this morning."

I asked where they lived, and she mentioned a number on Pleasant Street.

"Well," I said, "tell Susy not to worry. I shall get along nicely, and I will come to see her as soon as I can make time,—to-night, if not before."

"Yes, ma'am."

She went away then. She had a lazy sort of voice, and spoke lingeringly,—quite unlike the quick, characteristic utterance of little "Brains." How well I remembered that first day, and the brisk "Yes'm" that broke in upon my musings.

It was late in the afternoon before I could make time to go to Pleasant Street. I found the Morys living in the third story of a comfortable-looking house. I went first into a room which seemed to serve as a kitchen and sitting-room. Mrs. Mory, a tired-looking woman who had been pretty once, was stirring something in a saucepan over the fire. She turned to greet me, and invited me to go into the next room, where Susy was. It was a small bedroom, but every thing was neat and clean. There lay poor little "Brains," with a bright flush burning on her cheeks, her eyes glittering, and her poor little body shaken by a paroxysm of coughing. As soon as she could speak she put out her hand.

"Thank you, Miss Macgregor; it was very kind of you to come. I didn't mean to give up this way, and disappoint you. And I suppose you will have to get some one else. I thought first that perhaps 'Body' could do my work for a week or two, until I got better; but I don't suppose she'd answer."

"No, I fear she wouldn't; and besides, while you are ill, your mother will need her at home. But I'll keep the place for you. I shall have to get some one else, to be sure, but I'll get them with the understanding that you are to come back just as soon as you are able, and they must be ready to give up to you at any time."

"Oh, how good, how good you are!" the poor little morsel cried, with kindling eyes. "I was so afraid I should lose my place that it was worse than the sickness."

Her gratitude touched me profoundly, for it seemed to me, even then, that she would never get any better; and it was so hard to think of that poor little patient life going out so early, quenched in its dawn.

It brought on her cough to talk, so I did not stay with her long. On the way out I said to her mother,—

"Do not be troubled by any fear of want. I shall pay Susy her wages just the same as if she were well. I can well afford it, for I am prospering in my business, and if she wants any thing that you cannot get her, you must let me know."

As I went out of the house I caught a faint red glow of the March sunset, shooting up high enough to show a glimpse of its splendor even to the dwellers in brick walls. Would little "Brains" see many more days decline? I longed to take her away into the country, and give her, before she died, one glimpse of wide-stretching fields, of sunsets, and sunrisings. But it was too late. She was not well enough to be moved, and if she should never get any better she would see a light before long such as no sun ever kindled, breathe airs of healing, smell flowers that grow not on any earthly soil. Her "country" would be brighter than any of her dreams,—the land that lies "very far off."

The next day I went to see her again. I had not thought of going so soon, but a spell seemed to draw me. It was reward enough to see her poor little face brighten, and her eyes grow eager with welcome when I went in. But she was no better. She never would be, I thought. I asked her mother what the doctor said, and she answered me, with a burst of sobbing,—

"I don't think he has much hope of her. He says her lungs are very much inflamed. He thinks it might have been better if she had staid at home when she first got her cold, but I couldn't keep her. She was such an ambitious child. Oh, ma'am, if God takes her, how shall I bear it? Since her father left me, little as she is, she's been what I depended on."

I could well understand it. The girl had one of

those natures on which weaker ones rest instinctively. She was thoroughly reliable, with a courage, a patient hope, a quiet strength, utterly out of proportion to her tiny frame. I could not say any thing to console her poor mother, for I knew too well what she was losing, and it seems so idle to talk about heavenly consolations to ears deaf with misery. The soul is so seldom ready to accept them until after the blow has fallen, and God himself speaks to the stricken one through the darkness of desolation. I could only say, —

"We need not quite give up hope yet, and we ought to think of *her* now, — of making her as comfortable as we can."

Then I went out again into the March twilight.

Every night after that found me at Pleasant Street, I could not stay away. Besides all my interest in her, an unaccountable impression took possession of me that she was in some wise associated with my own fate. I was going, so it seemed to me, straight toward my destiny, — a destiny in some dim, undreamed-of way connected with "Brains" and her little room.

I have said that from the first I had not much hope of her. My hope lessened every day. She would never come back to the place I had engaged another to fill till she got well. I should never watch again her tidy little ways, or be amused at her quaint womanliness. I had not thought it was in me to care for her so much, but my heart grew heavy as I saw her fading away. She suffered terribly with her racking cough, and the constant wearing pain in her side and chest; but she did not lose her bright cheerfulness. For a long time, too, she continued to make light of her illness and tell me that in a little while she should be back doing my errands as of old.

The first time she said any thing else was one April night. I went to her a little later than usual, and found the doctor with her. I had never seen him before, this Dr. John Sargent. His name seemed somehow strangely familiar, though I could not recall at the moment where I had heard it. He was bending over poor little "Brains" when I went in, but he raised his head and met my eyes with his own, so kind, so pitiful, so serious, that I felt drawn toward him at once. The child put out her hand.

"You'll have to keep her, Miss Macgregor," she said, with a sad smile.

I did not think at first who she meant, and I asked her.

"The girl that took my place, you know. I've been asking Dr. Sargent, and he doesn't think I'll ever be able to go back any more."

She was so calm that for very shame I tried to be calm also, but the tears would come, and I went out into the next room without speaking. Soon Dr. Sargent joined me.

"It is very sad," he said. "I have seldom been so much interested in a case. Such a bright, patient little thing as she is, and so wonderfully womanly. She asked me herself, to-night, if there was any hope, and I had to tell her. You see how she bears it."

After he had gone I went back to little Susy. I had brought her a bunch of violets, which I saw in a shop-window as I came along, and her very pleasure in them made my heart ache. How she loved all beautiful things. How much she was capable of enjoying, and how little she had had to enjoy in this world, poor child. And now she was going.

I think she guessed my thought, for she touched my hand with a timid, caressing motion, and said, very softly, —

"There will be brighter flowers there, Miss Macgregor. 'It hath not entered into the heart of man to conceive,' you know. It is well for me; only it will be so hard for mother and Jane. But their Father will take care of them. You know what it says about the widow and the fatherless."

How unconsciously she reproved my lack of faith. I bent over her, and pressed my lips to the little cheek where the hectic burned. How many times I had doubted God, and what faith she had. She seemed to infuse into my soul new strength. As I went through the other room to go home I found Mrs. Mory crying very softly, so as not to disturb her sick child, in a quiet, dreary way, inexpressibly pitiful. Poor "Body" was kneeling with her face buried in her mother's lap, fairly shaken by the violence of her suppressed sobbing. I only said, as I went by, —

"Don't grieve *her* by weeping. She has been telling me that God will take care of you."

When I reached home I sat down and tried to think

what I had known before about Dr. Sargent. It carried me back to Horace Weir. John Sargent was his friend, I remembered, — a classmate, and the *fidus Achates* of his early manhood. Did they occupy such a relation still, I wondered. Would I be mentioned between them? But no, Dr. Sargent knew of me only as Miss Macgregor, the fashionable dress-maker for whom little "Brains" had worked. He would never associate me with Helen Bryce, even if Weir had once made that name familiar to him. What was there to arouse such tumult of hope and memory in my heart? I remembered little Susy, and the world where she was going, and tried to grow calm.

For a fortnight after that she failed fast. Of course I went to see her every day, and it carried me strangely near to the eternal world whither her footsteps tended. You cannot think what a change it seemed to come back to the thoroughly earthly atmosphere of my fashionable establishment, — to see the bright-hued silks, and laces white and dainty as hoar-frost, — to hear the perpetual talk about what was stylish and what was becoming, and be complimented about my invention, my charming taste. It was like turning back to earth from the gate of Heaven.

At length there came a day — it was toward the last of April — when I went earlier than usual to see little "Brains." She had been so weak the day before that I felt anxious. I carried her the first May flowers I had seen. The little creature had a sort of passionate fondness for flowers not unusual in such an organization. She loved and cherished them as if they were of her own kindred.

When I went in I saw Dr. Sargent was in the room, and with him, his back toward the door, another gentleman. The doctor heard my footsteps, and came out.

"A friend of mine is there," he said; "Dr. Weir, from New York. He came on to visit me, and I brought him to see the child. There is no hope, of course; but he might think of something to relieve her that I did not."

I felt my face turning crimson under his searching glance. But neither he nor I made any comment. As soon as I felt sufficiently mistress of myself I went into the room. Calmness stole like balm over my spirit as I crossed its threshold. I felt as if I were in the presence of waiting angels. I met Horace Weir's eyes, but I scarcely knew it as I went up to Susy, and saw the strange, seraphic light which made her little wan face seem as the face of an angel. I gave her the flowers, and she took them and my hand together into her clinging hold.

"Dear, kind Miss Macgregor," she said, fondly; "you won't have to bring me any more flowers. I am going where they blow all the time. What should I have done without you? How thankful I am that I went to your shop."

"But if you hadn't come there, perhaps you would have lived," I said, as well as I could for the sobs which were choking me. She thought a moment, then she shook her head.

7*

"No, I should not have outlived God's time; and you have made me so much happier. If I can pray for any thing after I die, I shall ask *Him*, when I get to His feet, to bless you for evermore. Can you stay with me a little while?"

I took off my shawl and bonnet, and sat down at her bedside. Dr. Sargent came up to bid her good-night.

"I must go now," he said; "but I will come very early in the morning. Will you stay a while, Weir, in case any thing should be wanted?"

"Certainly," answered a voice, every tone of which I knew well.

Little "Brains" looked up with such a bright smile, —

"How kind every one is," she said. "How kind you've always been, Dr. Sargent. Good-by."

Moved by some sudden impulse of tenderness, Dr. Sargent bent over and kissed the little wistful face of the child he had tended so long and patiently. Next time he sees her it will be after he too has gone over the river. He will not be sorry then that he "did it unto one of the least of these," Christ's little ones.

Weir sat down in the outer room. I stayed by Susy. Her mother came in and out restlessly, with white face, and eyes full of anguish and longing. "Body" had cried herself into a state of exhaustion, and she sat on the floor, her head in a chair, sleeping heavily. Shall I ever forget the glimpse I had that night into the heart of that dying child? Holding that little hand, looking into those eyes so full of meaning, and so soon to close for ever, I drew nearer than I ever had before to the mysteries of death and of life. It was midnight, I think, when a sudden light illumined all her face, and, as if in answer to a call we did not hear, she said, —

"I am ready."

Her mother clung to her in a passion of tears and prayers. Her sister, wide awake now, was sobbing at her side. She kissed them both fondly.

"God loves you," she said.

Then she looked at me with wistful eyes. I bent down and kissed her, my tears falling fast on her white face.

"God loves you, too," she said; and then a moment after, she spoke again, as if that voice we could not hear were once more calling, —

"*All* ready."

Then she turned her face, with that last smile on it, to the wall, and went home.

An hour afterward she lay, as we had robed her, in white garments, with shut eyes, and a look so calm and sweet upon her face you would have thought her sleeping. I had to go then. I knew my mother was waiting for me anxiously.

"May God comfort you," I said, going up to Mrs. Mory to bid her good-night. She did not turn her eyes away from the dead face on the pillows.

"Yes," she answered dreamily, "*she* said God loved us."

As I went down the stairs Weir followed me. When we were in the street he drew my hand through his arm, and spoke to me for the first time.

"Helen, that dead child has given us to each other. But for her should I ever have found you? Sargent knew how vain all my inquiries for you, since I came back, had been. He had seen a photograph of you which I carried—perhaps you have forgotten it—across the sea with me. He felt pretty sure that he recognized you from it the first time he saw you; and he knew, besides, that Macgregor was your middle name. So last week he wrote to me, and I came on to find you out."

We buried poor little "Brains," two days after that, in the cemetery at Forest Hills, under the shadow of a great rock. You will see her tombstone if you go there,—a little white cross, on which there is no word save "SUSY."

We left her there on the last day of April, under a sunshine bright as June. We put white flowers round the little white face, and into the hands that would never be tired any more. And on the sod piled above her grave we left sweet blossoms to lie there and give forth their sweetness, and then die as she had died.

It was not long after that before I gave up my business to a successor and married Dr. Weir. We have enjoyed since then a happiness that sometimes seems to me too blessed to last. But we try to sanctify it by making ourselves ministers of God's bounty to His children. What we do for Mrs. Mory and Jane is no charity, for we consider them a bequest from little "Brains," at whose bedside we found each other anew.

TWELVE YEARS OF MY LIFE.

"We all are changed. God judges for us best.
God help us do our duty, and not shrink,
And trust in Heaven humbly for the rest."

I SAT alone in the room whence my mother, my sole remaining earthly friend, had been that day borne forth to her burial. It was a large, comfortable apartment, up two flights of stairs, in a New York boarding-house. The bed was shut up in a wardrobe; a few engravings which we had brought there with us hung upon the wall; a canary in the window sang all day to a red rose and a white rose blooming below him; in the centre of the room was a table flanked by two easy-chairs, in one of which I was listlessly swaying to and fro, — in the other *she* had been wont to sit; but alas, she could never sit there again, save in the fancy, by means of which I seemed to see her slight, wasted figure, her pure, patient face, in the accustomed seat.

A bright fire burned in the grate, and, lit up by its glow, the room looked quite like a parlor. I had congratulated myself on this six months before when I engaged it, and rejoiced that it would not seem to my mother entirely devoid of the comforts to which she had been accustomed in her old home. She was gone now, and I sat there alone, a homeless, friendless, I had almost said hopeless orphan, not quite eighteen.

Outside it was a wild October night. The rain fell heavily, and upon the long, lamenting blast seemed borne the wail of lonesome spirits, seeking rest and finding none. I shuddered as I heard the rain-drops plash upon the pavement, for only the cold sod was between *her* and the pitiless storm. Does not every one who has lost dear friends feel it harder to leave them under a relentless sky, a sobbing blast, a driving rain, than if moon-beam and star-beam shone on the new-made grave like the visible promise of a Father's love?

It would have been a luxury to abandon myself to my sorrow; to walk, in thought, through the beloved and memory-haunted past, and gather up every word that had fallen, like scattered pearls unheeded at the time, from the dear lips which Death had frozen into eternal silence. But even in that hour which should have been consecrated to love and sorrow, the Future confronted me. Stern and unsparing she looked into my eyes and bade me talk with her. "Wait a little, only a little," I cried out, trembling before her; but the storm was not more pitiless than she.

In March, after a long illness, my father had died. He left us poor. He had been a literary man, diligent, studious, and illy paid. Perhaps the delicacy of his fancies, the subtlety of his thoughts, failed to appeal to the comprehension of those on whom he depended for his fortune. We, at least, — his wife and his daughter,

— believed his writings above the times and the market; but we may have been too partial judges. At all events, the pecuniary rewards of his efforts were never abundant, and we were in no danger of being led into temptation by superfluity of riches.

He had the refined and exacting tastes peculiar to such sensitive organizations, and we lived, though entirely aloof from society and the world, much more expensively than the bare law of necessity demanded. His last hours were saddened by the knowledge that he was leaving us lonely and destitute; but he did not feel this so keenly as it would have been his nature to feel it, because God, who tempers the wind to the shorn lamb, mercifully sent upon him that sort of lethargy, that prostration of the reasoning faculties, which so often follows their too constant and severe exercise. Sometimes a terrible dread of the future for us two helpless women would rack his heart, but, as a whole, he possessed the most thorough and childlike faith in the Almighty and Eternal Father which I have ever seen. His very last words, as he held our hands in his, and sought our faces with his loving, longing eyes, were, —

"The widow's God, — a Father to the fatherless, — the Bible says so. Trust, my darlings, trust."

And he lapsed into death peacefully, as one might drowse away into sleep, with a smile upon his lips born of that serene trust in God. It was there still when we buried him, — we shall know him by it in the resurrection.

It is not needful that I should say how we two — wife and daughter — had worshipped him; how we had reverenced his genius, found rest in his strong heart, and loved back his love. When we had left him in the village church-yard and returned to our desolate home, we felt that for us the sun of life had set for ever. Stars might indeed arise and make our night holy; but no matter how bright the stars shine, when the sun is gone neither bird nor blossom has ever forgot that it was night still, or been deluded into song or bloom.

Perhaps it was well that the stern necessities of life were upon us. The inevitable fact that we must *do* something gave tone and stimulus to our lives. By the expenses of my father's illness and burial, and the mourning habiliments which we had purchased, our little hoard in the bank was more than half exhausted. There remained to us now not quite three hundred dollars, besides the small sum likely to accrue from the sale of our simple household furniture. The lease of the cottage which we occupied would expire on the first of April, and in the two weeks intervening we must settle upon some plan for the future.

It seemed to me that my mother could never endure to remain in Woodstock. To keep house where we had been living was simply impossible. We had no means of paying the rent; besides, we could no longer afford a servant, and neither of us had ever been used to household labor. As for boarding there, I could see no way of obtaining any employment for our support; and even if I could, I thought it would kill my mother to live on where he had died, — where they had passed so many happy years. In this extremity my thoughts turned to New York. We had occasionally passed a winter there with my father, and I knew more about it than about any other city. It seemed probable that there would be something in that vast industrial hive which my hands could do; besides, — and this reason had great weight with me, — I should there be able to procure for my mother the best of medical advice. I had already begun to see in her the same symptoms which heralded my father's decay; and a terrible fear haunted me, which I strove in vain to banish, that she had not watched over him so long and so lovingly without inhaling from his lips the breath of the Destroyer.

So I went to New York. I engaged there the room I have described, and returned to Woodstock to superintend the dissolution of our household, and the sale of our possessions. I retained the engravings which my father had collected from time to time, and his small but well-chosen library. For things like these there was no sale at Woodstock; besides, they were endeared to us by too many memories to be parted with willingly.

In two weeks we were domesticated in our new place of abode. At first the entire change, the removal from all early associations, seemed to do my mother good. I made strenuous efforts to find an occupation that I could pursue at home. I did not think of teaching, for I feared I had neither the patience nor the tact to be successful in that employment; besides, I possessed no accomplishments, technically so called. My education had been chiefly imparted by my father, and was not only desultory, but of a very unusual kind for a girl. I knew some Greek and a good deal of Latin, was thoroughly familiar with English literature, and a more than tolerable mathematician; but these are not what most parents wish to have chiefly taught to their daughters, and they stood me in poor stead of showier knowledge.

I succeeded, after a time, in procuring some embroidery to do. I worked upon it early and late, and managed to earn about half enough to pay our expenses. I soon, however, discontinued this attempt. As the warm weather came on, my mother began to fail rapidly, and the physician whom I called to attend her took me aside and told me there was no hope. He said her constitution was thoroughly broken, — that consumption had already seized upon her, and in an organization like hers its progress could not be slow. She could not live longer than till the falling of the leaves, perhaps not so long. In the mean time all that could be done was to keep her as quiet and as happy as possible.

When I went again into our room she saw the trouble upon my face, — she, who from childhood had been able to read my every thought. A person older and more discreet than I might have evaded her inquiries, — I could not. I had never kept even a momentary secret from her. I threw myself on my knees beside her and sobbed out all that the doctor had said. Her lips moved. I knew she was murmuring an inaudible prayer. Then she bent over me and folded me in her arms.

"Oh, darling, darling, how can I be sorry that I am going to *him?* And yet, if it were God's pleasure, I would gladly stay with you, my poor, helpless girl. Do not weep at our Father's will, Gertrude. It becomes His children to submit to it, — no, not to submit, — to receive it thankfully; for we know that beyond all our asking or thinking He is good."

From that day I gave up all employment for the one duty of waiting on my mother. I nursed her; I read to her; I talked to her; I guarded her from every pang which love could ward off. I knew we had money enough to last us while she would be spared to me; farther than that I did not think or question.

That summer, with all its pain and sorrow, was a blessed one. I went down with her into the night, but looking up out of its darkness I caught glimpses of the eternal morning, fairer than any morning of earth which was to break for her *there.* From afar its glory shone even on me. I almost saw the waving of the heavenly trees, the gleam of the heavenly waters, — almost heard the eternal new song which the hundred and forty and four thousand are singing for ever before the throne of God.

Late in October she left me. Was it death, or was it translation?

During the three days in which her dead body lay in the room which her living presence had consecrated I sat beside it in a sort of trance. I shed not a tear. I think I scarcely experienced a pang of anguish. All selfish sorrow was subdued by a strange feeling of nearness to the infinite world, — a profound sense of the glory and majesty of that change which we call Death.

But this state of exaltation passed entirely away from me, leaving me hopeless and almost helpless, like a child alone in a boundless desert, when I had left her in a grave at Greenwood and come back to the room where I could no longer see the glory of the strong angel's presence, but only remember the darkness of the shadow of his wing.

Now I would fain have sat down and indulged in the luxury of grief. But, as I said, the Future was stern and inexorable. She rose up and would have speech with me. Long enough, she said, had I forgotten the cares of this world. How much had I left now in that purse which had never been the purse of Fortunatus, — how much between me and starvation? This last word goaded me into listening. I took out my purse and counted its contents. When the expenses attending my mother's funeral had been paid I should have but twelve dollars in the world, and, at the end of the week, half that would be due to my landlady. What should I do? I was slow at my needle, and, save in fancy work, little accustomed to use it. I had already tried the experiment of embroidery, and I knew I could not depend on it. I might teach young children, but then I had no means of obtaining such a situation, and my necessities were immediate. I took up an evening paper, and ran over the column of wants. I could see only one opening at all adapted to my needs. A well-known fancy goods dealer advertised for a saleswoman, — the salary, at first, to be five dollars a week.

Of course this occupation would be most unsuited to my previous habits of life, and uncongenial to my taste, but I could not afford to be too particular. Any thing was better than the horrors of destitution. On the sum thus offered I could *live.* I had clothes enough to last me for some time. At my father's death both my mother and myself had been supplied with mourning garments, not only plentiful, but even rich and handsome, — we deemed this but a suitable respect to his memory. In this regard, therefore, I was provided for. The situation as saleswoman seemed, if I could obtain it, to promise well. I believe I scarcely thought of the improbability that I should succeed in my application, with no experience and no references. I satisfied myself with the resolve to make the attempt on the coming morning, and then I shut out of my thoughts all future worldly troubles, and abandoned myself to the present reality of my loss.

Oh, with what homesick longing my heart cried out for the mother whom I had so loved. God grant that few who read these pages may be able to realize the intensity of my despair. I was alone in all the world. Not one human being lived to whom my life was precious, or to whom my death could bring sorrow.

I forgot the glory of the heavenly morning, the angels, and the new song. I only remembered that over my last friend blew the unquiet winds and fell the lonesome rain of this wild October night, and neither God nor man said any "Peace, be still!" to the tempest of my grief.

Brave and bright, after that night of storm, rose the October sun. It shone as gladly as if there had been no trouble in all the world. It will shine so on your grave and mine; for Nature has for her lost children no Rachel-voice of lamentation. The brave, joyful morning seemed a mockery to my grief. I dressed myself carefully in my deep mourning garments, and strove to look as well as I could, for the impression I should make was all I had to depend upon. The aspect which confronted me, as I tied on my bonnet before the mirror, was neither plain nor actually handsome. Dark and abundant hair was brushed away from a pale face, youthful in outline, but worn not a little with grief and watching. The eyes were like my father's, large and dark, brown rather than black, — the features were regular, and the mouth, my mother used to say, both proud and loving. My figure was tall; slender, without being thin. I had not much vanity, but a year ago I had cherished dearly whatever charms I might chance to possess for my father's sake, who, like all persons of a poetical organization, placed a high value on loveliness of person. I remembered this as I stood there, and thought, with an added sense of desolation, that no one cared for my looks now, — I had no one left for whose sake I need strive to be pretty.

And yet, despite my burden of sorrow, as I walked rapidly through the streets which led to Broadway, a hope or a wish stirred in my heart which was perhaps akin to desperation, — a longing to live in this world, only to *live;* no matter what troubles were in store for me: to live till I should be old, — to see my game of life played out, — to meet all that had been written for me in the book of Fate. It seemed to me then that I could accept joy or pain with equal fortitude, as only the accidents incident to being, laying them up as memories at which, in the long Hereafter, I could look back and smile. I consoled myself as did Æneas his old Trojans, —

" — forsan et haec olim meminisse juvabit."

By the time I had reached my destination, however, a little of my courage had deserted me. I went into the store and asked for Mr. Emerson. I was shown at once into a small counting-room, and a gentleman rose to meet me with an air of polite attention. With a rapid glance I searched his face. His expression was kind, and his countenance by no means destitute of refinement. In his eyes a look of habitual friendliness and real warmth of heart disputed the territory with the sagacions twinkle of the shrewd man of business. Now that I had reached the Rubicon, I felt a strange hesitation about crossing it.

"Mr. Emerson, I believe?" I said, half falteringly.

"The same, Miss —?"

"Hamilton," I replied, answering his intonation of inquiry. "I have called, sir, in reference to your advertisement for a saleswoman."

"For whom did you wish the situation?"

"For myself."

A thousand exclamation points and notes of interrogation twinkled in his eyes. I suppose neither my attire nor my manner had prepared him for such a disclosure. He looked at me a moment; then he said, still very politely, —

"For yourself? Have you ever served in such a capacity?"

"Never, sir."

"Have you any references?"

"No, sir, none."

I seemed to see a dismissal hovering upon his lips and waiting for utterance. My last hope for food and shelter was slipping away from me. I grew desperate. Before he had time to speak I interrupted him. In quiet, restrained tones, in few and simple words, I told him all my story. I did not dwell upon my grief; perhaps for that very reason he understood and sympathized with it the more. God bless his noble heart. He did not doubt for a moment the truth of my narration. When I remember him and all his kindness, I rejoice that human nature, even when seared by the cares and disappointments of the world and of business, is not so bad as it has been painted. When I had finished my story, I saw that his eyes were misty. He reached forward and shook my hand.

"Young lady," he said, "I have a daughter at home just about your age. Heaven save her from sorrow like yours, and Heaven send her a friend if such sorrow should come upon her. This situation is not good enough for you, — you should have one very different, — but, if you choose to take it until something better offers, you can come on Monday."

I tried to express my thanks, — to tell him that I hoped to prove worthy of his trust and kindness; but he interrupted me, —

"Good-morning now; you are weary and excited. If you will give me your address I will send my wife to see you to-morrow."

He glanced at the card which I handed to him, and as I was going out he said, —

"Would you not wish, Miss Hamilton, to change your boarding-place for one nearer the store?"

"I should, and it would be necessary for me to seek one less expensive."

"Very well. Mrs. Emerson shall manage that. Good-morning."

I went home with my heart lightened of one heavy care; but perhaps my sense of desolation was all the more bitter when there was no other emotion to contend with it in my thoughts. I will not linger upon my own feelings. I have dwelt on them too much already.

The next day Mrs. Emerson called. She was a kind,

friendly woman, — a worthy helpmeet for her husband. She took me with her to see about a new boarding-place. In a by-street, not very far from Mr. Emerson's store, a widow, poor but worthy, occupied part of a respectable house, and supported herself by plain sewing. She would be glad, Mrs. Emerson said, to eke out her scanty income by receiving a pleasant boarder. We went to see this Mrs. Gray, and I was much pleased with her quiet, civil manners and the neatness of her humble home. It seemed to me, in prospect, like a haven of rest. Before I left I had engaged to reside with her for the winter. That week I effected the removal of all my possessions. There was space in Mrs. Gray's sitting-room for the bookcase containing my father's library, and she seemed to take real pleasure in helping me to ornament the walls with the engravings I had brought. When we sat down to our toast and tea the apartment already wore quite a look of home.

I said I would dwell no more on my own feelings. I must also pass lightly over the outward trials of that period of my life. And yet, for the next two weeks, they were by no means trifling. Besides the one great loss, which deadened the force of all after-blows, I had to give up so much. I was living far more humbly than I had ever lived before. Every superfluous luxury, of which habit had made almost a necessity, was abandoned. Mrs. Gray, good, kind woman though she was, had no interest in my favorite pursuits, no sympathy with my tastes. Often had she been absent I should have felt less alone. Added to this were the trials incident to learning a new business. My occupation was even more painful and disagreeable than I had supposed. My life had been hitherto very quiet and retired. Though not diffident, I had an instinctive shrinking from contact with strangers. However, I struggled with my distaste for putting myself forward. I conscientiously strove to sell all the goods I could; and I had the satisfaction of knowing that, even in a business point of view, Mr. Emerson was satisfied with the result of his experiment.

One day, when I had been there a few weeks, a gentleman came into the store, and advanced to the counter where I was standing. I scarcely know why he should have attracted as he did my particular attention. It certainly was not because of any especial graces or charms of person. He had a lofty presence, a fine, commanding form; but it was not until long afterward that I learned to see any beauty in the stern lineaments of his face. The time came when I recognized the nobility of his expression, the power and firmness indicated by his features, and discovered into what gentle tenderness those calm eyes and stern lips could soften. But I saw none of these things then.

I think what interested me was a certain desperate and hopeless sorrow, of which I detected the traces in his face. Those who themselves have suffered are quicker to perceive and respond to the sufferings of others. He made some trifling purchase, and went out; but, for the first time since I had entered the shop, I was roused from my selfish sorrow into a genuine interest and curiosity about another person. I speculated a long time that night, sitting silently before Mrs. Gray's fire with a book between my fingers, as to what trouble could so have left its mark and seal of hopelessness upon his countenance; and he a man, allowed by the world's creed to go where he pleased, to choose for himself friends and amusements. I was a woman, — desolate, bereaved of every friend whose love had made my life rich and desirable; yet surely my face had never worn, in the darkest hours, the impress of such absolute despair.

It was not many days before I saw him again, and after that he came quite frequently to the store. He always seemed to prefer making his purchases at my counter; and my interest in him strengthened with every time I saw him. He treated me with as delicate a courtesy as he could have shown to an equal in society; and this formed such a pleasant contrast to the haughty arrogance of some of my customers, and the rude familiarity of others, that I began to mark the days on which he came with a white stone.

At length a week passed without my seeing him. I should have blushed to acknowledge, even to myself, how much difference this made to me, — how often I thought of him, and how many conjectures I wasted as to whether I would ever see him again. Do not infer from this that I was at all what story-books call "in love" with him. I can safely assert that my heart had not, at that time, approached even the verge of that dangerous precipice. But it was pleasant to encounter now and then, amidst the stagnation of my life, some one whose face roused me from my apathy, stimulating not only my curiosity but my sympathy; the courtesy of whose manners recalled to me the agreeable associations of earlier days.

At length I went home one evening and found a gentleman in Mrs. Gray's little sitting-room. The circumstance, so unusual in itself, surprised me; how much more when I perceived that her visitor was none other than the absentee concerning whom I had wasted so many thoughts.

In accordance with her primitive ideas of courtesy, Mrs. Gray introduced us by name to each other; and then she added, —

"Mr. Lincoln has come, Gertrude dear, to get me to do some plain sewing for him; though how in the world he happened to hear that I did such work I'm sure I don't see."

Mr. Lincoln took no notice of the question so gently insinuated. He addressed a few courteous and agreeable remarks to me, in which he did not allude to the circumstance of his ever having seen me before, and then he took his departure. When he had reached the door, as if struck by a sudden recollection, he turned back, —

"By the way, Mrs. Gray, I forgot to bring you my pattern. I will leave it with you to-morrow evening."

After he went out my landlady became voluble at once. It was such a piece of good luck that he should have heard of her. He would pay her so much more than she could get at the shops. He was so polite, too, and so nice-looking.

She was turning over the linen as she talked with busy fingers, making calculations which I was too much absorbed to notice. I had taken, involuntarily, so much interest in this Andrew Lincoln, without even knowing his name, and now Fate had so strangely brought us together again. Should I ever be better acquainted with him, — ever be able to solve the mystery written on his face? Time would tell.

He presently, after this, became quite a familiar visitor. At first it had not struck me as at all singular that he had heard of Mrs. Gray as a neat and reliable seamstress; but when a second dozen of shirts succeeded the first, and these in turn were followed by other garments of various descriptions, whose construction seemed to require his particular explanations and directions, I began to think, with Mrs. Gray, that "he must be going a missionarying to some heathenish place where nobody knew how to sew," or, — the thought would haunt me, so I may as well confess it here, — that he found pleasure in coming to my boarding-place, and was determined to make a pretext for continuing his visits as long as possible.

After a while, however, he seemed to ignore any necessity for excuses, and, by the time Mrs. Gray had finished his sewing, he had fallen into the habit of coming to see us quite regularly. He was lonely, he said, at his hotel, and it was so pleasant to come where he could feel at home; only, if he was intrusive or in the way, we must give him a hint.

In an early stage of our acquaintance he had drawn from me, in the most delicate manner, the history of my past life. I hardly know how I was beguiled out of my reserve, — chiefly, perhaps, by his appreciation of my favorite books, and his warmly expressed admiration of the engravings which had been my father's pride. I was in some sort obliged to explain how treasures so at variance with my present mode of life came into my possession.

We had not been long acquainted, when, finding that I, as well as Mrs. Gray, was always at my needle when at home, he proposed to occupy the evenings he spent with us in reading aloud. I soon suspected him of a design in this manner to test my mental resources and study my character. He had a marvellous way of drawing out my opinions on various topics connected with art and literature, and then he would bring forward his own, — worth more than mine by as much as thorough knowledge and mental discipline are more valuable than mere taste and feeling.

As our acquaintance progressed, I had gradually almost ceased to speculate concerning the sorrow whose profound and passionate impress had awakened my first interest in him. Indeed, I think that the sign and seal of despair had been uplifted from his face. Looking back, I believe that the hours he spent with me did him good and not evil, — that he was a happier and surely not a worse man for my influence.

Was it strange that my life once more put on the colors of hope, — that flavor and tone and richness came back to it? I no longer repined at the disagreeableness of my daily task. Without my own knowledge or volition my feet had wandered to the very border of Love's ideal realm, and already every thing had begun to look brighter than its wont, through the soft haze of that enchanted atmosphere. The spell which was woven round my life was more perfect than the devices of the old magicians. *I* had no room for discontent, — no longing for the talking bird, the singing tree, or the golden water; or, perhaps, I had found them all. I do not mean that I had admitted, as yet, even to my own consciousness, that my heart had gone out from me, as Noah's dove from the window of the ark, and, like that, would return no more. For the nonce, judgment and reason slumbered. Soon, however, came the moment which roused them again from their repose.

A neighbor's child was sick, and Mrs. Gray went to take care of it through the night. I was to remain at home and alone. She had regretted this as she went out.

"If Mr. Lincoln would only come," she remarked; "but it is not his evening."

My heart echoed her wish. "If Mr. Lincoln only *would* come," I thought, as I trimmed my lamp, and drew my chair up to the little round table with an intention of reading. Books were before me which had charmed many an hour in other days; but somehow I did not care to read. I sat for half an hour looking listlessly into the fire; seeing there castles with shining turrets, flame-colored autumn woods, burning bushes bright as the vision of Moses. Remember I was but a girl, — barely eighteen.

At length I heard a familiar tap upon the door, and sprang to open it. Mr. Lincoln *had* come.

"Alone?" he said, as he entered and glanced around the room.

I explained the cause of Mrs. Gray's absence. A look not so much of gladness as of relief crossed his face. He sat down with an air of resolve and deliberation.

"It is fortunate that I came. I have been wanting to see you alone for a long time, and I intended to-night to have arranged such a meeting, but Fate or Providence seems to have managed it for me. I must tell you the whole truth, Gertrude, — a truth neither pleasant to tell nor to hear. You must know just how I am situated, and then you shall decide whether I can see you any more."

As he spoke the room seemed to grow very cold and dark. Struggling with the gloom, my eyes could only see his face, and on it sat more than the old despair. I felt a shuddering presentiment. The trouble which was coming nigh me seemed already to chill me with its icy touch. I folded my hands and nerved myself to listen.

I cannot repeat the story which he told me in his own words. It was briefly this: —

He had married, when quite young, a woman whom

he thought he truly loved; by whom he believed himself beloved in return. She was beautiful; a brunette, full of fire and pride; wayward, exacting, and capricious. For a time her beauty had enslaved him, her petulant humors held him in thrall. After a while, however, her exactions became wearisome. He was tired of playing the lover, — coaxing and submitting by turns. He felt it was time that the quiet happiness of a peaceful union should succeed to the fantasies of a year-long honey-moon. At this she rebelled. He found that her temper, as well as her beauty, was of the torrid zone. A calm existence did not suit her. She cared little for the pleasures of the intellect, little for the quiet peace of domestic life, — she would have worship or war. He made this discovery just before the birth of his first child, — his little boy. This event had reawakened all his tenderness for the mother as well as the infant.

Katherine was very beautiful in her illness, and toward her child she seemed to develop a patient love which was a new phase of her character. No sooner had she regained her usual health, however, than the customary miserable scenes of violence and contention commenced again. It might have been his fault even more than hers. He had been carried captive by her beauty, and had striven eagerly to obtain her hand, never pausing to consider whether her nature was really fitted to make him happy, and when she was his wife he had, like so many men, expected to find in her traits of character which she never had possessed.

In short, they had both mistaken for love a thoughtless youthful passion, which had presently consumed itself.

For three years after his boy's birth things had gone on thus, — there had been tempests of wrath fierce as a tropic storm, long-continued estrangements, and now and then an interlude of reconciliation, a gust of fondness. By this time his little girl was born, and after that there were no more glimpses, ever so brief, of sunshine.

For his children's sake he strove, for still another year, to remain under the same roof with her, but a time came when this was no longer possible. Mutual recriminations had again and again goaded them almost to madness, until both became convinced that the only relief must be in separation. They parted in anger, without one word on either side, of relenting or forgiveness. Four years had passed since that day, but he had not once seen the faces of wife or children.

When he had proceeded thus far in his narration he paused, and sat for a few moments looking into the fire. I would fain have broken the silence with at least a sentence of sympathy, to let him know that I understood him, — that I had not listened to him unmoved, — but I could not speak then. The time would come, no doubt, when I could forget my own anguish in my sympathy for his; but I believe the first impulse of every human soul, — at least every woman's, — in any hour of deathly agony, is selfish. With the poisoned arrow yet rankling in my own heart, how could I calmly strive to soothe in his a wound which had already begun to cicatrize?

At length he spoke again.

"I do not hate Katherine. God knows, Gertrude, that I pity her as fervently as I do myself. Nay, more; for she is a woman, and to a woman it is doubly terrible to know that she must live for ever with her heart's warmest longings repressed and stifled. But for me she might have married some one else, whom she could have made happy; with whom she could have been happy herself. Now her life must be like mine, — desolate."

"She has her children," I found voice to say.

"Yes, the children!" His face kindled. "They must be a great comfort now. Andrew is eight, and his little sister three years younger. You don't know, Gertrude, how I have longed to see those children. I dream about them nights. I hear their baby words, and feel the clinging hold of their little fingers, and then I wake to remember that perchance they do not even know that their father lives to pray for them. But, Gertrude, their love would not be enough to fill up all the voids in my life. I have felt this more than ever since I knew you, and more than ever have I pitied Katherine in her lonely, blighted youth.

"You know now that I have no right to talk to you of love; still, this once, I beseech you to hear all that is in my heart. When I first saw you I had little faith in love or woman. I should have rejected, as a simple absurdity, the idea that either could move me; and yet, by some unconscious magnetism, you attracted me at once. When I went out of the store I found myself recalling your pale, sorrowful face; your slight figure in its deep mourning robes; the grace and delicacy of your manners. I wondered by what strange chance you had been placed in that position, so unsuited, as I at once saw it was, to your tastes and your previous habits. My curiosity, — let me call it by some better name, — my sympathy was fully aroused. I went again and again to the store. At length I resolved to know you better. I followed you home one night, and then set myself to learn all the particulars concerning your place of abode. I found that your landlady was a seamstress, and that made my course clear.

"All this time, Gertrude, I had no thought of loving you. I had no right. To a man of honor his vows are as sacred in the untold wretchedness of an uncongenial marriage as if happiness had made it impossible to have a wandering wish. I believed myself incapable of breaking mine, even in thought. There was no reasonable ground on which the law could give me freedom. The release which is granted to crime is denied to misery. Even were it otherwise, I should not have sought it. I had always a horror of divorce, and not for worlds would I have entailed its disgraceful publicity upon my children. Freedom could come to me but in one way, and God knows, even when I have been tempted almost beyond my strength, I have never been mad enough or wicked enough to wish for that. Therefore I regarded myself as beyond all danger of falling in love. Indeed, in your case the idea of love did not cross my mind. You had interested me, and I had so few interests in life that I determined to follow this one out, — to ascertain the cause of your uncongenial situation, — if possible, to aid you.

"When I had visited here for a while I found I could not stay away. Your society had become a necessity to me. I believed you my friend merely, but I discovered that friendship was very sweet. At last the knowledge forced itself home that I loved you with all the strength of my nature. This love had stolen upon me so gradually, and now seemed so much a part of my life, that I could scarcely chide myself. Had this been all, Gertrude, I think you would never have heard the history I have told you. I would have schooled myself to taste calmly the dangerous delight of your presence; and when this was no longer possible, you should have seen me no more. But in the same hour that the conviction of my love for you was brought home to my soul, I discovered also that I had it in my power to win your heart. I had a strange feeling as if, in the native country of souls, yours and mine had grown together. I believed I had power to summon my other self to my side. Nay, I thought that, unconsciously to yourself, you did love me now. Forgive me, Gertrude, I know that I am speaking to you as man does not often speak to woman, but in this hour there is no room for disguise or concealment. I read your heart as I had read my own. Then I knew my duty. I must tell you all, that you might understand how hopeless was my future, — that you might conquer your coming agony before it was too mighty for you. I believe some men would have been tempted to keep silence, and strive still to win your love; but, thank God, I was left open to no such temptation. More than I prized yourself I prized the stainless purity of your heart and life; dearer to me even than my love was my unsullied integrity, by which only could I call myself your peer. I have told you all. Do you forgive me that I took for granted your love for me?"

I could not speak, but I reached across the table which stood between us and laid my hand in his. Then for a while we were both silent. He spoke first: —

"Gertrude, I shall never talk of these things again. I have shown you this once all that is in my heart. In return I have a right to make but one request. I have wealth; let me use some of it for you. I cannot bear to see you toiling day by day for your daily bread. While I have enough and to spare, you shall not, must not, wear out your young life in this drudgery. If you were my sister you would let me help you. Am I not as near to you as a brother? Does not my love give me as much right as brothers claim? Do not be angry, Gertrude. I hardly know how to utter my petition so as not to wound you. I beg only for this. Let me make a home for you among congenial people; let me surround you with the common comforts of life; let me feel that you are at least above and beyond the necessity of toil. Then I will submit to any thing else. If you prefer, I will never see you; or, if you will let me visit you sometimes, I will ask only for your friendship, — the sympathy you would give to suffering anywhere."

He paused, but I read an appeal in his face fuller of earnestness even than his words. I never for one moment doubted his honor or his heart. I knew that he respected me as deeply as he loved me, — that his care for me would be tender as that of a brother for a sister. But I was my father's daughter. I had my own pride to satisfy also. I could not accept a pecuniary obligation even from him. Still I did not wish to answer him then. I had my arrangements to make, — my future to settle. I would tell him in a week, I said, — not now. I was too tired, — too much exhausted. Would he leave me, and not come again for one week, — then he should know. He must give me time to think.

He obeyed me. He only held my hand for a moment, and then he went.

"Good-by, and God be with you," I said, as he stepped out into the moonlight. He did not know that in my heart I meant that farewell to be the last utterance of my lips to him, until we should meet again where victor souls learn the triumphal anthem of the angels.

I went back into the room where I had met this last and bitterest sorrow of my life. Soon my plan for the future was shadowed forth in my mind. Then I had a right to think over all that Andrew Lincoln had said. I reverenced him unspeakably. Little as I knew of human nature, I realized — I had read "Jane Eyre" — the ease with which he might have deceived me. I knew he loved me with a love as true and tender as pen of the romancers had ever portrayed. How I blessed him that it had been no selfish passion, — that his love for truth and right had been mightier. And yet, — answer me, heart of every woman who shall read this tale, — was my trial light? Because of his very goodness, because I could reverence his image in my soul, and look up to it as almost without taint or flaw of human imperfection, was it not all the harder to know that between us swept the tide of circumstance, — remorseless as death, pitiless as destiny?

And yet, in the midst of my desolation, it was something to feel that he could have loved me, — that had Fate given us to each other I might have made him happy, — might have been his happy wife.

I sat there until the first ray of the morning stole through the windows, I looked at the almost empty grate. Castles with shining turrets, flame-colored tints of autumn woods, burning bushes, all had vanished into the cold gray ashes, signifying desolation. Was it a type of what that night had done for my heart and life?

I walked toward the store that morning with a heavy heart. Once more I must fold my tent and go on alone into the desert. For a little time I had lingered beside an oasis of peace. I had tasted pleasure. It had proved a cheat, a mirage, it is true. No matter, it had gladdened my eyes while it lasted. Now I must give up all, — the home I had made for myself, the friends who had been kind to me, the work by which I had earned my bread. I must go, — where? In that moment, clear as if my guardian angel had stooped to whisper them in my ear, came to me my father's last words: —

"The widow's God, — a Father to the fatherless, — trust, my darlings, trust."

Had the invisible, strong arm ever failed me? Need I doubt it now? I walked on with renewed courage.

When I reached the store I sought an interview with Mr. Emerson. I told him that I had imperative need of change; that there were reasons why I was unwilling to remain any longer in New York; and I inquired if he could help me with advice or suggestions.

He told me, in reply, that he had felt from the first I ought not to be in my present situation. He knew the constant contact with strangers was repugnant to my taste; that I was capable of doing something better. Still he had honored me for submitting so cheerfully to necessity; for doing so well what I had undertaken to do. Ever since I had been there he had been on the lookout for some different employment, by which I could maintain myself more agreeably, but as yet he had found nothing very desirable. Yet, if I was so anxious for an immediate change, there was something, — an advertisement he had seen in the evening paper, — a governess wanted for two small children, in Eastern Virginia. It did not seem to promise much, yet I might like it better than the store.

I thanked him eagerly. I do not often weep, but the tears choked my voice. It was not gratitude, though his kindness touched me deeply; but I was leaving so much, — so much that he could never know.

That morning a letter was dispatched to the address indicated in the advertisement, giving, as I afterward discovered, as much of my history as Mr. Emerson himself knew: praising me far beyond my deserts, and stating that, if my services were accepted, I would be ready to commence my duties immediately.

Five days of my week of trial had already passed before an answer was received to that letter. In the mean time I had trembled lest I might not, after all, be able to get away, — lest I might be obliged to see Mr. Lincoln again, though I was convinced such an interview could only be productive of additional pain. At length my suspense was ended. Mr. Emerson's recommendation was accepted, and he was requested to inform the young lady that a carriage would await her at the —— station on the afternoon of the twenty-seventh of April. The letter had been delayed one day in its transit, and I should just be able, by starting the next morning, to reach my destination at the appointed time.

That night, with Mrs. Gray's assistance, I made all my preparations. I did not confide my plans for the future even to her. I told her enough of the circumstances in which I was placed to convince her that, for the present, it was better she should not know. I had previously secured from Mr. Emerson a promise of secrecy. He was to be deaf and dumb to all inquiries, should any be addressed to him.

It was late in the night when I sat down alone before the sitting-room fire, and prepared to write a letter to Andrew Lincoln, which Mrs. Gray was to give him at his next visit. This was the hardest task of all, and yet in writing to him for the first and last time there was a troubled joy. I confessed to him that even as he had loved me so had I loved him, — loving better only God and the right. At the same time I bade him an eternal farewell. With a love in our hearts which it would be deadly sin not to conquer, I showed him that it would be worse than madness for us to meet. There was no safety but in parting for ever. I told him how impossible it was that I should accept from him any pecuniary assistance, and assured him that I was going to be so circumstanced as not to need it. Then I bade him good-by, thanking God that when he read the words he would never know the pang they had cost me. I suppressed the cry of anguish which would fain, through that dumb sheet, have made itself heard. If my tears fell, I took good care that they did not drop upon the paper. I signed my name firmly, and directed it on the outside to Andrew Lincoln, and then —

It was a lovely afternoon when I stepped from the cars at my place of destination. The Virginian spring, earlier than ours, had already clothed the earth with verdure. I could hear birds singing in the near woods, and the air was full of a sweet, subtile odor, betokening that it had lingered above beds of violets and the pale anemone. Just after the train stopped a handsome carriage drew up before the little dépôt, and an old gentleman, with silver hair and a kind benevolent face, alighted.

"Miss Hamilton, I conclude," he said, cordially extending his hand. "My name is Wentworth."

His appearance impressed me very pleasantly, yet it surprised me. I had pictured the Richard Wentworth, whose name had been signed to the letter received by Mr. Emerson, as a young man, the father of the children in whose behalf my services were required. They must be his grandchildren, orphans, perhaps, and already I felt my heart yearning over them, — I knew what it was to be an orphan.

"Here are your pupils," said Mr. Wentworth, as he handed me into the carriage. "Andrew, Bella, this is Miss Hamilton."

The little girl was shy. She retreated to the farthest corner, and hid her curly head behind her grandfather's arm. The boy, however, gave me his hand, with a frank, boyish welcome. As he lifted his blue eyes to my face a thrill struck to my heart. They looked to me like Andrew Lincoln's own.

"What nonsense!" I said to myself. "Has that name Andrew such a hold on your imagination that you cannot hear a child called by it without indulging yourself in fancies of an impossible likeness?"

The drive to Hazelwood was a short and pleasant one. I was not in a mood for enjoyment, and yet I was conscious of an involuntary sense of admiration at the sight of my future home. It was a gentleman's mansion of the olden time, large, hospitable-looking, and somewhat quaint, with its old-fashioned gables, and the piazza surrounding it on all sides. Mr. Wentworth alighted, handed me from the carriage, and led me into the house with ceremonious politeness. He threw open the drawing-room door, and begged me to be seated while he found his daughter.

"Mamma is in the arbor, — I see her dress," I heard one of the children say, and the three went out of sight.

"They are not orphans, then, after all," I said, as I threw myself back upon the sofa. I dared not trust myself to think. Night was coming, loneliness and silence. Till then I remanded my thoughts; I bade my heart be still. I took up, with some hope of distracting my attention, a book which was lying beside me on the sofa.

On its fly-leaf was written, "To my wife, Katherine Lincoln," with a date nine years before. I knew that handwriting. The book, then, had been Andrew Lincoln's gift to his wife during their year of honeymoon. The leaf had been partly torn out, as if in some moment of passion, and then spared by a tender afterthought. There were traces of tears upon the page. Her tears, — perhaps after all she loved him. If she did, God help and comfort her. Thank Heaven, my heart could breathe an honest prayer for her, even then.

My destiny had led me here, — here of all places, —

under the same roof with Mr. Lincoln's wife; to be the teacher of his children. The room seemed dizzily whirling round and round. Chairs, tables, mirrors assumed fantastic shapes, and blended together like the colors in a kaleidoscope. I knew the symptoms, but I would not faint, — I was determined not to lose my self-command. I sat bolt upright and fanned myself vigorously. Presently the mist cleared from my brain. I was thankful for the lady's delay, which gave me a few moments to reason with myself.

Providence had brought me here, — I ought not to leave, now. Indeed I had nowhere else to go. There could be no place where I was more safe from the danger of meeting him. This path had been opened to me, and my feet should walk on in it without faltering. Shall I confess that there was one gleam of troubled joy in the prospect? I could love *him* and serve him innocently, in loving and serving his children. It was not strange that the boy — his son — had looked at me with his father's eyes. It was not strange that I took him into my heart from that moment. I had made up my mind concerning the future, and fully regained my self-command, when a servant opened the door, and said: —

"Mrs. Lincoln is coming, ma'am. She will be with you at once."

She had scarcely ceased speaking when her mistress came into the room.

I rose to meet her, — face to face I stood with Andrew Lincoln's wife. Physically, she was the most choice and perfect specimen of beautiful womanhood I had ever seen. To this day I think I have never met her peer. The picture she made as she stood there will never fade from my memory. The crimson curtains fell apart at the western window, and the golden sunset rays lit up her dark hair into warm chestnut tints. Full, queenly figure, clad all in white, as suited the balmy April day, — bright cheeks, and lips of the reddest bloom, — eyes full of slumberous fire, — little hands, glittering with gems, — she charmed me like a figure from an Oriental romance.

Her husband had told me she was proud, but she never could have been haughty. There was a certain childlike impulsiveness in her manner still, — she would carry it with her all her life.

She took my hand and looked searchingly into my face for a moment.

"I am sure I shall like you," — she said the words with a warm, satisfied smile. "Let us be real friends, Miss Hamilton."

"We will." I answered her quietly, but in the silence of my soul I recorded the words as a vow. God knows I have kept it. I was her true friend from that hour.

Days wore on, and something which was not quite happiness, yet bore a strange resemblance to it, stole into my heart. I loved Andrew Lincoln's children as I shall never love children again, and I loved Katherine his wife. Her character must have changed much in the solitary years since her husband left her. She was not exacting now, — certainly not selfish. I have never seen a mother more tender or devoted, especially to Andrew, whose resemblance, in both face and manner, to his father, daily appeared to me more striking. Was this likeness the secret of the tears I so often saw in her eyes when she kissed him?

She had appeared to like me from the first. She sought my society, and seemed to wish me to consider myself not her children's governess merely, but her friend and her equal. One day, with a gush of passionate weeping, she told me her story. It was much the same which I had listened to before from Andrew Lincoln's lips, only she blamed herself more than he had blamed her. It was all her fault, she said. She had been a spoiled child, turbulent, and exacting, and she had played with his love until she had lost it.

"And did you love him all the while?" I asked.

"I did not think so then, but I am sure now that my real love for him never wavered. For a long time, though, I thought that I actually hated him. My fierce temper was in the ascendant. He provoked me, and I suppose I was half mad. I told him more than once that all I would ask in the world would be to have him go away from me out of my sight, and never torment me again with his presence."

"And he only took you at your word?"

She smiled bitterly. "*Only* that; but he had not been gone long before I knew that he had taken with him all I cared for in life. I am a desolate, heartbroken woman, Gertrude. I have my children, it is true; his children and mine. It is that, I believe, which has kept me alive; but I would give every thing on earth to feel the forgiving pressure of his lips, to hear him say, as he used to, 'Katherine, I love you.' Oh, if you only knew him you could tell better what I have lost, and what bitter right I have to mourn."

If *I* only knew him! Alas, alas, did I not know him too well for my own heart's peace? He was indeed all she had pictured him, — but what was that to me? He was hers only. He ought to be hers. She was worthy of him, too. I commanded myself perfectly. No one could have suspected that I was more than Katherine Lincoln's sympathizing friend, — no one dreamed that I had ever heard of her husband before. I asked, in quiet tones, —

"But why, if you think the chief fault was yours, have you not written to him to come back? Was it not your duty to make the first advances, if yours had been the first blame? Do you say that you love him and are yet too proud for this, Mrs. Lincoln?"

She shook her head sadly.

"It is not pride, Gertrude. Pride with me died a violent death, long ago, but I *love* my husband. What comfort would his presence be when I knew that his heart had shut me out? And yet I think sometimes, that he might love me now better than he used. I have tried so hard since he went away to grow up to his standard, — to be all that he admired in women. It has been the law of my life. Vain words. Men never tread the same path twice, do they? I was hateful to him when he went away. He might come back, if I sent for him, out of duty or pity, but if he loved me he would wait no summons."

There was truth in her words, and yet I felt that they must, in some way, be brought together. What capacities for blessing were in both their natures. Her love for him, despite all, was so true and so steadfast. He would love her if he were to see her now, — he could not help it. I longed to do something to bring about their reconciliation, — but how? There was nothing for it but to fold my hands and wait. Had I ceased to love him myself? Why torture me with this question? I strove then to put self and selfish feelings out of sight. I was trying to follow Christ, though it were but afar off. Should I shrink because the way was hard? From the time I came to Hazelwood I had never thought of Andrew Lincoln without thinking at the same time of Katherine, his true and loving wife.

For a whole year we lived on peacefully together, — Katherine, her children, and I. I had learned to love her as if she were my sister. I shared, I believe, all her thoughts, and I knew she was each day growing into purer and more perfect womanhood, — more and more worthy of being a good man's honored and cherished wife, — as she ought to be, as I trusted in God she would be soon. She was singularly gentle and winning now, but as sad as she was tender. We used to talk often of her husband; but when I prophesied that he would come back some day and make her happy, she used to say that I did not know him, — I could not dream how utterly he had ceased to love her. She should never see him on earth. Perhaps it would be permitted her to go to his side, and ask his forgiveness in heaven.

It was in April that little Andrew fell sick. We sent for a physician, but before he came I was well satisfied what we had to dread. "Scarlet fever," he whispered, as he bent over the bedside, thus confirming our worst fears. When he went out of the room my eyes met Katherine's. I understood her expression, and answered the question it implied.

"Yes, you must write to him. There can be no doubt about your course now. You say he loved his children dearly. How could you answer for it to him or to yourself if Andrew should die, and he not be here to see him? Think if you had been away from your child five years and could not even give him one poor, parting kiss before he was snatched from you for ever!"

"But Andrew may not die; oh, it will kill me if he should."

"And yet he may, — in any case, you have your duty to do." I spoke with decision and severity; I could not allow myself to falter. They must be reunited now if ever.

She went to a writing-desk which stood in the corner of the room and wrote for a few moments rapidly. Then she came and put the sheet into my hand.

"Read it, Gertrude. Have I done rightly?"

"MY DEAR HUSBAND, — Andrew, our little boy, is very ill. The doctor calls it scarlet fever. I thought that you would wish to see him. Your presence would be the greatest comfort. Your faithful wife,

"KATHERINE LINCOLN."

This was the note. Could it fail to touch that strong, true heart of his?

I had little time for speculations, or Katherine Lincoln for hopes. Andrew grew worse rapidly, until the question was no longer whether he would recover, but how many hours he could live. Neither of us left him for a moment except occasionally, when one or the other would steal away, to whisper a few words of comfort to poor little Bella, who was kept in a distant wing of the house in order to be removed from the danger of infection. But we could not go out of the room without those restless, preternaturally bright eyes missing us in a moment, and then the little, weak voice would wail, — "Mamma, Gerty, don't leave Andy, please." So we watched over him constantly together, neither sleeping, eating, nor weeping.

It was the afternoon of the fourth day since Mrs. Lincoln had dispatched her letter. A change had passed over Andrew's face sudden and fearful. We knew too surely what it portended. He was dying. In a few moments his soul would go forth, and leave the fair little body lying upon the pillows still and tenantless. Katherine's eyes met mine, with a look of stony, immovable wtetchedness in them that fairly chilled me.

"To think," she said, "that *he* will not be here,—that he can never see poor little Andrew again alive. Gertrude, this is my work."

I knew the step which came, at that very instant, so hurriedly across the hall. So did she, for she clasped her hands tightly upon her breast, as if to hold her heart from breaking. She looked as white as a marble statue, and as fair. I could see that, even in the midst of my sickening anguish over the boy whom I loved as if he were my own. I do not think Andrew Lincoln looked at her as he crossed the threshold. I think he saw nothing but the little wan, death-stricken face upon the pillows. He sprang to the bedside and knelt down with a groan of despair; he had recognized the impress on the pallid brow.

Do dying eyes see more clearly than living ones? Andrew was nine years old now; he had been only four when he saw his father last, and yet his face lighted up with a sudden, glad glow of recognition. "Papa, papa!"—he piped the words in his clear boyish treble, as joyously as I had ever heard him speak. He stretched up his arms, and his father caught him to the bosom that, for five years, had longed so vainly for the touch of that little head. "Papa, papa!" and the face and eyes brightened with a radiance as of dawning,—the pale, quivering lips sought the father's lips bending to meet them,—a shiver ran along the slender limbs, and then the golden head dropped backward. Andrew Lincoln's boy was dead.

Katherine saw it, and the energies so long taxed

gave way at last. She fell at her husband's feet in a death-like swoon. He kissed the white, still face ere he lifted her. "Poor Katherine!" I heard him murmur. Was there a quiver of love in his tones, or was it only pity?

"Had we not better take her into the next room? She ought not to be here when she comes to herself," I said, forgeting at the moment how strangely my voice would fall upon his ears. I had been standing in the shade of the bed-curtains, and he had not seen me before.

"You, Gertrude?" The words, with their accent of questioning surprise, came as if involuntarily from his lips, and then neither of us spoke again while we carried his wife into the next room, and busied ourselves in restoring her. I only waited until she opened her eyes and, putting back the hair from her white face, sat up and looked at her husband, before I went away from them. I did not stop to think; I knew it would not be wise or safe. I went at once to Mr. Wentworth, who was with Bella, to tell him of Andrew's death, and Mr. Lincoln's arrival. I had occupation for a while in soothing the little girl. Then with my own hands I made ready my boy — mine by the love I bore him — for the grave. I brushed the soft, curling hair round the still face, restored now to more than the beauty of life, and frozen into the last and sweetest smile of all. When I had arranged all things, I went again to his parents. They were sitting near together upon the sofa, and Katherine was repeating, in a voice broken with sobs, all the details of those last sad days. Even then, she thought of me with her usual tender consideration. When I went into the room she said:—

"This is Miss Hamilton, who has been to me the dearest and truest of friends. We can never thank her enough for all she has done for Andrew. He loved her scarcely less than he loved his mother."

How strange it seemed to have *him* speak to me in such words, constrained yet grateful, as a husband would naturally use to his wife's friend, who had been kind to his dead child. He had uttered such different ones when we met last. I was weak, I know, but I could not command myself sufficiently to answer him. I only said: —

"I have dressed our darling now. I thought you would wish to see him."

They rose and went together into the still room where lay their dead. I staid alone. Even my love and my grief gave me no claim on that consecrated hour.

Andrew had died on Thursday. On Saturday afternoon he was to be buried. I had passed Friday in my own room, keeping Bella with me most of the time. The poor child was almost frantic at the loss of her brother, and it was well for me to have some one besides myself to think of and to comfort. I believe Mrs. Lincoln passed that long, dreary day, for the most part, alone. Much of the time I could hear her husband's restless steps pacing along the piazza, and once I knew he went away for a solitary walk.

It was Saturday morning. Andrew had been put into his little casket, and I had just gathered a basketful of white and sweet-scented flowers to strew about him. I stole noiselessly into the room where he lay. I thought no one else was there; but when I had gone up to the coffin I saw, in the dim light, Andrew Lincoln sitting motionless at its head. He looked up, and our eyes met.

"God has taken him, Gertrude; I am written desolate."

There was such a wild pathos in his tones. They went to my soul. How I longed to comfort him.

"Not desolate," I cried, "surely not desolate. Bella is left you, and your wife,"— and then I went on, carried quite out of myself, half forgetful of even the presence of the dead, in my passionate longing, at whatever cost, to reunite those two and make them both happy.

"You wonder, doubtless, at my presence here, in your home; but I came ignorantly. I thought the best answer to what you said to me the last evening we passed together was to go quite away from you, before there should be any thing in our acquaintance which it would be painful to remember. This situation presented itself; I obtained it through Mr. Emerson, and came here, never dreaming — it was Mr. Wentworth who advertised — that the children I was to teach were yours. I had not been here a month before I loved your wife as I think I should love a sister. She was so true, so earnest, so unselfish. At length she told me her story, the same I had heard from you, only she blamed herself as you had never blamed her. All the fault was hers, she said. You were every thing that was noble. I knew how true her sorrow had been by the change it had wrought in her. There was nothing left in her character of pride or petulance. She was a sweet and gentle woman, the tenderest and most patient of mothers, the fondest and truest of wives; and therein lay the wretchedness that was breaking her heart. She dared not seek to recall you, for she believed that your love for her was utterly dead. She had no hope left in life. When Andrew was taken sick she sent to you because it was her duty, but she wrote, I knew, with more of fear than of hope. She loves you, Mr. Lincoln, as no words of mine can ever tell you. Thank God that in taking your boy to be an angel in heaven He has restored your wife to bless all the years of your life on earth."

He did not answer me. For an instant he took my hand in a grateful pressure. There were tears in his eyes, — through their mist I could not look into his soul. He left me and went out of the room. I knew he had gone to her. Their sorrow could not be all bitterness when it restored them to each other. But I, — where was my fountain of consolation? Death had taken the bright, noble boy I loved so well, and had given me nothing. I had a right to weep as I stood beside the dead and pressed my hot, throbbing forehead to the little cold hand. He had gone from me to a land where there would be no sin in loving.

Two weeks had passed since little Andrew's funeral, and from my seat under the pines I could see through the distant greenery the gleam of the white marble cross on which his name was graven. I sat there, where the shadows danced about me as the sunlight glanced fitfully through the boughs, looking listlessly at the beautiful landscape, and thinking mournfully about my life. Again had I come to one of its mile-stones. Again, yet again, must I take up my pilgrim's staff and go onward, into what strange scenes, amidst what perils, who could tell? Others, I thought, had friends, and love, and home, — sweet rest, safe shelter. Why had Fate dealt so hardly with me? I was not wont to repine, to be thankless and discontented; but this once I had consented to taste the cup of self-commiseration. I found its waters bitter.

"Gertrude," — it was Mr. Lincoln's voice. Screened by the trees, I had not seen him coming till he stood before me.

"I have been looking for you," he said. "I want you to promise to remain with us. Katherine says you talk of going away. I have told her the whole story of our acquaintance. She knows how dear you became to me once, how dear you will always be to me. She loves you, too, as one woman seldom loves another, and it is her prayer as well as mine that you will always live with us and be our sister. Do not refuse," — his eyes searched my face anxiously, — "we cannot give you up. You shall be in all things as if you had been born Katherine's sister or mine. I will not ask for your answer now, lest you deny me. Perhaps my wife may be better able to persuade you."

He stood there beside me for a few moments after he had done speaking, but beyond a mere expression of my thanks I made him no reply, and presently he went away. Then I sat and thought for a long time. Here was all offered to me for which I had been pining, — with the want of which I had upbraided my fate. Love, — for I knew they would cherish me tenderly, both of them, Katherine as well as her husband, — friends, and a home, — a safe shelter, from which I need go out no more until I should exchange it for the home and the peace which are eternal. Should I accept all this? Was it not too pleasant to be safe? Was not its very sweetness dangerous? Could I answer for my own heart? Was I sure that I could live for years under the same roof with Andrew Lincoln and never think of hours whose perilous happiness duty bade me forget for ever? *He* might be safe. Katherine was beautiful, and she loved him; but where was the fine-linked armor with which to shield my woman's heart?

No, I would not stay. They and I should be better apart. Our paths led far away from each other. They might wander wherever the flowers smiled or the birds beguiled them. I must go out into the world to do my work, to earn the bread I should eat. But the prospect which had looked so gloomy to me an hour before seemed changed. Things from which there is no escape always confront us with a sterner mien. Now that a choice had been offered me, and I knew that ease and leisure might be mine for the taking, I could accept work thankfully, recognizing its ministry as best for my soul's needs. I cheerfully made up my mind, and then I went into the house.

Mrs. Lincoln met me in the hall. She put her arm round me, and kissed me with a deeper tenderness in her manner than I had ever felt before.

"You are going to be our sister, Gertrude?"

"Gladly; I am most thankful to owe to friendship the tie which birth denied me."

"And we will be so happy, all of us together."

"But I cannot stay here. I will be your sister always, — your faithful, loving friend while life lasts; but it would not make me happiest to live here. I must be independent, even of those I most value."

This was my firm resolution, and I kept to it. In vain were all their entreaties, and at length they desisted from them. Perhaps Katherine's womanly intuitions interpreted my heart as no man, not even the best man, could do. When she found that I was not to be moved, that I would not go their way, she bestirred herself to help me go my own. I owe to her the situation in which I am passing the midsummer of my life. I am a teacher in a girl's school. Young, bright faces are around me, — young hearts gladden me with their love. I have no hopes or dreams of any other future in this world, and, perhaps, for this reason I do my duty the better.

It is ten years since little Andrew died, and Bella — now a young lady of sixteen — is the dearest of my pupils. Three years ago she came to me to be educated.

"I bring her to you because we can express how deeply we trust and honor you in no stronger manner than by giving you our only child to train. Make her like yourself, and we shall be satisfied."

These were her father's words when he put her hand in mine, and since then she has been my chief comfort. She was too young to remember the one sad episode in her parent's lives. I heard her just now discussing with two of her friends, as such young things will, love and marriage. I heard her say, —

"You are wrong, Fanny, if you think people always cease to care much about each other after a little while. My father and mother have been married twenty years, and you cannot find me two in their honey-moon who love each other more fondly or are happier."

She is right. Andrew Lincoln and his wife *are* happy, with that full blessedness which only love can give. I think of them daily, and rejoice in their joy. For myself, — if one's path lies always in the shadow, one will never die from a stroke of the sun, — I am content.

For this long ten years I have never been to Hazelwood. Its master and mistress come to see me every summer, and I know it grieves them that I postpone so long the visit I am always promising. I shall go some day. I want to see how the roses have grown about the grave where little Andrew has slept so long. I shall press my lips to that white cross which gleams above him, and offer on that spot my prayer of thanksgiving for life and all the blessings of life.

LITTLE GIBRALTAR.

IT was a lonely place. Every day, and all the day, as it seemed, the wind blew steadily from east to west, for the boughs of all the trees were bent for ever toward the sunset. On three sides the sea broke sullenly against the rocks of the small promontory, and went back again, repulsed and discomfited. The house and grounds which occupied the whole of this sea-girt nook formed an estate which was called Little Gibraltar. The name was not inappropriate. Thousands of years, doubtless, had the waves stormed those gray rocks, — thousands of years had the rocks stood firm and thrown them back again into the sea. One could imagine the assault going on for ever, — the repulse eternal.

Ten years ago it was that I saw the place first. I had a friend at school who won such foothold in my affections as no girl had ever won before. We were not intimate, as school-girls reckon intimacy. We had no secrets to tell, or, if we had, we told none. We made no rash vows by starlight and moonlight, but we liked to be together, and we had tastes and fancies in common. I have always loved beautiful women, and this Elinor O'Connor was "beautiful exceedingly."

It was not until I had known her a long time that I learned any thing of her history. When I did, I ascertained that her father was an Irish gentleman of considerable wealth, who had fled to this country years before with his bride, the daughter of a noble family, whom he had stolen, not against her will, from a convent. Leoline was the young wife's fanciful name. She had died five years after the birth of her first child, Elinor, taking with her to the world of spirits an hour-old baby. My friend could just remember her mother, and she told me that her manners were so winning and her beauty of so rare a type that the life-long effect of her loss upon the husband, who idolized her, was by no means unaccountable.

Soon after her death he had purchased Little Gibraltar, and having arranged the grounds and built the house after a certain fantastic plan of his own, had retired there with his young daughter, an efficient housekeeper, who also acted as a sort of nurse or superintendent to little Elinor, and a corps of good servants, who had ever since retained their situations.

Elinor's description of her home had abundantly excited my interest and stimulated my curiosity, and I accepted with extreme satisfaction her invitation to pass the long summer vacation — our last before graduating — at Little Gibraltar. At first I hesitated, lest my intrusion should be unwelcome to the master of this strange domain; but when I was assured that his consent had been solicited and obtained before the invitation was extended, I set aside my scruples and anticipated only pleasure.

The last week in June school closed. A staid serving-man came for Elinor, and took all the trouble of our baggage and bundles. We had a five hours' car ride, and then we got out at a little country station. John, the serving-man aforesaid, went to a stable across the road, and came back with a sort of family coach drawn by two powerful black horses. We got inside, and he mounted the box, and off we drove. It was three miles, I should think; but long before we reached our journey's end we could see Little Gibraltar gleaming stately on its rocky height, with the sea climbing for ever at its base. Elinor pointed to it, as she said, with more eagerness than she had been speaking before, —

"Home, Aria!"

"*Is* it home?" I remember I asked her. "It looks to me like an enchanted castle of Mrs. Radcliffe's times. It is strange, and in a weird sort of way, very beautiful; but it does not seem homelike."

"Perhaps it isn't, as most people reckon homelike; but it's all the home I have ever known since I was old enough to remember. I don't know where it was that I lived with my mother. It is singular that I should recall so clearly as I do her wonderful beauty and wayward grace. There is one thing I ought to tell you, Aria. My father, sane enough about every thing else, believes that he sees *her* now, — that sometimes she comes and calls him, and he goes out and keeps tryst with her. I know not whether it is madness, or a clearer vision than has been given to others."

Elinor's face had kindled as she spoke, and there was such a strange, far-seeing look in her eyes that I should not have been surprised if she had told me that she, too, had this clearer vision which could pierce through the veil of mysteries.

We were near the place by this time, for John drove rapidly. The house was a rambling, castle-like building, —

> "With its battlements high in the hush of the air,
> And the turrets thereon,"

built of some pure white stone, which glittered in the sunset. A long flight of winding steps led from the entrance hall to the carriage road below, and at the foot of these steps stood, ready to welcome us, Reginald O'Connor, his hat lifted, his whole manner full of courtly grace. Unconsciously I had formed an idea of him. I had fancied him a sad, silent, elderly mourner, bowed and wasted by grief, indifferent to all the small observances of life. I saw, instead, the handsomest man, the stateliest gentleman I have ever met.

He was not yet quite forty, and he scarcely looked ten years older than Elinor. He had dark eyes, penetrating, yet with a curious, dreamy, speculative look in them. His heavy, black hair was brushed back from his high, thoughtful brow, — a brow a little too narrow, a little wanting in the indications of combative force and strength, without which a man may be good, and gifted, and graceful, but never great. I had been interesting myself in Spurzheim and Lavater, so I analyzed his head and face, while he stood waiting, before the carriage stopped. I discovered that his was the temperament of a poet, — that he had ideality, veneration, and a wonderful power of personal magnetism, — that he could enjoy and suffer keenly, but that he lacked fortitude, and perseverance, and hope, — that there was a certain weakness in his character which was consistent with the highest physical courage, but which made him helpless before that mysterious something which, for want of a better name, we call Destiny. He could never, therefore, rise above a great sorrow. If I had not made this analysis then I should never have made it afterward, for there was something about him, as I found presently, a certain nameless charm, which defied criticism.

As the carriage stopped Elinor jumped from it into his arms. He gave her a quick kiss, and then extended his hand to me.

"This is so kind of you, Miss Germond," he said, as he helped me out. "You are a pioneer, too, — the first lady who has ever visited at Little Gibraltar. You had need of good courage."

"It did not require a great deal of courage to bring me with Elinor."

He looked at me inquisitively, as if he wondered how genuine my words were. Then he smiled.

"I believe you and she do honestly love each other,

in spite of all the sneers about girls' friendships. I can answer for Elinor. I have heard, for two years, of nothing but Aria, until I have learned the sweet name by heart."

He had given me his arm, and was leading me up the stairs. Elinor was running on before us, gayer than I had almost ever seen her. She looked back, nodded laughingly, and said, —

"That's right, papa. Vouch to Aria for my devotion."

In a moment we stood in the entrance hall, — a lofty apartment lighted by a dome, and in the midst of which a circular staircase wound upward. It was paved with tessellated marble, and hung with pictures which, as I learned afterward, Col. O'Connor had himself painted. On one side a door was thrown open into a conservatory full of choice flowers, beyond which was a spacious library. On the other side another door opened into a large and lofty drawing-room. Into this latter apartment my host led me, having paused by the way to introduce me to Mrs. Walker, — the housekeeper, to whom I have before referred, — who continued to matronize and superintend the establishment. Elinor lingered a little to talk to her, and the Colonel and I walked into the drawing-room alone. Opposite the door an immense pier-glass filled the space between two great windows, and as we stepped in we saw ourselves reflected in it; I still leaning on his arm, and he bending toward me with his air of courtly deference. A sudden and curious presentiment thrilled me like a suggestion from some one unseen, — a presentiment which told me that in some mysterious way my fate and his were linked. And at the same time I heard a whisper, distinct yet low, as if it came from far, — "Beware."

I seemed, in some way, to know that this whisper was not meant for me, but for my companion. I felt sure that he heard it also, for he released my hand which he had been holding upon his arm, and offered me a chair. I saw that his face was pale, and his lips had a nervous quiver. Then Elinor came in, with Mrs. Walker, and a sober, middle-aged lady's maid, ready to show me to my room; and her father told us that dinner would be served in half an hour. I thought he was glad to have us go upstairs.

My room opened out of Elinor's, and looked, like hers, toward the unquiet, shimmering sea. I refused the maid's assistance, and when my door was shut sat down a moment to look out of my window and think. The waters had a curious phosphorescent glow and glitter. They seemed mysterious and infinite as the fathomless sky which bent above them, — mysterious as destiny, infinite as immortality. What puppets we human beings are for Fate to play with, I thought, — beneath the dignity of actors, — not knowing even our own parts, or whether it were tragedy or comedy in which we should be called to perform, — whether the play were in five acts or in one.

My vacation was to be two months long. I felt as if I were going to *live* more in that time than I had in my whole life before.

I opened my trunk. My drama must begin, like many another, with dressing and dining. I had never been able to decide whether I was handsome or not, — though I knew my style was unique. It was certainly not that which those unfledged youth who haunt the steps and dog the walks of boarding-school misses most delight in; for I had never received a compliment in my life, unless the look in Col. O'Connor's eyes this afternoon had been one.

I had a low brow, round which the dark hair drooped heavily, a clear, dark skin, and the coloring in all respects of a brunette, except that my eyes were blue as turquoise, — a bright, light blue. This contradiction between my eyes and the rest of my face made me striking, peculiar: I must try my power before I could tell whether or not it made me pleasing.

I put on a black dress, which suited me, for it drooped in heavy, rich folds about my figure, which was full and tall. Soft, old lace was at my wrists, and was fastened at my throat by a brooch made of an Egyptian scarabæus, and which glittered like an evil eye at my throat. Then I was ready, and had ten minutes more, while I was waiting for Elinor, in which to wonder as to the meaning of the strange whisper I had heard. She came for me at last, and we went downstairs.

The drawing-room was lighted now, and I noticed, as I had not before, the extreme richness and elegance of all its appointments. One would have thought that in furnishing it the master of Little Gibraltar had been arranging for gay feasts and grand festivals, instead of fitting himself up a refuge in which to hide away his sorrow.

One recognized everywhere traces of that exacting ideality which would not be satisfied with less than perfection. At the farther end of the room folding doors were thrown open into a dining-room, where a table glittered with plate and crystal. Col. O'Connor met us at the door, and, giving me his arm again, took me in to dinner, Elinor following. The dinner was conducted with ceremonious stateliness, and, watching the high-bred courtesy of my host's manner, I understood in what school his daughter had acquired that grace and repose which had been at once the envy and the despair of Madame Miniver's young ladies.

Just here I begin to feel that I have undertaken a hopeless task. I have succeeded, possibly, in conveying to you the impression of a home, fantastic but superb, — of my stately host, and the friend whom I loved so well. So far words have served me; but now they begin to seem vague and pointless. They will not render the subtile shades of that midsummer experience. I cannot tell you the strange spell which drew me toward Reginald O'Connor. Fascination does not at all express it, — it was at once finer and stronger. Sympathy, magnetism, psychological attraction, — choose your own term. I only know that I felt, in my very soul, that I had met the one man in the universe whose power over me was positive as fate.

I did not deceive myself about him in the least.

I knew he was not wiser, or grander, or nobler than other men, — not wise or grand, perhaps, in any high sense at all. But, just such as he was, I felt as if I would rather have been loved by him, and die, than be the living darling of any other man. All the time, too, there was the sense of entire hopelessness, — the belief that he *had* loved as he would never love again, — that Leoline dead was more to him than the whole living world. We passed all the days together, — we three, — riding, driving, rowing; and, after a while, I sitting for my portrait, and Col. O'Connor painting it. It was after one of these sittings that Elinor said to me, —

"Aria, I think my father is beginning to love you. I have never seen him as he is now before. If he were not too old for you, — if you *could* care for him, — I think it might be to him like the elixir of life. To me, you know what it would be to have you with me always."

"You deceive yourself," I answered, with forced composure. "You have told me the effect which your mother's loss had on him, and how his whole life since has been full of nothing but her memory. He will never love again."

She looked at me curiously. I knew that my face was turning crimson under her gaze. She sprang up and kissed me with impulsive fondness.

"My darling," she cried, "I believe that you *could* love him! With you the mistress of Little Gibraltar what a different thing life would be to me."

She went out without giving me time to answer her; but after that she left me more alone with her father.

He painted on at my portrait, and grew absorbed in his task. He was never satisfied, — he said my face changed with every change of my moods. He made me give him sitting after sitting. To-day he deepened the eyes, to-morrow he altered a wave in the hair, or changed a curve of the lashes. I began to believe that I was beautiful, as I saw myself glowing, a radiant vision upon his canvas. One day he threw down his brush. It was the week before we were to go back to Madame Miniver. He cried, with a sort of suppressed passion, —

"It does not suit me, Aria; it never will. You must give me *yourself*, Aria, child, darling" —

He stopped as suddenly as if an unseen hand, cold with the chill of the grave had been laid upon his lips. His face turned white.

"Forgive me," he said, "I must go."

He went from the room. I remembered what Elinor had told me, — that sometimes his dead wife called him, and he went out to keep with her a ghostly tryst. I believed that he had gone now in obedience to some such summons. I sat on where he left me. I did not dare to think what I was doing. I had a vague feeling, which I would not suffer to crystallize into a thought, that there was a rivalry between me and his dead bride for his love. Had not I a right to win? I remembered what Elinor had said. I believed that he would be better and happier with a warm, living love, in place of this haunting, ghostly memory. But I knew not which would triumph; I could only wait. At last I heard the door open, and he came to me softly in the gathering twilight.

"Aria," he said, "I love you. It is Heaven's own truth, and I have a right to tell it to you. But I am not free to ask you to be my wife, — I do not know that I ever shall be. I promised Elinor's mother, when she was dying, that I would never marry again. I am bound by my vow unless she releases me from it. I thought then, Heaven knows, that it would be easy enough to keep. I loved her so well that I fancied there was no danger of my loving any one else. I should least of all have feared loving you, — you, yet in your girlhood, and my daughter's friend. But it was curious the charm you had for me from the very first. As we stood in the drawing-room that first night a whisper came to me, which I knew was Leoline's warning, 'Beware!' To-day, when I began to speak to you, I heard her voice again, — a sudden, imperious call, which I could not resist. I went out and saw her, as I always see her, walking to and fro upon the balcony, with her baby, a little white snow-flake, in her arms. Aria, I begged her, as I would beg for my life, to release me from that vow. She could have answered me, — she has spoken to me often enough, — but she only looked at me, with eyes full of reproachful pain, and her lips uttered no word."

I remembered the whisper which I too had heard, that first night, and wondered that I had not also heard to-day the voice which summoned him. Perhaps that first warning had been meant for me as well as him; but I had not heeded it. A ghostly, numbing terror began to creep over me. I sat still and did not answer him.

"For Heaven's sake, Aria, speak to me one word," he said, coming close to me. "Am I a man or a monster? I loved Leoline. She had a right to my constancy; and yet, God knows, I love you. Oh, why did you come here?"

"I *was* going next week, — I *will* go to-morrow."

The words seemed to drop from my lips against my will. They sounded cold and hard. I felt as if life and sense were failing me. In a moment Col. O'Connor was kneeling beside me.

"*Don't* look at me so, Aria. You are turning to stone before my eyes. Don't hate me, — it is enough that I must hate and scorn myself, — that I, who thought my honor stainless, must live to know that I have broken at least the spirit of my vow. And yet, am I to blame? I could not help loving you. But I am old and sad, — I could never have won a young, fresh heart like yours."

The misery in his voice touched me indescribably. It was like the turning of a weapon in a wound. It tortured me into a sense of keen life, and gave me power to speak.

"I don't blame you," I said. "It was fate. But I *could* have loved you. It was a vain dream. Let us forget it and live."

"No, I am ready to curse fate and die."

He looked into my eyes.

"Aria, this is bitterness beyond what a man can bear, — to feel my happiness so near, and yet so out of reach, — to love you, to feel that I could win your love, and yet to renounce you."

He bent forward and drew me with firm hands close to him. I felt his lips on mine for one moment, — fond, quivering, thrilling to the centre of my being. Then he released me.

"There, Aria, that is all. Forgive me if you can. You will not hate me, I know. You shall not go back until the time comes; but you need not see me again after to-night. We should never have met, or we should have met in some other sphere. Well, child, it is possible to bear most things. Come, we cannot escape life. We must go to dinner."

At the table a strange gayety seemed to possess him. He ate nothing, but he covered his lack of appetite and mine with quip and badinage and brilliant turns of thought.

After dinner he went into the library to look over the evening mail, and presently sent for Elinor.

She was with him a few moments and then came back. She looked me in the eyes like an inquisitor as she said:

"Papa has received a letter which will take him away from home to-morrow morning; we shall probably have to leave without seeing him again."

I expressed my regrets courteously, but I made no sign, nor did she ask me any questions.

We went back to school. What a mockery it seemed to me, with girlhood lying as far behind me as infancy. My thoughts ran tumultuously in one channel. I cared for none of the old delights or ambitions. I could not study. I had learned a lesson which swallowed up all others, as did Aaron's rod the rods of the Egyptians.

In the midst of the term an epoch came which gave me independence, — my twenty-first birthday. I was three years older than Elinor, — late in finishing my studies, as, on account of my extreme delicacy in childhood, I had been late in commencing them. I was an orphan, and at twenty-one I became mistress of myself and my fortune. I should have left Madame Miniver's, but I had no tie anywhere so strong as the one which bound me to Elinor, and I staid on for her sake.

Early in December she came to my room with a letter in her hand.

"Aria," she said, "I am summoned home. My father is failing mysteriously. He wants me with him, and he says, 'Tell Aria that, for her own sake, I must not ask *her* to come, though her presence would be the greatest comfort.'"

What to me was "my own sake" in comparison with his comfort? What if I suffered a pang or two more? The worst suffering of all would be to know afterward that he had missed me. I went with Elinor.

We got there in time to see the last of him whom we both loved so well. We watched beside him night and day for three days, and then, in the wild winter midnight, "he heard the angels call."

He had been speaking calmly enough about his plans.

"I have given Little Gibraltar to Aria," he said to Elinor, as she bent over him. "You will be rich enough without it, and you would not care to live here. It will have a deeper worth, a different significance for her."

Then he sent her from the room, on some pretext, and talked to me.

"It is all a mystery," he said, "strange as sad. Can a man love two women? I loved *her*. Heaven knows it, and my long, solitary years since her death have borne witness to it. And yet, if it be not love for you that is wasting my life away, what is it? We shall understand it all in the next world, I think.

"She has come to me often since last summer. She waits for me always on the balcony outside, and I know she is there by the tune with which she hushes the baby on her breast, — always the same tune, — one she used to sing to me in other days. I go out when I hear it, and meet the sad upbraiding of her eyes. But she has never spoken to me since that day. I have pleaded a hundred times for release from my vow, but her lips will never open. I wonder if she will turn from me with horror in her eyes in the world of spirits; or whether, for her baby's father, there will be pity and forgiveness? Wrong or right, I could not help loving you; it was my fate."

I could not answer him, but I bent and pressed my lips to his mouth. Now, with him floating away from me on the unknown sea, I felt no scruples. But at the moment my lips touched his I heard, as distinctly as I ever heard any sound in my life, a strain of wild, sweet music, — a tune I had never heard before. His eye kindled with recognition as he caught the sound, and he tried to rise. I turned to listen to Elinor, who was opening the door.

"Aria, the tide is going out," she said.

I looked back to the bed, and answered her, —

"He has gone out with it."

And we heard the music, both of us, fainter, lower, farther and farther away, until its sweetness died on the waiting air.

Believe my story or doubt it, — it does not matter. I have told it because some force outside of myself seemed to constrain me. I have never loved again, — it does not seem to me that I ever shall. You see me in the winter as the world sees me, gay and careless; but I go every summer to Little Gibraltar and dream over again the old, passionate, troubled dream. Elinor comes, too, sometimes, with her husband and her children; but I like best to be alone with the dead days in that nook haunted by memory, where rise the fantastic turrets toward which the sea climbs eternally, where the white walls glitter, and the wind blows all the day, and every day, from the east toward the setting sun.

HOUSEHOLD GODS.

IT would be hard to imagine any young, strong, healthy woman more apparently helpless than was Marian Eyre after her father's death. She looked her affairs in the face the day after his funeral, and confessed to herself this fact.

Her mother had been dead so long that she could scarcely remember her; and during all the years since she had lived with her father, and been educated by him, both living and educating going on in the desultory, inconsequent, fragmentary manner in which a man who was half saint and half Bohemian and wholly dreamer, would be likely to conduct them. As to morals, St. Anthony himself was no purer than Reginald Eyre. His Bohemianism was only the outgrowth of his restlessness. It suited him to breakfast to-day with the dawning, and climb an Alp before sunset; to lie in bed to-morrow till noon, and sup coffee as lazily as a Turk in his Oriental-looking dressing-gown.

He liked to winter one year in Rome, another in Florence, and a third in Venice, web-footed, melancholy, and princely. Paris he did not much affect. Life there was too bustling, too melodramatic. The French recklessness and *laisser-faire* were of quite another kind from his own, and therefore did not suit him. But half over Europe he and Marian had wandered together. She had learned languages from hearing them spoken; and art-history from studying among galleries and ruins. This wandering, beauty-worshipping life suited her, and made of her what she was, — just Marian.

I would I could make you see the face of clear, healthy paleness; the eyes which had caught the color of so many skies and moods, and never seemed twice the same; the sensitive, proud mouth; the head set like Diana's, and as small and stately. She was her father's idol as well as his companion, — the fair embodiment for him of womanhood. He always saw, through her eyes, her mother's soul; and he had never loved any woman but those two.

He had inherited quite a little fortune; but after his wife died, and his wandering habits began to grow on him, he turned it all into an annuity, because its ordinary interest would not keep him and Marian in the roaming way that had grown to seem to him the only life he could endure. In every thing else his moral standard was of the highest; so I will wait until I find a flawless soul, which has won by virtue of its own spotlessness a right to question, before I try to reconcile for him his idleness with his conscience. In truth, I do not think the matter had ever troubled him. He believed himself to be educating Marian, and so doing his duty in his day and generation; and perhaps he was. If he had sold salt and potatoes at home, and increased his banking account, would he have done more, or better? I am not casuist enough for such questions.

His annuity, of course, was to end with his life; but he had sufficient forethought for Marian to deny himself many a lovely bit of wood-carving, many a choice old missal, many an antique, for which his soul longed, in order to insure that life heavily, and pay each year therefor a large percentage from his annuity, so that when they two could roam together among the wonders of art and of nature no longer she would not want the means for making her life beautiful without him.

At last they had come home to New York.

Though they were far more familiar with half a dozen foreign towns, they always called New York home, because there Marian's mother had died, and in an old down-town church-yard her dust lay blossoming into roses and pansies when the summer suns shone on her grave. They had always had a theory that they were coming back there to settle, when Marian's education was completed. Now she was twenty-three; but Mr. Eyre saw that his mission as educator might still be prolonged with advantage to her and ever fresh delight to himself; so he compromised with the old theory by coming home for this one winter, intending to go back in the spring.

They had plenty of cousins in New York, on whom

they had no especial claim; but these Eyres and Livingstones and Brevoorts received them with much eagerness. They liked to see Marian at their parties. There was something unique and distinguished-looking about both her face and her toilets. The soft-falling Italian silks she wore, and the antique ornaments, suited her calm, proud face and her manner of graceful repose. But from none of these people could Reginald Eyre or his daughter have been willing to receive, or felt free to ask, any thing beyond this courtesy, which, after all, claimed more than it conferred.

They had rooms at the St. Denis,— these two,— and had unpacked for their adornment whole trunks and boxes of treasures, — choice carvings in wood and ivory, illuminated missals, old line engravings by dead masters, cameos, coins, bronzes, and a few pictures, brightening the gray New York of mid-winter with glimpses of Italian heavens.

Here, in the midst of this gay season, — in which, however, despite the gayety, Reginald Eyre was secretly homesick and restless, — he had been taken suddenly very ill. A few moments' delay in the drawing up of their carriage, after they came out of the heated air of a large party, was the only discernible cause of an attack of pneumonia so severe that it terminated his life in a week, in spite of the best medical skill and the tenderest nursing.

He died, as he had lived, like a dreamer: no thought of neglected opportunities or neglected work troubled his last hours. He spoke to Marian, in the few intervals his sharp pain allowed him, very tenderly; but he gave her none of the traditional death-bed counsels and exhortations.

"I think God has loved us, my darling," he said once. "I have missed nothing in life but your mother, and I shall find her now."

Marian was lifted out of herself by the calm expectation of his mood. She did not shed any tears over him, or utter any moans. Time enough for that in the long hours afterward. He saw her to the last, as he had loved to see her, with her fair, unstained face, her true, hopeful eyes. The last words he said to her, an hour before he died, were only, —

"We have been good comrades, Marian. You will miss me in the old places, but not for long. Nothing is long that has its sure end. It seems but yesterday since I kissed your mother's lips when she was dying."

Just at the last the pains of death shook him cruelly. He could not speak, and his only good-by to Marian was the clinging hold of his fingers upon her hand, which did not relax until those fingers stiffened and grew cold.

The morning after his funeral Marian looked listlessly into the paper. She had done every thing listlessly in the three days since her father died. Sometimes she thought her soul had gone out of her, and only her body remained, ruled by dull instinct and old habit. She unfolded the paper, and looked it over with no interest about what it might chance to contain, but simply because it was her morning wont.

On the second page an item caught her eye, and roused her. The office in which her father's life was insured had failed, gone utterly to ruin. She understood her situation perfectly. She knew how resolute he had been in making this provision for her; how entirely it was her sole dependence. Her very first thought was one of profound thankfulness that he had been spared this blow; that he had died without anxiety for her. The next was the question which has confronted so many other helpless women with its blind terror, — the problem society would find it well worth its while to aid them in solving, — what should she do?

She loved music passionately, but she had never learned its theories; poetry, but she had never written it; pictures, but she could not paint them; sculpture, but she had never thought of modelling. Of course teaching came to her mind for a moment, as it presents itself to most women similarly circumstanced, but it seemed clear to her that she had no vocation for it, and there was no one thing she could have taught well enough to satisfy her conscience. Besides, the world was full of teachers already, to whom the calling belonged by right of possession. She would have shrunk, in any case, from entering their already overcrowded ranks. But what *could* she do?

She looked around her and reckoned up her worldly possessions. A few hundred dollars remained of their last quarter's funds. Besides, she had two rooms full of carvings and pictures and bronzes, — a sort of museum of art. They had been selected, she knew, with taste which could not be challenged. They were rare, all of them, — some of them very valuable. If well sold, they ought to bring her a good deal; but she had heard how ruinously such things were often sacrificed at auction. The commissions a regular dealer would require for disposing of them would be large, and that method of effecting their sale would be slow.

At this moment an inspiration visited her. What if she should take a room and dispose of them herself? She understood art well enough to be sure that she could arrange them so as to show to the best advantage. She would need the countenance and assistance of one experienced saleswoman; and while she was thus engaged in turning into available funds her own sole inheritance, she would be getting a little knowledge of trade, and might perhaps be able to find employment afterward in some picture store or art gallery. At any rate, there appeared this one step to take, this one beginning to be made, in answer to her problem, and doubtless the rest of its solution would come afterward.

In this emergency she needed a friend, and she ran over the list of her acquaintances, as she had previously that of her possessions. She could not apply to any of her hosts of more or less far removed cousins. Eyres and Livingstones and Brevoorts, one and all, held themselves grandly above all trade of lesser degree than sending out ships to fetch home silks and velvets. Especially would they hold a woman's hand so soiled by it that no floods could make it clean. Her father's friends had been for the most part men as impractical as himself. But there was just one of them, a man of different type, to whom in this emergency her thoughts turned. So she sat down and wrote a note to Mr. Nathaniel Upjohn, and that evening he answered it in person.

He was a man of thirty-five, with no air of trying to be younger than that, no attempt to catch at the youth slipping for ever away from him; but yet a man whom you would never associate with coming age; who seemed strong and resolute enough to stand still here in middle life for ever. He had made his own large fortune by his own hard work; and yet he was not merely a worker. He liked whatever was best and worthiest in art and in literature, and these tastes had brought him acquainted with Marian's father.

I am telling too simple a story to require any disguises. I am quite willing you should understand that this middle-aged, busy, practical man was very much in love with Marian Eyre. In knowing so much, however, you are wiser than she was, for she had not even suspected it. He had come to see them only occasionally, and then his conversations had been chiefly with her father, though his eyes seldom lost sight of Marian. He had not meant to let her know what he felt for her at present, if ever. He thought himself removed from her by some subtile barriers which nothing in her manner had encouraged in him the slightest expectation of surmounting. But when her note came to him, when he understood by it that she would allow him—him of all others — to go to her in this time of her great sorrow, a wild, sweet hope sprang to life in his heart, which, however, almost her first words dispelled.

She came into the room in her deep mourning garments, a pale, sad creature, from whose face all the brightness seemed gone, but who had never been so lovely in his eyes at her brightest and her best. She gave him her hand, but there was no response in it to his tender clasp. She looked at him, but she did not seem to see him.

She began at once upon the business on which she had desired his opinion, and told him her wishes in a few direct sentences, as if she had arranged beforehand what she would say, and was afraid to trust herself to utter an unnecessary word. In five minutes he understood her position.

"That I should do something," she said, in conclusion, "you perceive to be a simple necessity. That I should do this very thing for a beginning, appears to me clearly for the best; and I sent for you because I knew no one else so capable of giving me good, sound, practical advice. I must have a suitable salesroom, and a proper clerk or assistant, and I suppose there are some means which I ought to take to bring myself, or rather my possessions, to the knowledge of the public. Can you put me in the way of all this?"

"If necessary, I suppose I can; but it seems to me there must be something else for you to do. I do not want to see the treasures my old friend collected with such loving patience scattered to the four winds."

"That will probably be no more hard for you than for me," Marian said, with a petulance for which she condemned herself the next moment. "Forgive me, but I have thought it over on all sides. It seems to me it is the only thing I can do; and we shall not make it any easier by lingering over it. You perceive that I could not even afford to hire a room in which to keep my possessions, therefore I *must* part with them. Will you help me?"

Some words came to his lips then which he had not meant to speak. He said them hurriedly.

"I wish, Marian, that you would let me help you to some purpose. I did not mean to tell you, for you have given me no encouragement, but I love you deeply and dearly; and if you *could* love me, and let your future be my care, you would be spared all this, which it is misery to me to see you suffer."

"I am no Circassian girl," Marian said proudly; "have you had any reason to think I could be bought?"

Her face was kindled now, — aflame with pride and spirit. Her cheeks glowed, her wide eyes held scornful meaning.

"Did I try to buy you?" he asked, with a gentleness which disarmed her pride. "I said if you could love me. Love is no matter of bargain and sale; but I believe I have realized from the first how vain my hope was. I will try to help you, in your own way, since you cannot let me help you in mine. I must have a little time, however, to think how it can best be done. So, if you please, I will go away now, and either come or write to you to-morrow evening."

"I do not deserve that you should be so kind," she said, very humbly, as he got up to go. "I know that you have done me great honor; but you can hardly understand how determined I am to help myself. The life I look forward to has for me no especial terrors, while to marry a man because I was destitute and he pitied me would be in my eyes a crime."

"It would be no less than that in mine. If you had loved me, you would not have misunderstood me. If I had not loved you first, I should not have dared to pity you. But I had no right to trouble you with my dreams. Will you forgive me, and let me be your friend?"

"If you will honor me so far. Perhaps you will be my only one; but that I shall not mind."

Then Mr. Nathaniel Upjohn went away, and Marian was left, as she had chosen to be, alone; but her heart was very lonely and desolate indeed, as she sat there among her relics.

The next day she waited anxiously for news from Mr. Upjohn. The afternoon post brought her two letters. The first one, bearing Mrs. Gordon Livingstone's scarlet and gilt monogram, she threw aside, and broke open the other, directed in a strong, compact, business hand, which she felt sure was that of her father's friend.

It contained a proposition, the result, as Mr. Upjohn wrote, of earnest deliberation upon her matters. He saw, with her, that the articles of *virtu* in her possession must be sold, though he was more and more convinced that she herself was not the one to sell them; while he entirely agreed with her as to the disadvantages which would attend intrusting the matter to a regular fine-arts dealer. But, in a building of his own, on Broadway, were two vacant rooms. Of the larger he proposed to make a storeroom, for the reception of the articles *en masse*, while the other was to be tastefully arranged as a salesroom, the things in it to be few in number, in order that they might be advantageously placed, while from time to time, as articles were sold, the vacancies could be filled from the other room. He had in his employ, moreover, and could well spare in her service, precisely the right person for a salesman, while he himself would undertake the necessary steps for bringing the sale to the knowledge of the public; which last matter, he thought, should be managed in a very quiet manner, as the patronage of half a dozen art connoisseurs was worth more than that of a hundred promiscuous buyers. As for the expenses of this arrangement, of course they would be paid from the proceeds; he would not even venture to offer his rooms rent free, but Miss Eyre might depend on being charged only the exact cost which was incurred, and would be saved from all extortion in the way of commissions. He made bold not only to hope, but to urge, that this plan which he had proposed might be resolved upon, since it seemed to him the only one by which she could at once fitly and advantageously accomplish her purpose.

The letter was somewhat of a surprise to Marian,— it was at once so cool and so kind, so simple and so business-like. Who would think that last night this man had been laying his heart at her feet? If there had been the least touch of love-making in his communication, however, it is very certain that she would have rejected his proposition. As it was, she began at once to consider it favorably. It is possible that all the time she had secretly shrunk from putting herself before the public in this unaccustomed way; at any rate she was not at all sorry to be relieved from it, and to feel that her interests were to be so thoroughly well represented without her aid.

Having reached this conclusion, she opened Mrs. Gordon Livingstone's scented epistle. It was the letter of a female diplomat. It began with condolences on the death of Marian's father, and passed to sympathy in the loss of Marian's fortune. But for this latter knowledge, she said, she would not have ventured to intrude, even by letter, upon her kinswoman in these first days of her grief. As it was, she wrote at once, because she felt impelled to open heart and home to her as a mother. Would Marian come?

Then followed some rose-colored sentences about admiration and appreciation, the pleasure she should expect from her young relative's society; and then came the true gist of the letter. She understood so well dear Marian's pride and sensitiveness that she had determined to bait her proposition with an opportunity for her cousin to make herself useful. Her children were provided with a good governess and competent masters; but if Marian would oversee their practicing a little, and talk French with them enough to impart to them her own perfect accent, she could relieve herself twice over from any unnecessary sense of obligation, and feel that she made Mrs. Livingstone very greatly her debtor.

A little smile of amusement crossed Marian's face. She was not wanting in shrewdness, and though it had not before occurred to her at what a premium such acquirements as her own in music and languages might be held, even unaccompanied by the gift or the inclination to teach regularly, she perceived it clearly now, through the flowery eloquence of Mrs. Livingstone's periods. This benign kinswoman of hers was not one to proffer benefits without having first made certain of her *quid pro quo;* so, as after all the proposition suited her, she felt no hesitation about availing herself of it.

She wrote a letter of acceptance, graceful and ladylike; grateful, too, but frosted with a little reserve and dignity. As her rooms were engaged up to the end of the month she preferred to remain in them until then. This would give her time to superintend the removal of her effects, and to make her preparations.

By the same mail she sent her reply to Mr. Upjohn, cordially thanking him, and putting her business matters unreservedly into his hands.

During the fortnight which followed she bore herself most bravely. All her father's cherished treasures — all the lovely pictures, and bronzes, and vases, and terra-cottas which they had collected with such pleasure and pride during their happy, wandering years together — were packed under her supervision, loaded into commonplace vans, and carried off before her eyes; and if she shed a tear over them, only Heaven and silence knew it.

During this process of removal she saw Mr. Upjohn frequently, and always in the aspect of her father's friend, — a middle-aged man, kind, quiet, thoughtful, and somewhat formal. At times she almost believed that she had only dreamed that this man once asked her to be his wife. The contradiction between those few strange moments when he had startled her with his love, and these cool, well-balanced interviews since, puzzled her for a time, until she gave the puzzle up, only too thankful to find in Mr. Upjohn what he was, — her one true, strong, faithful friend, in this time when she needed friends so much.

At length the whole thing was over. The last household god was gone, — not even a pensive Psyche or a winged Hope was left to bear her company. She had thanked Mr. Upjohn, and given him her new address, where she asked him to call and report progress; settled all her bills, and still she had half an hour before the time appointed for Mrs. Livingstone's carriage to come for her. She had meant to avoid this, and had lingered over her closing tasks that she might not have time to think. But still a space remained, and silence and memory confronted her, and would have their will of her.

It was a sharp wrench to go out of these rooms which she had shared with her dead, — where she had heard his last words, and kissed the cold lips when they could speak no more. She made no outcry, — why should she? Who was there to care for her mourning, or to comfort her? But perchance her own true dead, "from the house of the pale-faced images," heard the wail which only her soul uttered, and by some celestial mystery, of us uncomprehended, brought her comfort.

When the carriage came at last, that fair, calm face of hers bore no trace of conflict. She went quietly down the stairs, her long, soft, mourning robes trailing after her, and was greeted cordially by Mrs. Livingstone, who sat in the *coupé*. So her new life began.

If Mrs. Livingstone was prepared for any effusion of grief on Marian's part, and sympathy on her own, she was certainly disappointed. Miss Eyre was not one to wear her sorrow upon her sleeve, or shed her tears in company. She was quiet and graceful and dignified as ever. The most expansive of women could have found no excuse for falling upon her neck and weeping over her. So they made talk about indifferent matters, as people do in society, and by the time they had reached Murray Hill their further attitude toward each other was mutually well understood.

With infinite tact Marian slipped into her place in the household. She never failed to perform conscientiously the duties which could justly be expected from her; but also she never put herself for a moment in the position of protégée. Mrs. Livingstone understood clearly that she was securing for her growing daughters advantages in certain directions such as she could procure for them in no other way, but she also knew perfectly well that Miss Eyre would remain under her roof no longer than the position was made agreeable to her.

Agreeable in a certain way it was at present, — as much so, at any rate, as any home among unloving strangers could be made to this proud, tender girl, who had known nothing but love all her life, for whom the heart of her dead had been always so true and so warm. Her grief never came to her lips in words, or overflowed her eyelids, but there were times when the orphaned heart rent the very heavens with cries which no human ear heard, and reached out into the infinite spaces as if by the very force of its desire it could wrench back from them the dear old love.

Soon Lent began, — the cessation of parties and operas, at which Marian, in her deep mourning garments, had not assisted, and the inauguration of quiet, small dinners and high teas. At these lesser gatherings Miss Eyre was present; and the admiration of more than one man made Mrs. Livingstone fear lest she might possibly lose her fair inmate unfortunately soon; until, seeing the cold sweetness with which all advances and attentions were alike received, this fear gave place to a new one.

Tom Livingstone was the darling of his mother's heart, and the pride of her eyes; and Tom Livingstone was coming home in June. The only son among a household of girls, he had been made a sort of demi-god in the home circle, and had borne his honors loftily, after the manner of men. There were good things about him certainly, though he was not the hero into which his feminine worshippers had exalted him. He was handsome, in that young, haughty, unchecked manhood of his. He had no vices. Culture had made the most of a mind naturally shrewd and sensible rather than highly intellectual. Travel had developed his taste and stimulated his imagination, until really there was a good deal of charm about Tom Livingstone.

His mother remembered with a little secret dismay that June was near at hand, and that he had met the Eyres in Florence two years ago, and written home some very extravagant letters about Marian. What would be the result when he came back and found this "rare, pale maiden" domesticated under his own roof? She gave this girl, whom she had seen letting brilliant opportunities slip by her so coolly, credit for disinterestedness. If she smiled on Tom it would be because she loved him; but what girl could help loving Tom if he tried to make her? What if he should try? What could be done or said? Miss Eyre was a gentlewoman, — as well born and bred as any Livingstone of them all, — his cousin by too many removes, moreover, to have the ghost of an objection conjured out of the relationship.

She knew by experience that Tom was ill to drive; and she knew also that he must marry money, or make a vast social descent from the family scale of living.

Gordon Livingtone's million, divided into eight or nine portions, could not make any of his heirs rich, as Mrs. Livingstone was accustomed to reckon riches. Tom must mate money with money, or come down in the world grievously. She perceived that she had done a very indiscreet thing in setting a snare for his feet with this pretty, portionless temptation; but she did not so clearly see her way out of the position, so she waited for the future with what patience she could, and a daily prayer that Miss Eyre's heart might be touched by some one else before the conquering hero came.

Marian herself, meantime, went on with her life patiently but wearily, and quite unconscious of these speculations about her. This living without the ceaseless tenderness which had been her daily food so long begat a hunger of the heart so intense that it seemed to her sometimes as if it could not be borne; but she was never once tempted by it to feed on the husks of a love for which her own heart held no response, which attracted her only by what it promised, though of such opportunities she had more than one. But her loneliness wrought into her manner something gentler and more appealing than she was aware.

Mr. Upjohn felt this change on the occasions when he called to render an account of his stewardship, though he did not gather from it any hope. He never thought of trying to persuade her to revoke his sentence, which he had so well understood to be final. Possibly a bolder and more self-confident man might have caught a hint from her mood, and stormed her heart into his power; but perhaps Mr. Upjohn might not, after all, have cared to hold what he had been forced to win by storm. It was, however, certain that she was strongly drawn toward him in these interviews, though by no attempts of his own. He was so true, where all else seemed hollow; so earnest, where all others seemed formal; so devoted to her interests, that she felt at last that the man whom she had begun by regarding simply as her father's friend had become now her own personal property, — only her friend, it is true, but at the same time her only friend.

He had certainly met with excellent success in her service. Week after week substantial sums of money were transferred to her banking account, as one rare and costly article of her father's collection after another was disposed of at a just and generous valuation. What means he took to bring about these sales, or who purchased the articles, she never inquired. Having once given the matter into his hands, she cared to hear no particulars, and she never once went to the salesrooms. Having once gone through the parting with these household gods of hers, she did not care to renew the pain.

In June the family went to their summer home on the North River; and soon after this Tom came. There were a good many fine traits in his character. He was direct, straightforward, honorable, and in earnest, though he was no flower of knighthood, no miracle of constancy. If he loved a woman, and his love were returned, it was in him to love long and well; but he would never waste much time in despair for the fair woman who was not fair for him. Neither himself nor his kindred, however, had suspected this healthy, elastic, recuperative power of his healthy, elastic nature. He was just a hearty, generous, well-cultured American gentleman, — as fine a type, too, when thorough-bred, as one is likely to find, — clear-eyed, quick-witted, and courteous.

He was about Marian's age, familiar with her best-loved haunts in the Old World, and an old acquaintance in the days when she had been happiest. It was very natural that his coming should give her pleasure, and she showed it in the frankest, most unreserved way. Talking with him, she felt herself more at home than she had been before since her father's death. She brightened into her own softly radiant self, — a fascinating creature, with her pure, proud face, her red, smiling lips, her dusky, drooping hair, and the eyes which changed with every thought, took a new color with every mood.

The young hero in Panama hat and Magenta necktie lowered his colors before her. She had swayed his fancy curiously in their few meetings in the old days, and he had never forgotten her. But now her graver sweetness stole into his heart, and he was ready to offer her the half of his kingdom.

She had been so used in her father's time to cordial friendship and free companionship with men, — friendship touched often with chivalry, but never warming into love, — that she went on, unconsciously enough, in this path along which young Livingstone was gallantly leading her. They rode and drove together, or passed long summer twilights hanging in a boat 'twixt crimson sky and crimson river, and Marian had not enough of ordinary young-ladyhood about her to guess where it all was tending.

Quite unintentionally, it was Mrs. Livingstone who opened her eyes. Going one day past the door of that lady's morning-room she heard the words: —

"It is true that Marian is all which you say, but it is equally true that you cannot afford the luxury of marrying her."

She hurried on instantly, with glowing cheeks. It was all plain now. She had been blind. Tom loved her, and had been trying to let her see it, and taking encouragement from her frank, free manner, while she had never once guessed his meaning. She smiled a little over Mrs. Livingstone's notions of poverty. To say nothing of the hundred thousand likely to come by and by, Tom had fifty thousand of his own, now; and on an income less than that would yield what happy years of pleasant wandering she and her father had known. If she loved him, certainly his mother's opposition, based solely on the question of finances, would not deter her from marrying him, or feeling that he had a right to please himself. The question became at once whether she might, could, would, or should love him, — a potential of which the indicative was hard to determine. She really did not know, herself. If you, my reader, are so clear-headed, so subtile in your intuitions, that you could never be in doubt about such a matter for a moment, turn compassionately this leaf which reveals to you Marian in her indecision, her poverty of self-knowledge; but, for my part, I think most girls who have never had an accepted lover, or been accustomed to speculate about love and marriage, would have an epoch of similar uncertainty at the instant when a most agreeable, eligible, and altogether unexceptionable friend should stand before them suddenly transformed into an expectant suitor.

That night the whole story of Tom's hopes and fears came out. He took courage, perhaps, from a new shyness in Marian's manner. At any rate, he told her how dear she was and always must be, and then waited for her answer.

"I am portionless," she said, gravely. "If there were no question about any thing else, I think your family would not approve the marriage for that reason."

"They would get over that," he protested, eagerly. "They all think you are perfection. They only fear that I am too good-for-nothing a fellow to help myself, and not well enough off to make you comfortable. But I could do any thing, with you for my inspiration; and in this one greatest thing of my life I must please myself. If you can love me, Marian, nothing else is wanting."

She looked at him, — his handsome, eager face so full of longing tenderness for her, so lonely, so sorely needing it, — young, strong, fond, ready to do and dare for her sake. Surely she *must* love him, — surely this thrill at her heart *was* love. But — was it? Marian was romantic; that is to say, she had high ideals. Love to her meant a grand, heroic something, which would be strong and steadfast through life, and outlast death. Would all her skies be dark, she asked herself, her days empty, if the shining of Tom Livingstone's eyes were quenched? Was he so much to her that without him the rest of life would be barren? Her heart uttered no affirmative, and yet she had been accustomed to think that this and nothing less than this was love. The "Yes" which had almost sprung to her lips shrank back again, and she said, instead, very humbly: —

"I dare not answer you, for I do not know myself. It seems to me that in marriage there is no half-way. One must be ineffably happy or ineffably miserable. I would not trust myself to be any man's wife unless I was sure, beyond a question, that I loved him with all my being. I cannot tell whether I could ever love you like that, for I never thought of you, until to-day, as other than my pleasantest of friends."

He ventured on no prayers or protestations, for the quiet solemnity of her mood awed him. The matter which she looked at with such serious eyes took on new sacredness for him. He dared not be responsible for this woman's happiness, unless indeed she could love him so entirely that there would be no doubt about his making it. So he told her, gravely and gently, that he would wait for her to understand herself; and though, whatever her decision might be, he must always love her, he would never blame her or accuse her of having held out to him any false hopes.

Then they sat silent in the evening stillness. He had hoped to have that graceful head of hers upon his shoulder, to kiss the serious, smiling lips of his promised wife, to be happy in her sweet and frankly given love. Instead, he sat a little apart from her side, with a distance which seemed like the sweep of eternity between their souls. Would he ever come more near?

In the weeks that followed Marian grew thin with anxiety. She meant to do right, at whatever cost; but it was so hard to know what right was, to evolve certainty from the chaos of her emotions. There was so much to incline her heart toward him in his handsome, graceful, courageous youth, in his ardent yet reverent devotion to herself. Sometimes she thought she could ask no more; but slowly a conviction grew on her that in him was not the strength on which she longed to lean. She might be his inspiration, as he said, — he never could be hers. She must look at him with level eyes, and it was in her nature to long to look up. The daughter of Reginald Eyre, "Puritan Bohemian," was not likely to have any religious cant about her; but she had strong spiritual needs. A steadfast sense of personal responsibility to a personal God underlaid her life and made it solemn. Tom Livingstone was worthy of a better love than hers, she was ready to grant; but, when she began to think of seeking her rest and shelter in him for ever, she discovered that that gallant, generous heart of his lacked something without which she could never be satisfied.

At last she told him so, with that sad tenderness a good woman always feels for the man who has loved her in vain.

True to his promise, he accepted her decision, and held her blameless. He only said once, with despair in his eyes: —

"If you could but have loved me, O Marian!"

And she answered, in a low voice, which seemed to him sadder than any wail: —

"Oh, if I could! Don't you *see* how desolate I am?"

If the family had known any thing of this probation and its results they never alluded to it before Marian; but Mrs. Livingstone's manner was most cordially gracious just after this final decision; though she made only feeble attempts to combat Miss Eyre's resolution to go back to New York early in September and go into lodgings. Marian offered no explanations, — she was not addicted to them, — she merely announced that she felt it desirable to make different arrangements for the next winter, and must go early to town in order to perfect them.

Then she wrote to Mr. Upjohn. Somehow in every difficulty it seemed very natural to turn to him, — he was so strong and so self-reliant, so eminently to be relied upon. She felt no hesitation about asking him to secure her suitable apartments, — a little parlor and sleeping-room in some quiet and not too expensive boarding-house.

He had managed her business matters so admirably that she had quite a little provision for the future, and could afford herself a space of leisure in which to map out that future to her liking. She had somewhat changed her ideas about teaching. She thought now that she could without difficulty make up from among her acquaintances a class of young ladies who had finished school, but who would be glad to read the modern languages under her tuition; and she much preferred the independence this course offered to a longer residence beneath the Livingstone roof-tree. Tom alone was urgent that she should remain under his mother's protection. He was going abroad again at once; and he should be so much more happy and at ease if he left her, as he found her, there. Mrs. Livingstone seconded him courteously; but I think Marian's presence was somewhat embarrassing to her at this juncture. However that may have been, her courtesy and her son's entreaties were alike met with polite but firm decision. Early in September Marian removed to her Fourteenth Street apartments; and the next week Tom Livingstone's name was registered among the passengers of the "Arago."

Miss Eyre felt a strong, sweet delight in her self-sovereignty as she went into her pleasant parlor and looked around her. In one corner stood a Psyche, which surely she remembered; in another a wingèd Hope, by some disciple of Canova. One picture, a face of Saint Catherine, with eyes full of courage and of faith, lips strong for prayer and tender for praise, — hung over her mantle, on which flowers bloomed in crystal vases. It was like coming home to come back to these old, beloved objects; but she did not understand their being in her possession. She felt sure that Mr. Upjohn would come to inquire after her comfort, and she waited for an explanation from him impatiently. When at last he came, and her question followed her greeting, he only smiled and said:—

"I thought it would not be good for you to have too much money. The rest had sold so readily that I ventured to keep these for your own pleasure."

He was repaid for all his trouble by her bright, cordial thanks. Somehow they had grown singularly good friends since the night when he gave up all hope of their ever being more than friends. She felt very near to him, very comfortable with him, this evening, as she told him over all her plans, profiting by his clear sagacity, made hopeful by his hopefulness for her, catching the contagion of his strength. She looked at the rugged manliness of his face, and found something noble in it, which she wondered that she had failed to discover before. She was not quite desolate, surely, since she had this one friend, who had loved her father, whom her father had loved, and who, she felt now, would be her friend for all time.

She had no difficulty in arranging her class upon satisfactory terms. She laughed cheerfully with Mr. Upjohn, who came to see her as often as once a week, about being an independent, self-supporting woman; and she found an interest in her regular task, which really made life brighter and better worth living for her.

Sometimes, as the winter passed on and she saw more and more of Mr. Upjohn, finding in him always the same cordial, earnest, but unlover-like friend, she began to wonder whether he had really ever loved her at all, or only been moved by sympathy in her distress on that one night which she so well remembered. Did *he* remember it as well, unconscious as he always seemed? She began to long to know. She recalled his words: —

"If I had not loved you first I should not have dared to pity you;" and, knowing that he was truth itself, she felt that he must have cared for her then, though his strong manliness had helped him to overcome it so utterly now.

She believed honestly that she did not regret the lost opportunity, but every week she saw more clearly how much he was to her, even as a friend, which Tom Livingstone never could have been. Was it that, after all, the world's workers must ever be nobler than the world's idlers; or that a larger outlook on life had given him a wider horizon; or that in his nature, as God made it, there was capacity for nobler issues than in the other's? She could not tell. She had only a subtile consciousness that, let her soul take wings as it might, in no height of her aspiring could she ever soar beyond his capacity to stand beside her.

She was still too shy in her confessions to herself, or perhaps too wanting in self-knowledge, to fully divine how different her answer would be likely to be now, if he were to ask the old question over again; and he, on his part, understood himself so well, and was habitually so sure of his own emotions, that it never occurred to him to doubt whether Marian was equally self-poised, — whether her "no" once spoken must needs be "no" for all time. He was not at all likely, therefore, to give her an opportunity to change her mind. But just here an accidental turn of a conversation, a lucky chance, — I speak after the usual fashion, but I believe in a heavenly and special Providence, — occurred to set them both right.

He came in one evening, and found her warming her slender fingers by the fire blaze. She looked so lovely, so homelike, so entirely gentle and womanly, that, despite the seal he had long ago set upon his wishes, his heart went out toward her in a great wave of love and longing. But he only spoke to her with the calm friendliness of his usual manner.

"I am cold," she said. "I have just been to Murray Hill to make a call of congratulation. The second Miss Livingstone is soon to be married to Colonel George Seabright."

"Seabright! Why, he is as old as I am, and Maud Livingstone is very young, is she not?"

"Nineteen last autumn; but what is that if she loves him, and I think she does."

"But do you think it no sacrifice when a woman loves and marries a man older than herself?"

"I think no marriage is a sacrifice when a woman loves."

Some glint in her eyes inspired him. He looked into her face.

"I think you felt differently once," he said, slowly.

"I was not very well worth loving in those days. I neither understood myself nor any one else."

"But you do understand yourself now, and I do not think you have changed your mind."

"If *I* have not, I presume *you* have," she said, archly.

Both her hands were in his in a moment. Pride, passion, power, all looked together from his eyes, and then were succeeded by and lost in a strong, pure tenderness.

"You will," — that was the first impulse, — "I mean, will you, Marian, will you give up your class at the end of this quarter?"

"For what?" the bright archness lingered in her tone, but her pale cheeks flushed with the dawning of a new day, and her eyes were too shy to meet those which sought them.

"To be my wife."

Was it the same Marian Eyre whom he had wooed in vain before whose hands staid in his now so willingly, whose lips he kissed with the glad audacity of a happy lover?

"The patient are the strong," a tender ballad says; but certainly in this instance the strong was not the patient. Perhaps Mr. Upjohn thought that a man who had waited thirty-six years for his happiness had waited long enough. At any rate, he hurried Marian with her preparations until he had shortened his probation to the briefest possible space. There was a little talk about a bridal journey, but that she put aside.

"I would rather go home," she said, honestly. "You know I never had any home, never in all my life."

So, not at all reluctant at the change of programme, he busied himself in making home ready for her.

She had been used to relying on him so long, in matters of business, that for him to assume all responsibility seemed natural and proper; and it never occurred to her to wonder that in these arrangements of his he neither consulted her taste nor asked any assistance from her. She went on quietly with her own preparations, more simple, indeed, than they would have been once, but not without a certain distinguished elegance, lacking which Marian would not have been herself.

At last, one afternoon, they were quietly married in church, and drove away together to their home in a pleasant up-town street.

When she stepped into the hall, with her husband's welcome spoken low and tender in her ear, Marian began to recognize some old acquaintances, — certain bronze knights in armor whom she saw first, years ago, in the shop of a noted Roman fabricant; a cuckoo clock on a bracket of Geneva wood-carving; an antique table with a curious vase upon it.

Watching her face, Mr. Upjohn led her through the house. Here a soft-eyed picture hung; there a shape in marble gleamed; yonder a well-known group in terra cotta told its old story. In her own room, her Hope and her Psyche and her soft-eyed Saint Catherine kept watch and ward. They had been removed while she was at church to the place appointed for them. Everywhere was some beloved relic of the old days, — not one of her treasures missing.

"*You* bought them all?" she asked, at last.

"Yes, dear; with no thought or hope, then, of this happy, happy day, — but because, even then, I loved you too well to see any thing you had helped to select, or care for, pass into the hands of strangers."

"You know I cannot thank you," she began, but just there she broke down utterly, a very woman in her happiness, and wept such tears as all true women who have loved happily can understand. Round her were all her household gods, and she had found, at last, her rest and her home.

THE JUDGE'S WIFE.

"WHOSE house is that behind the elms?" asked a stranger, one summer morning in 18—, of Israel King, landlord of the only inn the good town of Essex could boast. Strangers frequently made this inquiry, for the house in question was by far the most noticeable in the little village. The situation, on the top of a gentle hill, was in itself fine. Noble old trees, stately enough to have been the pride of some English park, surrounded it, and between their foliage you could catch tempting glimpses of a large, hospitable-looking stone mansion.

"Yes, that is a hansum house. You are not the fust one, by a good many, to ask who it belongs to," commenced the landlord in his circumlocutory fashion, rubbing his hands and sitting down as who might, if he was urged, a tale unfold. "I calkerlate it's about as hansum a house as you'll find in a country village anywhere, and Judge Elliott, the man who owns it and lives in it, is a fine man,—a master fine man, *I* call him, though there's been some hard talk about him, but that's neither here nor there;" and Israel shut his lips together as one not to be induced to tell any thing more, — at least not without urging.

By this time, however, the stranger's curiosity was really aroused; besides, he had a lonely morning to pass before he could attend to the business which had brought him to Essex, and what could while away the hours more agreeably than to listen to a story, — a veritable New-England romance? So he fell in with the landlord's humor, and *urged* the worthy publican to his heart's content.

"Waal," commenced the narrator, "I dunno as I mind tellin' ye, seein' yer a stranger here, an' it can't do no hurt, ef it don't do no good. It's nigh onto fifteen year ago; let me see, — yes, '*twas* seventeen year ago last spring, — how time *does* fly, don't it? — when Jacob Elliott, he wan't judge then, come to Essex and hung out his shingle. He was a master smart young lawyer, an Englishman born, and he'd larnt most of his law in England. Anyhow, he'd got admitted to this county bar some way, and he'd practised a year over in Simsbury afore he come here. I never see any young man come up as he did. 'Twant long afore he was on one side or t'other of about every hard case that was tried in Har'ford county, and the side he was on most gen'ally come off ahead. When he'd been here seven year they chose him Judge of the County Court.

"But I'm gittin' afore my story. He hadn't been here long when he got acquainted with 'Lizabeth Mills. I dunno as you'd a called her hansum, — most o' folks didn't, but somehow I liked the looks of her better'n any girl in Essex, and I guess 'Squire Elliott was pooty much o' my opinion.

"She wan't small, — ruther above middle size, I guess you might call her neither slim nor stout. She had kind of a stately form, and my good woman used to say she made her think of our horse-chestnut tree, — not a bit too large for her height, and not a bit too tall for her size, but shaped just as true as a die, and kind o' lofty lookin', as if small things couldn't git nigh her. *She's* kind o' poetical, Miss King is, and she allus thought a master sight of 'Lizabeth Mills. So did everybody, for that matter. All the old folks was greatly took up with her, she was so perlite and respectful and willin' to talk with 'em. The young girls all liked her. She was so neat and so smart, — she knew how to twist a ribbon or tie a bow better'n the best of 'em, and she was allus ready to help other folks. Besides, she never interfered with their sweethearts. The little children, — it did beat all how *they* took to her. She allus had some nice story to tell 'em, and she made 'em rag-babies, and did a heap o' things for 'em the other girls was too full of beaux and finery ever to think o' doin'. When she went amongst the little ones they was allus all over her to once, and she never seemed a bit put out by 'em. Her face would kind o' kindle up when she see how they loved her, and my good woman said the smiles she would give 'em it did her heart good to see. 'She ought to be married and have some of her own, she loves 'em so well,' says Miss King. I was pooty much of the same opinion, but we used to think it was main doubtful whether she ever got married; the young men was all afraid of her. Truth to tell, they was the only human critters who was oneasy in her company. Old folks and young folks, children and grandparents, all felt free and easy with her, but the young men hung off. Girls that wan't good enough to tie up her shoe-strings got courted and married, but she got along to twenty-three, and I don't believe any chap had ever so much as walked home with her from meetin' or singin' school, exceptin' her own brother William.

"Her father — everybody called him 'Squire Mills, he'd been Justice of the Peace nigh onto twenty year — was one of our fust men. He owned the best farm in Essex, and folks kind o' looked up to him. They lived in hansummer style than most on us, 'specially arter 'Lizabeth grew up. She had a mighty sight o' taste, that girl had. Their parlor used to look, of a summer day, like a little garden, with pinks and roses put all round in cheney saucers and little glass dishes. He hadn't but them two children, 'Squire Mills hadn't, and they did think a main sight of one 'nother. 'Lizabeth was jest two years the oldest, but William was taller than she was, and they was allus together.

"But you'll think I'm steerin' a good ways from my story. Truth is, I ain't so young as I used to be, and my thoughts have got slow 'long with my steps, and like jest about as well as my feet do to stop among the old places and rest. Never mind, it all has something more or less, to do with Jacob Elliott. He come to Essex when 'Lizabeth was jest about twenty-three, and I calkerlate he wan't fur from thirty. As I was sayin', 'twan't long afore he got acquainted with 'Squire Mills' folks, and he and 'Lizabeth seemed to take to each other from the fust. He was over there most every night on one excuse or another; and they read together, and talked, and walked about under the trees; but somehow I didn't think the courtin' seemed to git along very fast. The young man grew thin and pale, and somethin' seemed to worry him mightily. You had to speak to him twice afore he'd hear you, and everybody noticed how absent-minded he was. Most o' folks laid it to his bein' 'fraid of 'Lizabeth; she had carried sech a high head to all the young men. But my good woman sees about as fur into a millstone as anybody, and, says she to me, —

"'Israel, you may depend 'tain't no sech a thing. He understands 'Lizabeth too well to feel 'fraid of her. He's got somethin' to trouble him that we don't know nothin' about. Maybe he feels too poor to be married.'

"The time come afterwards that we understood those symptoms better, but my good woman was right when she said he had somethin' to trouble him that nobody knew on.

"Waal, things went on in that fashion fur some time, and one night — it was a summer night, and dark as a pocket — I was outside of the house, sittin' down to git cooled off under the horse-chestnut tree, in front there by the road, and I see 'Squire Elliott come out o' 'Squire

Mills' gate, — *that* is 'Squire Mills' house, the third one from here, on the other side of the road. I could see him in spite o' the dark, — I'd been out so long my eyes had got used to it. I dunno as I told ye he took his meals at our house, but he lodged in his office, just beyond here. As he come along by where I was sittin', I heard him say to himself, he spoke kind o' firm like, as if he'd made up his mind, —

"'Well, I shall taste happiness now. Dear girl. God knows I would die before any harm should come to her, but I cannot tell her my secret. She would never see the matter as I do.'

"Arter his office door had shut, I went into the house and told Miss King what I'd heerd. My good woman never was no gossip.

"'Waal, Israel,' says she, when I'd told her, 'keep it all to yourself. If 'Squire Elliott don't choose to tell his secrets, don't you go and let on that he's got 'em. He knows his own business best, and he'll do about the right thing, I guess. He's a good man; he shows it in his face.'

"Waal, I took Miss King's advice. I didn't say any thing, and the next day we heerd that 'Squire Elliott and 'Lizabeth Mills had promised to have one another, and would be married that fall. From that day 'Squire Elliott seemed to have put off his trouble, whatever it was. He had a quick hearin' and a kind word for everybody, and his face — he was a master hansum man — seemed all kindled up with hope.

"Where his stone house stands now was a good,

roomy two-story wooden one then, and 'Squire Mills owned the place. It was ruther old-fashioned, to be sure, but it had been a good house in its day, and all the trees and every thing o' that sort was jest as hansum then as they are now. Jacob Elliott wan't wuth a great deal, but old 'Squire Mills give a deed o' the place to 'Lizabeth, and fitted it up a little, and that fall they was married and went to livin' in it.

"You never see a happier couple. For the next five years I don't believe they knew what trouble meant, only I reckon 'Lizabeth would have liked some children, and they never had none. Babies came thick as hops to folks that had nothin' to take care on 'em with and didn't want' em, and 'Squire Elliott's practice grew bigger, and he made more and more money every year, and there was only they two to use it. Maybe 'twas my notion that 'Lizabeth wanted any more. At any rate, they was all bound up in each other, and they seemed happy as the day is long.

"At last the 'Squire concluded to build, and they went home one summer, and staid to old 'Squire Mills'. In the mean time the old house was tore down, and that big stone one put up in its place, and in the fall they went to housekeepin' again. There didn't seem to be any human comfort wantin' to 'em then. That winter 'Lizabeth jined the church. She allus had seemed as good as a saint to me, but Miss King said, after this her face was like the face of an angel, and her voice was so tender and full of love to everybody that it most made the tears come in your eyes to hear it.

"The next year they chose him Judge, and now Judge Elliott was quite a great man among us. They looked up to him more than ever, and folks that hadn't seen any beauty in 'Lizabeth Mills' face begun to think her a 'mazin' fine-lookin' woman, now her husband was Judge, and she wore silks and satins stiff enough, as Miss King said, to stand alone. Most folks would 'a been set up, in her place, but she hadn't half so high and mighty an air to anybody now as she used to put on to the young men when she was 'Lizabeth Mills. She was a true Christian, if there's one on earth, I b'lieve, and she did all the good she could to everybody. It seems main hard that heavy trouble should come to any one so good as she was, but the Scripter says that the Lord chastens those He loves, and maybe, though we couldn't see it, her heart was sot too much on this world.

"The next summer arter the one Jacob Elliott was chosen Judge there came a stranger to my house, — I've kept tavern here for twenty-five year, summer and winter. He was a gentleman, I saw that the minit I put my eye on him. He looked somethin' like Judge Elliott, I couldn't help thinkin'. He was younger, and his featers wan't much like the Judge's, only there was a kind of a look, — what you might call a family likeness. He told me if he found it pleasant here, he might stop several days, and he should like to git acquainted with some of the people in the village. He was an Englishman, he said, travellin' in America for pleasure, and he thought the best way of judging of a country was to know somethin' about its inhabitants. Then, says he, kind o' careless like, as you asked me this mornin', —

"'Who lives in that hansum stone house behind the elms?'

"I told him it was Judge Elliott, and that he was an Englishman. He seemed mightily interested at once, and I went on and told him all I knew about the Judge, so fur; jest as I've told it to you, only I didn't speak o' the words I'd heerd him say the night arter he got engaged to 'Lizabeth Mills.

"When I'd got through, says he, — 'Thank you, Mr. King,' — he was a mighty perlite, smooth-spoken man, — 'I have been very much interested in your story. Would you feel free to take me over to Judge Elliott's, and introduce me? I should like to make his acquaintance very much.'

"'Free,' says I, 'bless your heart, anybody feels free to go and see Judge Elliott, — there isn't a kinder or more hospitable man anywhere.'

"With that I went into the house and brushed up a little. Then I clapped on my hat and started off. It wanted jest about two hours of dinner time. It happened that the Judge himself came to the door.

"'How do you do, neighbor King?' says he, in his pleasant, friendly way, and then his eyes fell upon the stranger gentleman. I could have sworn that he turned as white as a sheet to his very lips, but the next second I doubted my own eyes, for his smile was so composed and pleasant, and his manner so natural that it didn't seem as if any thing could have stirred him up enough to make him turn pale a minit afore.

"'Perhaps,' thinks I, 'it was only in my eyes, and perhaps it might have been a suddin pain come over him.'

"So I took no notice. Says I, —

"'Judge Elliott, this is Mr. Robert Armstrong, an English gentleman, who would like to git acquainted with you.'

"He shook hands heartily with the stranger, — he was allus a master cordial man, — and then he invited us in. The time passed quickly, and, fust we knew, it was dinner time. We had sot talkin' two hours. To be sure *I* hadn't talked much, I reckoned it warn't my place; no more had Mr. Armstrong, fur that matter; he'd seemed satisfied to sit an' hear the Judge talk and look at him, and sure enough I'd never seen Judge Elliott more sociable, and he allus was a mighty good talker. When I see it was dinner time I made a move to go, but the Judge wouldn't hear to no sech thing. We must both stay and take dinner with him, he said. Fust I thought I'd go home and leave Mr. Armstrong, but arter a good deal o' pressin' I agreed to stay too.

"Jest then Miss Elliott come into the room. You've no idee how grand and kind o' splendid she looked in that hansum parlor. It seemed jest made for her to live in. She had on a silk gown, sort of a dove color, and it trailed along behind her on the carpet when she walked. She had more hair than any other woman I ever see, and it was braided that day, and wound round her head somethin' like pictures you've seen of queens. She couldn't a looked more *like* a queen ef she'd been born one, — so stately as she was, with her silk dress, her pale face, and her dark eyes, with pride and kindness both in their looks. I tell you I was a little set up to have the Englishman see in a Har'ford County Connecticut girl a woman they'd a' been proud of in Queen Vic's court. I see he was struck all of a heap with her, to once. He talked with her very quiet and respectful, and she was sociable and yet dignified to him, and real friendly to the old tavern-keeper she'd known ever sence she was knee-high.

"It didn't want very keen eyes to see that the Judge was prouder o' her than of house and lands; and every now and then, in the midst of her talk, she would look at her husband, with eyes runnin' over full of love. I tell you, stranger, it ain't every man that gits looked at like that in his journey through this world. I could see Armstrong noticed her looks and understood 'em as well as I did.

"Waal, pooty soon we had dinner, and a nice one it was, too; and when it was over, the Judge invited us to walk out into the grounds. Miss Elliott, she stayed in the house, and arter a little *I* got kind o' strayed away from 'em. I hadn't any idee of their having any privacy to talk, but I thought they might get better acquainted without me than with me.

"There's a double walk round back o' the Judge's house. Three rows of pine-trees are planted thick together, in kind of semicircular fashion; a middle row and two outside ones. Between the middle row and each outside one is a walk where you can never hear a footstep, the dead pine leaves cover the ground so soft and thick. Somehow the shade looked invitin', and arter a little I went into one of these walks. It was the outside one, furthest from the house, and pooty soon I heard Judge Elliott's voice, and knew't they were in the other one.

"Bimeby I looked through, between the trees. I knew the green was so thick they warn't likely to see me, and I thought I'd jest give 'em a good look, as they walked slowly along, and see ef it had all been my imagination about Mr. Armstrong's lookin' so much like the Judge. They were pacin' under the pines, and the Judge made some remark and seemed waitin' for an answer. Just that minit Mr. Armstrong — he was a little ahead — turned round suddenly and stood full in front of Judge Elliott.

"'My brother,' he cried out, with sort of a tender yearnin' in his voice, 'my own dear brother Alfred,' — I was lookin' at the Judge and I saw that same strange look pass a second time over his face, turnin' it white to the lips. But, as afore, it went away in a minit, and he gave Mr. Armstrong kind of a puzzled, surprised smile.

"'Do not deny me, you cannot,' the stranger went on, his voice gatherin' up passion and energy. 'You *are* my brother, my own elder brother Alfred. Did you think *I* would believe you were dead? Did you think I would never find you? I loved you too well,

— my heart clung to you as to my life. I felt in my heart that the world still held you. I have hoped and waited all these years, and at last it came about in the very strangest way. I happened to see a few numbers of the *North American Review*, and there were some articles in them which I knew were yours. There was no name to them, but I could not be mistaken. They advocated some of your favorite old theories; they had exactly your cast of mind, your very turns of expression. I thought no labor too much by which I might hope to find my brother; so with only this clue I crossed the ocean. I came to Boston and learned the name and address of the author of those papers, and then I came here to find you. The landlord strengthened my conviction by telling me you were an Englishman, and had not been in this country more than nine or ten years. And now I have seen your well-known smile; heard your well-known voice; felt the touch of your hand. Do you think you could deceive me *now?* Oh, Alf, Alf, you will not try to shut me out of your heart?'

"At that moment he made a movement as if he would throw himself on his brother's neck, and Judge Elliott drew back real quiet and dignified. Armstrong had forced me into believin' him by his earnestness, but I must say I was staggered by the Judge's cool, calm manner. I couldn't believe any brother could put it on arter listenin' to sech words. I begun to think the stranger must be on a wrong track.

"'I am more than puzzled by what you say,' answered the Judge, in his grave, perlite way. 'My name is not Alfred Armstrong, but Jacob Elliott. I am an Englishman, it is true, but I think if you will look at me again you will convince yourself that we have never met before.'

"'Oh, Alf, Alf,' cried the stranger again, 'this is too cruel. I cannot bear it. I will not. To have hoped for this meeting for ten long years and then be cast off like this. I know that woman I saw in the house would be an excuse for a good deal, but I swear to you I will not interfere with your happiness. I will not ask you to take your first wife back. I will not betray you to a soul on earth; only call me brother; only let me into your heart,' and he made as if he would have thrown himself at Judge Elliott's feet, and still the Judge drew back and answered calmly, and yet sort o' cuttingly, —

"'I should be sorry, my dear sir, to suspect you of being a monomaniac, but I am at a loss to account for your vagaries in any other manner. The only wife I ever had is Mrs. Elliott, the lady I had the honor of presenting to you. I have no brother, and never had, and if you persist further in this strange talk I shall be obliged to bring our interview to a close.'

"I declare, sir, I wish you could a' heard how that Armstrong *did* beg. I can't tell it over, rightly, so I won't try, but it acterly squeezed the tears out o' my eyes, and I ain't one o' the cryin' kind. He couldn't a begged harder fur his life. He kep tellin' over all sorts of boy capers that he said they had cut up together, — he talked about his mother, and how she told 'em to love one 'nother when she was dying; and he promised to go away satisfied if the Judge would only call him brother once, and let him go off thinkin' they two loved one 'nother as they used to.

"But 'twan't no use. The Judge didn't flinch a hair. He wan't apparently no more moved than a stone. He kep jest as perlite and smilin' as ever, until at last he seemed to git tired o' listenin', and then he put a stop to the talk ruther sternly, and turned to walk away. I never *shall* forgit how Armstrong's face looked that minit. Somethin' like pride seemed riz up in him at last, and he cried out in a firm, strong voice, —

"'Alfred Armstrong, I will trouble you no more, — I will *never* trouble you again. Cast me off and deny me, if you will, — forget your dead mother and your poor old living father, and scorn every tie of blood! Go on in sin, yes, *sin*, and the time will come when my face shall haunt you; when you won't die easy without my forgiveness, which you must *ask* for before you have it.'

"The Judge never made no answer. There was a mighty strange look on his face as he walked away, as if he had fixed all his features jest so, so't they shouldn't tell no story. I *was* puzzled, you may depend. I didn't know what to make of any on't. When you heerd Armstrong speak you couldn't help believin' him, and then again I thought he must be mistaken, 'cause I didn't think any nateral born brother could a' stood it out agin them words as the Judge had. And then I see some things that didn't look quite reasonable to that view o' the case, so I had to give it up. I was mighty shamed o' listenin', I confess to you, but I hadn't had no notion o' doin' on't in the fust place, and I dunno but most men would a' done the same thing if they had stood in my place, arter they'd heerd the beginnin' on't. Anyhow, I went out o' the other end o' the pine walk, and dodged about among the trees, and went into the parlor, and I don't think Judge Elliott ever mistrusted, from that day to this, that I heerd him.

"It wan't more'n ten minutes afore he and Mr. Armstrong come in together, as perlite and civil as possible, but I didn't think there seemed quite as much friendliness betwixt 'em as there had afore dinner. Mr. Armstrong apologized for keepin' me waitin', and pooty soon we started for home. You may b'lieve 'twan't long afore I'd told Miss King all about it.

"That's one o' the prime comforts o' havin' a good wife. When you want to tell somethin' so you can't keep it in no longer, you can go to her, and it's jest as safe as it was afore. She didn't know what to make on't no more'n I did, but she charged me to keep it all to myself, and I may say I didn't need no caution on that pint, for Judge Elliott wan't a man a body'd like to git sot agin him, and indeed I liked him and his wife both, too much to want to make 'em any trouble. Ef there was any thing at all to Armstrong's story, wife and I concluded that the Judge had had a wife in England and been divorced from her, and was afraid to have it come out for fear 'Lizabeth wouldn't live with him; knowin' how strict she was about them matters. Ef that *was* the case, Miss King said there was some excuse for his not ownin' his brother, for we all knew that he sot his life by 'Lizabeth. But we were fur enough from guessing the truth. We wan't much surprised when Mr. Armstrong paid his bill and left the next mornin'. We kep all these things to ourselves, and I may safely say that's more'n some people would a done; maybe more'n I should a done ef I hadn't had my good woman to help me.

"Arter this time it seemed to me that I could see a little difference in the Judge. I reckon no one else noticed it, but I could see that he was more silent, and when he wan't talkin' there was a look in his face as if some heavy trouble had settled down on his heart. I guess he was more'n ever soft and tender to 'Lizabeth. Folks said, laughingly, that he seemed to be afraid he should lose her if she was out of his sight a minit; and, true enough, when he was to home they wan't never long separated.

"It went on three months, and then, 'long the fust of October, the Judge was suddenly took down with brain fever. I 'spose all these things had been a harassin' him till he couldn't keep 'em under no longer. From the fust day he was took down he was jest as crazy as a loon. Miss King allus was a master hand at nussin', and she thought so much o' 'Lizabeth that she went right over there and told 'em she'd stay by, pretty much o' the time till the wust was over. After she'd been there twenty-four hours, she come home to see to things a little, and she told me it was enough to break a body's heart to hear how the Judge went on. Sometimes he'd start up and say, real firm, — 'My name is not Alfred Armstrong. I am Jacob Elliott.' Then sometimes he'd cry out, *so* pitiful, to his brother to come back, — that he never meant to send him off, — he did love him, and allus had. Often and often he'd say, as humble as a little child, — '*Won't* you forgive me, brother Robert? You told the truth, I can't die easy without it, — oh, Rob!'

"Other times he'd shout out to him to be gone, — that 'Lizabeth was his wife, the only wife he ever did have, or would have, — nobody should take her away. Then again he'd put on a smilin', perlite face that was wuss than any on't to see, and he'd say, —

"'I never saw you before, no, sir, never. Excuse me, but you are entirely mistaken.'

"I 'spose Miss King understood these things a good deal better'n 'Lizabeth did, but, of course, she couldn't explain nothin'. He kep goin on so, day arter day.

"Gen'ally I used to see my good woman once a day, and she told me it did beat all how 'Lizabeth bore it. She was jest as white as a sheet, Miss King said, but she kep over him night and day, and never seemed a bit tired nor sleepy. Wife had a sofy in one corner o' the room, where she used to lie down and sleep nights, for she was determined not to leave 'Lizabeth, and, spite o' restin' a good deal, *she* was pretty well tuckered out; but she said 'Lizabeth didn't seem to know what tired meant. Miss Mills, 'Lizabeth's mother, was old and feeble now, so't she couldn't be there, and wife tried to be a mother to the poor, troubled critter as well as she could. 'Lizabeth was one o' them kind that don't love easy, but when they do love it's deep. Miss King said if the Judge died she thought they'd both go together.

"One mornin', when he'd been sick a little more'n a week, I got up early and went out door. It was jest about the finest mornin' I ever see. The sun was comin' up red and round, and the trees was green as ever in some places, and in others they looked as if they'd jest been sot afire. I don't pertend to think much o' sech things, but somehow, that mornin' took right hold of me, and made me feel soft-hearted, but maybe I shouldn't remember it so well ef it hadn't been for what came arterwards.

"Jest then I see Miss King a comin', and I went to meet her. Somehow I was 'mazin' glad to see her. There hadn't been a soul to stop to the house sence the Judge was sick, and there hadn't been no partikler need of her in a business pint o' view, but somehow things allus look lonesome to home when a woman ain't about.

"When I come up to her, though, I see pretty soon that somethin' more'n common had happened. At fust thought I didn't know but the Judge was dead, and I asked her.

"'No,' says she, 'but I dunno but he'd better be afore all comes out that's got to.'

"She wouldn't say no more till we'd got into the

house and sot down together, all alone. Then she told me how, the night before, as she lay on the sofy in the corner, and Miss Elliott sot by the Judge's bed, he woke up, and she could see in a minit that he was rational again. She said she'd been talkin' with Miss Elliott the minit afore, and as long as she knew of her bein' there she thought no harm o' lyin' still, though perhaps she'd ought to have got up and gone out. The Judge was dreadful weak, but he managed to put out his hand and touch his wife's. In a minit she was bendin' over him and kissin' him as if he'd been a baby. Says he, —

"'You do love me, 'Lizabeth. All this time when you thought I didn't know any thing I've felt that you was hoverin' round me and taking care o' me.'

"As he said that, Miss King said the tears gushed right out, and his wife kind o' soothed him, and then, pooty soon, he broke out again. He said he couldn't keep his secret no longer. It had well nigh killed him, or made him crazy for life, keepin' it so long. Then he went on and told her how, when he was a young man, not much more'n a boy, he'd been married in England. He didn't love the woman, nor she didn't love him, but she was rich, and somehow his folks and hern fixed it up between 'em, and he didn't make no objections. He'd never been in love then, and sech things was more common there than they are here. So he lived with the woman a number o' year, and, from not carin' any thing about her in the fust place, he got to most hatin' her.

"She didn't suit him no way, and he began to feel

as ef all his futur was spilt by marryin' her. But he was too reasonable to lay it all to her. I guess he blamed himself the most. Well, arter a while, he found out, pooty nigh for certain, that she hadn't been true to him. He said he s'posed he might a got positive proof of it ef he'd a tried, and ef he'd known what was comin' arter, he *would* a tried. But as it was, he didn't think he should ever want to marry again, and he pitied her, and felt like bein' merciful to her. He thought it wan't her fault, marryin' as she did, — that, maybe, ef he'd a loved her, and been tender and lovin' to her, she'd a' kep strait. So he concluded to leave her her good name, and all the money he had married her for, and go off in sech a way that folks would think he had killed himself, and she could marry the man she liked ef she wanted to.

"It was pooty hard to leave his old father, and harder still to leave his younger brother, who had allus been nearer to him than any thing else in the world, ever sence his mother died, but he was pooty nigh desperate, and when he'd made up his mind he didn't flinch. He come to America, and took a new name. He had studied law in England, and he went into 'Squire Holmes' office over to Simsbury, — he'd happened to git acquainted with the 'Squire in Boston, where he landed, — and pooty soon got admitted to the bar. He'd no thought of ever marryin' at that time, but when he come here and see 'Lizabeth Mills, he found out what love was.

"'Twould e'en a most melted a stone, my good

woman said, to hear him tell how he loved her, and what a fight he had in his own mind afore he could make out what to do. He thought some, fust, of going back to England and tryin' for a divorce, but he s'posed they'd all gin him up for dead there; he didn't know as he could get one, and he knew that 'Lizabeth was dead sot agin 'em.

"Finally, he concluded that, whatever Alfred Armstrong had done, Jacob Elliott had never been married, and he didn't think there was one chance in a thousand that anybody'd ever know them two names meant one person. Take it all in all, he felt perfectly safe in gettin' married agin; and arter he'd once made up his mind his conscience never troubled him. He persuaded himself that he was doin' right. I've allus noticed it was pooty easy to do that when a man's whole heart was sot on any thing. His life had been as happy as any human bein's need to be till arter his brother come.

"He told her all that story, — how his heart had yearned over his brother, but he had loved her so much better he couldn't run the shadder of a risk of havin' to give her up, and so he had sent his brother off. But Robert's voice had sounded ever sence in his ear, — he couldn't silence it. Robert's last words had stuck by him. Livin' in sin, — he couldn't get that out o' his mind, and he had brooded over it until the fever came. He had never meant to tell her, but he couldn't go anywhere else for comfort, and he couldn't keep it in no longer. All the way through, Miss King said 'Lizabeth had listened without sayin' a word, but she could see by the lamp-light that her face looked as ef it was turnin' into stone, and when he got so fur a cry come out of her lips, not loud, but a sort of gasp like, as if her heart was breakin', and says she, —

"'Thank God that I've no children to bear this with me.' Wife said she couldn't help thinkin' then how often we see that God is blessin' us instead of cursin' us in keepin' back the very things we hanker arter the most. When 'Lizabeth had gin that one cry she bowed her head down on the bed, kind o' helpless like. With that, Miss King said, the Judge seemed as strong as a lion. He caught her in his arms and kissed her cheeks and her eyes and her white lips. He told her she was his wife, — his only wife; the only one he had ever loved or would ever own, and, now she knew all, they would be so happy together. Surely she couldn't think, for one moment, that first marriage was binding before God, — nobody could. A woman he had never loved, who had never loved him. Besides, he was Alfred Armstrong no longer. He was another man now, and she was his wife, his own true wife, and no power on earth had any right to separate them. Then, when she didn't say any thing, he began callin' on her to forgive him, and tellin' her if she didn't, he should die there afore her eyes. At last this roused her, and she kissed him once.

"'Oh, Jacob,' says she, 'forgive you! I forgive you as I hope to be forgiven. How you have loved me.'

"By this time he was all exhausted, and she soothed him and made him go to sleep. I s'pose, in his weakness, he thought 'twould be all right now, — she had forgiven him, and so they should live right along, jest as they did afore; but, ef he did, he didn't know 'Lizabeth. Arter he had got well to sleep she left him and come along to where wife was lyin'. Miss King said it seemed as ef she'd grown ten years older in that one night. Says she, —

"'You heard it all?' Wife told her she did hear it, and that she pitied her as ef she was her own child. There was some pride left in her, gentle as she was. I s'pose she didn't like to be pitied, and she cut Miss King short by askin' her not to mention what she had heard, for her sake, till the Judge got better. Then it must all come out, but till then she'd be thankful to have it kept secret. Of course wife promised, and she didn't consider that she broke it by tellin' me, fur we never had no privacies from one 'nother. Neither of us said a single word to any outsider, but I tell you our hearts ached in them days for 'Lizabeth. Miss King was over there pooty much o' the time till the Judge got better, and, as fur as she knew on, the subject was never mentioned again betwixt him and Miss Elliott. But all this time, she said, 'Lizabeth was jest the tenderest nuss. She built him up as nobody else would a' had the patience to, and at last, when he had got comfortable, she went out of the house one November mornin', and over to her father's; and, pooty soon, we see old 'Squire Mills hobblin' along arter the doctor.

"She had borne up as long as she could, and now

she was took down with a fever herself; and for some six weeks we half hoped, half feared she would never get up again. I say half hoped she wouldn't, fur it didn't look as ef there could be any more comfort fur her in this life. We all knew how she loved the Judge, and we knew, jest as well as we knew her, that she'd never live with him any more.

"When he heard she was sick he was nigh upon crazy. Jest as soon as he could, he used to crawl over to 'Squire Mills' and sit beside her. Even her best friends, now it had all come out, hadn't the heart to reproach him. It was clear to everybody that he'd sot a great deal more by her than he did by his life, and he wan't no more the same man that he was six months ago than two persons. Trouble and sickness had broke him down as twenty years o' common life couldn't have begun to.

"It was Christmas before 'Lizabeth begun to set up. Everybody called her 'Miss Elliott' jest as they used to, and I s'pose 'twould a' come hard to her to give up the name she had been called by through all the happiest years of her life. When she was toler'ble well and strong she asked to see the Judge alone, one day. It was the fust time she ever *had* seen him alone a minit, sence she went out of his house. They had a long talk. Nobody knew what they said, but I s'pose she made him understand that they must never be nothin' more'n common friends to each other again. When it was over she went upstairs to her room, and wan't seen again that day by anybody, and the Judge come out and walked slowly along to his own house, where he must live alone all the rest of his life, and his face looked a'most as if he was struck with death.

"Arter that he didn't go there no more for some time, —then he got to goin' again, maybe once a week, and she would sit in the room with her old, feeble mother and talk with him fur an hour together. But I should a thought 'twould a been about as bad as not seein' one 'nother at all. All this time she was urgin' it upon him to go to England and make it up with his brother. Besides, she told him it was his duty to find out whether he hadn't been mistaken about his wife, and, if he had been, to live with her again, if she wanted to live with him. I couldn't see no duty o' that sort about it, but 'Lizabeth had got it into her head, and she could allus make him do jest about what she thought was right.

"So the next spring he sailed for England, and it was nigh upon fall afore he got back again. He had found his father alive, and he and his brother had made it all up. As for his wife, the man that he thought she was in love with had been dead a number o' year, and he heard a good character of her everywhere, so't maybe he'd been mistaken in what he thought about her in the fust place. But she told him she never had loved him no more'n he had her, and that, so fur from havin' any desire to live with him, nothin' short o' force would ever make her do it. So he come back, as he went, alone.

"He went to see 'Lizabeth the fust thing, and she

was well pleased that he had done his duty, but she knew her'n, and she could never be nothin' more than friendly to him again. I don't rightly understand the law o' the case, but he couldn't git a divorce from his English wife, though she might a got one from him ef she'd chosen, but she didn't.

"I forgot to say that as soon as the matter had come out he had resigned his office, but folks call him Judge Elliott still, and I s'pose they allus will. He's had chances enough to practise, for 'most all that knew his story pitied him more'n they blamed him, but he hain't done much business sence. 'Twan't long afore his father died, and he got some consider'ble money from England. He paid 'Squire Mills more'n what the old place where he built his house was wuth, and I s'pose he'll allus live there."

"How long is it since?" asked the stranger, as honest Israel King concluded the narrative to which he had been an absorbed listener.

"Waal, I should think a matter o' nine year. Let's see. Seven year arter he fust came here he was chose Judge, and the next year this affair come out, and he's been here in all seventeen year this spring."

"And he has lived here nine years, only a few steps from the woman he loved so well; who had thought herself, for seven years, his true and lawful wife, and neither of them are dead or mad?"

Honest Israel smiled, a shrewd yet sorrowful smile.

"No, they wan't weak by natur, either of 'em. Plenty of women that didn't love half so deep as

'Lizabeth would have broke their hearts and died, but hers broke and she lives. It's somethin' like Moses smitin' the rock for the water to gush out, my good woman says, for her life has been a constant stream of kindness and good deeds ever sence. She don't shet herself up in any selfish sorrow, but I guess she goes to the best place for comfort, arter all. She does jest what God tells her. She's kinder than ever to the old folks, and I guess she's nigh about the best idee the children have got of an angel. She sees the Judge pretty often. He goes there every now and then and spends an evening with her and the old folks. Anybody'd s'pose that would be a sorrowful kind of comfort, but it seems to do him good; and every now and then they meet when she's on some of her walks, and he talks with her a little while, and then goes back into his hansum house alone. I should s'pose it must be a pretty hard tussle for him to live right along where she used to live with him, but Miss King thinks it's the very reason he want's to live there. *She* thinks he can kind o' fancy, sometimes, that 'Lizabeth's sittin' in the old places, and hear her voice when it's all still and quiet round him."

The landlord paused, and his guest was silent also. Both were lingering in pensive thought over sorrows not their own. At length the old man touched the stranger's arm.

"There she comes now," he said, almost in a whisper. "You can go out and walk kind o' careless along the road, and you'll get a good sight at her."

The stranger's interest was too much absorbed for

him to pause and consider the questionable delicacy of this course. He went out of the yard, and sauntered along the street. He saw a woman of forty, more beautiful, to him, than any younger face he had ever seen. She looked, as Israel King had said, a grand woman, strong in body and soul. Her face was still, and pale, and fair. Round the lofty forehead was braided hair as dark and luxuriant as ever. Under it shone large, clear eyes, full of a glory and a light not of this world. Heaven's own peace sat on her features, and smiled in the mouth, sweet as a child's, but firm as a martyr's. She wore a quiet, gray dress, which suited her as well as the silks and satins of earlier days ever could have done. Her step was lofty, her port worthy of an empress.

"Fit for earth or fit for Heaven," he murmured involuntarily as he looked on her, — "fit for one because fit for the other." He could see that "the tranquil God, who tranquillizes all things," had sent calm upon her life.

As she walked by Judge Elliott's stately house, he saw a man go out and speak to her, — a man, to whose life calmness, unless it be the calmness of despair, was yet to come; a man, old beyond his forty-eight years, sorrowful, downcast, lonely. He saw this man's face brighten as she talked with him, and, finally, he saw her gather from the hedge a rose full of dew and fragrance, and give it to him, and then go calmly on her way, leaving some of the glory of her presence behind her.

He went slowly back to the inn.

"That was Judge Elliott," said the landlord, meeting him as he approached. "Poor things! Poor things! I s'pose it'll be all squared up and come out right up *there*," and he lifted his old, weather-beaten face to the calm blue of the summer morning sky. Did he see, through and beyond the azure, a glimpse of shining turrets, the gold and pearl and amethyst of the city not made with hands?

It is just ten years since my friend, to whom the Connecticut innkeeper related this strange story, recounted it to me. It interested me deeply at the time, and it was many months before I ceased to think of it. It was obscured, at length, by the interests of my own life, and passed out of my heart as such tales will, when we have never seen the faces or heard the voices of the people. Perhaps it would never have come back to me, but for a strange chance, or Providence. Looking over, in an idle hour, the deaths and marriages in a file of English papers, sent me by a friend, my eyes fell on this: —

"Died, at Birmingham, Susan Armstrong, wife or widow of Alfred Armstrong."

With feelings stronger than an idle whim I marked this item, and sent it to the address of the man whom, in this "ower true tale," I have chosen to call Jacob Elliott, but who was known by another name to the denizens of Hartford County. Perhaps he already was aware of his first wife's decease, and had wooed and wedded again the Elizabeth of his love; or, perhaps, one or both of them may have gone long ago to the land where, we are told, is neither marrying nor giving in marriage, but where, I love to think, those who love truly here will love on for ever. I know not. Heaven is higher than earth, and nothing is left to blind chance. Those two were God's care, for they were His children. Pray for them, all kind souls!

A LETTER, AND WHAT CAME OF IT.

WE were two girls together, Margaret and I. Our mother was dead, and now that we were through school, we kept house for our father, and were under very little restraint of any kind. Margaret, our friends said, was her mother's child, I my father's. I had, in fact, inherited all that I was from him. Strong, muscular organization; black eyes and straight black hair; olive skin; firm, yet pleasure-loving lips; haughty forehead; fiery, yet easily soothed temper; warm affections,—these were his, and he had given them all to me, his oldest daughter.

Neither of us could remember our mother, but a portrait of her, taken just before her marriage, would have answered equally well for Margaret. She died at the birth of this her youngest child, passing from earth gently and sweetly, like a flower which exhales its soul in perfume. I have been told that my father's agony was terrible. Grief with him was as the storms in tropic climates; it swept every thing before it with a resistless flood, to which neither reason nor religion could for the time oppose any barrier. For weeks he could not bear to look at the infant thus left him. When at length the calm succeeded to the tempest, and he heard, in the quiet, the still, small voice from heaven, he learned resignation, and turned for comfort to the ties which yet bound him to life. The little, white thing, lying upon pillows in the nursery or nestling to a stranger's bosom, looked up to him with the eyes of his early love. He named her Margaret then, because it means pearl, and no other name seemed so fitting for the frail, fair babe. Besides, he had given for her all he had, and to him, therefore, she was indeed a pearl of great price.

My sister was fair. She looked like the women whom the early painters chose for models when they painted angels. She had hair of tawny gold, — you saw such if ever you paid your respects to Page's Venus. Her eyes were, in color, like the sky where its blue is deep and cloudless, and a light shone in their depths tender and tranquil as a star. Moreover, she had small and delicate features, a mouth to which smiles came not too often, but like returning children to their home, — you have seen faces where the smiles were aliens, and you felt as if they required a safe-conduct, — a skin transparent and faultlessly smooth; a shape tall, slender, and graceful, and you have Margaret, as charming a blonde as the most ardent admirer of that type of beauty could desire. She was firm, too; those fair women always are. Her character had plenty of tone and fibre. It is we brunettes who are easily moved and governed, after all. I could outstorm twenty like Margaret. While she sat calm and quiet and apparently submissive, I could raise a tempest and put the whole house in commotion. But I always ended by doing precisely as she wished. We passionate souls always yield, if only we find people firm enough to remain unmoved by us, quietly persistent in their own will.

I think it was because Margaret and I were so different that we were friends in the true sense of the word. I suppose sisters always love each other. There is duty, natural affection, and all that; you know what, if you've read Mrs. Ellis. But they are not usually *friends*. Ripening on the same vine, they are as like as two peas. There is no charm of novelty. Their society cloys each other like sweet wine. In our case the wine was spicy and pungent. We could never thoroughly analyze its taste, and returned each time to the draught with new zest and new curiosity.

You know something about us now, and I will proceed to tell you what we did.

It was early in the month of June, and a leap-year. We were living very quietly out of town. Every afternoon at five o'clock papa drove out, his business being over at that hour, and often brought with him some mercantile friend to dine and go back in the evening, or, if he were not a family man, to occupy a spare chamber and drive into town with him in the morning. Margaret and I never saw much of these visitors beyond making ourselves agreeable to them at dinner. We voted them old fogies, and never imagined any possibilities of entertainment from their society. We saw very few young people either. We had so many sources of amusement at home and in each other that we did not trouble ourselves about beaux and parties, and were enjoying a pleasant season as grown-up daughters at home, which is very rare, now that girls are permitted to step from the school-room to the ball-room, to waste their first bloom in the dissipations of fashionable life.

We loved fun dearly, both of us, and that June we determined to seek it in a new and not exactly legitimate channel. The most frequent of papa's guests was a Mr. Thorndike, — Ignatius Thorndike. He was a man some years younger than our father, but we thought he could not be much less than forty. We were respectively seventeen and nineteen at that time, and forty seems fearfully old to girls in their teens. We had never thought much about Mr. Thorndike, — he was the gravest of all those grave merchants, — but we knew that he was unmarried. We had heard that he was too poor to marry when he was young, and, now that he had been successful in business, even beyond his hopes, he did not dare to seek a wife, because he had lost all faith in his own ability to please, and feared lest he should be accepted for the luxuries it was in his power to bestow.

To this grave merchant we resolved to send a letter, making the freedom of leap-year our excuse, and so wording it that it might prove the commencement of a correspondence which we thought would be vastly entertaining. I hardly know which of us first suggested the idea, but we were both quite carried away with it. The composition of this precious document was our joint work. I have retained a copy of it, which I have by me to-day. It reads thus: —

"MR. THORNDIKE, — I have hesitated long before writing you this note. I should not venture to do so now were it not that I am emboldened by the license accorded to leap-year. To a different man I would not write it for worlds, but I am sure your character is of too high a tone for you to pursue a correspondence merely for amusement or adventure. If you think I am indelicate in addressing you at all, — if you do not desire my friendship, you will let the matter drop here, — you will never reply to me, or bestow a second thought on one who will, in that case, strive to think no more of you. But should you really value the regard of a girl who is fearless enough thus to disobey the recognized laws of society; honest enough to show you her heart as it is; good enough, at least, to feel your goodness in her inmost soul, — then you will write. Then, perhaps, we shall know each other better, and the friendship thus unconventionally begun may brighten both our lives. Remember I trust to your honor *not* to answer this letter if you disapprove of my course in sending it, — if by so doing I have forfeited your respect. Should you reply, let it be within three days, and address,

"GRATIA LIVERMORE,

"*Boston P. O.*"

It fell to Margaret's lot to copy the epistle, as she wrote far more neatly than I. In fact, she was my superior in every thing requiring patience or grace. We sent the missive, and, for three successive days after its probable reception, we despatched a messenger into town to inquire for letters for Miss Livermore. None came, however, and we at length concluded that our attempt at fun had proved an ignominious failure. All that delicate flattery had been wasted. Most likely Mr. Thorndike despised his unknown correspondent too thoroughly even to be amused by her. We were vexed, both of us. We called him a fussy, cross-grained old bachelor, and said, even to each other, that we didn't care; but we did care, we were mortified and disappointed. That afternoon, when papa came out to dinner, we noticed as he drove up the avenue that he was not alone. We were both of us watching from our window, but Margaret was the first to recognize the visitor.

"That odious Mr. Thorndike!" she cried. "Well, thank fortune, Laura, he never would think of suspecting either of *us*. Scorn to reply to that letter though he may, I'll wager he'd give at least one bright eagle to know who wrote it."

We both of us dressed ourselves as tastefully as we could. Mr. Thorndike's well-known avoidance of women made us resolve that he should at least think his friend's daughters not ill-looking.

Margaret's dress was a pale rose-color, just the shade of the spring peach blossoms. It lent its own soft flush to her cheeks. A spray of wisteria was in her golden braids, and her arms, with the hair bracelets on them, shone fair through her thin sleeves.

I was in white. It toned me down better than any thing else. In fact, I looked well in it. I twisted a few roses in my hair, and put a bunch of them at my waist. Great hoops of barbaric gold were in my ears, and bracelets of the same were upon my arms. I liked Margaret's looks, and she liked mine. We were too dissimilar to have any petty jealousies.

When we went into the drawing-room Mr. Thorndike rose.

"Good afternoon, Miss Otis; good afternoon, Miss Margaret," he said, as he placed chairs for us. He added a pleasant remark about being so frequent a guest, and then returned, apparently quite forgetful of us, to his conversation with papa.

We left them at the dinner-table at the earliest possible moment, and went out of doors. The grounds around our mansion were well kept and spacious. Papa liked breathing room, and did not choose to be overlooked by his neighbors.

We sought a nook which we both loved, where a dusky clump of pines crowned a hill. In the centre was a rustic seat, resting on which we could look out between the tree-boles toward the west. The air was full of the rich, balsamic odor of the pines. Under our feet the fallen leaves were piled so soft and thick you could not hear a footstep. The winds among the boughs talked together all day overhead, and our hearts interpreted them; and now, looking afar over other hills, we saw the crimson glory of the sunset. We both, for different reasons, liked to watch it. I, because it seemed to belong to me. I could fancy myself in harmony with those gorgeous colorings, those fantastic clouds. The phantom shapes hurried on without rest were like my thoughts; changeful as my moods; wayward as my life. Margaret liked them by the law of contrast. She was self-centred and all rest, — a still noon, or a midnight lit by a full moon. She enjoyed vivid colors, hurrying storms, sudden changes, — they deepened the sense of her own calm. Silent, with the dreamy speculativeness of untried girls, our hearts were questioning the future which seemed hiding itself behind the clouds and the sunset.

"I think it is a ship. Do you see the spars and the trim masts?"

We both looked up, and there beside us stood Mr. Thorndike. We had not heard his step on the soft pine leaves. He stood there, looking, as he always looked, calm and grave and strong, — much such a nature as Margaret's, only deepened by masculine elements. There was enthusiasm in his eyes, softened by half-poetic melancholy. They were fixed, not on us, but steadily on the sunset. Perhaps the light in them was a reflection from that crimson distance. He went on speaking, as much to himself, apparently, as to us.

"Yes, it is a ship, surely. See, it is sailing on a flame-colored river, and the port whither it tends no man knoweth. Life is like it.

"'Our beginnings, as our endings,
Rest with the life-sender.'

We were not, we are, and we shall be. I always liked pictures in the sunset, as in the embers. The cloud-pictures are best though, for they are on a grander scale. There is more room for fancy to fill up."

I stole a glance at Margaret. His discourse, so unpractical, so far removed from business, was as much a surprise to her as to me. But it was in harmony with her thoughts; while at first I did not like it, because it seemed incongruous with the man.

"I never heard that castles in Spain were merchantable property," I said, with perhaps a latent irony in my tones. Mr. Thorndike looked at me, and the poetic enthusiasm in his gray eyes was replaced by the shrewd analytic expression which betokened the keen man of business.

"Very true, Miss Otis. You think, and justly, that castle-building is a curious pastime for one who has been the architect of any thing so rugged and real as his own fortune. You are right. It was certainly quite a different subject upon which I designed to speak to you. In advance, I must implore you both to forgive my plainness of speech. I am a business man, little used to ladies' society, and accustomed to say my say in the fewest and most simple words. I received a letter three days ago signed 'Gratia Livermore.'"

Margaret was pale, with a look like marble in her face. I felt my own cheeks turn crimson. Angry tears rushed to my eyes, but I forced them back. I beat the ground nervously with my foot. It is a trick I have, when I need great self-control and yet my impatience must find some outlet. "Well?" I said, inquiringly.

"Well," he calmly proceeded, "I knew the handwriting. I have often seen Miss Margaret's delicate chirography in her father's possession. I recognized it, and I recognized you in the composition, Miss Otis."

"And so you despise us, and have come to tell us so?" I spoke defiantly, and looked into his face with eyes which strove to scorn his displeasure.

"No, Miss Otis; a moment's consideration would convince you that if I despised you I should surely not have taken the trouble to speak to you about this matter. I believe I am just,—just and honest; but I do not pretend to be a man of disinterested benevolence. Your father is my best friend, and among my few female acquaintances none stand so high as his daughters in my regard. I was therefore the more pained that you should have written this letter. I was not influenced by personal feeling. I quite passed over the light esteem in which you must have held me to think my vanity so susceptible, so easily touched. I thought only of yourselves. Had you had a mother this would never have happened; or, if it had, I should have found it hard to forgive you. But I always held that the best man in the world is not fit to have the sole charge of daughters. He is away from them too much; he does not understand their tastes or their temperaments. When I read that letter how I pitied you, because you had been left motherless. Perhaps I should have taken no notice of it, had I not thought my friendship for your father imposed upon me a duty toward his daughters. It was but a girlish freak, and its repetition was scarcely to be assumed as a probability. Still I wanted to say to you that no young girl can be too careful how she trusts her handwriting in the keeping of any man. In good society an anonymous letter is considered almost a crime; and as to letters under a lady's own name, perhaps I am conservative, but it is my opinion that, except upon business matters, they should never be written to any gentleman save a near relative or a betrothed husband. I have no right to say all this, but I have spoken as a brother would, to you who have no brother. Am I forgiven?"

Margaret went up to him and offered him her hand. Her aspect was pale still, but no longer like marble in its repose. Her lips quivered. Her soul shone transfiguringly through her face, and kindled her eyes into tenderness, which her rising tears served to heighten. Her voice was full of feeling.

"Not forgiven, sir, there is no need of that; but you have shown yourself our true friend, and we thank you, — I and my sister. Do not fear that we shall fail to profit by your kindness."

He held her hand a moment, then he placed in it our silly letter and turned away.

I caught the sheet from her, tore it into fragments, and scattered them to the winds.

"What would I give," I cried, "that we had never written it. To have disgraced ourselves so in Mr. Thorndike's estimation, — it is too bad. I shall never bear to see him again; shall you, Margaret?"

"Certainly: I shall see him with far more pleasure than before; for I know now what a true man he is. I did not think one met such out of books. I can almost forgive myself for having written the letter, because it has shown me such a noble page of human nature."

That evening, despite our mortification, was a very pleasant one. Mr. Thorndike had never before taken such pains to make himself agreeable. We found hitherto unsuspected delight in his conversation. He had thought much and read to good purpose. He had lived his forty years with open and observing eyes.

Music was proposed after a while. I "performed" well, — so said my teachers and the few critics who had heard me. I played difficult music; grand, stately symphonies from Mozart and Beethoven; and Mr. Thorndike listened — he could not have deceived me — with the soul of a genuine music-lover. Margaret succeeded me, and she sang a few ballads, — simple Scottish lays, solemn and tender with love and death, — accompanying herself with low, sweet chords, which one might imagine the wordless melody of an accordant spirit.

"Margaret's music is best," said papa, wiping the

tears from his eyes when she concluded, and I knew she had been singing some of our mother's old-fashioned songs, calling back the romance and melody of his youth. Mr. Thorndike said nothing, but I thought I discerned a treacherous mistiness in his eyes; and when she was through he closed the piano, as if, having heard those ballads, he wished to hear nothing more. Presently he retired.

During that summer we learned to know our new friend well, and we both liked him. We had respect for his opinions, and even for his prejudices. We revered the unswerving integrity of his life, and we found more pleasure in his society than we had ever found in any man's before. True, we did not know many with whom to compare him. We were not yet "out," and young men were seldom among papa's visitors. Perhaps it was well for us, before we went into general society, to become so well acquainted with a strong, true man like Ignatius Thorndike. After that it would be hard to impose upon us counterfeit coin in lieu of sterling gold.

I think he took all the more pleasure in our acquaintance because his life had heretofore been too much occupied with business for him to cultivate friendships among women. He was certainly very attentive to us. After dinner we used to leave papa to his nap and the evening papers, and wander off, we three, into the woods and dells which lay not far from our home. None of us knew enough of artificial enjoyments to spoil our zest for the simple pleasures of our quiet life. We rejoiced, like happy children, over a rare flower, a curious leaf, or a pretty stone. We talked about every thing, — politics, religion, poetry, fashion, business, and finally we got one day to talking of love. Mr. Thorndike had no patience with flirtations. He spoke of them in terms of unmeasured severity. He also inveighed bitterly against the selfishness of many marriages. He could not understand, he said, how a man could ever venture to ask a woman not half so old as himself to marry him. Only the strongest love, he held, could make marriage safe or happy, and certainly strong love on the wife's side, where there was such disparity of age, was too rare to be reckoned among the probabilities.

"And you think it is wrong to marry without a love as romantic as the love of novels?" asked Margaret.

"I think, Miss Margaret, that Hawthorne has written a great many strong and true words, but nothing truer then when he said, 'Let men tremble to win the hand of woman, unless they win along with it the utmost passion of her heart; else it may be their miserable fortune, when some mightier touch than their own may have awakened all her sensibilities, to be reproached even for the calm content, the marble image of happiness, which they will have imposed upon her as the warm reality.' There are women whom we know instinctively to be above all mercenary motives in marriage; but perhaps such, from their very tenderness and purity, would be the most easily persuaded to believe that to be love which was only its cold counterfeit. And when such a wife awoke from her delusion to the knowledge of all that might have been and was not, I should pity her husband, if a true man, even more than herself; inasmuch as I believe it would be easier to bear through life the burden of an unsatisfied hope than for a generous husband to feel that he had snatched the possibility of happiness from the woman of his choice, — that he had condemned the best part of her nature to perpetual solitude. I allude now to cases where a man's only fault is want of consideration, selfish haste, neglecting to make himself certain of his absolute empire over the heart before he accepts the hand. Those other cases, where the sacrifice of a heart for wealth and a name is deliberately made and accepted, are beneath even the discussion of high-minded men and women."

Margaret had listened silently while he had spoken; now she drew her shawl around her and shivered.

"It is chilly," she said. "I feel the damp. Let us go in."

At the time this struck me as singular, for Margaret was rarely cold. I used often to envy her insensibility to the cold of winter or heat of summer; her temperament so calm, or so perfectly balanced, that the weather had no hold on her. For myself, I liked nothing but sunshine. Few days were too warm for me; but I suffered from cold like an East Indian, — grew aguish in the slightest draught, and believed devoutly in furnaces and hot air. But I was not even chilly, now. However, we obeyed Margaret's motion, and the subject of love and marriage was not afterward renewed between us three. It was clear enough, from what Mr. Thorndike had said, that he would never seek to marry a young girl; and even had we been, which we were not, match-seeking young ladies, it was warning enough to us to think of him only as the friend he had proved himself.

His attentions during that pleasant summer were pretty equally divided between us; if any thing, the larger proportion fell to my share. We did not go into town very early that year. We could not bear to return to brick walls and paved streets while Nature was holding her high festival of harvest time. Oh, those glorious October days! Grain waving on the hill-tops; grapes purpling on the vines; fruit blushing on the boughs; fire-tinted leaves rustling slowly downward; prismatic haze floating over all. If you never were in the country in October, you have missed something you can hardly afford to forego.

It was November before we were settled in our house in town, — a pleasant house, large and commodious, looking upon the Common, where the waving of the tree-boughs, and the Frog Pond, with its blue water and fleets of juvenile ships, do their pleasant best toward a little fiction of country life, — a sort of vignette. A maiden sister of my father was sent for, and promoted over our heads to the post of housekeeper. This was in deference to the proprieties, for we were to receive company this winter, and go into society, and needed a chaperon.

At first Mr. Thorndike came to see us frequently;

but as soon as we had collected round us a gay circle of acquaintances he began quietly to withdraw himself from our intimacy. Out of town, where there had been no fear of his attentions interfering with any one else, he had given us most of his leisure; but now he evidently thought the young men who surrounded us must needs be more agreeable. That this was not the case I could have answered, — for myself, at least. I missed him sadly. Compared with him, the young men of our circle — youths well-born and well-bred, who had never known the slightest necessity for exertion — seemed sadly vapid and uninteresting. I began to suspect myself of quite as much regard for him as any prudent damsel would care to bestow on one who, by his own showing, was not a marrying man.

If Margaret missed our old friend as much as I did she made no sign. Reserved, self-contained, and cold as she really was, to all but the few, she was so sweet, and gentle, and courteous in society that she was very popular, — far more so than I, who carried my heart upon my sleeve. It was not long before the attentions of one, at least, of her admirers began to seem serious to me, an interested looker-on.

He was a young divine, of the poetico-romantic school, who was just then making quite a sensation. He was handsome; graceful in manners as in person; with one of those eclectic natures of which saith the proverb, "All's fish that comes to that net." Milton, Shakspeare, godly George Herbert, gentle Elia, Festus Bailey, Carlyle, Dickens, — who was there, ancient or modern, serious or profane, poet or essayist, who had not contributed to enrich his sermons?

"Words, dears," said papa, when we had coaxed him to go and hear Mr. Staunton; "a great many very fine words; but where is the soul? I'm too old-fashioned to judge, perhaps, but I confess I like the old grey-beards who were young when I was; who learned their theology from the Bible; and who utter their own thoughts in their own simple phrase, a great deal better."

Upon this Margaret defended the young minister warmly, and when I said to her, after we were alone, that I had no idea she was so much interested in Mr. Staunton, she colored, and, with more of temper than I had almost ever seen in her, answered that I had no right to infer any special interest on her part, but she did like to see every one dealt with fairly.

At all events, there was presently no doubt of Mr. Staunton's estimation of her. He showed it by many unequivocal demonstrations, and yet not in any way which made it possible for Margaret to repulse him, or obliged her, on the other hand, to encourage him. His attentions were such as friend might show to friend, but accompanied by looks and tones which evidently pointed home their moral. I do not know whether all this was noticed by outside observers; I thought not. It surprised me a little when, one evening, Mr. Thorndike spoke to me upon the subject.

He happened to call when Mr. Staunton was there. Margaret was singing in the music room, which opened out of the parlor. Of course the minister was bending over her, and for a few moments Mr. Thorndike was alone with me.

A little while we both listened to Margaret's voice, which floated out to us clear and sweet. My companion had been leaning his head on his hand, thus concealing his face; but when he looked up I saw an unfamiliar trouble in his deep eyes. He spoke hoarsely: —

"Is she, is Margaret going to marry Mr. Staunton, Laura? Perhaps I have no right to ask, but you know you have treated me almost like a brother."

"I have no idea," I answered, honestly. "You have seen as much, I imagine, as I have. He is very attentive, but she is reserved, even to me. I have no means of guessing her intentions."

He tried to smile, but it was a ghastly failure.

"Well," he said, "God bless her, whomever she marries, wherever her lot is cast. She will decide wisely. It is absurd for me to question it. Her own pure instincts will not mislead her; but Mr. Staunton, — Laura, I can never think he is good enough for her. Take my word for it, there is poverty of heart and soul beneath that fine exterior. The soil is too poor for wholesome grain where all that exotic luxuriance of transplanted flowers springs up."

In a few moments more he left. When I urged him to stay and see my sister, he answered in a voice I should scarcely have known, it was so constrained and unnatural: —

"Not to-night. To-night, at least, you must excuse me."

I needed no more words to tell me that he loved Margaret with a love as pure and as strong as his manly heart. Had he so loved me, I was conscious that I should have returned it. I esteemed him as I esteemed no other man. Perhaps I had unwittingly striven to please him; but it was here, as in all else, I who had failed, and Margaret, my calm, pale, firm sister, who had won what she seemed not to value after all. Well, thank Heaven and the common sense I inherited from my father, I should not die for love. I had no story-book sentimentality about it. If a good man, like Ignatius Thorndike, had truly loved me, and Heaven had separated us, I cannot answer for my fortitude; but, while I recognized the possible hold he might have had on my heart, my affections not having been sought, were still in my own keeping, and I was quite capable of being a true sister to him, and entering with unselfish warmth into his love for Margaret and all its accompanying hopes and fears.

That evening when I was alone with my sister, I told her all that had passed. I did not omit to describe the expressions which had swept over Mr. Thorndike's face or the inflections of his voice. She listened silently. Her back was toward me as she stood letting down her hair before the mirror. I thought her fingers trembled a little, but I could not be sure. When I had concluded she turned round for a moment. I could not read her face distinctly, it was shrouded so by the golden hair sweeping round it; but I could see that her eyes glittered, whether with tears or pride, and that her cheeks were glowing. Her voice was steady and unmoved as usual.

"Thank you, Laura," she said, quietly. "It is unnecessary to speak to Mr. Thorndike again upon the subject, but should any one ask you hereafter whether I am going to marry Mr. Staunton you can say no; as I shall certainly tell the gentleman himself if he ever gives me an opportunity."

She said no more. I longed to sound her as to her sentiments toward Mr. Thorndike, but I could think of no way. Open as a child in all her acts, Margaret was reserved about her feelings; and this reserve had even grown upon her of late. She went on undressing as tranquilly as if I had not told her that Mr. Thorndike loved her, and then knelt down, with her childlike instinct of reverence, to say her prayers, for neither great grief nor overwhelming joy had as yet taught her how to *pray*.

We went out of town early in the spring, as we had come in late; but before we went Mr. Staunton's visits had nearly ceased. I conjectured, though Margaret did not tell me, that he had offered her his hand and been rejected. His sermons about this time took a melancholy tone. He dwelt much on the fact that we are pilgrims and strangers, and have no continuing city here; he bewailed the vanity of life and the unstable nature of earthly hopes and dreams. He quoted largely from that school of bards whose constant longing seems to be to have the grass green and the snow white above their graves; the storms whistling and the flowers blooming over them, all at once. In this phase of emotional development he was more popular than ever, especially with the young ladies of his flock. The dear creatures seemed to have an affinity for tears, and take naturally to lamentations; and as not a few were rich and some handsome, he was in a fair way to console himself in time.

When we were settled in our suburban home we missed Mr. Thorndike's frequent visits still more than in the city. There was a different reason now for his not coming to us. It was the spring of 1858. The commercial earthquake which had commenced in the fall had been rumbling all winter, and bursting out now and then to overwhelm its victims with a financial ruin sudden and terrible. Toward spring the failures grew perhaps less frequent but more severe; for firms which had struggled so long, if they went down at last, wrought a devastation as fearful as when Samson, blind and old and persecuted long, pulled down upon himself the temple of Dagon. Few merchants had time for much social civility. It was all they could do to fight their way in the hand-to-hand conflict going on around them. Papa said Mr. Thorndike was struggling with the rest, — that he had a great many bad debts, and it was doubtful how long he would be able to meet his engagements.

"Couldn't you help him?" I asked, when he told us this.

Papa shook his head.

"I offered to, but he obstinately refused to involve

me in any way. 'No one can do more in these times,' he said, 'than look out for himself. You have children, and I have none. You are an older man than I, and not used as I am to struggling and privation. I shall remember all my life this friendship, when so few would dare to be friendly; but I must stand or fall alone, — I don't know which it will be.' He is a noble fellow, girls; not many like him in these days, when people hold honor and faith and friendship as mere fictions."

I turned to look at Margaret. I wanted to see how she was affected by this praise, but she had gone out of the room.

That day papa, not feeling very well, did not go to town. After dinner we were all together in the dining-room. Papa was at the window, where the sunset brightened his silver hair. Margaret was half-sitting, half-lying on a lounge in the back part of the room, and I was on a stool beside her. I think we were all partly asleep, papa smoking and watching the blue rings float up and away, and we girls dreaming each her own dreams. The sound of a horse galloping up the avenue aroused us. We heard the rider dismount and speak to Patrick, who was at work on a flower-bed not far from the house. Then, the doors being open, he came without ringing into the hall, and along to the dining-room. It was Mr. Thorndike. He evidently saw no one but my father, and neither Margaret nor I made any movement. He went straight up to papa and stood before him. His face was very white, but calm. His voice did not tremble, but there was a sadness in it deeper than tears.

"Mr. Otis," he said, "my struggle is over. My paper was protested to-day. These last failures have been too much for me. I have done my best, but the fruit of my life's toil is gone. I shall give up every cent, and no man can lose much by me; but I must begin again at the foot of the ladder, I who am no longer young. But, thank Heaven, I have no one dearer than myself to suffer through my misfortune. I have repined at my loneliness sometimes, but it comforts me now."

Papa was betrayed by his sympathy into suggesting a thought to his friend which he would never have accepted for himself.

"But can't you save enough to go into business again? It is custom; every one does it nowadays. No one gives up every thing."

Mr. Thorndike smiled with an indescribable expression of patient pride.

"Dear sir, you would be the very last to temporize with duty yourself. No, I must preserve my honor at all costs. I shall go into business again, I hope; but it will be as a poor man, as poor as I was twenty years ago. You must feel that this is right."

"It *is* right." It was Margaret who spoke. I had never seen her so stirred from her usual calmness. She sprang from the sofa and walked to Ignatius Thorndike's side. "Yes, my friend, you are right; *you* could do no other way. There is no absolute ruin in life save the ruin of integrity; no utter wreck but the wreck of honor. Gold is tried and purified by fire; only the baser metals are destroyed."

He held her hand, her white, delicate hand, that did not look as if there were any strength in it to labor. He glanced at her figure, so slender and so graceful, arrayed with such costly simplicity, — a woman whom it seemed no poor man could venture to win. Then he looked steadfastly in her eyes. What did he read there? They were luminous, as on that night when he had given her back our silly leap-year letter,—when she had first discovered how good he was. A flush like the dawning was on her cheeks. A noble pride, kindled rather for him than herself, shone in her face. She looked fit for a hero's bride. But what read Ignatius Thorndike in her eyes? He held her hand for a moment, gazing at her steadily. Then he said, with less composure than he had shown before, —

"God bless you, Margaret; I cannot even thank you," and turned away. As he went out of the door I, who was nearest to it, heard him murmur, "I could have borne all but this. This makes the cup too bitter."

I understood then that Margaret's soul had revealed itself to him in her look, — that he felt sure of her love. I know his first, despairing thought was that he could never marry her; that love had come too late, — come but to mock him with tantalizing glimpses of what might have been. I was not troubled, however, for I had faith in the true hearts of them both. I believe that when two belong to each other so that apart their being is incomplete, — so that, in life or death, no other could usurp the throne, — it is seldom possible to separate them, even in this world. Through pain and weariness it may be; over paths rough with rocks and thorns, or lying among shadows; still, were it from far antipodes, they will draw near to each other. By and by Mr. Thorndike would come to understand that to deprive Margaret of himself, of his love, would be to do her a heavier wrong than to subject her to one meal a day and an attic. Not, however, that I apprehended any such romantic catastrophe. The wife of a business man, who possesses strong health and active energies, can never know hopeless poverty. Besides, papa was well enough able to assist them. There would be only he and I left; he could give my sister her fortune now.

I did not mention any of my speculations to Margaret. She did not allude to Mr. Thorndike beyond a simple expression of her sympathy in his misfortunes; and I respected her reticent delicacy. We did not see him again for more than a month. From time to time I inquired of papa concerning his affairs. He had behaved nobly, — given up every thing, and refused an offer from papa, and two other of his warm friends, to lend him a sufficient capital to start again. He had sturdily adhered to his preference for independence, and was going to establish himself in a commission business. I believe I exulted in him — in the integrity which no temptations could shake, the self-respect which no misfortunes could lessen — as much as if his love had been mine.

It was June when he came to us again,—just a year, as I happened to remember, from the day at which I dated the real beginning of our friendship. He looked a little worn by anxiety and labor, but hopeful and resolute notwithstanding. For the first time he asked Margaret to walk with him, and omitted me in the invitation. I saw them, a few moments afterward, from my window, pacing slowly under the trees, her light dress gleaming through the summer greenery. They were gone a long time. When they returned Margaret came directly upstairs. A tender, womanly light was in her eyes; an expression of entire happiness upon her face. She sat down beside me, and laid her head against my shoulder, with a caressing manner which was unusual in her; for, though deeply and fervently affectionate, she was seldom demonstrative.

"I am not half worthy of him, Laura," she said, hiding her eyes from me; "not half worthy of being Ignatius Thorndike's wife; but I have promised to be so. I don't know what he sees in me, that noble man, — the best man I ever knew, — strong and true as an angel."

I could tell very well what he saw in her, — a bride whom any man might be proud to win; but those who love truly are always humble. I did not dispute the point; I only rallied her a little.

"Do I hear you rightly, Margaret?" I asked, with apparent incredulity. "Why, don't you remember all Mr. Thorndike said, last summer, about men who asked women a great deal younger than themselves to marry them,—how wrong he thought it, how hazardous?"

"That was when they asked hastily; when they wooed women who were not sure of their own hearts; when they married without knowing, beyond doubt, that their wives loved them."

"And he has no doubt of your love, then?"

"Thank Heaven, none; nor I of his."

Her sweetness and frankness had quite overruled my attempts to tease her, and banished the desire. I caught her in my arms instead, and wept over her passionately, —not, Heaven knows, because I was sorry; every thing had happened as I most wished. I could give up my beloved sister to her husband without a single apprehension as to her future. Nevertheless the tears would come. They are most women's safety-valve, and answer quite as well for occasions of extreme joy as for those of sorrow. Mine were contagious, and we had a good cry together,—we two, who had been the dearest upon earth to each other almost all the years of our young lives. I could be dearest to Margaret no longer. Was there any unworthy jealousy in my tears?

"What will papa say?" I asked, when we had got quiet again.

"Oh, he is pleased. Ignatius spoke to him first; and indeed, Laura, what could he have hoped for me half so good? As he himself said, he can give me to Mr. Thorndike without a doubt or a fear. I know it was a long time before Ignatius could make up his mind to ask my hand, because he is poor now, and he could not bear to have me share poverty with him; but finally" —

"But finally he bethought himself to do you better justice, and not sacrifice your heart and his own to what is, at worst, but a doubtful fear."

I went donwnstairs presently to see and congratulate my brother-in-law elect. Margaret staid behind; she had need to be alone, she said. I think she *prayed* then.

It was not long before Mr. Thorndike left. I was going with him into the hall, but I saw a rapid figure flitting down the stairs to join him, and I retreated, to leave them to exchange together their first lovers' farewell.

They were to be married in the early fall, before we went into town, and we commenced the preparations at once. I wanted to have superintended Margaret's *trousseau*, and I thought nothing could be too costly or too elegant for her. It was a real annoyance when she quietly refused to have this and that, because it was not fitting for the wife of a man whose fortune was yet to make. But she had always had her own way, — she did so still. Her quiet, persistent mildness was all-powerful.

In respect to style of living and expenses I could see there would be perfect harmony between her and her betrothed. Both were independent, and entirely above vanity. I went into the parlor one day, and found papa fussing and fretting in a manner quite unusual for him.

"What is the matter?" I asked, as I went up to him.

"Matter enough! One likes to see a very young man Quixotic, and heroic, and all that; but Ignatius Thorndike is old enough to take a common-sense view of life. I have been telling him I was going to buy Margaret a house and furnish it, and transfer some stock to her name; and instead of thanking me, behold, he will have Margaret and nothing else. He is not willing I should do any thing for her. If he were rich, he says, he should not mind; but, as he is not, he would prefer beginning his married life as suits his altered fortunes. It's absurd, — absolutely ridiculous."

"And what does Margaret say?"

"Oh, agrees with Ignatius, of course. She understands him so well that I suppose she thinks it would make him unhappy to owe too much, even to her."

It was possible, too, I thought, that Margaret preferred to be dependent on her husband. I had begun to understand her nature now.

She and Ignatius — the two firm, quiet ones — had their way. Papa only gave them their furniture, their silver, and linen. Mr. Thorndike rented a small, pleasant house in town, and it was all fitted up ready for them to go into before they were married.

It was the first of October when they went away from us. They had a very quiet wedding. Margaret wore white muslin, in lieu of the satin and point lace I would fain have selected; but with all her simplicity of attire she could not help looking like a queen.

Nature had stamped her *regina*. There was an unutterable content and peace in Ignatius Thorndike's face when he came from church with his wife, — his young, true, fair wife; and Margaret looked as if the ducal strawberries would have elevated her less than the unadorned honor of being Mrs. Thorndike.

They had no bridal tour. It was not only that the new-made husband had no superfluity of time or means, — in any circumstances neither of them would have fancied it. Their happiness was not of a kind to require change of air and scene. They needed no company besides each other. We knew this, — papa and I, — and did not intrude upon them much at first. After a while, however, we fell into the habit of spending with them some portion of every day. In fact, we cannot stay away, it is such a pleasant home to visit. A neat little house, simple in furniture and adornments, but with a few sunny pictures, plenty of choice books, and always fresh flowers in the crystal vase on Margaret's table. I do not know how the one tidy maid contrives to keep every thing so neat, and bright, and smiling. I half suspect Margaret of assisting her; but her hands are as white and ladylike as ever, her dress as faultlessly neat and elegant. She never talks about her domestic affairs. She is content to love us dearly and welcome us heartily, without presenting constant drafts on our sympathy in household grievances.

Her husband is all Margaret's husband ought to be, — loving, proud, honest, and fearless. I think he forgets that he is just beginning the struggle for fortune at an age when he hoped to be able to leave it off. Cheered by her brave, hopeful love, he knows no regrets. He puts mind and brain into his business during many hours of each day; but he comes home to rest and refreshment, and his heart has a sure anchor. Already he is successful. When patience and industry join hands with tact and skill the reward is sure. I should not be surprised if Ignatius Thorndike were one day to be numbered again among the rich men of Boston. But can he ever be a richer man than now?

OUT OF NAZARETH.

A QUEER little town, among hills and streams, where, under the thrifty, painstaking New England farming, the very rocks had blossomed into gardens, and every little brook had to turn a big mill-wheel. A place that might have been poetical, if it had not been so severely useful; with skies blue as Italy, and peaks which made you think of Switzerland; and yet a place where no tourists went, and which nobody ever thought of talking about.

The site for the little red school-house on the hill-side had been chosen because the land was rocky and therefore cheap, as well as because it was near the centre of the district. By the merest accident it was the most picturesque nook in the whole town. At its back a wood crowned the hill, — a pleasant wood, where there was little underbrush, and the school-boys kept all the snakes killed, so that timid girls could go there and gather flowers in spring and summer, and fill their dinner baskets with chestnuts when the early frosts opened the burs. The meadow, stretching out green and level at the eastward, was a capital place for strawberries and playing "gool;" and the hill, sloping so steeply from the school-house door, — what royal coasting there was down it in winter. All the juveniles appreciated these points of attraction; and Miss Amber, the teacher, appreciated what the rest forgot, the picturesqueness of a landscape which would have enchanted a painter, — if you could fancy a painter ever going to Nazareth, — and so all were satisfied.

Miss Amber had taught school in Nazareth, summer and winter, for five years; but then she began when she was seventeen, — so she was not very old. She was an orphan; but the townsfolks had loved her father, and she did not lack for friends. Parson Amber had been for thirty years their minister, and when he died, and his fair invalid wife, whom he had married late in life, laid her head down on his dead heart, and died in time to be buried in the same grave, every home in the little country town was open to his only child, and every heart was ready to give her welcome. But she chose independence, and asked for the post of teacher of the district school.

She retained the small but pleasant cottage which her father owned, and the woman who had been at once housekeeper and maid of all work for her parents; and so pleased herself with the semblance of a home to go to when her day's work was over, though the cherishing love, which had made those lowly walls so dear, was gone from the earth.

Miss Amber made a good teacher. I do not mean by this that she liked it. I do not hold to the creed that to teach well one must be in love with one's work. One must have ability to impart knowledge, and a respectable fund of knowledge to impart. Beyond these it only wants self-control and a conscience, — two things which Miss Amber had. So she did her duty in the fear of God, and did it well. It was not in the nature of things that she should particularly enjoy it. Her father had been a man of literary tastes and thorough culture, and after she had mastered the tedious first rudiments of knowledge he had been her teacher. To one who had walked among the stars, dreamed through the classics, was familiar with the daily lives and ways of the poets as with the faces of her neighbors, — one whose soul was full of subtile perceptions of beauty, undeveloped powers of imagination, longings all the stronger because unspoken after the glory, and romance, and fervor, of a full life, there could be little attractive in the task of thumping A B C's into naughty curly heads, or kindling torches of illumination to guide benighted intellects through the Rule of Three. All the more glory to her, I say, therefore, because she did her work well. All heroes do not lead regiments. She always passed her "noonings" at school, and staid at night to mend pens and prepare copy-books, — so for eight hours of every day she was not her own. Her moments and her thoughts were paid for, and she gave them every one faithfully. Then she went home, put on her home dress and her home face, and was her own mistress.

Did I say that Miss Amber had many friends in

Nazareth? I should have been nearer the truth to say she had but one. All cared for her. Partly for her father's sake, and partly for her own, the minister's little girl was dear to each and all. But if friendship means something more than liking; if it means companionship in pursuits, exchange of ideas, community of thoughts, she had one sole friend, — Adam Russell. And even on him she secretly looked down a little, though nothing in her manner ever gave a suggestion of it. She was exquisitely refined. Her mother had been faultlessly bred, — her father was a gentleman of the old school. To a dweller in Nazareth such refinement, inherited and cultivated, was no blessing. It was hard sometimes to conceal her annoyance at neighborly familiarities, awkward country ways. But her kind heart carried her safely through, and she wounded no mortal's self-love.

Still she wished — she could not help wishing it every night when he sat by her side — that Adam Russell were less rugged; less noisy in step and voice; had more softness, more social adroitness. She liked him heartily, nevertheless.

He had been her father's pupil. For three years before Parson Amber died he had taught the two together, — girl and boy. After his death they had kept on with their studies. It would have been so solitary to give up all old habits. After the first wild spasm of grief was over, and Grace had begun to grow familiar with her loneliness and sorrow, and recognize it as something that was not to be confronted or shaken off,

— a quiet guest rather, to sit with her at board and fireside until her own death day, — she began to feel the need of keeping up old ways. When Adam Russell came, timidly enough, not dreaming of books or study, but only to bring her a late flower or two which the autumn blasts had spared, and show her in his sad eyes and mutely sympathizing face how sorry he was for her, she brought out the last book they had been reading, and asked him quietly if he would stay and study with her a while. When he went away, she said, struggling with something that rose up in her throat and seemed to choke her: —

"Perhaps you had better come every night as you used, and we will try how we can get on together without a teacher. I think papa would have wished it."

Then she shut the door hurriedly, almost in his face; for she felt a storm of sobs and tears bursting forth which he must not see. How grief shook her. What bitter, bitter cries smote the very heavens from those orphan lips. With what unavailing anguish she called for voices to answer her, to bless her, which must be silent evermore, until she, too, should learn the secret password which opens the portal of eternity. How, at last, came merciful exhaustion, and then, through the stillness, a whisper faint and sweet as of a ministering angel: —

"He is a father of the fatherless, — even God in His holy habitation."

Little she knew, little she would ever know, how her sorrow was shared even then, — how he stood outside, that simple country-bred boy, not daring to seek admittance again, or proffer any comfort, and yet longing, in a passion of tender grief, and loving pain, to bear it all for her, — to shield that graceful head from every storm of life. He did not go away until the moans, that had penetrated faintly to his ear, were still, and the glow of a just-lighted lamp shone out softly from Miss Amber's window.

He was only sixteen then, and she was seventeen. He did not think about love. No dream of possible possession, no longing to call her his, blent with the humble sincerity of his worship. He only felt that to have died to make her happy would have been easier than to stand outside and know her shaken with a sorrow he was powerless to soothe.

Since that night five years had passed. Miss Amber had taught the village school. Adam Russell had worked the days through upon his father's farm, serving with faithful hands, but with heart and mind often far enough away. Evenings they had met almost daily. In the summer they took their books out of doors, or sat, when it was stormy, in the old window-seat; in winter at the fireside, with Aunt Prudence Fairly, the housekeeper, in the other corner nodding over her knitting. No one ever gossiped about Miss Amber; perhaps because she was open and frank as daylight in all her ways. Then, too, she held herself grandly above gossip, and, doing what she knew was right, would never have thought or cared what speech it might provoke. Moreover, there was an atmosphere of womanly dignity about her which would have forbidden foolish jesting with her name. If any one speculated, country fashion, that it would be a match some day between her and young Russell, she never knew it, and the thought of it had never entered her head.

She was twenty-two now, and he twenty-one in the summer gone by. She remembered his age as she sat waiting for him in the early autumn evening, and thought with a real regret that he would soon be going away to try his fortune elsewhere, as he had always said he should after he was of age. The books they were reading lay beside her in the old-fashioned window-seat; but she would not open them until he came. She sat with still face and wide eyes looking out toward the sunset.

She was beautiful just then. Ordinarily she was only distinguished-looking. She was tall and well-made. Her face was pale usually; clear and healthy, but colorless. There was character enough in her proud features, and a look of resolution and self-will about the corners of her mouth and in her dark gray eyes. But there were moments, as now, when her soul looked out through those eyes as through open windows, and they grew luminous with the inner light; when roses glowed on her cheeks and rivalled the bright bloom of her lips. These moments of transfiguration were when she looked at sunsets, or read poetry, or heard music. I think the sea would have wrought the same miracle; but her home was inland among the hills, and she had never seen it.

Adam Russell came in before the spell had ceased to work, while still the sunset's brightness was reflected in her changeful face. He had a love for the beautiful as quick and keen as her own; and, though neither of them knew it then, he had more power and more genius. Indeed, of genius, strictly speaking, she had not a bit. She was intensely appreciative, not creative.

Yet his face told no tales. He was not handsome, but he looked strong and in earnest: true Saxon,—large of limb, tough of muscle, with brown hair and blue, resolute eyes; Roundhead rather than Cavalier. Miss Amber turned and took up a book as he entered.

"Not to-night, Grace," he said, putting it away; "at least not now. Give me a little time to talk."

His accent touched her; for there was in it a certain pleading inflection, unconscious and tender.

"I don't know when, after to-night, I shall be here again," he went on, half-sadly, half-expectantly, as if he longed, yet scarcely hoped, to move her regret. "Shall you miss me at all?"

"I shall miss you more than you can guess. What a lonely five years these last would have been but for our evenings together. I am not of a temperament to relish solitude without some one to whom I can say how sweet it is. But are you really going? When do you go, and where?"

"I am really going. I staid here thus long only because they needed me at home. Father must make his next year's arrangements without me. You know

I never thought farming would suit me for a permanent thing, — or New England either, for that matter."

"And yet she is a good mother."

"Yes;" and the slow blue eyes kindled a little, and then softened. "I hope you are not thinking I don't love home. If I were rich, I think I would live and die here; but I must have room to grow. I must make money faster; for I want what it will bring. Why should I weary you with reasons? I think you've heard them all before. You knew my purpose, and now the time is come. I shall go to-morrow; where, I don't know yet, but out toward the sunset. I have three thousand dollars, which my grandmother gave me when she died. When I have made them ten times three, I think I shall be ready to come back. Simple people could live well enough on thirty thousand, couldn't they, Grace?"

He asked this question, and then he bit his lip with vexation. He had meant to ask her for her love, and here he was talking about money. Still he wanted so much to know what sum she would think enough for comfort, — when he might venture to come back. He had outgrown a little in these five years his boyish ignorance and simplicity of heart. He was no longer content to worship without the thought of return. He loved Grace Amber, and he *wanted* her, — to be his own; to meet him, with those proud, sweet eyes of hers, when he came in; to belong to him, with her red lips, and her dark shining hair, and her proud, pure woman's heart. But he had not outgrown his boyish shyness; and his very sense of her goodness and grace made him awkward. He had longing enough, but little hope. I am not sure that women do not like a self-confident wooer better. He started from his thoughts as if from a trance, when, after a moment's silence, her sweet voice broke upon his ear:—

"I don't know much about money, but I should think thirty thousand dollars, two thousand a year, enough for luxury. We never had more than half that income in my father's life, and we surely lived in comfort."

"And when I have that much may I come back for you? Oh, Grace, Grace, I don't know how to tell you, but you must have seen that you are all I care for in this world. Your sorrow pierces me to the heart. Your smiles make me glad. I would give every moment of my life for your happiness. I know I'm not good enough or polished enough for you. I know I'm not half what you deserve; but oh, who will ever love you so well? Who *could* love you so well as I, who have loved you all my life? If I grow better, worthier, will you promise to love me, to keep your heart for me?"

"Let me think,—wait,—give me time to tell you."

The silence that fell between them only lasted five minutes. It seemed to Adam Russell like a cycle of eternity.

Grace Amber's brain reeled a moment, and then grew steady. His declaration had been the greatest surprise of her life. During all the hours they had passed together she had never thought of his loving her. Could she give him what he asked? She stole a stealthy look at him as he sat with his eyes turned away. It was not the face or form of her ideal. She loved softness, gentleness, poetry of motion, grace of aspect. She *needed* most of all something to rely on, — strength, courage, truth, — but she did not know her own needs as yet. Her quiet life had developed her so slowly that she had not learned to understand herself. What she fancied now, she would not love five years hence. Still she could only answer from present knowledge. She cared more for Adam Russell than for any one else in the world. She would feel the pain she must give him to her own heart's core, but he did not satisfy her taste. She could not feel for him one throb of the soft, sweet tumult of passion which she supposed love was. She noticed the square, ungraceful shape of his stalwart figure in his ill-fitting country-made clothes. She looked at his hard, rough hands, browned with the summer's work in plow-field and hay-field. She did not see in him one thing to please her fancy. Plenty of good sterling qualities to make her honor and trust in him, — but not the eloquence of dark eyes and silver tongue, — not the magical charm, the persuasive witchery which could win her love.

She spoke at length, tenderly, deprecatingly, pitifully, with tears in her voice and her eyes: —

"I can't, Adam, I can't. I have tried, but it is of no use. I do love you, I love you dearly; but oh! forgive me, it is not in that way."

"Forgive you! Forgive you for not loving me, Grace! Did you think I could blame you? I hardly hoped at all. I knew I was not good enough, — I said so. Forgive me for troubling you. I have pained you, made you cry. Don't, Grace, you will break my heart," for, moved to the depths by his words, she was sobbing passionately.

"I don't wonder you couldn't love me. I only wonder I could have been so mad as to think it possible. God bless you. God make you happy. I know you are my friend, my true, good friend, and that is enough. It must be enough. You will be my friend still when I come back, won't you; wherever you are, married or single?"

A great gulping sob shook him in spite of himself as he said that, — he was not strong enough to bear the thought of finding her married to some one else. She could not answer him, for her tears were falling fast; but she put out her hand, and he took it and held it in a close pressure. After a moment he let it go, and for her sake forced himself to self-control and calmness.

"I brought you a book," he said; "one you like, and I want you should keep it to make you think of me sometimes when I can read with you no more."

He laid it in her hand, an edition of Shelley, bound as Shelley should be, in leather the color of the sea, and printed on fair, creamy pages, in type it would be a luxury to read. It was an English edition. He had been to Boston and back for it the day before. He said nothing of another gift he had purchased for her there, — a ring with a pearl white as milk, faintly flashing, — he had given up all hope that she would wear that now.

He received her thanks with a sad smile, and soon after he went away. He turned back on the threshold to say, looking at her with tender, sorrowful eyes: —

"If ever you want a friend, Grace, — if ever there is any thing a brother could do for you, — let me know. Promise me. My father can always tell you where I am, so it will be easy to send me word. No matter how far it is, I will not fail you."

When he was gone Grace Amber went back into the room where she had received her first offer. She had it to herself. Aunt Prudence was doing fortnightly duty at a sewing-society, and there was no one to notice her mood. She tried to read a little in her Shelley. Then she shut it and fell to thinking. She could not turn her mind all at once from the true, honest love that had been laid at her feet. She thought it all over, — what he had said, — how he had looked at her, — how generous and patient and earnest he was. If she could have loved him she knew he would never have failed her. She could have looked forward to a future fixed and safe and sheltered. But of what avail all this when she could not give him her heart? — that wilful, fluttering thing waited for the voice of another charmer. Some one there must be in the world who would look at her with the eyes of which she had dreamed, — whose tones, silver sweet to her ears, would woo in poet phrases, — a lover after her own heart.

But she pitied Adam Russell, her old playfellow, her fellow student, her one friend for so many years. She went to bed, at last, with a heartache for his sake; and his familiar, kindly face blended strangely in her dreams with the dark eyes, and smile half-sad, half-tender of the true Prince who was to come some day.

That was autumn; and the winter which followed was insupportably long and tedious. She had never thought that she could miss her old friend so much. Her school duties seemed harder and more monotonous, — the children more hopelessly stupid and the days longer. Then the evenings, — those still, dreary times, with no one to read to her, or hear her read, and the silence broken only by the steady, drowsy click of Aunt Prudence's knitting-needles. There was no one to notice the bit of scarlet ribbon with which she brightened her winter-dress, or the new ways she did her hair. She was not one whit more in love with Adam Russell than ever; but his going away and leaving no one to take his place made a terrible blank in her life. She grew thin. She looked not only pale, but listless. She found her solitude and the dull monotony of her days insupportable. She resolved to change it. She began searching the papers. In some of them, she thought, she would be sure to see the opening she waited for. Her evenings, devoted to advertising columns, became a little more interesting.

At length she chanced upon an advertisement for a governess whch seemed to promise something. All the wisdom of Solomon was not, for a wonder, required of the applicant. She was not expected to sing like Patti, play like Gottschalk, and dance like Mademoiselle Cubas. The accomplishments, so called, were to be taught by masters engaged for the purpose, — the governess was expected to train her pupils in the ordinary branches of an English education, to direct their reading, and criticise their manners. Miss Amber had no fear but that she was qualified. The only trouble was the references required. To whom could she refer, — whose indorsement, of all she knew, would establish her credentials?

She was frank by nature, and she solved the question in the directest way. She wrote a letter to the address given in the advertisement, in which, with straightforward simplicity, she set forth the details of her birth, breeding, and acquirements, — all her past life, in short. Perhaps nine advertisers for governesses out of ten would have passed such a letter by unheeded. Fortunately she had chanced upon the tenth one, who appreciated it, and understood her at once. She received in reply a communication nearly as frank as her own.

Mrs. St. Clair, the lady who desired her services, was a widow with two daughters to educate, of whom the younger was ten and the elder twelve. She resided in New York in the winter, in summer upon the Hudson; and she wished a governess who would be no less a companion for herself than an instructress for her daughters. If Miss Amber chose to accept the engagement she would be treated in all respects, social and domestic, as one of themselves. She concluded by naming a salary which sounded munificent to one accustomed to the wages of a district school-teacher in the country.

Miss Amber answered the letter by return mail, accepting the situation, and agreeing, as had been proposed, to join the family at Riverdale the second week in May.

This done, she dispatched a note to the school-committee of Nazareth, informing them that she must resign her post at the end of the winter term.

Her next task was to settle matters with Aunt Prudence. The little cottage where they lived, with the books and furniture it contained, was her inheritance from her father. She could not have borne to have it pass into other hands, or to see it shut up. She proposed to her housekeeper to remain there, and keep a home always open for her return, — promising to send her from each quarter's salary a remittance sufficient to keep her in comfort. The proposal was accepted with thanks, after a few vain remonstrances on the evils of young girls going to strange places, the dangers of city life, and sundry kindred topics.

So all was settled, and then Miss Amber had a pleasant employment for her leisure in making her preparations. It was marvellous how far her money went, aided by the contrivances of her deft fingers, for she was her own dress-maker.

School closed, and she parted from the children, the last day, with more real regret than she could have imagined it possible to feel for them. They were a link to her past life; and the future, now that she was drawing near it, seemed so dim, so vague, so untried, that she shrank from it a little, and turned to the past with a strange tenderness. She shed not a few tears for the days gone by, as she roamed again over her old haunts, and went round among all her old, kind friends to bid them farewell.

Still, when she had fairly left Nazareth behind her, and started on her way to Riverdale, her spirits rose. The prospect of change exhilarated her. She seemed to breathe freer. Her pulses thrilled at the thought of new scenes and new faces, — perhaps, who knew, the real story-book lover at last. It was time, she said to herself, with a smile and a blush, — she was almost twenty-three, and if he did not make haste, "the invisible, unknown he," she would be old and faded before he came for her.

That night she passed on the Sound. The next forenoon she reached Riverdale station. The other passengers who got out there marched away, as if each one knew where he was going. She was left nearly alone, when a respectable-looking coachman asked if it was Miss Amber, and conducted her to a carriage where a middle-aged lady and two little girls sat waiting. It was kind of them, she thought, to meet her. She went forward with a pleased smile on her face that made her lovely. Mrs. St. Clair looked at her critically. She liked the graceful figure in quiet, lady-like travelling garb; the pale, high-bred face; the simple yet elegant manner. She congratulated herself. She had not done ill in trusting to her intuitions. She welcomed her governess cordially, and introduced Helen and May, her daughters.

In the mean time Miss Amber's cool eyes had taken her measure also. They saw in her a shrewd, reasonable, kindly woman, — no enthusiast, yet not without impulse, — a true lady, — a mother who would be judicious and faithful, but one whose affection would never be idolatrous or unreasonable, — a person whose whole character was well-regulated and consistent; whom she should like sincerely, and get on with serenely, but about whom she could never be enthusiastic.

They were satisfied mutually.

That was a pleasant summer. Mrs. St. Clair had notions of her own about governesses, and recognized a lady when she saw one. Miss Amber fell into the ways of the household without difficulty. She had quite as much time to herself as was good for her. She found Mrs. St. Clair a pleasant friend; and the children, if no better than other children, were no worse, and had been trained to be obedient and not exacting.

Gradually she became familiar with the family history. Mrs. St. Clair, not more than thirty-five now, had been her husband's second wife. Besides her own two little girls there was a son of the first Mrs. St. Clair; a young gentleman of twenty-five, who had been living for several years in Italy, and was expected home by and by. About this absentee, "brother Paul," as they called him, the children were very enthusiastic. He was so handsome, so generous, — above all, he painted so beautifully. He must paint Miss Amber's portrait when he came home.

Mrs. St. Clair spoke of him with a certain kind of affection. That he was her husband's son was a claim on her regard which she would never have thought of ignoring. Still there was no difficulty in perceiving that he was not to her taste. A very real woman, she had not much sympathy with the ideal. She was just the kind of person to look coldly on artists, and distrust poets. So her curt and slightly sarcastic comments on the children's rhapsodies only amused their governess.

Unconsciously to herself Miss Amber was beginning to make a hero of this unknown "brother Paul." It would have shocked her if she had realized how much she thought about him, — how much reference she had in her choice of books and studies to the probability of their future meeting, and the subjects she should want to discuss with him. She would have laughed at the idea of the rich Mr. St. Clair falling in love with his sisters' governess; and yet, underneath her acknowledgments that such dreams would be impossible of fulfillment, and absurd of conception, I am not sure that there did not lurk a hidden something, not vivid enough to be called a hope, less tangible than a fancy, which pointed to him as the true Prince.

After a quiet, pleasant summer the family went back to New York. Miss Amber was more than ever charmed with her situation, as indeed she had reason. Mrs. St. Clair had taken a hearty and honest liking to her, and meant to afford her every enjoyment and advantage in her power. If she had been a daughter of the house her position could hardly have been more agreeable or independent. She had, to be sure, her hours for lessons, when she taught with zeal and thoroughness, — but she might have done as much had May and Helen been her own young sisters. Outside these hours they were quite as much in their mother's charge as in hers. She enjoyed this luxurious life. She delighted in the ease and elegance of her surroundings, — handsome furniture, spacious rooms, attentive servants. When she thought of Nazareth, in those days, it was almost with a shiver of self-pity. How had she lived so long with such commonplace associations? What would tempt her ever to go back to that rugged life, so bare of all luxury and grace?

In New York Mrs. St. Clair introduced her in society as her friend. Probably few guessed at her position; or, if they did, they politely ignored it, perceiving that they were expected to receive her on the footing of one of the family. At first she remonstrated against giving up so much time to society; but when she saw it was really Mrs. St. Clair's wish, she yielded to the natural, girlish enjoyment it gave her, only taking most conscientious care that her pupils should never be neglected, or their hours for study set aside.

She met with admiration enough to have turned some heads. Not that she was called a beauty. The women, indeed, could see nothing to admire in "that pale girl;" but the men seemed to find something. Perhaps it was partly the oddity of a woman who did not sing or play or dance, in a circle where every one else at least attempted these accomplishments. Then her style was so peculiar. She dressed so simply, yet with a taste so faultless. Her conversation was so piquant, so fresh; her moods so independent; her bearing so quietly regal. It was the difference between a nature pure, inexperienced, unhackneyed, and one which an artificial life had warped out of all originality; cramped remorselessly down to conventional standards. Mrs. St. Clair smiled to herself now and then to see how her protégée was becoming the fashion.

Her smiles changed to half-vexed astonishment when two offers of marriage came from two of the best matches in the city, and were successively rejected.

"I do not think you know your own mind, or have any true idea of your own requirements," she said in a provoked tone, on the second of these occasions.

"Why? Because I do not love Mr. Desmond or Mr. Vanderpool? I know no harm of them; but I cannot help it if they do not touch my heart. It bores me and tires me out to talk with either of them an hour at a time: what would it be to see their faces opposite me for ever? Are you in haste to look out for a new governess?"

"I should be sorry to part with you, — I need not tell you that, — but I am not selfish enough to wish you to forget your own interests, and lose your chances in life for the sake of being my governess. However, you must gang your ain gait."

"Waiting for Paul, I know it!" Mrs. St. Clair soliloquized in an annoyed tone, as the door closed upon Miss Amber. "She is romantic, and those children have made him out such a wonder. A selfish, luxurious dreamer; he isn't half good enough for her."

It was just about that time that one of Aunt Prudence's occasional letters came, with an item of Nazareth news in it of more than usual interest. Adam Russell's mother had died suddenly. He had been sent for, but only arrived in time to stand over her grave. He had seemed very much overcome, but had only staid in Nazareth a few days. The night before he went away he had called at the old parsonage. It must have been to ask after Grace, for he had not talked of any thing else, and spoke little even of her. He took down some of the books, and went and sat in the old window-seat, and turned them over; and after he had sat there a while he got up and went away.

This letter touched Miss Amber's heart strangely. She had been Adam Russell's true friend too many years not to feel his sorrow. She knew by her own memories of anguish what it must be to him to lose his mother. It would seem to sever his connection with Nazareth; for between him and his father — a stern, rigid man — there was no great attachment. Perhaps she should never see him again. How strange it would be, after all those years of friendship. How good he had been to her; how much he had loved her. She wanted to write to him and try to comfort him a little; she thought she would if she had known where he was. But she did not know. There was no way but to send the letter to his father for him; and then it would be speculated about, and grow old and cold before it reached him. So she gave it up. Perhaps something whispered that since she could not give him what he had asked her for, any thing else which she could give him would be worth little. The thought of his lonely heart, his unshared sorrow, haunted and saddened her for days, — until, in fact, it was banished by a new and most potent excitement.

"Brother Paul" was coming. He had started in the "Arago." She was nearly due. He might be there any day. May and Helen were wild with the eager excitement of children. Miss Amber's expectation was quieter, but not less intense. The daily lessons were hard work for both teacher and pupils.

At last, one day, in the very midst of study hours, there was the bustle of an arrival in the hall. The girls sprang up and tossed their books to the ceiling. The governess attempted no restraint. She, too, would have liked to join the wild rush down the stairs. She retreated, instead, to her own room, and, like a sensible young woman, improved the time to make her toilet. It cost her more study than all the parties at which she had assisted that winter. She did not acknowledge to herself the half of her real interest. She wanted to have him for a friend, she thought, — to hear him talk about Italy; she must not shock his fastidious taste by her first appearance. She tried half a dozen things, and ended with a plain but rich black silk, which fitted her figure exquisitely, finished with soft laces at wrists and throat. Black became her. It seemed a sort of continuation, in effect, of her soft, dark hair. It made her pale face look clear. Still, when all was done she was not satisfied. She did not like the slight, pale girl she saw in the mirror. Something seemed wanting of grace and sparkle, — some charm she lacked in her own eyes that she knew not where to borrow. I do not know but she would have dressed over again if Helen, at the door, had not saved her the trouble.

"Mamma wants you to come down. Paul has been asking for you. He laughed at May and me for writing so much about you, and he says he wants to see the paragon."

Indiscreet tongue of childhood! Miss Amber's cheeks blazed, — her eyes glittered. They had been making her ridiculous. Well, she would be indifferent enough. Her excitement supplied the lacking charm. If she had looked in the glass now she would have seen no want of life and sparkle.

She went into the drawing-room haughtily. Haughtily she received Mr. St. Clair's salutations. Silently and coolly she took her place at the window. He was enchanted. Surely the half had not been told him. None of them had written of her as handsome. What else did they call this radiant creature, with the wide, luminous eyes, the dusky, soft-falling hair, the pale brow, and the rose tint on cheek and lip?

You perceive there was a certain exaggerative romance in his manner of thinking. He was both poet and painter, — not great in either art, but with enough of an artist's soul to color his conceptions.

Miss Amber, on her part, despite her vexation and her cool ways, lost not an inflection of his voice, not a shade of his expression. It thrilled her with a new emotion when he looked at her or spoke to her. Here were the dark, eloquent eyes of which she had dreamed, — here the silver tongue, the high-bred, faultlessly elegant manner. Of course he was nothing to her; but with such a man in the world for a standard of comparison, what chance was there for the Desmonds and Vanderpools of society? She was cool and self-possessed as a veteran, however. No one could have guessed from her manner the new, overpowering fascination which swayed her heart. Even Mrs. St. Clair gloried in her quiet dignity, and began to hope that she was not going to be foolish enough, after all, to fall in love with Paul.

Is there any need to tell how the days and weeks of their acquaintance went on? how the spell of those unaccustomed charms stole over Miss Amber's dreaming heart, innocent, childlike, and almost as susceptible at twenty-three as in early girlhood? She lost her power to criticise, and believed in Paul St. Clair's genius as he believed in it himself. She listened to him with pulses that kept time to the melody of his voice as he lay on an ottoman at her feet, and said his own rhymes to her, looking up now and then into her face with the dangerous sweetness of his dark eyes. She grew to find every hour spiceless, insipid, that was not passed in his presence. And yet she kept up to herself the pretty fiction that he did not, and never would, love her, that it was only his genius which charmed her; and so she blinded her eyes as to whither she was drifting.

As for him, he had had fancies many, and loves many; but he felt in her presence that he had never loved before. I know not how real his passion was. His own faith in it was profound.

Mrs. St. Clair looked on with a certain degree of such patience as one has with the vagaries and petulance of a sick child. She thought that the flame would consume all its oil and go out after a while, at least in Miss Amber's heart. For her step-son she was not much concerned; she believed thoroughly in his power of recuperation.

Before they left town in the spring she found, to her dismay, that affairs were assuming a more serious character than she had anticipated.

Miss Amber waited on her one morning with a cool announcement of her wish to resign her situation. A question or two elicited the cause. Mr. St. Clair had proposed to her, and she had promised to be his wife. Of course she could not with propriety continue to teach there; and probably Mrs. St. Clair would not wish it, — this speech, with a curious look and an air at once deprecating and defiant.

Mrs. St. Clair considered a moment. Matters had certainly gone farther and faster than she expected. She had judged Paul by his past flames, and so failed to do him justice. She had not given him credit for so much direct resolution and energy. Her chief concern was for Miss Amber, for whom she entertained a true, practical, common-sense, yet most earnest friendship, more real and tangible, as well as more judicious, than one woman in ten is capable of feeling for another. She appreciated the girl's intense, affluent nature; she thought it too rich a freight to be wrecked on the lee-shore of an unhappy marriage. Still, if it were possible that the marriage would not be unhappy; if she herself had not done Paul justice; if they indeed belonged together; then, in Heaven's name, let them marry. It would be giving her a daughter-in-law after her own heart. But, at any rate, they should have time to know whether they really and thoroughly suited each other. She spoke, after her silent consideration, deliberately: —

"I am not willing to release you. I want you should stay with me through the summer, as much for your own sake as for mine. Do not suspect me of being opposed to this marriage. If *you* could be happy in it, it would give me undisguised satisfaction. Paul has no occasion to marry for money; it needs only that his wife should be a gentlewoman. All my concern is that you should not make a mistake. A man can bear an unhappy or an unsatisfying marriage without ruin — the world offers him so many resources. To a woman, such a woman as you, it would be fatal. Stay here, therefore. Learn to know him well; and when you are satisfied by a fair trial that he fulfils all the demands of your nature, marry him. I believe if I were your mother I should hardly feel for you more anxiously, and I could not counsel you differently than I do now."

Miss Amber's eyes overflowed. For the first time she took Mrs. St. Clair's hand, and pressed her lips upon it with heart-felt tenderness. Then she lifted her face with a smile and a blush.

"What will *he* think? I told him I must positively leave,—that it would not be right for me to stay."

"I will settle it with him. You shall not be compromised; and I assure you he will be only too glad."

In her secret heart Miss Amber was glad also. She had dreaded to go back to Nazareth, even for a time,—to her dull, ungenial life there; the rude ways, the work-a-day habits. She had dreaded yet more to leave Paul St. Clair. In that stage of her love-malady his presence was the one charm of the universe. Take that away, and sun, moon, and stars would refuse to give their light.

So they all went up to Riverdale, and she basked in that marvellous brightness, morning, noon, and night. He had the freedom of the schoolroom now, and he haunted it incessantly during lesson hours. Indeed, when the warm weather came he persuaded his mother that both his sisters and their teacher were in need of a vacation; and for the months of July and August lessons were interdicted altogether.

Then, of course, he must paint her portrait,—the natural pastime of an artist in love. There were long sittings, in which he painted little and made love much.

He sketched her in every attitude, every costume,— never able to decide in which she was most charming.

At last she grew tired. She thought it was the warm weather, or the long, fruitless sittings. Mrs. St. Clair smiled shrewdly, and said something to herself about a surfeit of sweetmeats. If Paul would but have let her have her own way his power over her would have lasted longer. She longed to go off by herself and rest; to think her own thoughts, and have a few free breaths out of his atmosphere. But he could not understand it. He drew strength and refreshment and constant pleasure from her larger, deeper, stronger nature. How was he to know that this, and not the weather, was exhausting her, wearing her out?

She bore it as long as she could. The very effort to keep up the spell weakened it. Trying to delude herself into thinking that she was as happy as ever, as much entranced in his presence, only made her real discontent and weariness more tangible. Then, too, her nature was, as I have said, singularly honest,— honest to herself as well as to others. She had never been accustomed to self-deception, or to tampering with the truth. When she found that she was tired of Paul, of his dark eyes and soft tones, his poetry, his painting, his Italy, she was too truthful to wear a mask. She wondered at herself. He was certainly her ideal. She ought to have been satisfied for ever in his presence, only — she wasn't. She had taken more real comfort with Adam Russell in the old window-seat at Nazareth, fagging at Virgil and Cicero, than she seemed ever likely to find sitting in the perfumed air of Paul St. Clair's studio, and listening to his honeyed words and soft rhymes. The wine had been too sweet. Was she to blame because it palled on her taste?

Still she did blame herself intensely. It well-nigh broke her heart. She almost resolved to bear on in silence, for ever. How could she tell him when he loved her so; when he had said so often it would be death to part with her? Perhaps she would even have gone to such length of self-martyrdom as to smother for his sake the remonstrance of her own soul, and go on with the fiction of love when the reality was dead, if it had not been for Mrs. St. Clair.

That lady found her crying one morning, and made use of the opportunity to wrench the truth from her. Indeed, after the first pang which it gave her pride to confess that she had been mistaken, it came easily enough. It was such a relief to tell the whole truth; to lean a little on the strength and judgment of another. When she had said all that was in her heart she smiled with a little touch of self-scorn.

"How weak you will think me, — how weak I am! I don't know that I understand myself. Perhaps I love Paul as much as ever. Perhaps it is only this oppressive weather that makes me feel tired of every thing, and when a cool, fresh day comes I shall be myself again."

Mrs. St. Clair looked at her kindly, but with a shrewd comprehension, as she answered her: —

"I think you do love Paul just as much as ever, because I do not think it was ever love which you felt for him. You had an ideal, and you thought he fulfilled it. His dark eyes and soft words, his poetry and painting and dreaming, bewitched you, — but the back-bone of love was not there. It was impossible that it should be, for you were the stronger spirit of the two; and I think no real woman loves where she cannot lean. With you he would have become like a parasite. He would have drawn all the life out of you. You talked of how tired you would be of Desmond and of Vanderpool. I tell you either of them would be rest itself compared with Paul. The mind cannot dwell for ever in an artificial atmosphere. One must touch bottom sometimes. I am only thankful that you have found out the truth in season."

"But I cannot break my word. I know Paul loves me. I am not bad enough to requite love with cruel wrong."

"Humph! To my thinking the cruel wrong would be in marrying him when you don't want him. He would find out soon enough how you felt. The very selfishness of his nature would make him keenly sensitive to any coldness; and you know you are no hypocrite. Trust me, even if you loved him, he would be better off without you. He would lean on you till the little strength nature gave him would have died of inaction. He will be twice the man married to a woman weaker than himself, — one who looks up to him, — whom he must sustain. If you dread telling him, let me."

"No; if it is right to tell him I must do it. I will not delegate my duties. I will go now; but I seem to myself like Judas when he betrayed his Lord. To have received his love, four months ago, with joy and pride beyond words, and now to scorn it and reject it! Let me go this instant, or I shall never have enough courage."

How she got through the interview she never knew. When she went into his studio he was retouching the outlines of her portrait, looking at it with lingering, loving eyes. He sprang, when he heard her step, to meet her, radiant with welcome. She almost thought again that she loved him, as she met the ardent gaze of the dark eyes, and listened to the familiar music of his voice. She felt guilty and hopeless, as the strong Roman when he met the glazing reproachful eye of the master he had murdered. But she plunged desperately on, and told him the truth.

His burst of passionate grief, his upbraiding, his despair, pierced her heart. She sat very still; but she grew terribly pale, and her breath seemed to forsake her. When he paused she said, — it was all she could do to speak, and her tones were so low he thought them icy cold, —

"If you wish it, if you say so, I will marry you; but I do not love you in that way at all."

"You are mad, Grace, my darling, — my darling. You could not so have deceived yourself and me. You have told me you loved me so often."

Low and clear fell the slow, controlled tones: —

"I am not mad. I know my own heart now. I know it was not love. I am not deceived, though I was then."

He thought her pitiless, her tones fell so evenly, her eyes were so cold and dry. He little knew how near her heart seemed to breaking. It roused his anger. He asked, bitterly, —

"What is my crime? What have I done?"

"Nothing; only I have found out that I do not love you."

If she had felt less she would have shown more emotion, been more tender; but she could not trust her voice for an unnecessary word. At her icy stillness his passion burst all bounds. He forgot himself, and overwhelmed her with reproaches; pierced her with arrows of scorn that quivered in her very heart. She rose at last, and looked at him with sad, imploring eyes.

"After so many happy hours, I hoped we could have parted friends."

"A man forgives his murderer sometimes," he sneered, "who shoots him in fair duel. I never heard of one who shook hands, at parting, with a masked assassin."

With these words for the end of so much loving she went out of the room. She went upstairs, still firmly and tearlessly, and packed her trunks. She could not trust herself to rest or pause. When she had arranged all her possessions, and dressed herself for a journey, she went to Mrs. St. Clair.

"The next train leaves in half an hour. My trunks are all ready. Can I be sent to the station?"

Mrs. St. Clair saw a resolution in her face which it would be useless to oppose. Indeed she did not wish to oppose it; for she knew her well enough to recognize her need of change and solitude. She only asked, after she had ordered the carriage, —

"Will you come back to me when we go to town again in the fall?"

A shudder shook Miss Amber's frame; she answered, with almost a groan, —

"No, Mrs. St. Clair, never. I love you, and I love the children; but I am done with governessing for life. I am going home. If there is less to interest there, less to please, God knows how much less pain there is. Mere safety is something."

"I understand your feeling so, now. If you ever change your mind your place here will never be so filled that it will not be open to you to return."

When the cars whirled Miss Amber away she gave no look backward. She had but one longing, — to get home. She had been out into the world, and gathered herself apples of Sodom. The fair hues which looked so bright in the distance had all faded. In the pleasure-gardens stones had goaded, thorns had pricked her. She asked now only rest. Nazareth was rough, and rugged, and commonplace as ever, doubtless; but no paradise of promised delights could have seduced her from it. During all the journey she allowed herself no backward thoughts. She would suffer her self-control to run no risks till she should be beyond the reach of curious eyes, within the chamber where she had dreamed all her childish dreams, before her world's work and world's trouble came.

The next day she reached Nazareth. Drawing her thick veil down to escape notice, she walked home across the fields, leaving her trunks to be sent for. Just past her twenty-fourth birthday, and done with life, — so she thought.

Aunt Prudence Fairly was a kindly soul, and, thanks to the silent influence of her residence in Parson Amber's family, not curious. She welcomed Grace with genuine delight, and in the next breath told her how pale she looked, — "dead beat out."

"I know it. I am sick."

"Well, you just go to bed, and I'll make you a nice bowl of penny-r'yal, and put some draughts to your feet, and have you round as chipper as can be in a couple of days."

Miss Amber smiled faintly at the thought of such medicine for her pain. But she felt too desolate not to value the kindness of the intention. She laid her fingers on Aunt Prudence's withered hand with a gentle touch.

"That would not help me," she said, kindly. "I am not ill of any thing but weariness. If you will let me go to my room and not come out of it for the next three days I shall be all right. I want a thorough rest before I can bear to see or speak to any one, even you."

The good old soul had the grace to submit, though it was about the hardest task Miss Amber could have imposed. She longed to ask and answer questions, — at least to look at the returned wanderer, and tend her, — but she took her disappointment patiently.

For three days Miss Amber staid quite alone, only taking in periodical cups of tea, and slices of toast, which she ate and drank mechanically, because they were brought, but which did her much good nevertheless.

In those three days she grew better acquainted with her own heart. She thought a great deal about Paul St. Clair; and she began to understand how imaginary had been her love for him, even while it was most entrancing, — how little it would have been capable of withstanding the rude buffetings of actual life in this most real world. She pitied him with all the compassion of her heart in his present pain; but she had faith, after all, that it would be a wholesome tonic, — that the bitter draught would give him strength. Involuntarily she recalled the past of two years ago, and contrasted it with the present. How boyish, undisciplined, unworthy, seemed Paul's anger, his rage at the truth, his refusal to part friends, when compared with Adam Russell's unselfish patience. She could not help seeing where was the finer fibre of manhood.

She thought of the hard, rough hands, and ungraceful air which had seemed so intolerable to her then. Of how much less moment they seemed now. She was learning to look beyond externals, to that which can alone endure the heat of the furnace. She began to see Adam Russell as he was, — strong and faithful and self-denying, — the true gentleman. She half wondered that, in those old days, she had not loved him, for the very thought of him now was like the fresh cool wind blowing over the hills.

She looked out of the window at the rugged, beautiful landscape. She longed to climb the steep paths; to feel the free, life-giving air. She felt as if she had been surfeited with flowers and sweetness and luxury. She liked better this simple life, which lay before her now, in the town where her father and mother had died. She thought of the past with no regret, save for the pain she had given Paul. Her own share of suffering did not pay too dearly for the knowledge she had won. She dressed herself carefully, — it was the evening of the third day, — and went downstairs.

"I am well, now," she said, with a smile which made Aunt Prudence think of sunshine after a long storm.

"You won't go back for a week or two, I reckon?" asked the old lady, looking at her with fond eyes.

"No, I'm not going back. When the school is vacant again I shall take it."

"Will you be contented?" — with a shrewd, questioning glance.

"Yes, never fear. There will be no relapse into that restless mood which drove me away. I have seen the world, and it is no better than Nazareth."

"Well, then, I guess you can have the school by asking for it. Sally Perkins has been teaching, and she's goin' to be married this fall. School was out the day you came home."

Miss Amber had sat down in the window-seat, and was looking at the sunset fires burning beyond the hills. She wanted to inquire for the old friend who used to sit there with her, and she felt a singular diffidence. She did not look at Aunt Prudence when she spoke.

"This window-seat makes me think of Adam. It seems a long time since we used to study here together. Do you know where he is now?"

"Not rightly. Somewhere out West. He hasn't been home since his mother died, but they say he's making a power of money. He has something to do with railroads, and he's a great politician. He sent home some of his speeches, and I got 'em to read after they'd done with 'em over to his father's. I don't believe but what they're here now."

She bustled round to find them, and Miss Amber went on with her own thoughts. She did not read the speeches till the next morning, when Aunt Prudence was busy, and she could have them all to herself. She did not care much for politics; but if their subject had been the Government of Timbuctoo they would have interested her, for they made her better acquainted with her old friend. She felt, as she read, that she was in presence of an intellect more subtile and clear and powerful than her own. She recognized now and then touches of genius; and she saw how a fancy was held in leash by the subject, that might be full of exquisite grace. She began to wonder how he could ever have loved her; and to think it was because in those old days he had not learned to appreciate himself. I think she was not far from being in love with him, only she was judicious enough not to see it, and only to think of him as her best friend. Her past experience was her security against being morbid or sentimental.

The first of November she began again her old work. It tasked her energies. It was a very different thing from teaching May and Helen, her quick, graceful pupils. These untrained imps were stolid some of them, roguish some of them, stupid some of them, uncultured and undisciplined all. Still she was not discouraged, and seldom vexed. She seemed to have acquired some of Adam Russell's patience. She was as forbearing with error and stupidity as he would have been; and so, in brief space, she won love, and conquered all disposition to offend.

Her life went on monotonously enough until the next summer, when it was varied a little by a visitor. Mrs. St. Clair came to see her, and staid a week. She brought her a letter from Paul. Having outlived his despair, his natural good-nature made him penitent for having parted with Miss Amber in anger. He wrote to tell her so. Moreover, he had something else to communicate which he knew she would be glad to hear. He was engaged, with every prospect of a happy future. His betrothed was charming as any of his dreams, and she loved him without doubt or question. He believed that they suited each other utterly; and, dear as Miss Amber had been, sad for him as their parting had been, he was constrained to confess that she had, questionless, decided rightly for him as well as for herself.

When she had read it through she raised her eyes to meet Mrs. St. Clair's smile.

"I told you I had no fears for him. I never thought you were the one it would be best for him to marry, any more than I was deluded into believing he could make you permanently happy. His Lily is just to his taste. She will look up to him, and lean on him, and think him the first of created beings. They will be married this fall, and then I want you to come back to me."

This was the true object of the visit. Probably Mrs. St. Clair had not a doubt of success. But Miss Amber was firm. No persuasions moved her. She found herself best and happiest in Nazareth, and there she would stay. Her friend left her behind reluctantly, but was her friend too truly to indulge in any pique.

How little would Grace Amber have believed, two years before, that she could have refused such an offer without regret, — chosen Nazareth before the world. Now it must be some other lure than luxury and ease and a city life which would wile her from those rugged hills.

Living there, teaching still, the years went by her and changed her little. Spring violets bloomed, summer roses blushed and faded, autumn fruits ripened, and winter snows whitened the fields, bringing her little variety. Still she was content. She smiled as she looked at herself in the mirror on her twenty-ninth birthday, tying on her bonnet, to think that when the next year came round they would call her an old maid. There were no silver threads in her soft dusky hair, for the years had been kind to her. You would scarcely have known she was older than at twenty-two, save by the deeper meaning of her face.

It was Sunday. She had staid at home in the morning to nurse Aunt Prudence through an unwonted attack of sick headache; but in the afternoon she went to church as usual. It was September. The fields were green still, and the skies bright. But there was the breath of autumn in the air, and it braced her nerves and quickened her footsteps. She walked on cheerily, and there was a bright glow on her cheek as she took her seat in church. It deepened a little when some unconscious magnetism drew her eyes to the Russell pew, and she saw sitting there an old friend.

Time had changed Adam Russell. He looked fully his years; indeed, at twenty-eight he might well have been taken for thirty-five. His face was calm and kindly, but with a look of thought and power, — a masterful look, as of one who had struggled with the world and conquered it. He had lost nothing of his old friendly honesty, but he had gained that indescribable something which the world recognizes as the distinction of a gentleman.

It was no wonder that Miss Amber heard little of the sermon. Try as she would, her thoughts proved rebels. She stole no more glances after the first look; but more than once she felt that his eyes were on her face. She hurried out when the service was over, but fast as she walked it was not long before his free, firm steps overtook her. There was no awkwardness or embarrassment in his manner. He took her books from her hand as quietly as if a week, and not seven years, had lain between their last meeting and this. He even called her Grace, with the pleasant freedom of their old, long-continued friendship. At first he did most of the talking; but soon they were chatting together as of old. When they reached the gate she asked if he could come in to tea, or would they wait for him at home?

"Come in!" he answered. "Surely I can, if you are good enough to ask me. The only one who would have missed me at home is waiting for me in another home, now."

Then they talked about his mother, and his sorrow and her sympathy drew them still more into the old manner of intimate friendliness.

After tea was over Aunt Prudence, worthy for once; of her name, found her head getting to be more troublesome, and judiciously made her exit. So it chanced that they sat down together at the west window, where lay the Shelley, in its sea-green covers, just as the sun was setting.

"It makes the years seem short," he said, "to sit here again; and yet they were long enough in passing. But I did my task. I have brought home the thirty thousand dollars, Grace. I know I did not suit you then, — you thought you could not love me. I meant to grow fitter for you with the years, — more worthy; for I had always one fixed purpose, — to come home, and, if I found you free, ask you the question I asked you that night over again. Would there be any more hope for me now?"

"It is I who am not good enough for you now," she answered, faintly.

Then she told him the story of her year and a half away from Nazareth, — the story of Paul.

"Did you think that could trouble me?" he asked when she paused. "If you are left to me, do I care for the dreams which never proved themselves real? Can I be too thankful for any thing which taught you self-knowledge? I have never lost hope, or ceased striving, that I might grow fit to be your choice at last. See, this is what I had for you that night; it has never left me. Will you wear it now?"

He drew the ring from his breast, — its pure pearl faintly flashing, — and Miss Amber held out her hand. And so, with the ring upon her finger, and her hand in his, the twilight found them, and folded its soft shadows round them like a blessing.

She had won her life's rest at last.

"Do you love Nazareth too well to leave it?"

This question came the next day, when they had grown familiar with their joy.

"We will live where you choose," he went on, seeing that she hesitated in her reply. "It will be no sacrifice for me to live here, if you like it best. I have left my work behind me: it is for you to say whether I go back to it or begin a new life here."

She thought a little, silently. Nazareth was dear, — dearer than ever now. All the pure joy of her life had found her there; but *he* was dearer, — his interest the first thought. She would like to see him in his true sphere; to cheer him on in his work for God and man.

There was little for him to do in the quiet New England town. He wanted more room, she knew. So she put her hand in his and answered him, —

"Let us go back to your work. I shall have no regrets. Where thou goest I will go. Thy people shall be my people, and thy God my God."

So, three weeks after, true husband and true wife, they went hand in hand out of Nazareth.

Cambridge: Press of John Wilson & Son.

www.ingramcontent.com/pod-product-compliance
Lightning Source LLC
LaVergne TN
LVHW010136110826
845151LV00002B/365

* 9 7 8 1 4 2 5 5 3 9 3 6 8 *